'A chilling, addictive read.'
Woman & Home

'Dark, disturbing, compulsive. I was genuinely terrified reading this.'
Adele Parks

'An incredibly addictive thriller that examines women
in the workplace, ageism, and the clash of generations.
It's creepy and unnerving, with observations that
are often dead-on. A breath-taking debut.'
Samantha Downing

'A deliciously dark, addictive and twisted page-turner.'
Alice Feeney

'Guaranteed to start the mother of all office fights between
Generation X and millennials. Monks Takhar's enjoyably poisonous
debut updates *All About Eve* for our image-obsessed age.'
The Independent

'A taut, sharply written thriller about two women and
their toxic obsession with one another. Sexy, scary and
satirical, [it's] a cat-and-mouse tale on steroids.'
The Bookseller

'What a debut! Twisty, explosive, and hugely compelling,
with hints of *Gone Girl* . . . Excellent.'
Will Dean

'A hypnotic dance of obsession, gaslighting and revenge
that doesn't let up until its final unnerving reveal.'
People

'Monks Takhar tackles workplace dynamics, aging,
feminism, mental illness, and the hotly debated generation
gap, all within the framework of a tightly plotted
revenge thriller. A wickedly sharp first novel.'
Kirkus starred review

'Scarily, addictively dark. My mouth was hanging open for the last third of the book. Wow – what a brilliant read!'
Cressida McLaughlin

'If you like dark and twisted thrillers with venom in their veins, add this to your wishlist!'
Anita Frank

'A brutal beauty – twisted, terrifying, pitch-perfect storytelling that gets under your skin. WOW.'
Miranda Dickinson

'Deliciously dark, gorgeously written; an absolute powerhouse of a debut!'
Emma Cooper

'OMG! Loved the twisty-turning end. I couldn't put it down.'
Josie Lloyd

'A thrilling, wicked, thought-provoking book every woman should read.'
Roxie Cooper

'[A] dark and disquieting debut . . . Monks Takhar delivers an excruciatingly tense slow burn that's rife with twists that shock and devastate.'
Publishers Weekly

'*Precious You* promises to be one of the best!'
CrimeReads

'*Gossip Girl* meets *Single White Female*. One to add to your reading list.'
Northern Soul

'Messed up and BRILLIANT.'
Liz Loves Books

Helen Monks Takhar has been working as a journalist, copywriter and magazine editor since 1999, having graduated from Cambridge. She began her career in financial trade newspapers before writing for national newspapers including *The Times* and *The Observer*. Originally from Southport, Merseyside, she lives in Stoke Newington with her husband and two young children. *Precious You* is her first novel.

Precious You

Helen Monks Takhar

ONE PLACE. MANY STORIES

This novel is entirely a work of fiction. The names, characters and incidents portrayed in it are the work of the author's imagination. Any resemblance to actual persons, living or dead, events or localities is entirely coincidental.

HQ
An imprint of HarperCollins*Publishers* Ltd
1 London Bridge Street
London SE1 9GF

This edition 2020

1

First published in Great Britain by
HQ, an imprint of HarperCollins*Publishers* Ltd 2020

Copyright © Helen Monks Takhar 2020

Helen Monks Takhar asserts the moral right to be identified as the author of this work.
A catalogue record for this book is available from the British Library.

ISBN: HB: 978-0-00-834014-8
TPB: 978-0-00-840202-0

MIX
Paper from
responsible sources
FSC
www.fsc.org   **FSC™ C007454**

This book is produced from independently certified FSC™ paper to ensure responsible forest management.

For more information visit: www.harpercollins.co.uk/green

This book is set in 10.9/15.5 pt. Sabon

Printed and bound in Great Britain by
CPI Group (UK) Ltd, Croydon, CR0 4YY

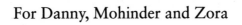

For Danny, Mohinder and Zora

Snowflake generation

noun

informal, derogatory

The generation of people who became adults in the 2010s, viewed as being less resilient and more prone to taking offence than previous generations.

COLLINS ENGLISH DICTIONARY. COPYRIGHT
© HARPERCOLLINS PUBLISHERS

'Oh, little snowflakes, when did you all become grandmothers and society matrons, clutching your pearls in horror at someone who has an opinion about something, a way of expressing themselves that's not the mirror image of yours, you snivelling little weak-ass narcissists?'

BRET EASTON ELLIS

'There is no one with a greater sense of entitlement than a millennial.'

WWW.DAILYMAIL.CO.UK ARTICLE, 'MILLENNIAL FURIOUSLY RANTS
ABOUT HOW MUCH EASIER LIFE WAS FOR HIS PARENTS'

'A lot of offensive stuff is happening. Why should people not be offended? People are offended but they're using that feeling of being offended to bring about change. Things are so dire sometimes that it's necessary. If I want to carve out a safe space, why shouldn't I?'

LIV LITTLE, EDITOR WWW.GAL-DEM.COM

Katherine

I've lost you in the neon river of high-visibility vests and chrome helmets flying ahead of my car towards the junction. You lot all look the same. *Is that what they think of* us? I can hear Iain say. I fight my exhaustion, rub my gritty eyes and try to find you again.

I slept in my car last night. I had that dream again, the one I told you about, the one I've had every night since I laid eyes on you. I'm back at my mother's farm. A darkness soaks into my bones; a black sky marbled with thick red veins envelopes me. Through the gloom, I see my top half is me today; a short swish of black hair, my strong arms shielded by a leather biker jacket. The bottom half is twelve-year-old me; my mother's dirty cast-off jeans hanging off stringy legs. I'm starving. Barefoot, at first I'm treading on stubbled grass, but the terrain quickly changes; I'm stepping on burnt pasture, like a thousand tiny razors under my bony feet. My blood begins to wet the parched scrub below. Suddenly, the ground begins to separate into hundreds of deep gullies. My instinct is to freeze, but I know I must go forward; ahead of me is the gate to the far paddock and I have to reach it to end this nightmare and stop my hunger. And I can't see her, but I know my mother is watching. She thinks I'll never make it. She thinks me too weak; she always tried to keep me so. She's willing me to stop, but I keep pushing forward, despite the pain, despite the hungry chasms at my feet that want to swallow me, I force myself to place one foot in front of the other to reach the gate.

I woke up aching, bent double in the backseat of my Mini. My life has come to this because of you: an existence played out slumped in Costa armchairs and the car I can't afford to insure anymore. This morning I'd decided to drive. I didn't know where or why until I spotted you on your bike. Then, I knew exactly what I had to do.

I stop-start, tracking you through the clog of traffic edging towards De Beauvoir and into Shoreditch, then the City. At Liverpool Street you snake your way through stationary vehicles and out of my sight. Then, the jam begins to shift, allowing me to edge forward and mark you again, keeping just a few metres behind you as the traffic pushes down Gracechurch Street.

We're nearly there.

Five cyclists have died on the junction ahead in the past year. Five young lives, just like yours, lost.

The car in front turns to give me free passage to the edge of the advanced stop line at the junction. I've got you in my sights. It's as if the world has finally decided to take my side, but no sooner than I start to move forward, cyclists flood into the void ahead. I'm surrounded once more by glinting handlebars and fluorescent young bodies.

I'm stuck.

I search desperately for you up ahead, then in my rear-view. But you've disappeared. You're going to enjoy another day on this earth; another day in my job, going home to my flat, tucking yourself into the bed my partner and I chose together.

Then, there you are.

You've pulled up right next to my door, your eyes focused on the lights ahead. Your body, that close to me again, makes my blood rise. You're inches from me, I could reach out, grab your arm, and beg you to tell me once and for all: Why? When I was ready to help you, why did you set out to snatch everything that was mine?

You start to move away, squeezing through the other cyclists to the very front of the pack. You flash that smile of yours. Of course, they let you pass. That devastating smile. That smile is like the warmest sun and the brightest light. That smile has undone my life.

Behind you, I move ahead too, breaching the cyclists' zone and causing various slaps on my Mini's roof and cries of *What the fuck do you think you're doing, you stupid cow?* to erupt as I force them out of my path. You swivel round to see what's causing the uproar, but quickly turn back towards the lights, knowing they'll change any second. You don't notice my car creeping up right behind you, and you don't wait for the green light before deciding to strike out on your own; up off your seat, powerful calves bearing down onto the pedals as you begin your acceleration. But it's time you were stopped from getting ahead of me.

Your back wheel fills my sight.

I wonder what your body will feel like under me, as your bones crunch and collapse. I can almost smell your blood, running hot in the final moments before it gushes from you, cooling as it flows out onto the tarmac to drip into the waiting drains and down to an impassive Thames.

Only when this happens can I really begin again.

The lights change to green. I slam my foot down hard on the accelerator.

CHAPTER 1

Katherine

Six weeks earlier

I'll never understand why they weren't worried, those young things I saw every day at the bus stop, stretching free of their crammed houseshares and parental buy-to-lets in my neighbourhood, at least a mile from the nearest place they would actively choose to live. Why didn't they care we hadn't seen a bus for twenty minutes? I made a mental note to ask Iain why no one under thirty seemed arsed about being late for work anymore, then texted my deputy, Asif. I was hoping he'd have words of reassurance, something I could use to soothe my latest work-related crisis. That Monday was the first day of a brave new world at the magazine I edited: new owners, a new publisher, a shot at a new start. I knew it was critical I made a good impression, but the world was already screwing this for me by making all the buses disappear. I messaged Asif:

No bus. Confess late now or busk it?

And got back a not particularly helpful:

Nice weekend? New publisher already here. Not sure.
Good luck. xxx

I can see myself that morning, gazing in the direction of my flat, the edges of its dried-out window boxes just visible from where I stood. I wore the oversized high-collared shirt I'd bought the day before, an ankle-length pencil skirt split to the thigh and the black biker I always wore to work. I wanted to show up looking just-pressed, but edgy and not desperate to fit into the new corporate regime I was facing, even though, of course, I was.

Mondays were already hard for me, even before that day. It wasn't just that after twenty years I seemed to be getting worse at my job, not better, nor that the youth, hope and unbounded energy of my interns shoved the frustrated promise of my own formative years right back in my face with greater force every day. No, it was the awfulness, the horrifying dread, of the interns asking me, 'What did you do this weekend?'

Compared to when I was at the height of my potential in my twenties, I felt invisible most of the time. But on Monday mornings I felt suddenly watched. I tried, as I so often did when I was surrounded by millennials, to minimise the damage to my pride. While they recounted their energetic tales of running around London, meeting other bright young things from north, south, east and western corners, as I had once done, I sat tight. I had done next to nothing with no one but Iain, and this could be exposed at any second. I'd sometimes manage to arrange phone interviews for 9 a.m. on Mondays, so I could block out their weekend lives and avoid their social and creative endeavours showing up my dead existence. If anyone got to ask me The Monday Morning Question, I'd recently taken to out-and-out lying, telling the interns, 'We caught up with some old friends.'

That Monday, my anxiety was soaring when I caught the glow of a taxi's light far up the road. I watched it furtively at first, until I realised I was the only one inching towards the edge of the pavement to hail it. Of course, none of the bus stop lot had the money for a black cab. No money, but plenty of time. Their lives were rich with activities and all the time they had to do them: arts, crafts, queuing for artisan toast, curating photographic records of their fizzy lives on social media and generally being creatively incontinent. I felt the hum of self-belief and productivity whenever I was around younger adults and it left me feeling singed.

I double-checked behind me for any would-be competitors for my cab. I saw you.

You were something quite different.

You had their air of creative confidence, the one I could only assume comes from parents who cheerlead your every trifling achievement, but you seemed to carry a hunger about you too; some neediness in your eyes. Out of nowhere, I got the sense you were a young person with whom I might possibly have some common ground.

Because unlike the others, you seemed like you *were* bothered by being late for work. Less like them, more like me. Such an odd sense of time and age I felt you emit: undeniably as young as them, but somehow seeming older and more desperate, like me, all at once. And do you remember, you wore that tiny leather skirt? I have one just like it and I used to wear it to work too. Your skin was as pale as mine, but fully taut and shimmering, except for a dirty stripe of oil on the right side of your forehead. I couldn't take my eyes off you. You were like looking into a mirror, or more like a window into a different time in my life, not long past, but just out of reach. I wanted to know more about you, to see if you really could be anything like me. When the taxi began to pull over, I began to wonder if I should invite you to share it.

I glanced back at you again. A finger on your left hand fiddled with the string tag on the yellow laptop case you held against the front of your thighs. You switched your weight from hip to hip and occasionally flicked the nails of your right thumb and index finger under your chin. I took the door handle and turned around to take you in one last time, before the ebb and flow of a London day separated our paths. A thought needled its way to the front of my mind: your face would return to me throughout the day and I'd have to exorcise you by telling Iain over dinner about *The Girl I Saw at the Bus Stop Who Reminded Me of The Old Me*.

But you were watching me.

As you looked over, you bit your bottom lip, painted hot orange like the sunrise in summertime, and flicked your nails against your skin again before moving your black eyes off me to the non-existent bus on the horizon.

I could let you in to my cab, but I wondered what we would possibly talk about. Or maybe you'd just sink into your phone, like people your age do, and I wouldn't get to talk to you at all. And how would you pay your way? People like you never have cash on them, so would I give you my bank details so you could transfer your share of the fare? Was that wise? Was that *cool*? Wasn't there an app for that, one I'd be embarrassed to say I haven't downloaded or even heard of yet? Or would you ask to meet me somewhere at lunchtime to give me my twenty quid? Would we then end up having a burger? Find ourselves talking for ages?

Go on, girl, you show 'em what us old ravers are made of, I could hear Iain say.

No.

No, I should leave it.

I didn't need to over-complicate what was already shaping up to be another day I'd want to forget. I opened the taxi door and readied myself to leave you on the pavement, but suddenly you were there, right behind me.

You made me jump.

'Hi there, you must be heading south? Mind if I get in?' When you spoke to me, your mouth split to reveal the most fantastic teeth.

'Yes. I mean, I'm heading to Borough, but—'

'Perfect. Me too. Wait a sec, sorry, I've just realised, I literally don't have any cash.'

Behind you I saw the bearded and big-haired gaggle were agog that you'd thought of hitching a ride and they hadn't. If I refused you, I feared a group of them would initiate some kind of collective action, gathering their grubby coins together in a bid to get in.

'It's fine, just get in.' One of you had to be better than three or four.

'Is that alright? You're absolutely sure?'

You gained and double-checked my consent. It was a technique you would use again and again on me when I didn't understand what I was agreeing to. One of your many gifts.

'Sure.'

I obediently slid over to the far seat to make room for you. You bent low to get in, your head suddenly so close to mine I could smell you'd just washed your hair. It was still wet at the roots, cooling the blood in your scalp. I was about to tell the cabbie where to go, but your youthful scent made me falter.

'Borough, please. I'd avoid Old Street if I were you. Dalston then Gracechurch?' you said. Smiling, you waved your phone in my direction. 'Good for you? I've just seen there's a burst water main near City Road. I mean, if you'd rather go your way?'

I saw your screen was blank.

I looked to the driver for some response, but was distracted by the faint reflection on the glass screen in front of me: a decidedly middle-aged woman, short ink-black hair framing a smudgy face. I was struggling to recognise myself again. I hadn't admitted to Iain yet, but in the build-up to that day, I could feel my illness creeping back with its full force, exactly how it had when the last crash happened fifteen months ago.

An extended Christmas break, followed by six weeks pock-marked by regular sick days, followed by my GP signing me off work as a beige cloud surrounded me, washing the colour out of everything. Recently, that familiar filter of dread which had only recently lifted felt like it was on the descent again. If I went back to my GP, I suspected he'd want to put me back on my antidepressants again. But Citalopram had given me weeks of terrible side effects so that I suddenly needed help to achieve even the basic requirements of life: eating, concentrating, remembering both what had happened that day and things I'd done years ago. I felt sleepy constantly, primally drawn to dark rooms, my bed or under a blanket on my sofa, like an old animal looking for a quiet place to die. Eventually, getting to work became impossible and the pills made all of it worse, with a mouth like cotton wool and a supressed sex drive to boot. My GP said I'd only need to take it for a few months to 'jump start myself again'. My former masters at work were understanding, and anyway, they were too distracted by finding a buyer for the struggling business at that point. I doubted whether the new owners would be so sympathetic, or their attentions as diverted.

When Christmas rolled around again last year, I'd been off for nearly ten months. I knew I had to bed myself back in before the new team took over. I had to persuade them and anyone else who was looking that I was back to 'normal'. By January I'd come off my pills and was back at work, but in my heart, I knew I hadn't been 'fixed'. The beige cloud was lying in wait to blow in again; I could see the faint shape of it growing larger on the horizon the day I met you.

Lily, when you came along you were like a flash of hot pink, cleaving through the paper bag tone threatening to take over my world again. I think this is why it was so easy for you to do what you did. If you ever flattered yourself by thinking for one moment you'd sent me to rock bottom all by yourself, you really have no idea what state my life was already in.

I knew the route to Borough you'd suggested would add at least ten minutes to my journey to work, meaning I had no chance of making my first meeting with the new publisher, Gemma Lunt, on time. She'd know I was missing in action for the greater part of last year and why. I was sure she'd be looking for signs of weakness.

'We'll go your way.'

When these words left my mouth, it was my very first act of knowing submission to your will. This was the precise moment my life, such as it was, started to end.

We didn't talk at first. I looked out of the window on your side and waited for you to thank me, as you had to, surely. You couldn't have failed to notice the banks of increasingly forlorn faces on the 141's route up to De Beauvoir. But you were silent, holding your laptop case on your legs in what I'd soon recognise as the buttoned-up, butter-wouldn't-melt way you choose to hold yourself. I said nothing, waiting for you to speak. But my curiosity finally got the better of me. 'I don't think I've seen you at the bus stop before,' I said. 'You just moved here?'

'Yeah, but with any luck, I'll just be passing through.'

You must have seen the flicker of offence on my face, 'Not that Manor House isn't awesome. I mean, it's so super-easy to get everywhere. I cycle mostly.' You turned your head away again to watch the world from your window as we crawled up Kingsland Road.

'Well, if you're not wild about Manor House now, you should have seen it round here twenty-odd years ago. The whole place was a red-light area. Hard to imagine now.'

'That sounds pretty dark.' You didn't seem to think very much of my corner of the capital. It seemed that just like the constantly-changing bus stop crew, you'd use Manor House as a stepping stone; once you started earning more than me, as you all seemed destined to, you too would be off to a more desirable postcode than mine.

It struck me that your poise and your choice of words added to the sense that you were some kind of chimera; stilted mannerisms that tried to convey control and maturity, but then you'd defaulted to a childish Americanism: 'awesome'. Young and old at the same time, just as I'd guessed by looking at you. Your accent was unanchored too, a southern clip with northern vowels.

'Are you a native Londoner?'

'So, I was born here, but I grew up all over the show. Some time here, on and off. Right now, my mum has a little bolthole and she wanted me to move in with her, but I told her it's time I took responsibility for myself, because that's important, isn't it? You should take ownership of your life, don't you think?'

'I think that *is* important.' I was thrown by the sudden panorama of your sentence, but I liked how you now seemed to want to share your thoughts with me.

'Well, anyway, for now I'm on my own in one of those vile, gentrifying Woodberry Downs high-rises – right behind the bus stop – you probably totally hate.' You turned to look me up and down. 'You look like you've probably got a beautiful Victorian house, tonnes of character, lots of beautiful things. My place is kind of a nowhere place.'

I was taken aback by your flattery. It was the nicest thing anyone had said about me for a long time, besides Iain, of course. An unexpected compliment. How good that had felt. As your eyes moved urgently over my face to assess my reaction, I suddenly got the notion you were lonely in that newbuild tower of yours. Maybe you needed a friendly neighbour. I wanted to think this because, Lily, I was so lonely too.

I considered admitting I had a Victorian flat, not a house,

but you didn't need to know the limits of my success. Not yet. I wanted more from you before I let you go at Borough. I pointed to the dirty stripe on your face, 'I think you've got oil on your—'

'Oh god – puncture. Trust that for a Monday.' You lifted the back of your hand to the opposite side of your forehead to the smudge.

'Other side. Here.' My fingertips reached the skin on your face.

I didn't mean to touch you, but it happened. My blood seemed to surge towards the surface and I know I felt yours too, coming forward to meet mine, like iron filings to a magnet. You blinked and pushed yourself back into your seat, saying, 'Thanks, I think I've got it.'

The cab was suddenly hot and small. I thought about texting Iain, but it was way too early in the day for that, so I cracked open the window and tried to move the conversation on.

'What is it you do?'

'I'm a journalist?'

Not *Training to be*, or *Hoping to be*, but *I'm a journalist*, already, though no one had probably paid you a penny for a single word yet. People your age are incredible. I didn't tell anyone I was a journalist until my second promotion, when I'd just about stopped living in fear of someone telling me I wasn't good enough to be there. We didn't have 'Fake it 'til you make it' in the nineties. Neither did we have parents who had us believe we were the centre of the universe and that universe was rightfully ours.

'Who do you write for?'

'Myself mostly, I guess. I blog.'

'What about?'

'You know. This and that. My life…What I see.'

I thought and I waited. I enjoyed that moment before I said what I said to you next, 'I edit a well-thought-of trade title. We're always looking for interns if you're in the market for the next move.' I anticipated your breathlessness, the sound of your body turning towards me to give me your full and urgent attention. But it didn't happen, so I kept talking, 'I usually have between four and six interns working for me – one on design, another on picture research and at least two writers.'

Nothing.

'I've seen people your age really learn their trade working in a professional environment, so, have a think, maybe. Opportunities can be hard to come by. Maybe this is fate?' I tried to laugh, but it didn't come. I sounded so old, so *seasoned*. I was forty-one, but I wanted to feel fresh and relevant, not like someone who says things like *Your age* and *Learn your trade*. I still felt young inside, but then thought, *Isn't that what old people say?*

You looked at the road ahead and muttered, 'I'm actually starting at a trade today. Interning.' I noticed your fingers were gripping your laptop case. Clearly, you'd have liked it if I'd just stopped talking. You made me feel something I was suddenly aware I'd been closing in on without being able to badge it: you made me feel like an *old fool*. You continued, 'It's about management and stuff. Interviews with businesspeople. Things bosses care about. It's called *Leadership*?' You didn't look at me as your voice inflected upwards again at the end of a sentence in a way that made you sound unambiguously young and annoying.

The next words formed in my mind, but they seemed to lose their power as soon as I went to say them. The offhand way you described the magazine told me you wouldn't be deeply impressed by what I was about to say. And if I didn't find myself remotely impressive anymore, why should anyone else, least of all you?

'I edit *Leadership*,' I said quietly.

You looked right at me, 'Oh. That's literally where I'm heading right now.'

'That's a bit fucking mad, isn't it?' I said. I didn't register it then, but would learn later that you winced whenever I swore.

'Wow. I guess it is.'

But it couldn't have been that exciting, because you already sounded bored. It was the tone of a cooler person you meet at a party who spots someone more interesting over your shoulder and grabs a superlative out of the air as a sign off. I used to do that, but now it's people like you who do it to me, young people who use my magazine as a mere departure lounge that allows them to soar somewhere brighter and better, me existing only to on-board the next batch of interns who would leapfrog my life.

'Do you know who'll you be reporting to? I wasn't expecting a new intern today.'

'Gemma Lunt, the publisher. It's her first day too.'

'Right, well, don't worry, I'll explain why we're late. Stick with me, and my deputy Asif. You'll be fine.'

'Should I be worried?'

'No. Not really. Just keep your head down. You'll probably be set up in my team.'

You nodded. 'Sounds great. I'm super-focused on what I need to do, like you say, being somewhere I can learn from older people?'

A spike. The sense of the smooth, hard finger of youth prodding my loosening life. Subtle, and few would deny the barb if they heard it themselves. But I would learn very quickly that every single person in my world would take your side first, always give you the benefit of the doubt before they would me. A privilege given to the young and beautiful, a privilege I didn't know I had until I lost it.

I watched you for a moment from the corner of my eye as the first inkling there was something less than innocent about you prickled my stomach. I didn't yet know if it was just paranoia; a wild idea sprouting from an already unreliable mind. I never fully realised how much danger a person is in when the individual they trust least is themselves. After you, Lily, I'll never ignore my first instincts again.

'It's great you're so ready to learn…I'm Katherine, by the way.'

'Lily.'

You offered me your narrow palm, but gave no indication you knew exactly who I was.

The minutes dragged as we passed Liverpool Street. It had gone nine. I was supposed to be in Gemma Lunt's office in fifteen minutes. I'd only agreed to the early slot so I could avoid the usual Monday morning social interrogation. I thought about dropping her a line to manage expectations, then decided I'd chance getting there on-the-knuckle and avoid my first communication with her being about something I'd failed to execute effectively.

The cab suddenly picked up speed and we caught a couple of green lights. For a moment, it seemed possible I might just be OK.

You leant forward to speak to the driver, 'Hi, could you pull in here, up on the left?' and we swerved into a side street. Turning to me, 'I have to pick up something from my mum? I'll be so quick.'

'But I'm already late, couldn't you—'

'It's OK. I can square it with Gem, promise.'

'Gem?' You knew my new boss. How?

I tried to remember what I'd only that hour told you about my work. When I struggled, a fresh anxiety rose in my chest. Another symptom of the beige cloud: forgetfulness followed by panic about what might have happened in the gaps.

Before I could say anything else, you were out of the taxi, running through a carved stone archway. When you clearly thought I couldn't see you anymore, you stopped running and instead walked slowly towards a heavy lacquered door. You pressed on a buzzer and spoke sullenly into an intercom, all urgency gone. In my head, I begged you to yank the door towards you and race through it like your life depended on it, but instead you pulled it carefully and stepped gently into the building.

9.03.

9.05.

At 9.07 I drafted an email to Gemma, trying to convey confidence, a lack of guilt, but also some necessary undertones of contrition. I noticed your laptop case next to me.

9.12.

I wanted to know what the hell you were doing. I thought about telling the driver to get going, but you were apparently on intimate terms with 'Gem', the very woman who'd masterminded the buyout of *Leadership*. I couldn't leave you there, even if I wanted to. The day had felt like a huge test I needed to pass. You were making me fail it.

When it got to 9.17, the meter bust forty-five quid and I was getting seriously pissed off. Not only because I'd lost all hope of not being late, but also because once it got past £60, I'd have to submit a 'business case' with the receipt under the new staff code of conduct.

I looked at your laptop case again. The driver thumbed his phone. The courtyard was empty. I let my hand inch over to the far side of the back seat. Your case was made of suede, soft as butter. It felt expensive. The closing mechanism was a string and leather tag wrapped around two buttons. Anyone wanting to sneak a peek would have to remember exactly which direction you'd tied the figure of eight around the buttons. They would have to be quick about it.

Before I could stop myself, my fingers had unspun the twine and flapped the case open. Your phone number and your name in sensible black ink capitals:

LILY LUNT

So, you were some relation to Gemma Lunt.

Well, wasn't *that* a neat detail you'd chosen to keep to yourself. I wondered what else you might be opting to not tell me and what you would divulge to Gemma from the information you'd gleaned from me so far.

The driver stirred, saying something like, *Here we go.*

I looked up to see you sweeping out of the door and into the courtyard. My fingers were suddenly sodden. Was the string wrapped round the top button first or second? From the left or the right? I tried one way, it didn't look right. I tried another, it still looked wrong. I quickly glanced up again. You were still a few seconds away, but on seeing me, broke into a quick jog, a wholly fake display that you gave a shit over how late you were making me. I fumbled desperately. You were at the other door and your perfect little figure of eight had been replaced by a damp, slack tangle. You climbed in, and if the mangled thread didn't tell you I'd been tampering with your things, then my sweaty guilt surely would. I'd have to distract you and hope against hope you wouldn't notice. So although you should have been apologising to me for royally fucking-up my morning, instead, I found myself over-brightly asking you, 'Everything alright?'

'Yes, good thanks. Hi, we can go?' you said to the driver.

Your eyes rested on your case.

You knew.

You were carrying a black cube with the words *Caran d'Ache* embossed in silver. I didn't know they were a luxury pen maker until I googled it later. This, the family business and a mother working in the City? You had to be made of money.

'Something for Gemma?'

You pulled your eyes off the dirtied twine and breathed as if you were saying *Look, Katherine*, without actually saying it.

'I'm so, so sorry. I didn't want to make things, like, at all awkward. So, Gem is my aunt. I know a bit about optimising content, that sort of thing, with the magazine and the website, I guess it seemed a bit of a no-brainer, me helping out? Gem and my mum, they haven't always been best buds.' You tapped the box with an alabaster finger. 'Sorry. *Family* stuff. Look, I'll explain to Gem it was me. I made you late. My bad, honest,' and your dark eyes flickered down onto your laptop case again before returning to my face.

Optimising content. We used to call it 'good writing', and once upon a time some, just a few of us got our jobs on merit, not because of the luck of birth. Now I was going to end up walking in with you, like I was in on it. My team were going to disrespect me even more than they already did.

'Don't worry about it. Really. How about we start again from the beginning?'

You smiled: surprisingly wide and meaningful, some strange energy coming off you as your sunny lips stretched over tombstone teeth, eyes darting across my face again. My anger started to recede. That smile of yours. Another one of your gifts.

'You got it. Let's start again.'

A minute later in Monument, the traffic was dire. My stomach turned with dread. I couldn't afford to feel this way. I summoned what Iain would have said to me: *It's not so bad, is it, girl? Let's get a bit of perspective, will we?*

OK.

Maybe I wouldn't have made it on time anyway, and now I'd rescued the boss's niece from a puncture and missing buses. Perhaps this was a good start after all? Maybe I was actually winning.

Come on, it's a good day, no?

We reached the open air of London Bridge and I let the thin March sun reflecting off the river lift me. I nearly loved

London again in moments like that, when your eyes sweep left and right over the Thames and it feels like the Southbank, Big Ben, Tower Bridge and good old HMS Belfast exist just to make you feel it's good to be alive. *Today will be a good day.*

'So, have you been editor for very long?' you asked from nowhere.

'Some might say too long,' I replied before I could stop myself.

'Would they?'

'I've been there about twenty years now ... I still love my job.' The sound of 'twenty years' in my mouth felt like a great stone I wanted to spit out. I thought, for the thousandth time, about how it had got to such a vast amount of time. Thankfully, you seemed to have lost interest before I'd even finished faking the joy of my two decades at the same place.

We crossed the river and pulled up outside the office. I needed to pay by card. You sat forward on the edge of the back seat, your legs pointing in the direction of the door.

'You go ahead while I sort this out,' I felt obliged to say, as I tried to add a tip in a way that made mathematical sense and didn't look tight, but still kept the total south of £60.

'Thank you. Is that OK? You're sure?'

'Out you go.'

'I'll be super-quick with Gem.'

'That's not—' I said, pressing the button that added 15 per cent on top of £57.50 in my distraction.

'Thank you, Katherine.'

The first time you said my name.

You gave me a thousand-watt smile which I returned in a kind of wonder.

'That's fine,' I said to the air as I watched you skip towards the revolving doors of my office building.

Out on the pavement, as I stuffed my card back in my purse and tried to regroup before heading in, I felt a tap on my shoulder.

'Thought you could do with this today.' Asif handed me a tall black coffee. He smelt of a recent spritz of his beloved cologne, *Fierce* by Abercrombie & Fitch, his forehead glistening in the strengthening sunlight, hazel eyes gleaming under dark, soft curls that made all the interns swoon. At least I had him in my corner.

'My god, you fucking star.' I took a sip that burnt my tongue. 'You been in yet?'

'I have.'

We went through the doors, swiped our passes and started to mount the marble stairs to our floor side-by-side. 'And?'

'And it was fine, she's fine. A bit … you'll see, I don't know. We should be alright.'

He seemed to be holding back, trying to protect me.

'Emphatic stuff. Have you met the niece yet?'

'Niece? Not another hopeless bloody intern? Not yet. When did *you*?'

'It's kind of an unfunny story.'

Asif and I walked in as you emerged from a hug with Gemma, a woman with hen-brown curls pinned into an insubstantial French twist. Like me, she was in her early forties, but with her corporate skirt suit and sensible hairdo, she seemed so much older than me. I'd heard she had built and sold many businesses, and that she'd bought *Leadership* practically on a whim once she'd identified 'the brand's multi-platform potential,' whatever that meant. She had no kids and a fancy duplex in Marylebone, a house in Norfolk and some kind of Alpine ski chalet. Imagine.

I watched you and her inside the recently-constructed glass office she'd commissioned for herself. They were actually on the verge of building me my own office, just as things started to turn at *Leadership*. The end of year accounts came out and the directors suddenly went from signing off my every request to stalling on my requirements, then actively sidestepping contact with me so they could dodge admitting the perilous state of *Leadership's* balance sheet to 'their girl', the junior reporter they'd 'groomed for greatness' and then appointed youngest-ever editor nearly twenty years earlier.

In that office, which in a better world would have been mine, Gemma grasped your shoulders with both hands. I could see you were staring at the floor as she tried to force you to look her in the eyes. You wouldn't meet them. She gave up and scanned the office over your head, drew you close to give you a quick kiss on the head before finally letting you go. You kept gazing down before visibly gathering yourself and flouncing out of her office and into the open floor. It took just a couple of strides to get you to your assigned desk space, diagonally opposite mine. She wanted to keep you close to her, and close to me. And even then the reporter in me was asking why. *What are you?*

As you moved, I saw Asif take in every centimetre of you and your legs – solid stripes of muscle tense under black opaques, disappearing at the very last moment into a pelmet of leather. Asif, my one-time intern, my protégé who'd even chosen his login to please me when he'd first joined (StephenPatrick59, in honour of my love of Morrissey), someone who stood by me during the worst of it. He had seen me at my very best, just before my illness, before anyone understood the old company's catastrophic finances, when it seemed me and my merry band could go on writing away, propped up by a semi-loyal base of subscribers and a modest advertising revenue, forever. These were the days before the first 'tough conversation' with the old directors on the 'hard realities' we couldn't run away from anymore: the world had moved on and we hadn't. Shortly after came the first redundancies, when we said goodbye to senior reporters who'd come up the ranks like me and who we couldn't afford anymore, then the second round, where we lost our grizzled sub-editors, the connective tissue that always held the bones of *Leadership* together.

But even in those changing times, I'd been able to lobby for us to switch off below-the-line comments to encourage an elevated debate at real-life events where we'd document the outcomes. But that period, when people couldn't hide behind their keyboards and usernames, was gone. Comments were now activated and often spilled over into the, at turns banal and cowardly, Twittersphere. Integrity and discipline were wholly lost in this modern world where people like you and, worse than that, those my age, feel it's somehow both appropriate and interesting to share the first thing that comes into their heads. And as I watched Asif drink you in, something else I once understood was altering before my very eyes. I suppose you know, when you walk into a room, something in the air changes. I used to be capable of doing that.

'She's ready for you,' you said as you passed by me, then,

'Just be yourself, Katherine.' I felt your breath on my ear, smelt your clean, warm scalp again. I shuddered.

'Hi, come in, come in. Wonderful to be able to put a face to the name, finally. I'm sorry it's taken this long to meet, I've been neck deep in the strategy, the financials and so on, but I know *all* about you.' Gemma gestured towards a swivel chair I knew to be broken, though she didn't. I nodded and perched on the crap chair without letting my weight bear down.

'Likewise.'

'We're a bit late, so I'll cut straight to it.'

My stomach fell. I knew she and her new board had been discussing 'my future'.

'Nothing formal or anything. No need to look so worried!'

'I'm not, I'm just ... Sorry, I had a bit of a nightmare this morning. I hate it when one of my team shows up late and goes on about the failures of the Jubilee Line, or whatever,' I tried to smile over the familiar thrust of cortisol in my veins.

'Lily explained. Did she tell you much about her background on the way in?'

'That she's your niece?' And as I thought about it, I realised we'd been together in that taxi for almost an hour and all I knew was that you blogged. (Who doesn't? Besides me, of course.) I should have asked you a million questions, but there I was, armed only with a scrap of information on your relationship with Gemma.

'That's right. She's also very bright and very young, but I wonder, could I ask you, in confidence, to keep an eye on her? Asif says you're much stronger than you seem on paper.'

I was confused. Damning me with such faint praise didn't sound like the Asif I knew. I looked over at him, walking towards the space behind your chair, then placing his hands squarely on the back of it, right above your shoulders.

'Right. Thanks. I *am* really strong,' I flustered.

'You probably understand it was a bit of a tussle with the new board to keep you on, but I won and I'm really glad I did.'

'No. No, I don't, exactly. A *tussle*? Could you ... what does that mean?'

'Oh, Lord, I assumed they'd kept you quite close to the process ... Well, it was the board's preferred option that we maybe start afresh. New look, new management, new editor. But I thought it right and proper you got to be part of the new now, so here we are.' She smiled, as if she expected me to thank her for letting me keep my post at a magazine I'd lived and breathed since I was almost a girl, a title I'd shaped. I had no choice but to play along. I needed my job, my second home in the world, so I couldn't get as angry as I was entitled to.

'OK, well, thank you, Gemma. You can count on me to ... I'll always keep going,' I garbled. My once-familiar territory as unstable as the broken chair trembling beneath me. Gemma began speaking again, talking at me like she'd made index cards beforehand. I knew if I could muster the energy, I'd already despise her.

'They tell me you've put a huge amount of effort into the first new-look issue. I can't wait to read it all tomorrow, I'm so glad to hear you've committed so much to what I really hope is going to be an exciting new chapter for all of us.'

I was glad she'd noticed. I'd gathered enough resolve to make sure we'd come out of the blocks under the new owners with a strong issue, getting the interns to set up most of the interviews, do the background research and fact-checks, but writing the lion's share of the features and profiles myself. My picture byline would be all over the magazine and website by the following day. I can't say my heart and soul went into those pieces, but sweat and elbow grease certainly had. I am a fighter by nature, Lily. As soon as I feel my back on the wall, my fists go up. My primal instinct.

'Thank you, Gemma.'

'Now, was there anything *you* wanted to discuss?'

'No, not really,' I said, but then you waltzed by outside the glass and I swear you winked at me. Behind you, Asif's eyes followed your arse until it disappeared into the kitchen area. 'But I suppose it'd be good to know if there's anything else I should know about Lily?' My opening move.

'Well now, perhaps there is. It's actually down to Lily we're here. When she read *Leadership* was in trouble, she thought it had *huge* potential. She was excited. It was wonderful to see. I was looking for a new project, she was living with me at the time – I'm really her second mum, if you must know – she could see what it could be and brought me right into her vision. So there you are.' Gemma beamed at the memory, and I imagined the two of you holed-up together in some palatial slice of prime central London real estate, plotting how to give old lady *Leadership* some commercial CPR, rescuing her from the demise of which I was the figurehead.

'So your buyout, it was all her idea. That's quite a vision for someone so young. Young people are so different now to how I was, how things used to be.' I was unsettled, almost sure you'd given no indication whatsoever that you were in the driving seat of the buyout. And wouldn't this mean you'd have known who I was when you muscled your way into my cab? Because for more than twenty years, up until that day, I *was Leadership*. Perhaps you were embarrassed, too modest to draw attention to your ability to see the latent opportunities in my ailing empire.

But then I watched you again through the glass.

You'd returned to your seat and Asif had come round to lean at the same level as your screen. While you spoke, pausing occasionally to gesture towards the images, he nodded in the general direction of your sideboob. You clocked him doing so and flicked your fingernails to your throat to maintain his attention.

'Now, I'm glad you've mentioned how things used to be, Katherine.'

'Yes,' I said, without really listening, as I watched you call my picture research intern over to you. She obeyed and was soon nodding along with you and Asif.

'I've had a bit of *feedback* from your team. There's clearly a lot of admiration there for you.'

'OK.' I finally had to look away from you as you corralled my team around you, doing what, I didn't know yet, but I had a feeling I wouldn't like it.

'An appreciation you come from a tradition of journalism that has some really excellent traits, one of those being a certain *resilience*. But certain elements, it might be that some of them are a bit of a hangover, you might say.'

'A hangover from what?'

'From maybe the atmosphere of an old-school newsroom. A bit of banter with the interns? Fine, of course, but it may be we need to think about …toning it down a bit.'

'Toning down what?'

'I think it's probably a vocabulary issue as much as anything. One of your team said you'd called them "soft" when they'd been nervous about calling a consultant who'd just lost their business; another individual said you liked nothing more than to refer to them as precious "Snowflakes"?'

'Who said that?' Really, it could have been any one of the current crop of interns and I wasn't surprised they'd swooped on the opportunity to plead their case to Gemma. I was more alarmed the Snowflakes had found such a ready advocate in a woman of my generation. But of course, this conversation, all of it, was about you, not them. Gemma wanted to arrange the world so it worked better for you, matched more closely with your lofty expectations, where any challenge to your status quo was banned. Five minutes in and you were already well into the process of reshaping my office into something closer to your liking. I looked over again to see the picture researcher offer you a palm to high five. You slapped it meekly, smiling at your feet.

'I'm not going to get into who said what, but let's take this as an opportunity to think again about the kind of place we all want to work. It should feel inclusive. It should feel safe. I know you'll want to get on board with that.'

'Of course, yes.' I was hobbled, but I needed to keep fighting somehow. 'Is there anything else I should know? Anything more on what the interns fed back?' I paused. 'Or anything else about Lily?'

The corner of Gemma's lip twitched. 'No. Nothing else that springs to mind.'

'Well, OK then.' I didn't move towards the door yet. I wanted her to know I didn't feel this conversation was really over. You see, I could tell your aunt was hiding something. People like you and me, Lily, we're excellent liars, aren't we? People like Gemma? Not so convincing.

'Oh, one more thing, Katherine. Sorry, I forgot to ask … How are you? Would you say you're feeling well?'

'I'd say I was stronger than ever.'

'Great, well, just to let you know, I'm going to have to keep asking you. It's part of our new *Wellness Policy*.'

'Good to know the new team are committed to caring.'

She nodded and gave me a squishy smile. She believed me. Excellent liar, see?

I got back to my desk, avoiding the eyes of my team, and you. But as I booted up my machine, I heard you say, 'How did that go, then?' Casually, as if you'd known me for years; more than that, as if you were my peer. You didn't even look away from your screen, which you already seemed to be filling with prodigious amounts of copy. Who did you think you were? You thought you'd saved my sorry arse from unemployment. You thought my world was your empire because you were the niece of a chequebook publisher. Lily, there are some postcodes you can't just buy into.

'You didn't say how lovely your aunt is,' I said loudly enough for the other interns to hear. 'Let me get organised and we'll talk about some background research you can help Asif with.'

You moved your hair behind your ears with your fingers.

'Oh. Should I clear this first?'

I thought I heard a stifled snort from the IT intern in the far corner of our bank of desks. I couldn't let on I didn't know what 'this' was.

'Go for it.'

'You're sure?'

'Yep.'

'I mean, Gemma wanted me to focus on writing this curtain-raising piece for the awards, but I can prioritise your work if you'd rather—'

A request for consent twice. Signature play. Inserting yourself into the most visible and important areas of my work, also what I'd soon identify as a classic move.

The *Leadership* awards were the biggest night of our year, our shop window and a rallying cry for readers and advertisers to stick with us for another twelve months. You were already worming your way to the front and centre of it. As I hadn't been well enough to attend, let alone lead on last year's awards, this year's would be my chance to reassert my authority, reinstating my reputation by showing everyone I was alive and kicking, on the outside at least.

You turned back to your screen and started typing again without waiting to hear my mumbled, *No.*

'Oh, I should probably also flag, I was just introducing myself to the team and got brought into a little pow-wow about the cover for the reprint of the mag for awards night? I have a couple of ideas on tightening up the cover lines, maybe going for a sharper image. I mean, it's practically the same, just a teensy bit more contemporary. I'm sure you're going to love it, but they're only ideas. Feel free to push back.'

Those dark eyes danced below raised eyebrows, a certain mischief on that smooth pale forehead, your orange lips, perfectly arranged into the faintest of smiles. *Well, what have you got for me?*

'I'm sure I don't have a choice,' I said quietly to the air.

'Katherine. You're so funny,' you said without a hint of laughter.

That afternoon, when Gemma headed to a board meeting, I watched you brazenly go into her office, close the door behind you and start rifling through her in-tray. You opened a stiff brown envelope, removed what looked distinctively like a corporate credit card, and slipped it into your pocket. I was outraged, not just because of the lunacy of giving an intern her own card on account of being the pretend daughter of the boss, but because I'd been waiting weeks for the replacement one I'd been promised by the new owners.

When you walked out you went directly to Asif's desk. Whatever you said made him jump out of his seat, pull on his corduroy blazer and accompany you towards the double doors out of the office. It was nearly 3 p.m., the time I'd normally go for a coffee with him. It seemed we wouldn't be heading out together that day. Neither would I go for coffee with him the next day, nor the day after that.

After watching you disappear with my only remaining ally at work, I dialled a department recently created under the new management.

'Is this Talent and People? Katherine Ross here. I've got a new intern, started today. Trying to work out how best to use her, could you ping over her CV?'

If I was going to get one step ahead of you, I needed to get to know you better.

Lily

5th March – The First Day

I so love the ritual of writing this at the end of my day. The stiff cover, the rustle of real paper, a safe space for me to unload and observe, and so much more *intimate* than my MacBook. Vintage, like a proper diary, one I can't delete or undo. This notebook is perfect.

I should have been long gone by the time Katherine Ross showed up at the bus stop. It was so weird. She kept turning around, blatantly staring, which got me thinking. Why don't I blag my way into the woman's cab? So I do. Easily done.

At first, all I get from her is the generalisable hate she has for people my age. It was radiating off her, the way she looked at everyone at the bus stop. Total disdain. But then she lets herself talk and the hate starts to lift. She likes chatting to me, I can tell. What's more surprising is how much I enjoy talking to her, watching her speak. It's like there's a whisper of something warm, and I get the feeling she's throwing me a rope she wants me to grab onto. I've only felt it once before in my life. When I realise it's happening again, and with KR of all people, I have to stop myself from massively over-sharing.

Don't ask me how, but at one point she ends up stroking my face. Now that, I was not expecting! It feels pretty intense when I have to keep my head straight. I also need to make my life easy wherever I can, so I decide to pick up Mum's gift for Gem as I'd promised. I have it that we swing by one of the offices she cleans on Mondays. God knows how many fat cats' bins she had to empty to pay for that pen, but Gem will, and I guess that's the point – to make Gem feel crappy on a day she should be feeling good, guilting her out about how much Mum would have toiled to buy something Gemma could pick up with the change in her Smythson purse.

When I get back to the cab, I can tell KR had been looking at my MacBook. For about a second, I brick it, but she looks so guilty, I know she'd not got very far. I kind of feel sorry for her.

Gem gives me The Talk the second I walk in. I make all the right noises, of course. When it comes to telling people what they want to hear, I am, of course, something of an expert.

KR is scared of Gem. When it's her turn to go into Gem's office for the first time, she looks petrified, so I see an opportunity. I do what any supportive subordinate would when their boss has an important meeting, I give her a bit of friendly encouragement that might help keep her on her toes. Isn't that what 'normal' female friendships are all about? Show me even the best of friends who don't have to watch what they say, bend over backwards to keep everything on an even keel, all the while trying to make the whole thing look like it's not really hard work.

I also make a point of showing KR I'm onto way better things than the grunt work she'd inevitably give me, the freshest of the fresh interns, the lowest of the low. I get a couple of pieces published, make them change the front cover of the awards reprint.

I invite the right-hand man Asif out for coffee. He jumps at the chance. Too easy.

She's made sure everyone knows I'm there because I'm The Niece. She didn't tell them I wasn't being paid though did she. Gem tells me I need to be seen to 'earn my stripes' first and wait for an opening. The ground is already shifting, even if she, and KR, can't feel it yet.

CHAPTER 2

Katherine

When I got home from the gym that night I looked at my flat again with new eyes: your eyes. Every inch of our 730 square feet had been maximised. When we planned to sell up, I'd encouraged an old mate to do a piece on the place for 'Homes & Property' in the *Evening Standard*. The headline: 'The next big thing', the sell: 'How one budding novelist styled the life into her conversion in up-and-coming N4'. The piece detailed how I'd turned walls into bookcases, high ceilings into display mezzanines, bedroom stairs into storage, with feature walls created not by wallpaper but oversized Damien Hirst prints. With that article, I felt like I'd really done it. I'd left the old me at my mother's farm where she belonged. I was no longer insignificant, no longer provincial. I was urbane. Successful. Someone you wanted to be. Someone you wanted to know. Now I barely remember being that person.

We paid for doing up the place with the rent from Iain's flat in Holloway, which he owned outright, having the foresight to buy it practically on his credit card back in 1990. My friend had written that I was a journalist and 'writer-in-waiting' and it was almost true. Two literary agents had asked for the rest of my latest manuscript and only one had passed by the time of the interview. Iain, meanwhile, was still flying high as a senior copywriter for ad agencies and was about to land a gig on the writing team of a sitcom pilot. It seemed we were approaching some terrific threshold: the tantalising possibility of unqualified London success, so close we could taste it in the air and on each other. Our many and varied friends pumped us up.

We'd sell my place, use the equity to shoot for a four-bed fixer-upper on the edges of Highbury and use the Holloway rent to help pay for the works. Iain was in his mid-thirties by then, I was about twenty-six. Life was so good, we just didn't realise it yet.

'So, how was it, then? I've been waiting for the call all day!' Iain shouted at me from the kitchen. It was just Iain and me, as you know. We were getting on for twenty years together when I met you. Those years, all the times we'd relished together, all those we'd survived as a couple, had stitched us into each other. That's how it felt. Not every woman would let Iain be who he was, live the life he enjoyed, and not every man would fit to me. For one thing, I had always been adamant that I never wanted children. I suppose you could say I was a victim of neglect as a child. Iain was the first person I wanted to tell. I also told him I couldn't risk putting someone else through anything like the experiences I'd gone through. It was too terrifying and, anyway, Iain knew we didn't want sober lives where we'd have to lock down at six o'clock. Us with kids, who would we be? Not us at all. We agreed early on to leave the breeding to people less interesting than us and focus instead on having a fantastic life together, one that would allow our creative selves to thrive. I believed the narrative was holding.

'Hello, gorgeous.' I kissed Iain's cheek, damp with steam from the pan he was hanging over.

'Hello, you.'

He and I still looked broadly the same as we did in the pictures for the *Evening Standard* spread. I've always looked after myself. I run. I go to the gym. I run *to* the gym. I don't wear leggings unless I'm *at* the gym. And it is only relatively recently I seem to have found myself in that specific category of invisible I didn't really understand existed until, one day just before I got ill, I realised I hadn't told a single slowing van driver to fuck off when I ran to the gym. I could now run all the way down Green Lanes wholly untroubled. Not a single beep. At first it felt liberating, this mid-life cloak of invisibility, for that purpose at least. But I suppose I never thought it would sweep over people like me, and so emphatically, especially when I wasn't even old yet. Or perhaps I was.

A couple of weeks before I met you, I'd pulled out some short shorts I'd not worn since I was thirty-odd. I ran and waited for the cat calls, but nothing. It seemed white van men were able to age a woman by her calves and thighs alone, but what exactly was old about mine? I hated that I cared. Women like me were supposed to be better than this.

'How *was* it?' I repeated Iain's question back to him. I'd been wondering what to tell him. I wanted to talk about you, but I also knew if I said what was really on my mind, I'd sound completely neurotic. But I did need to confide in him. Because he and I were best friends. Each other's only friends.

We'd had many lives together. The one shortly after the

Evening Standard spread is where our luck started to turn. London itself seemed to move against us. Iain's pilot got pushed to midnight, the series dying quietly at birth. My latest manuscript, my final attempt at writing sustained prose in my own voice, was rejected by the second agent and then it seemed like I'd run out of things to say.

'I'm wai-ting,' Iain sang, his fingers squeezing the black plastic valve of boxed red he would have started on a couple of hours earlier, sending a drink for me gushing loudly into an expectant tumbler.

Soon after the sitcom was canned, he was made redundant. There was no justice in it, but as he passed forty, Iain was ageing into a professional leprosy. He could only get bits and bobs of freelance work. We started to lose a bit of confidence. By the time I'd been at *Leadership* for the best part of ten years, I was being paid an editor's salary, but the fixer-upper crept up to £400,000, then £450,000, then suddenly £700,000 and after that, we stopped looking. We upped the rent on Iain's place and decided to stay put at mine until the bubble burst. That first day I met you, we were still waiting for the pop.

'Well, I'd say today certainly feels like the start of "An Exciting New Chapter".' I repeated the subject line of Gemma's first all-staff email (and in gauche title case too) as I hung my jacket up. My eyes caught the poster that darkened my hall, hovering over our lives for the last five years. It was the real reason why I still lived in what should have been my bachelorette flat.

It was a one-off poster of The Film. The Film was supposed to be the start of An Exciting New Chapter for me and Iain. Perhaps Iain would tell you one version of the story, but let me tell you mine from where I think it starts.

As my father had the temerity to die on my mother when I was nine, it had been instilled in me at an early age that no one can save you from yourself, especially not a man. My mother spoke to me only when she sought to remind me that we are all truly alone and no white knight will come to your rescue. This is the one thing my mother and I agreed on. I had looked to my writing to save me, but as I got past thirty, something changed. I lost the will to write for myself. I thought about writing all the time, but the memory of my second manuscript being rejected for the final time, when I felt I'd so nearly become published, hurt too much to put myself through the process again.

The ideas didn't come. I started a couple of drafts, but somewhere I'd lost whatever it is you inherently have, what I had for a short window in my twenties: the innate belief in what you say and the expectation your words will always find a willing audience. Because that's how people like you carry yourself about the world, isn't it? You think someone should always be primed, waiting to listen to you. Maybe not being able to write for myself was the very earliest sign of the beige clouds swirling. While my creative life was in stasis, Iain was still trying to make his happen. Then a way for me to ride his wave came along; a chance for him to save me from myself.

He invited me and most of our old mates to go in on a film he would write and produce. It didn't take much for us to put our money in; we were all going to be Executive Producers. It proved irresistible to me and everyone else whose dreams had faltered as their fortieth years approached. We put our faith in Iain's ability, some of us, admittedly, with fingers crossed behind our backs. Because it wasn't necessarily that we believed Iain was a born auteur. Ultimately, the film fulfilled the belief there had to be *something* that would provide a final chance to make good on our lives, to snatch victory from the jaws of middle-aged defeatism.

All my savings for the fixer-upper went into the film, and when more money was needed, I wanted to believe re-mortgaging my Manor House flat to the hilt and adding Iain to the deeds to extract even more from the lender would be the penultimate paragraph on a story that ended marvellously, historically, for him and for me. But no matter what you said about the film, it was not good. It was appalling. It did not rescue us. It died a death and killed our friendships with all those who'd let themselves believe Iain would produce a work of excellence that would generate life-changing money for all investors. Iain said sorry over and over, but there was nothing to say sorry for, not really. He'd made no promises, but he had tried, hadn't he? *We* had tried. The one thing your generation excels at is making stuff with your iPhones, pouring your innermost thoughts into your tweets and your blogs until you get better at it and/or something finally sticks. For people like us, things aren't so easy; and they certainly didn't come as cheap.

But I admit, I made a mistake. I looked outside of myself for salvation.

It got so that our friends stopped calling us. Part of me was relieved because whenever I saw them, at some point the conversation always turned to The Film. What might have been. What was lost. We had to find new bodies to come back to ours, buying the last round and plenty of coke for those who would venture to Manor House. But soon enough, we found ourselves going home alone together, and at some point a couple of years ago or so, we stopped going out much at all. Then, when we weren't really looking, we became truly middle-aged.

You don't need a specific reason to suffer from a mental malaise but I know your lot, always seeking a 'trigger' to understand my illness, so, take your pick for mine: the fact I could no longer deny the London life I'd built wasn't strong enough to save me. It would not put a clear blue ocean of money and creative success between me and the desperate child on a farm in Derbyshire. Nor would it solve the problem of the management consultants circling the magazine, or the failure to move house, or my body starting to do dreadful middle-aged things; chronically dry skin on my shins no moisturiser could address, robust whiskers on my chin I had to pluck away every single day, the first grey pube, then another, and another. I felt so let down by my body, but more by my pathetic attitude to it.

Altogether, things big and small made me feel as if I was breaking down until eventually I was a broken thing. And let me tell you something, Lily, you really learn who your friends are when you become needy and unglamorous. It turns out none of my old girlfriends wanted to know the ill version of me when I tentatively reached out to them again. On a good day, I told myself it might have been different if they hadn't invested in the film, or if the film had provided them with the stellar returns we'd all hoped were possible. On a bad day, I knew they only loved me when I was flying high. How could I find fault with them when I felt broadly the same?

Iain always smiled as he stirred whatever he was cooking

for me. When I was ill, he'd cooked me back to life. It wasn't that nothing tasted good, it was that everything tasted of nothing: no texture or depth. Iain had to keep me alive like the pathetic rejected lambs my mother forced me to bottle-feed as a child. He couldn't get out of the habit of hand-rearing me; cooking elaborate, time-consuming, fattening meals; boiling vats of bones all day long, as if he could borrow the distilled marrow of dead animals to give the essence of life back to me in a bowl. That's what you think we do to your generation, isn't it, Lily? Steal your young lives for our own self-serving ends?

Iain stirred his stew so vigorously, I noticed while his arms were getting thinner, his stomach trembled above his belt. Mouse-coloured hair, now silvering. But he was still attractive, with well-set grey eyes, a wide symmetrical smile, and a liking for looking at me a little longer than he needed to; he made me feel truly seen. Did you feel that way too when you first met him? What did you really think of him, of us, in those early days?

'I know what'll cheer you up,' my Iain said.

'Who says I need cheering up?'

'Some Hungarian New Wave. There's nothing a little Béla Tarr can't solve. A spot of *Damnation* will put it all in perspective.' He squeezed the last drops of the wine out, having liberated the silver bag from its box, holding it between his torso and underarm like a bagpipe. My partner was what your lot might call 'an alcoholic', but you figured that out soon enough, didn't you? What you'll never understand is how this wasn't an issue before you. Perhaps one day your generation will grow to see how life doesn't cleave along binary lines:

hopeless addict/functioning citizen; mentally well/mentally ill; good person/bad person.

'Well, why ever not?' I looked into my glass.

'What's Gemma really like then?'

I turned on my stool, my back to Iain and the breakfast bar that divided the tiny open kitchen from the living space in my flat. Some instinct made me think twice about introducing you to the conversation, to say your name in my home, to let you invade my domestic space, but still, I felt compelled to speak of you.

'Oh, she's alright. Earnest, in an HR-sanctioned way ... But she's landed me with her jumped-up niece.'

'*Another* intern is it? How many's that now?'

'Six? Seven? I can't keep track anymore. Anyway, she flounced into my cab this morning. The 141 decided to take the day off and I managed to flag a cab and this *millennial* jumps in and eventually tells me she *happens* to be the boss's niece. What she doesn't tell me is that she's the one who gave Gemma Lunt the bright idea of buying out *Leadership*. She definitely would have known all about me, but played dumb and let me rabbit on about my job before the big reveal. Creepy or what?'

'Maybe she didn't recognise you.' Iain, already on your side. I glowered at him. 'Well, anyway, is she any good? Going to make your life easier? Worse? Too soon to say?'

I breathed, 'Well, she's clearly privileged. Imagine me at her age having a maiden aunt who could go out and pick up a magazine for me to write for? She's walked in off the street, jangling her family's money, fresh out of uni, with the cheek to demand we change the front cover. *And* she starts writing a piece on the awards off-the-bat. Just like that.'

'How very dare she, and at a magazine too.'

'Oh shut up, you know what I mean.'

'Not really,' he laughed.

'When *I* did work experience, you just assumed you'd be making coffee, doing the photocopying, dodging the boss's busy hands. Or not, depending on who the boss was.'

'And when *you* started out, they still called it "work experience," it lasted two weeks before you were made "senior reporter" and people still used photocopiers … and sent faxes.'

'That was probably before she was even born. Fuck, she didn't even exist when I was at peak possibility.'

'Hey. You. You're not even close to that yet. Not even close,' his mouth slopped around on the last 's' sound, but he meant it. He still believed in me.

'And young people knew their place. Fuck, we're old.'

'We are that. And aren't you just a wee bit glad about it?' He took another gulp from his glass, then watched me swinging around on my bar stool.

'Go on. What's really pissing you off about this girl? Is she fit?'

I shook my head. 'No. She's not *fit* … She's an absolute knockout.'

'OK, so let's see now: she's got youth, beauty, privilege and nepotism going for her. No wonder she's writing the cover story on day one.'

I said nothing.

'And no wonder you're jealous.'

'I am not,' I lied. 'Come on, let's not let her ruin our evening. Where's my *Damnation*?'

I pretended to look about the flat and again thought of how

56

you would see it. There were indeed all the beautiful things you'd imagined surrounded me: Provençal pots, Ashanti masks, Balinese ceramics, all evidence of a life lived wide and well. Once. I viewed them each afresh with your eyes and saw far too many things. Items fighting for space on bookshelves and display mezzanines I couldn't face dusting anymore, the cleaner long sacked. A collection of dull silver trays clustered above the door. There was hardly a square inch of wall that didn't have something on it. No cupboard door sat flush. So many things seemed like they were trying to burst out; I bruised my hips on the corners of overstuffed drawers poking out; I had to duck for cover every time I opened a cupboard, knowing some plate or culinary gadget of Iain's might fall and hit me. The whole place looked and felt like a life double-backed on itself, looped over and over. Sun-faded Hirst prints. Dusty Moti tapestries from India. Iain's old gig photography. There was no space anymore. No space for more stuff, no space for new thoughts, no space to create; no real space for the future at all.

I seemed to have collected masks from every corner of the world without ever intending to. So many masks. My own face, now a mask. An exhausted skin caught over a mind struggling to accept it was no longer young. I was beginning to realise something I should have looked hard in the face, then warned you and all women like you about: there's a big secret only revealed when it's too late: how you feel in your twenties is an illusion. That unique flavour of power and self-knowledge, you'd never know it at the time, but it dissolves. I should have told you from the off to prepare to save yourself from being caught unawares by the passage of time as I had been. When age moves against you, make sure you've built your self-worth around what you're capable of doing, not the beauty of your youth. And if I'd have done that, who knows, maybe then you wouldn't have changed my life like you did.

I'd forwarded your CV to my personal email and read it on the bus home. It showed an urbane life. A long list of posh schools, a year out before English Lit at Leeds and what looked like more time out, (travelling on 'Gem's' generosity, no doubt), making you twenty-four to my forty-one. Obscene. The charmed life of a graduate, and a hugely privileged one at that, brazenly stretching ahead of you; a long corridor lined with doors blown wide open by your confidence and your utter gorgeousness. *That used to be me*, I thought, now it's other people; now it's you.

'What's her name? Just so I can really get on board when you're bitching about her.'

I turned my head towards the ceiling, the only clear white space in my whole flat.

'Her name is Lily.'

'Lily. They're always called something like Poppy, or Daisy or Lily. She sounds like a proper Snowflake, love. You might need to watch yourself.'

Damnation is a tale of desire, betrayal and despair. I'd agreed to watch it only to humour Iain really, doing a bit of work on the side. But while he was out-cold after the first twenty minutes, I watched to the bitter end. It spoke to me.

When it was over, I shut my laptop and watched him asleep, or unconscious, his mouth agape in a classic grandad-after-Christmas-lunch way. And I loved him.

'Iain. *Iain?* Come to bed,' I shook his shoulder and touched his face, trying to wake him in the same way I did every night. But he never stirred when he was like that. He'd come round in a couple of hours and throw himself down on our bed. So, as usual, I left him, crept to the bathroom, locked the door and inserted two fingers into the back of my throat, letting go of all the fat and sugar Iain had put in me.

You see, Iain needed to feel he was doing something, anything, to contribute to our life and my happiness. Food was his medium. In the day, I retained the foods I'd chosen for myself. Come the night, I had to let my partner fulfil his role, but I couldn't have his food pillowing me out into full-frontal middle age. You wouldn't understand, but this purging ritual was an act of love. It was one of the many secrets of our long and happy relationship.

When I slept that night, I had the dream where I tried to reach the paddock gate for the first time. I cried out for the child in me; the dreadful sense of my mother's hate relived for the first time in years.

Lily

5th March – The First Day, continued

Stay late in the office. Get a couple of stories up online. Think twice about the picture byline, but I'm actually really proud of what I've produced, so I go for it. Asif assumes it's Gem's idea, she assumes it's his. No one tries to stop me.

I get inside my building as I always try to – without the concierge seeing me.

When I came down to London with Gem, I was desperate to avoid staying with her or Mum. They want too much from me, from what my life could be, or maybe now, what it could have been. Everything they say wears me down to less than I am. Especially Gem. She's so over-invested, there's no way she could ever get a decent return. She always demands the best by reminding me of the worst, 'You can *do better*. You can *be better*.' It's too much to keep up with being the version of me Gem expects at work and at home.

It started the very first day we moved in with her.

We'd celebrated my eighth birthday by getting evicted. Mum had been late again with the rent, the landlord wanted us out and was keeping the deposit. We packed our things and schlepped from where we were in Newham to Gem's place in Marylebone. I'd been there before and other people will say it was a completely gorgeous place. Huge. But to me it was like travelling to another planet. All I wanted to do was go back to our old flat and my old school where everyone knew me. When we'd visited the Marylebone place before, it seemed like there was too much space. I never felt comfortable. From the moment we had to live there, I knew I was never going to fill the place. I also knew from the off that was the one thing Gem expected. I was there to plug the gaps in her life.

Gem's challenge was that investing in a relationship to produce children was too high risk for her. The chances of getting what she wanted out of it were too open. Owning a child ready-made by someone else took away that risk factor. Enter me.

I remember us turning up with our backpacks and carrier bags of my cuddly toys. Gem opened the door and scooped me off her step and swung me into her hallway, triumphant. My mum had conceded: she needed Gem's help to raise me and I was now in her home indefinitely. She would get to be a parent.

'Welcome home, my darling. I'm so happy you're here. Now, how about you and I make a deal. You know what a deal is, don't you, Lily?'

'I think so.' Gem, always with the 'deals' and 'negotiations', every bit of her life, even the most personal, based on a hustle rigged so she walks away with more than she deserves.

'I'll be the best aunt in the whole wide world, I will make sure you always have a home with me if you can promise to be the best Lily you can be. Can you do that for me?'

I nodded. I could feel the weight loaded into the words. I've always felt in deficit with Mum, like I owed her a favour and now I guessed Gem was doing the same. I wanted to ask her what I had to do to make things OK, but I could feel the sobs trying to tear their way out of my lungs and I didn't want to lose it, I guess because I already had an idea that wouldn't be what 'best Lily' would do.

To my mum, Gem said nothing. She held the door and watched her sister walk in. There was nothing to say. Gem and Mum's parents were apparently dirt poor, but Gem had 'pulled herself up by the bootstraps'. My mum, on the other hand, had continued the family traditional of bad jobs and bad housing. She never understood Gem's belief that stacks of cash were all anyone could desire. All Mum wanted was a simple life – husband, kids, little house, little job, which drove Gem mad; she hated Mum's *life choices*. 'Elaine, your problem is you aim so low. There's so little margin for error, one tiny wobble puts you on your knees,' I heard Gem say once, with relish. The final eviction had proved Gem right: my mum couldn't even do the basics. There she was, homeless and alone with one child she'd apparently 'waited a long time for' but whose existence she blamed for pushing my dad out the door.

Mum and I climbed up the staircase that smelt like a church to our rooms. When we got to my room, my mum told me, 'Don't listen to what she says. You don't belong to her.'

I told my mum, 'I don't belong to anyone. Not you either,' because I don't. I was right and she knew it.

From nowhere, she said, 'I do my best, Lily. I know that's not good enough for you, it wasn't enough your father.'

Dad the Disappeared. The taboo I was never allowed to speak of, but she could lob at me whenever it suited. I wanted to make her pay for saying his name and for putting me in that big stupid flat and the dumb new school I knew I'd be dragged to soon enough.

'But you *can't* look after me. That's why we've had to move in with Gem, isn't it?'

'Listen to me. She is *not* your mother. I am, for my sins.'

I looked at her right in the eyes and asked, 'What's a sin, *Elaine*?'

She was quiet for what felt like a long time, her rough fingers gripping legs covered by a cheap denim skirt. 'Come down when you've unpacked your things and washed your hands.'

So, from that day, I knew it was going to be a case of one of them thinking, 'If I press this button, will she come closer to me than to her?' or, 'If I dangle this carrot, promise her this, will she bend my way?' Gem wanted her trophy 'daughter' and Mum wanted to keep control over the one thing she had and Gem didn't. That's not love, is it? People assume because I had not one but two maternal figures, I grew up in a kind of paradise. But I was not *nurtured*, I was *experimented on* as they tried to beat each other using me. The only way I was going to survive was by pitting the two of them against each other.

This rule applied for years, all the way up to Gem buying *Leadership*. I'd planted the idea of Gem thinking about her legacy. What was she working towards? What was she leaving behind and who to? I carefully led talk of 'legacy' towards the idea of 'dynasty'. 'Gem, don't you think it would be incredible to find something we could both take a role in growing, not just to sell it on, but to become our family business? For me, then maybe even for my children, your grandchildren … ? I've read about this magazine that's in trouble but has massive potential.'

Mum could see what was happening and didn't like it one bit. 'School fees are one thing, Gemma, but buying a company so she can have a go at playing journalist? Isn't that a bit much, even for you?' To which Gem said, 'At least my hard work has bought her an education and more. How have you ever helped her? How were *you* planning to get her out of the mess she's in?' (Once it was done, Gem never discussed what happened to me at uni in terms that actually described the events. Always 'the mess', 'the problems.') Mum said, 'How dare you say I don't work hard? And if she's got into a mess, it's trying to be someone like you who'd flog their grandma for a quid.'

When we knew the *Leadership* buyout was definitely hap-pening, I let both of them know I needed to move. My mother had only just managed to get away from Gem by moving to a miniscule rented flat in Mile End. She didn't want me staying with Gem anymore, but she didn't want me living with her either, not really, although she told me I could 'have the living room' at her place if I 'really wanted it'. She made a seriously half-baked attempt to look like she actually cared where I lived, 'Get your own place, keep on with Gemma, it's your choice, but do *not* make out you couldn't have stayed with me if you wanted to, Lily.' Ok, Mum, you can say you tried to help me now.

I told Gem I didn't think it was a great idea if I lived with her once we started working together. 'It's going to look so much more professional for us if we don't introduce ourselves to the business as a "mother and daughter act", but two individuals serious about making the magazine a success.' She didn't *quite* buy this, telling me, 'Do let me know when you've touched down in the real world. I'll keep your room made up in Marylebone.'

Of course, there was no way I could afford anywhere on the meagre allowance she gives me to keep me from 'working in jobs like your mother's.' But I had to show her she wasn't right about everything. So, I am now fully immersed in the real world, thanks Gem.

I knew I had to be away from both of them and somewhere I could focus on what I need to do, but I was about two minutes into my search when I realised rent, even in unsexy Zone 3 North East London, is *completely* insane. I mean, I couldn't even afford to live in one of those places where you're the one sleeping in the living room, let alone somewhere with a real room of my own and a proper space where I could eat a meal with a flatmate, sit on a sofa and talk, maybe even make a friend. Today, living rooms are another basic that's become a luxury for my age group. *Why aren't we rioting, people?*

I googled 'Rent-free accommodation N4' in an act of hopeful desperation, as I'm sure hundreds of others like me must have done before. I saw this:

Sympathetic homeless female 18-24 req. for discrete rent-free use of mod high-rise apartment N4. Apply w/ photo.

I went to see the place, to see the concierge who'd posted the ad. He is in his forties and completely repulsive. I negotiated the 'erotic arrangement' with him down to one hour every Wednesday in exchange for the use of the flat and the promise to keep it quiet from the absent owner, a Singaporean, he tells me. The time with him seems to come around so fast. Sometimes it feels like a week of Wednesdays.

When he's sweating on top of me, behind my eyelids I imagine a map of London with tiny little flashing red lights for every one of us swapping the use of our bodies for the use of a home. Were all of them damaged like me? Or were some of them normal, with friends who worried about them, mates who would eventually say, 'That's enough. You need to come and crash with me'? Maybe they would one day find themselves somewhere warm and not toxic, protected from it all – dysfunctional parents, exploitative rent and 'erotic arrangements'. Was it ever possible that one day we would all find ourselves safe, in jobs that pay us money, with the possibility of a real future?

I honestly don't know why more people my age aren't more like me. Why aren't they angrier? We're not much more than playthings to those older than us, to people exactly like KR. Her so-called Generation X are the *worst*. KR and her contemporaries think it's their right to take us for everything we have, everything they think they can get away with, then minimise our pain and undermine us for our choices over the few things we can control.

Each week, when the concierge goes after his hour, I swallow my tears down like a meal, something to make me stronger. Afterwards, when I take my shower and scrub my body down with salt and honey, it's very hard not to give in and cry. But I never do.

I've just pulled over the deadbolt and safety chain and put some soup on, my mum's words ringing in my ears, a last-minute plea to create the impression she really did want me to stay with her: 'You'll never manage on your own. You can't even boil an egg.' To which I reminded her, 'I don't eat eggs.'

I log on and start to type, only remembering the soup when I smell the pan burning dry. I just hate it when the adults are right.

Time to show one of them how wrong they can be. In the morning, I'll pop my head into Gem's office and tell her I've thought of a great way to help Katherine Ross get back to her best, like she and I talked about.

I know I'm paying a high price to stay in this flat. But I can see KR's place from here. I'm less than 100 metres away but from the darkened glass of the tenth floor, I am invisible to her.

For four weeks now, I've got to see her spill out onto her front steps every morning. I know what times she comes and goes. I know how weak she's feeling before she puts on her daily 'I'm doing fine!' mask for the rest of the world as she drags herself to the end of her road and across Green Lanes to the bus stop at the foot of my block. I know on Sundays she tears around the park like something is chasing her, and in the afternoon strides to the pub with The Partner like they're late for an important appointment.

All this insight makes the price for this apartment worth paying.

CHAPTER 3

Katherine

This is how catastrophic change begins. Small disturbances at the surface, the first suggestion of the sinkhole opening beneath; the moment in the horror movie the protagonist sees something out of the corner of her eye and dismisses it witlessly. I used to love horror movies. I can't bear them now.

Even though I felt uneasy about you, I couldn't wait to see you that second morning. I couldn't give what I felt a name. I still can't. The best I can do is say it felt like a kind of imprinting. I'd been let down by my life and orphaned by my friends. I hadn't talked properly to anyone who wasn't my partner in so long, it was as if I had an overflowing store of friendship backed-up in me. You. Yes, Lily, even though I wasn't sure about you, I was *that* pathetic; I was ready to bury my doubts. This is who you become when no one returns your calls, and the only people troubling your mobile are your GP, your partner, or Vodafone.

On Tuesday morning I spent ages choosing an outfit that might make me look fresh and relevant and not mutton dressed as lamb. I hopelessly tried to do my makeup to achieve a dewy sheen. I wondered if the time was coming when I should let my natural colour come through, or dye my hair something other than black, which seemed suddenly blocky and incongruous against my dulling face. I desperately wanted to collapse the years between someone like you and someone like me.

Part of me was glad when you weren't at the bus stop. I was disturbed by the horrid dream I was struggling to shake off, but buoyed by the fact my articles would be live on the website and in the shiny new editions on everyone's desks by the time I got in. You may have changed the cover for the issues they'd distribute at the awards, but this edition would be all mine.

I got to my desk. Still no you. And no coffee from Asif either. I turned to find the two of you nestled next to each other on the old sub editors' desks, huddled around what looked like proofs of the most recent issue.

'Good morning. Time for a quick catch up? Katherine?' Gemma tried to get my attention from the doorway of her office.

'Be right there,' I said distractedly, watching Asif run his fingers over his beard as you looked to gauge his reaction to something you'd just said. I watched until I couldn't anymore, closing Gemma's office door slowly on the sight of you throwing your head back in glee. Asif looked as if he could just climb right inside you there and then.

'Congratulations on this.' She threw a fresh copy of *Leadership* towards me over her desk. 'Some great foundations we can really build on.'

'Thank you.' *Is that it? For 12,000 words from your most senior writer? Patronising.*

'What I want to talk to you about, today, is how we're going to achieve that.'

'Yes?'

'I hope you'll take what I'm about to say in the spirit in which it is intended … I'd like us to talk about reorganizing our content, making a few tweaks to your writing. So, to that end, I've asked Lily to look at what's working and not working on the website. I should probably tell you, early indications on the two articles she posted—'

'Two articles? I didn't see any copy from her.'

'Asif edited them yesterday evening. Well, they've already had more click-throughs and longer combined viewing times than all of your content in the last four weeks put together.' I watched you through the glass. You were now flicking your fingernails under your chin, before biting your bottom lip as you started to type. I was ready to assume it was your picture byline driving your traffic. 'She's young, but she's a quick learner and she knows how to give online readers in particular what they want, so I've booked some time away from the office for you and her. She's going to help you look again at your writing. There's no shame in needing to re-boot. You could find this is the best thing to happen at this stage of your career. Details to follow. Now, are you up for the challenge?'

What a slap in the face. The humiliation. *You* were going to teach *me*. I didn't yet know you would teach me the lesson of my life.

I had no choice but to say, 'Of course I'm up for it.'

You kept trying to talk to me all day, but I gave you the brush off. I needed more of an idea of what I was dealing with before I let you know anything else about me.

I read your pieces. A horrifying truth dawned. You were

actually pretty good at this. A natural attention-grabber. Your headlines were nearly as enticing as your picture byline; your copy was as taut as mine was saggy. When I re-read my features, they felt in the reading how they'd felt in the writing: hard work. I was angry, I thought it was at you and Gemma, but it was really at me, for being so tired of it all.

But what had Asif been thinking, putting up two pieces from a day-old intern like that? He sent the odd smile over from his side, but knew me well enough to give me some space. It wasn't until gone seven when the office had emptied that I heard him come up behind me to say goodnight.

I looked about. You weren't at your desk, but your machine was still on, so if you were going to file any more sparkling 'content', it would have to go through me.

'Late night at the office, K? Kind of reminds me of old times.' Asif, hands in his pockets, took a step closer. I guessed he was trying to get back into my good books and it was only to make him feel better that I told him, 'Ah, the days of yore. I miss them too. But you know me, Mr Khan, there will always be a part of me that's down with the brown.' I smiled and turned in my seat to face him.

And I don't know how, but there you were, right behind him; a millennial spectre clutching an orange Bobble water bottle, complete with a luminous shard of cucumber glowing within. You looked flustered, maybe because you were appalled at the idea of Asif's buff twenty-six-year-old body against my creaking bones as they had been once. I noted to one day tell you that just because you'd turned his head, you couldn't undo history. Not even you.

'Sorry, I thought I'd get a head start transcribing my— I can't concentrate in my flat.' You turned to Asif who was by then smirking at his shoes.

'Don't worry. I'm off. I'll bid you ladies goodnight. Don't work too hard.'

We both started typing and a difficult silence settled.

'Would you like me to pretend I didn't hear that?' you said eventually.

When did young people get so prissy, so unable to take, give, or hear flirting? I had seen this attitude in so many of my interns in recent years. The rebuffed compliment, the blatant distaste when I've said something, *anything*, even faintly sexual. This wasn't the first time I'd wondered exactly when and why a whole generation became so joyless, so sexless. Then I wondered if your indignation was fired because you'd heard I had a serious partner and believed there was only one way to do *that* right.

A pause.

'Shall I tell you something? My partner and I have a code,' I began. I wanted to shock you now, I had you on the ropes and this would be my one-two jab, to show you up for the wrong-headed innocent you were, give you something else to chew on. 'There are rules. I meet someone I'd like to have sex with, we discuss our feelings and he signs it off, or he doesn't. If he comes across someone he'd like to have sex with, I say yes, or I say no. My partner signed off on Asif, once or twice, but then we agreed I should stop. You see, we're a couple who are first and foremost for each other. That never changes. But if we're lucky, Lily, we're a long time alive, and a long time together. People my age are capable of believing there's more than one way of doing something. My advice to you? Don't judge what you haven't tried.'

Suddenly, displaying the full peacock tail of my sexuality, I felt restored; the real me rising from the ashes of the day. But this wasn't my one-two jab, it was your rope-a-dope: the art of taking blows, letting the other fighter expend themselves before going in for the kill.

'I wasn't talking about that, whatever you're talking about.' Your face was flushed with righteousness. 'Racist language in the workplace? It's a sackable offence.'

You should be careful. How right Iain had been.

And in that moment, I thought I knew what you were. You were here to get me sacked. Plain and simple. Gemma could be the acceptable face of sisters sticking together, middle-aged women doing it for ourselves, but you, her, the faceless head honchos now making up the new board, you all wanted me out.

If only it had just been this.

'I don't think I understand, Lily? Exactly what racist language did I use?'

'I, literally, don't even want to say it out loud.'

'Say what?'

'That racist phrase you just said to Asif.'

'You have to be kidding.'

You began typing again in silence.

'Language, between friends, old friends. It's complicated. Nuanced. Coded. Sometimes, Lily, it's perfectly possible you might not understand what you're actually hearing.'

You took a sip of your cucumber water then typed some more. I started to pack my bag as if I was leaving work as normal, trying to act like someone who was definitely not at any risk of being sacked for being racist.

'There's a code of conduct?' you said eventually, voice sweeping up at the end.

'What, so, we can all work in a "safe space"? There's a lot more to feeling safe at work than bleeding the joy out of every exchange between grown adults. Trust me.'

A pause.

'I guess I heard about your time off. I just thought you might need to possibly be a bit more careful?'

'I wasn't on holiday. And *I* was led to believe confidentiality was enshrined in the new *Code of Conduct*.'

'I'm sorry. I must have heard Asif or one of the interns say something.' You tucked your hair behind your ears and looked back at your screen before deciding to power down. I logged off too, watching for a second as the light drained away from my machine, mesmerised by the little white dot in front of me, feeling the exhaustion in my bones, my brain. A sensation rushed in around me with sickening familiarity: the compulsion to lie down and never get up again. I didn't even notice you'd come to stand by my chair, so when I turned to leave, your body blocked my path. I gasped. Awake again.

'Katherine. Would you consider going for a drink with me? Tonight? Now? Give me a chance to clear the air? I'm sorry, I think I've really overstepped the mark. I'm still feeling my way with this place. With Gem.'

Your black eyes seemed to plead with me. And I thought I saw it again, that loneliness. Your need to connect with another person. Perhaps we would end up getting a burger and talking like we'd known each other forever after all?

'Alright. OK,' I said, nodding dumbly, taken aback by the glint of a feeling shared.

You handed me my leather from the nearby coat stand.

'Shall we?' you said, smiling.

'Give me one second.'

I nipped to the loo to text Iain:

Snowflake wants to go for a drink. Don't worry about dinner.
See you later xx

I couldn't remember the last time I'd sent a 'Going for a drink, be home late' text over some spontaneous invitation, maybe one of the girls finding themselves on the Southbank or London Bridge and thinking *Sod it, let's see if Rossy's up for a drink*. Iain knew how good it would have felt for me to be able to say I wasn't coming home yet. He texted back:

That's fab. Enjoy xxxx

You and I left the office, and that's when we really started to talk.

I don't think I've ever really seen you laugh, but you're very beautiful when you smile. I remember thinking that you smiled a lot that night and how good that made me feel about myself. You were enjoying my company, my stories. You weren't watching the clock, not like my old mates towards the end. And unlike them, with you, there was no sense of you waiting for the moment when you might, in not so many words, suggest I 'pull myself together,' or inevitably get to asking if there was any way whatsoever it would be possible to get some money back after The Film. Talking without these things hanging over the conversation made me feel more like me again. And you asked so many questions that let me hear something of my old voice again. You knew how we all love a great listener, didn't you?

Looking back, I can see there was a tinge of something pre-rehearsed about some of your questions, and somewhere I clocked you'd all but had a personality transplant since your almost total indifference to me in the cab on Monday. But I jumped clean over my doubts and right into telling you my life story.

Chatting to another woman again about my career, my reflections on life so far, was like slipping into a warm bath. How I wanted to soak away the aches and the pains of the last few years. The imprinting process in full swing as I tried to forget all the friends who'd abandoned me. First, the ones who had babies left me, though I could understand why. I was terrible around children. Who would want the scary lady in the leather jacket who never smiled near their kids? Then, The Film did for some of the women I'd cared about most. That hurt, a specific pain I'd not known before. I suppose it was like being dumped, but I didn't know because I'd never been dumped. My luck had run clean out. My girls, my main girls were 'pressing pause' on me, that's what they said. But they never came back. Finally, there were a couple of remaining second circle friends who hadn't invested in The Film. But they didn't know what to do with me when the beige began to blow in. They left me too. Soon enough, the only things left standing were my work and my Iain.

'So, where did it all start for you, being a journalist? I'd love to know. I'm so early in my journey, I know how much I need to learn!'

'Well, I came down to London late nineties, worked in a pub for a bit, this was in the days when you could rent a room in Walthamstow for forty quid a week. I know, fucking ridiculous, right? I applied for work experience at every local paper all over London, but with no training, no degree and no connections, no one would look at me. Then one night, I was out seeing some mates in Islington and I saw these two guys start on some bloke. They had baseball bats. It was ... ugly. My mates ran off home, fair enough, but I watched from across the way, got out my notepad and started getting down the details. Someone called the police and an ambulance. I managed to get some other eyewitness quotes and something from the police too. I told them and everyone else I was a reporter from the *Islington Gazette*. Then, I scooted back up the Victoria Line to my room, begged one of my housemates to borrow his PC, and filed the story to the *Gazette*. Just 250 words, but it was enough to persuade them I could come and do work experience. Pretty cool, eh?'

'My god, yes! Amazing! Then what?'

'I got there, loved it, worked my tits off, got on staff. The money was shit though. I knew I'd earn more on a trade mag. Junior news and features writer on *Leadership* was the first thing I applied for.'

'And you got it.'

'And I got it.'

'And quickly became indispensable, then the youngest editor in the title's history.'

'Yes ... Yes, that's me. How did you—'

'I've been proofing biographies for the awards supplement?'

I nodded. It sounded feasible.

'I want you to know, I have, like, *so* much respect for your experience and how you've come up the ranks. It's inspiring. I also really want you to know, I'm so embarrassed about the Gem-making-us-do-copy-camp-thing. I basically begged her not to make us do it. But she's got her "own ideas" about how she's going to run things, even though she has basically zero experience in journalism. But who are we to talk her down?'

We.

I liked how that sounded, so much. Too much. It resonated around my loneliness, arousing something deep and dormant. You and me: friends. The cub reporter and the grizzled editor, an alliance across generations against 'the man', or woman, in this case.

'Don't worry about it. I'm sure it'll be fine,' I said, swallowing the end of my second gin.

'But I really do. I'm such a worry-wort. Are you a worrier? Sorry, I'm not talking about, you know, your time off or anything.'

'My *beige period*?' I tried to laugh.

'Could I ask … was there a trigger for what happened to you?'

I sighed and looked at you side on, my head cocked to show you I was trying to decide whether to share my private thoughts with you or not. But at that point, it was just that: a show. The sad fact was, I was dying to tell you everything about me. While I was still, apparently, thinking about it, you added, 'You don't need to worry about me. You can trust me.' And I wanted to believe you. I wanted to forget about the taxi ride and your holding back the truth about how you came to my magazine. I wanted to put all that to one side, chalk it up to coincidences and let myself believe the only thing for me to worry about *was* my failing talent. I wanted to let you convince me this was the case and at times like those, you were so dreadfully convincing.

'I'm not worried about you.' Probably the greatest lie I told myself about you, worse than convincing myself you were a friend-in-waiting.

'Because I think you'll find I could be very good for you. If you give me a chance.'

And your smile shone at me again as you moved one hand out across the table in my direction, reminding me of my young self again, that combination of steel and softness.

It's then I saw it clearly: I could mentor you. We could go through the whole copy camp charade, but I'd bring you round to my way of doing things, share with you everything *I* knew. I would mentor you and in return you could teach me the ways of your digital world. We'd be unstoppable. We'd propel the magazine and website into the stratosphere. More readers, more advertisers, more sponsors, more everything. I would initiate our partnership by conceding to your absurd millennial vocabulary.

'Triggers for my illness … Well, I would say it wasn't just one thing and I'm not sure I wholly believe in triggers, not for me anyway. I'd had hard times before and they hadn't got me down, not *down*-down. If anything, the dark days got me up, off my feet. Then when I got ill, it was just … total. I felt flattened, the world didn't look like the world anymore. It's hard to explain, but I don't think it was just a case of, "Oh my god, we're broke," or "Oh my god, am I really celebrating my fortieth birthday at *Leadership*?" or any one thing that pushed me over the edge. It was nothing and everything.' I shrugged, as if I was talking about some mysterious thing that had happened to me a very long time ago. You changed tack.

'Wow. So from the late nineties to now, that's like, a whole bunch of time. *Leadership* must be like a home-away-from-home.'

'It is, or it was, before everything changed.'

'Maybe it can be again?' you said softly and I had to look away so you couldn't see how much you'd moved me.

'Sometimes I … I feel as if I've let *Leadership* down. I've let myself down. I know we're going to be OK; I know we can survive using a rolling buffet of interns to keep the lights on and sponsored content to pay me.' You visibly bristled at this, I ignored it. 'But I can still see it, we're slipping behind editorially. Readers, they're so fickle these days. I've seen the data. They skip through a story that took a week to put together for the magazine in fifteen fucking seconds on the website and I don't know why. You know, I *did* see the digital revolution coming? I thought I could ignore it, but it got bigger and bigger, so much bigger than I thought it ever would, until it changed fucking everything and it feels like I don't *get* anything anymore.' I saw some bubbles of spit land on my sleeve on the 'm' of 'more'. I was literally, as you would say (correctly for once), frothing at the mouth. 'Sorry. I—' I began and you rubbed my forearm. 'I don't usually spill my guts like this.'

'Well, get used to it, boss. OK? Shall we get a bottle of something red and warming?'

'Yes! Allow me. Fuck it all, right?'

I noticed you recoiled slightly whenever I swore. I suppose I naturally swear a lot, but I'd always thought most journalists were prone to sweariness, whatever their age. As much as I believe people like you need to toughen-up, I didn't like the faint tell as the skin under your eyes tightened at each curse. Before too long into our night, I stopped the 'fucks' and 'cunts' and even the 'arseholes'. I started to feel less angry in doing so. You helped me soothe myself. Maybe you millennials were actually onto something.

It began to feel, as we sat there in the corner of The George that night, when tourists and beery workmates came and went around us unnoticed, that you and I were really communicating. I felt the warmth of a couple of gins and a bottle of Rioja and the full flush of releasing all the conversation I had pent up in me. And it was thrilling to observe your pristine complexion up-close, the swell of your cheeks, the way you tapped the white triangle of skin above your tangerine v-neck from time to time. My skin once glowed like yours.

We both looked at our glasses, only a drip in each of them. You poured the remainder of the bottle into my glass. I sensed our evening drawing to a close. I didn't want it over yet.

'Writing was a real escape for me. Not just journalism, writing my own stuff too. I wrote my first manuscript, just for me, to get my head together about … childhood stuff, I suppose. Does your blog help you get your head straight?'

'I guess. That and my diary. I try to work out my future by processing the past and reporting on the present there.'

'I used to keep my notepad with me at all times in case I ran into a story, but also if I had a thought about something or other I wanted to get down. Iain used to call it my "little book of lottery tickets". One of them had the winning line on it, the one that would help me write the next manuscript. The One. The one that would save me, get me out of *Leadership* and put my life where it deserved to be …'

'Wow. It sounds like, what did you say your husband's called again, Iain? He sounds super-supportive.'

'Iain. My partner, not my husband.'

You'd invited him into the conversation and then I really let myself go, encouraging you to excavate me, draw things to the surface. Because when I spoke about Iain, it felt so good to share all the gestures, big and small, that made him so wonderful. When our relationship seemed of interest to you, he and I became my proudest achievement. I seemed to be educating you about proper, grown-up partnerships. You asked me more and more questions.

'How did you know Iain was right for you?'

'I suppose I fell for him, hard. I sort of realised when I met him, I thought I'd been walking forward into my life. I mean, I had, but I'd been limping on one leg, because now I felt complete, balanced, a left leg to the right.'

And then I started telling you how Iain and I had come to sleep with other people, figuring I could educate you about the world, how things could be. 'We were at a party and I had this thought that we shouldn't deny ourselves, even though we knew we were going to be together for a long time, maybe forever. He knew exactly what I meant. That's why we work, Lily. We have rules, like I said. We talked about everyone before and after.'

'Who were the other guys you were with?'

'God, all sorts really. Contacts. Friends. Friends of friends.

A good many colleagues. Interns. *Lots* of interns.' I immediately regretted saying this as your face twitched when I said 'interns' and I instantly tried to cover my tracks. In truth, there had been fewer takers over recent years, which couldn't have helped me much. It suggested either that I wasn't as attractive as I was when I was younger and/or most of the millennial generation were as ridiculously puritanical about sex in the workplace as I suspected. It's hard to say which I found intuitively more disappointing. 'I mean, yes, interns, but not for a while. Mostly when I was closer to their age. The thing with Asif? We have a bit more of a connection than interns from back in the day. He's like my work-husband. We don't play that way anymore, by the way. My idea.'

'Sure,' you nodded, giving nothing away. 'So, what's Iain's type?'

'Well, he doesn't do wallflowers. He likes the firecrackers. Women who aren't backwards in coming forwards, if you know what I mean.'

I liked talking about the women of yesteryear, who I really was and how I played things before living made me sick. It was all so amazingly sexy then. Until it wasn't. Until it started to feel like an effort, like every other plate I had to keep spinning in my life. Even before I got properly ill, I'd barely looked at another man for months. Iain had calmed right down too. We'd fallen into a slower rhythm. Gone was the bed-hopping high summer, and in came a calmer September which risked heading to the freezing dead of winter if I wasn't careful. And I wasn't careful enough in the end, because of you.

'What about you? Is there anyone special in your life?'

'No, not at the moment. Hey, I'd love to meet Iain one day.'

And I let you leave it there. Because I immediately had an image of the three of us together: sat around a table, wine and conversation flying between us. We'd laugh; I'd catch Iain's eye and he'd send me a smile that told me he was glad I'd met you, happy I had someone new to share my thoughts with, enlivened by the idea you'd be good for me, and therefore, for both of us.

'What are you doing this weekend? Why don't the three of us have lunch?'

'Hey, that'd be perfect.'

We swapped numbers.

You made me take a selfie with you. It felt stupid and foreign, holding my phone on high in an unpractised way. You corrected the angle of my arm at first, your thin fingers grasping the muscles on the inside of my upper arm. I could smell all of you.

'No, higher up. You never done this before?'

'Erm, yeah, not as much as you lot …' Then, in friendly frustration, you took my phone off me before scrunching into my side and miraculously working out how to put on the flash and some kind of flattering filter before handing my phone back. I loved how good we both looked in that picture. How close. In age. In comradery. In friendship. You were giving me a direct line to who I used to be: young and fun, someone you would fight to be friends with, not avoid.

I've looked at that picture you took of us a million times. It was far enough away that you can't see my pissed redness, my dark circles, my desperation. Nor could I see the black energy hiding behind your eyes. Like our selfie, I vowed that at our planned Sunday lunch with Iain you would see the very best of me again.

It got to chucking-out time and you said you needed to get your bike from the yard behind the office. As we started to leave, I was overwhelmed by the idea of hugging you. I felt like we'd breached something, moved somewhere together. I stood up woozily. I remember you holding my forearm to steady me and that somehow becoming a prolonged embrace. I could feel something between us, something powerful. I didn't want the night to end. We finally pulled away from each other.

'You going to be OK, cycling half-cut? You could leave it overnight; I could pick up a couple of bottles along the way. We could keep talking.'

'Think I'll sit the next dance out, thanks all the same. I'm not actually that much of a drinker?'

I faltered for a second and clawed back an image of a finger of wine untouched in the bottom of your glass.

I was mortified.

I'd drunk and blathered on about myself and my life, while you'd listened on soberly, watching as I gulped down the booze, telling you another one of my difficult little secrets, throwing in a good amount of intimate and revealing details about Iain for good measure. You'd topped me up again and again, but you hadn't refilled your own glass once. Was it because you were one of those oh-so-serious twenty-odd-year-olds who barely drinks, needing to wake up with a clear head in order to *optimise* their days? Or perhaps you felt bad because you hadn't money to pay for any of the drinks? Or was it more deliberate than this? Paranoid anxiety needled me. But I didn't know who I should trust less, myself, or you. And I desperately didn't want to take the sheen off those moments where we seemed to connect.

Yet dread still rose to the surface of my uncertainty and embarrassment: the sense of you wanting me malleable, that you set out to expose me and you'd succeeded. I had the idea you somehow knew the ways to see me for what I really was. And once again, I'd spent time alone with you and discovered almost nothing about you in return.

I didn't say much else before I sloped off into the night, moving with the drinkers spilling out of Borough Market pubs in the direction of London Bridge, pissed and alone. I know you watched me as I walked away, waiting a minute or so before turning in the opposite direction. I felt it.

Lily, I knew somewhere you were no good for me, that I was unravelling again and you were tugging hard at the threads. But whatever your interest in me, you *were* interested.

I had been seen.

I wasn't invisible.

I had someone new to talk to, someone I could see on the weekend, someone who had some insight into my most ancient pains. So if it seemed to me you'd barged your way into my life and under my skin, I was ready to plough right back into yours. You can't unlearn how to fight.

And there was something else. Somewhere, I had the idea that you liked me even though you didn't want to.

Lily

6th March – Time for a Drink?

Down with the brown. Down. With. The. Brown. Seriously? This woman gets more and more clueless. She's talking about 'coded language' when we know this is code for, 'I'm not being racist but …' or worse, that jokey kind of racism people her age are prone to, which they think is funny and ironic but everyone with half a soul knows is just good old-fashioned racism.

But I can't stop looking at her, into those bright blue eyes. She can tell. She likes how it feels.

I ask her to come for a drink with me and, my god, she can unload: on The Partner, on her career, her depression, the lot. This crazy monologue she has to get out with only the smallest little nudge from me to keep it coming. Gotta admit, it's pretty fascinating, being this close to those eyes as they dance round her memories while she sweeps her fingers through that extreme black wave of hair over and over. She doesn't know she's still beautiful.

I liked listening to her, even with all the appalling things she said, the most disgustingly least self-aware ideas she thinks are absolutely fine: '*a rolling buffet of interns to keep the lights on and sponsored content to pay me.'* She thinks she's doing us some kind of favour. Offensive in the extreme but because she's so completely *othered* young adults, in her eyes it doesn't matter what she does or takes from us.

But still, sometimes her words fall out of her studded with tiny gems of something that feels like truth, like little pomegranate pips in a bowl of bitter leaves.

I needed to keep my usual guard up, but it was hard. I haven't found it this difficult since Ruth. That was the first, and until now, the last time I let myself open up. I wanted to be honest with Ruth about what Mum and Gem did to me and what I've done to other people. Ruth wanted to hear me and I wanted to tell her about everything that's inside me.

With KR, I feel like I want to tell her things about me too. Real things. And I find myself wanting to learn more about her. That's when I pour her another drink.

It was the plan to see her inebriated, get a view of what's behind the leather armour. I make sure she's fully drunk, so much so that when we leave the pub, she's all over the show. I actually have to stop her from hitting the deck. I grab her before she drops to the cobbles. I could have let her fall, I *should* have let her fall, but I can't believe it was actually my first instinct to save her.

I rescue her, despite all the times I've been allowed to fall and break into pieces by people like her, despite how many injustices and abuses people like me suffer at the hands of people on her level, casually using young people in their workplaces and their beds. Her bed. But even after she admits that's exactly what she thinks is her right, to have sex with unpaid graduates in a clear abuse of power that she can't see, I still want to help her. It's weird.

Eventually, she's off home, but not before she's tried to extend the night. Way too soon for that. She's stomping off to the bus stop in that way that's *so* her. I wait and watch and I'm thinking how KR always strides or stomps everywhere when she should be treading carefully.

CHAPTER 4

Katherine

I never bothered being quiet on the rare occasions I came home late, usually after a work do. Iain was generally unconscious by 10.30. When I got back from The George that night, I was desperate to talk about you, sound Iain out on the night and what I thought may have happened, but he was gone on the sofa and, as usual, I tried and failed to wake him.

I went to the bathroom, put my fingers in my throat and got rid of the booze you'd put in me. Then I went to bed and sleep arrived quickly.

I had the dream about the burnt ground on the way to the far paddock gate, my mother watching it all, unseen. I wanted to wake up before I had to watch myself falter towards the gate. But I was still too drunk to rouse myself. I had to watch my child feet not reach where they needed to be.

In the morning, dehydration woke me early, but it had woken Iain earlier. He was already in the kitchen fixing breakfast. 'Morning, gorgeous. Sorry, didn't hear you come in last night.'

'Just as well probably.'

'What's the matter?'

'Last night with Snowflake, it was a bit intense. And worse, I have to go on some kind of "copy camp" with her.'

'What?'

'I need to "re-boot my writing" and she's the one to help.'

'Fucking hell.'

'I know. A new low. It's got to be all part of the plan to get rid of me, right? Set me up to fail, generate some kind of paper trail to show they did everything they could to help me before booting out the last bastion of the old world.'

'You think?'

'I honestly don't know anymore … Snowflake, Lily, she only lives over on Woodberry Downs. I said maybe we'd see if we couldn't get together with her for lunch on Sunday at The Brownswood? Keep your friends close, enemies closer and all that.'

I hoped the fact I'd arranged something that meant he could start on the Bloody Marys, with 'cheeky' straight chasers, from eleven papered over the potential oddness of me inviting a brand new intern into our weekend. I couldn't bear to admit to Iain how desperate I was to bring my new friend into our life, and I certainly couldn't tell him I wasn't at all sure if you were friend or foe yet.

'Sorry if I seemed a bit paranoid the other day, about work and about Lily. I'm trying to be strong.'

He walked around to the other side of the breakfast bar and held me, held me so tight my whole body relaxed. 'You have absolutely nothing to apologise for.' He kissed my head. He kissed me on the mouth and I felt like I was home again. We ended up shagging right there in the kitchen. We still did things like that. You probably have no idea. You probably thought we were totally past it. We weren't. I wasn't.

As soon as he got in the shower, I opened my laptop and

googled you. I found the odd Lily Lunt, but none of them were right. No Facebook. No Twitter handle I could attribute to you. I couldn't find your LinkedIn, let alone the blog you said you wrote. There was nothing I could attach to you with any certainty. It was as if you didn't really exist.

'Hey, Katherine.' You'd crept up behind me as I approached the office building without me seeing, making me jump, as proved your habit. 'You look nice today,' you added.

'Good morning, Lily.'

'How you doing?' It was wintry that day, your black eyes glistened behind the rising steam of your breath. You seemed to search my face. I wondered what you were looking for: signs of my hangover, embarrassment, or maybe how ready I was for whatever you had planned for me that day.

'Good thanks. You?'

I almost told you I hadn't really drunk that much, for me anyway, the night before. I could handle a lot more and get on with life just fine. But when I thought about what that would achieve and how little it would impress you, I kept quiet. Once I'd thought about it, it didn't seem that cool to me either.

'Really well. Here.' You passed me a coffee from the square cardboard tray you were carrying. The lid of my designated cup was loose and dripping, 'Sorry, they were a bit sloppy today. Maybe they'd been out last night too!' I noted the other three cups were perfectly clean and dry. 'I think this is how you like it?' You thrust the cup at me so a scalding splash hit my hand. 'Whoops. Don't worry, I won't tell Gem you're under the influence!'

You tried to make it sound like a joke, but I don't think

you have much of a sense of humour, do you? People your age are so fucking serious and earnest, but you really need to realise before it's too late, that laughing about things isn't a slight on life, but a full-blooded affirmation of it.

'Thanks,' I said, meaning for the drink, but you used your free hand to squeeze my arm in a reassuring way: *Don't worry, I won't tell.*

Up in the office, it wasn't long before Asif came over to our desks. I briefly wondered if it was to speak to me, but knew it was to be close to you. Because you looked so perfect as you typed. Thoughtful, hopeful, young. My hungover mind scrambled for something flirty to say to bring Asif's attention fully to me, but then remembered the previous night's *allegation* and instead found myself adopting a matronly 'business as usual' demeanour as far away from casual racism and sex as it's possible to be. I really needed to keep my job.

'Morning all,' Asif said, perching on the empty desk next to me, his body twisted so he could look at both of us, but talk to me.

'What you up to?'

'Wondered if we could talk about the awards?'

'Sure. Why don't you find some time in my diary later?'

He looked confused at my coolness, so turned his back to you and mouthed, 'You OK?'

I nodded workishly. '3.30 any good?'

'Sure.'

'Would you mind sending me a quick agenda?' You were watching us from the corner of your eye. 'Invite Lily, I think we could really use her. If that's OK with you, Lily?'

This was a masterstroke. You were probably listening out for 'inappropriate content' and instead I'd put you on the front row of interesting work, while creating a three-way environment where neither workplace relationships nor low-level racism would be allowed to flourish. You didn't expect this. You struggled to sound contained.

'Sure, yeah. Great. As long as you're sure? Is that alright? Asif?'

'Sure is.'

I took a sip of the coffee you'd given me. There was an odd aftertaste, but I was so in need of a caffeine boost, I drank through it. As I reached the bottom of the cup, the last sip was so sour I nearly asked, *What the hell did you put in this?* Was this why you had been watching me? After about five minutes I was feeling queasy. I dismissed it at first, but before long, nausea came on me in terrible waves I couldn't ignore. I started to panic. What *had* you put in my coffee? *Ridiculous*, the rational part of me knew, yet as I sweated heavily the idea took hold: you were capable of hurting me. I dared not look at anyone in case they could see what I was thinking. And I couldn't let you see I was struggling. All but soaking through my shirt, I ran to the loo and locked myself in a stall, stripping down to my bra, cramps tearing through my gut. I sat there, panting, semi-naked. I needed to get a hold of myself. It was probably some kind of perimenopausal episode. Eventually I cooled down enough to get up and out of there, giving in and calling Iain, pretending I was fine. But I still couldn't shake the idea you'd actually tried to poison me.

Later that afternoon you and Asif disappeared for coffee again. He didn't even offer to bring one back for me.

At 3.25 p.m. you were up on your feet and ready for the meeting, iPad in one hand, your filtered water bottle with the smug vertical slice of bobbing cucumber in the other.

I wanted to print off Asif's agenda to scribble notes on it, but my computer flashed an error message: the printer was still empty as it had been since early that morning.

'Can anyone tell me why this printer's still out?' I shouted to the floor.

You sneaked up behind me and whispered, as if you were protecting me from humiliating myself any further, 'It's paper-free Wednesday? It's in the new Environmental and Ethical Policy?'

Of course it was. I wanted to scream 'For *fuck's sake*', but the interns were watching, so I walked back to my desk, grabbed an old invoice and stuffed it into the empty tray. The printer didn't agree with the paper, so I ended up walking to our meeting with what looked like a crumpled piece of rubbish.

As I walked in, my heart sank. You and Asif were squeezed around a red table in the meeting room. Asif was mashed in so close to you, you must have been thigh-to-thigh. I took my seat unsteadily. The nausea came again just as Gemma wandered by in the corridor outside. I closed my eyes and took a deep breath. When I opened them, she was suddenly pulling up a chair next to me. To my horror, she sat down and looked at me expectantly. The lines on my wrinkled agenda swam. I would rather have been anywhere else than there. With Gemma watching, I lost all clue about how I was going to get through this meeting.

'Gemma. Great you've decided to join us.'

'Well, as Lily said, if I'm going to get right up to speed on how we're making the rebooted *Leadership* Awards the best yet, I want to get a front row seat on the planning.'

I looked over at you. You smiled at me like butter wouldn't melt. 'That's ... great.'

Gemma and Asif were now gazing gormlessly at me as if they expected *me* to kick off the meeting. My brain tried desperately to catch them, but words evaded me. Boiling again, I opened my mouth and all it had for me was, 'Um.'

'Shall I start? Would that be OK with you all?' you asked and before I could speak, Asif said, 'Go ahead, Lily, what's on your mind?'

'I'm all ears,' Gemma chimed.

And from that moment on the meeting became The Lily Show.

'OK, so *please* don't take this the wrong way. Your social media strategy was a disaster at last year's awards. I mean, you do realise, I'm sure, it was essentially non-existent? Sorry, I don't want to offend anyone here, but if we're really serious about our awards being the premier management accolades, recognising the techniques that support organisational growth, particularly as more of them are using digital channels to innovate around their business models, shouldn't we at least *feel* part of the digital age on social?'

Your words, your innate self-belief, your tenacity, it all stung me. It was a feeling as old as time: the sudden and hor- rific realisation the whole world had got younger. I considered shouting you down for spouting your modern mumbo-jumbo, but knew in my heart, the real issue was I'd slipped quietly into obsolescence, nearly taking *Leadership* down with me, so I said nothing and let you go on to dazzle your aunt, and Asif.

'They may not have expected to see you being active on social in the past, but at the very least they're expecting you to be involved in the conversations everyone else is currently having *without* you. I don't want to sound, like, massively harsh or anything, but I think we're losing ground here, trading off an illustrious past which is being all but forgotten in what's now, I'm sure you'll agree, a very crowded marketplace.'

'And what should we be doing about it this year?' Gemma asked, wide-eyed in admiration, throwing a glance to me over to see if I'd noticed how well her little pet was performing.

'Yeah, how do we engage with *Leadership's* users in their digital hangouts?' Asif asked.

At this, I knew the best I could hope for was to leave that meeting broadly unscathed and the only way I could do this was by saying as little as possible. You and Asif became increasingly animated about the 'digital strategy' you were going to build around the awards while Gemma clasped her hands in rapture. As you were all but ignoring me, I tuned out, right up until you offered to write my opening speech for the gala dinner.

'I could help you hone the message this year,' you told me, smiling, the perfect picture of hopeful innocence.

'No thank you, Lily. I think I can manage on my own.'

'Well, let's keep an open mind until nearer the time, shall we?' Gemma said before pushing off to a board meeting, leaving me to stare at my pointless agenda while Asif continued to drool over everything you said. He barely looked my way, and under the heat of your energy, your bright ideas, I was shrivelling, lessening. I decided there and then to opt out of that side of you, get you to send your copy to Asif to edit so I could concentrate 'on the core business of the magazine'. Of course it was already becoming clear to me you were establishing yourself as the core business, the reason we'd live again. I needed to spare myself from having to look at your writing and your shining future in the face.

In that meeting, in what was once my space, I was burning up, out of control. I told you and Asif I had to make a call. I tapped at my desk for a minute before grabbing my jacket and getting myself to a bench in the graveyard of St George's Church nearby.

Did you know, the graveyard is on the site of the old Marshalsea Prison, a debtors' jail? That day, I sensed the bodies below my feet, cold and still. *No money worries for you*, I thought, letting myself smile a little as I weighed up whether to call Iain for another pep talk. I could just hear him say, *C'mon girl. You're better than all this shite. You're a fighter.* I took a deep breath and headed back to the office shortly after, ready, so I thought, for whatever came at me next.

When I reached my desk, I'd just been cc-ed on a message:

From: Acceptableinthenoughties@gmail.com
To: g.lunt@leadership.uk
Cc: k.ross@leadership.uk

Subject: A note on the Editor

Dear Publisher,
I have important information on the current Editor.

Are you aware that Katherine Ross runs her team like some kind of harem?

She'll take whatever she can. Brown, dark and white. She's not fussy as long as the flesh is young. Those poor interns will do anything for a leg-up. Some of them know exactly what it takes to get ahead. Shouldn't your illustrious rag be thinking about safeguarding the young from what amounts to corporate rape?

With concern

In her office, I saw Gemma place the receiver down on her phone before getting up to call me into her office. My heart thumped, my legs, jelly.

'Well, this is clearly wholly unacceptable,' she began.

'Gemma, I honestly don't know what this person is talking about.' In truth, Asif had made it onto staff around the same time our relationship became intimate. I didn't connect the two, but I knew others did.

'I've asked IT to delete it immediately. How do you feel?'

'I'm shocked … Stunned.'

'What I mean is, would you like me to take this any further?'

'I'm not sure I follow.'

'You'd be within your rights to ask for this to be investigated.'

'But?'

'But I was wondering how you'd feel about that.' Her lips pursed and shifted to the left side of her face. She suspected you could have sent the trolling message.

'I'm a bit shaken up, but I don't feel the need to pursue any action as yet. Chances are it's some sad case I've done a story on, wouldn't you say? Some misogynist idiot who thinks he can put the brakes on a successful woman.'

'I think you're almost certainly right.'

'So I don't think we need to give him the satisfaction of knowing he's rattled me.'

'If that's your decision, I'll follow your lead.' She and I watched each other for a moment. 'Well, I think you'd also be well within your rights to take the rest of the day off. Go home, have a nice cup of tea and try to forget all about it.'

She was desperate to get me out of there.

'I think that's exactly what I'll do.'

'And, Katherine, let's keep this between just us. Stay united. Stay strong?'

'Stay strong. You got it.'

I returned to my desk, logged off and put my jacket back on. You watched it all. You got up and approached my desk.

'Katherine, are you off? I think you're out of the office for the rest of the week at the photoshoot? I thought you might be too busy to remember we're having lunch on Sunday? With Iain?'

I was pleased you were confirming our arrangement, but when you said my partner's name I instinctively cringed inside. It was as if I knew somehow what was going to happen. You'd said 'Iain' like you already knew him and I didn't like that. Lily, you didn't know him, you still don't know him and you never will, not the way I did. You'll also find you don't know me very well, despite the closeness you manufactured when it suited you. 'It'll be so nice to talk, you and me, properly, outside of work. There are lots of things I wanted to tell you the other night,' and you sent that smile my way again. You apparently planned to share your secrets with me. For that, I couldn't wait.

'We'll see you Sunday at The Brownwood about twelve. It's usually packed by then, but we'll be in there somewhere.'

'That's alright. Just wear that green leather you save for weekends, you'll be easy to find!'

'Right.'

How exactly could you have known I wore that jacket on weekends?

I was so taken aback, I couldn't think of anything to say to this. I stuffed my papers in my bag and all but ran out of the door.

Had you been watching me even before you'd invaded my taxi on Monday?

As soon as I got in, I told Iain what you'd said, but he dismissed it immediately. 'You said yourself she lives this way. She's just seen you about the neighbourhood. What's so weird about that? I reckon you've had a tough few days, so why not give yourself a break from thinking the absolutely worst scenario possible.' He started fixing me a gin and then gave my shoulders a massage, ostensibly trying to take care of me. But this was him taking your side. He would always take your side, from the very beginning to the very end.

Lily

7th March – Katherine the Curious

It's funny who you bump into when you least expect it. I'm in the big bike shop on the tip of London Bridge when I see Samira, my best friend at my second junior school. That was just before Mum and Gem both got fed up of me not being whoever they needed me to be and sent me away, as if a child is something you can order online and send back to Amazon if they don't warrant a five-star review.

I arrived late in the year at Samira's school and there weren't many girls to choose from, so I chose her. Samira had two parents, brothers, sisters, one roof over her head her whole life and tons of money, but she thought her home life was, far, far worse than mine. She had no idea, just like I had no idea of what living in a normal family would be like. Her main beef was being the youngest. She said she never got any attention at home. She didn't know what luxury and freedom this was. Not to be scrutinised like I was, broken down into a series of parts, none of which measured up to whatever Mum and Gem thought I needed to be. Smarter, nicer, more normal.

Samira told me she wrote poetry to help get her through. I told her again and again, 'You should really read them out in front of everyone. No one will laugh, they're *so* amazing. Everyone will be jealous of you. Go on, ask Miss. You go, girl.'

So, one day, she gets up to read one of her 'best works' aloud.

It was one of my earliest wins. It showed me how ready people are to believe what you say when you tell them exactly what they want to hear. It's often as easy as that. As simple as a well-chosen compliment, or the right line of questioning to convince them their life is as interesting and exceptional as they'd like to believe it is.

They say children are cruel. I knew that already from the last school, when they'd rounded on me for exposing some boy's lies about his parents still being together. I knew a kid with a dysfunctional parental setup when I saw one. I called out his, they called out mine: I was a two-mum weirdo and had been dragged over the coals for it, especially when they found out I had a 'rich mum' and a 'cleaner mum'. But Samira had yet to discover the brutality of children. She deserved to be punished for not having any idea how lucky she was. When it was over, maybe she'd run home to her happy family and realise she had somewhere safe, away from criticism and cruelty. I didn't know what that felt like, not until later, when I set up home with Ruth.

My Ruth.

When the snickering at Samira's performance started, it was quiet at first, quiet enough for her to ignore. But the laughter spread like a virus. Before long Miss Whatshername's cries were drowned out by the sound of children laughing so hard they were crying.

Do you know, I really admired how Samira made like she didn't want to break down as she retook her seat next to me. I guess I respected her more when she didn't want to speak to me again, especially when the name 'Sonnet Samira' stuck (sorry, Samira, coming up with that one was too easy!). But we're adults now. Perhaps she'll be happy to see a familiar face in the city.

When I see her across the bike shop, she's holding something Lycra in front of her, wondering whether to try it on or not. I recognise her big sad face instantly. It's funny how some people carry around the child in them forever. Samira and I are like that, I'm guessing KR is too.

I'm going to surprise her, tap her on the shoulder. We'll catch up, I'll find out if she works round here too, see if she fancies going for lunch one day. But when she starts looking about for a fitting room, she sees me first. She jerks her head away in a really unnatural way before turning back, as if she's checking whether it's really me. It takes her three attempts to get the Lycra thing back on the rail. She can't take her eyes off me. Her mouth is open.

I wave to her.

'Hey. It's me, Lily!'

She swallows, turns and starts to stagger towards the exit.

I follow her outside. By the time I get there, she's at the kerb, checking behind her. I wave again.

The lorries and taxis screech and scream as Samira tries to cross the foot of London Bridge with the lights still on green. She runs down the steps towards Southwark Cathedral and I know I'll never see her again.

Later on, when the concierge is grunting on me, I make myself think about what I did to Samira. *Maybe I do deserve this,* I tell myself. I may have only been a child, I may have been damaged, but I understand I deserved how much Samira wanted to get away from me. So, I accept there will be no catch-ups, no meals, no walks, no time with anyone who isn't Gem or my mum, that is, until my lunch with KR and The Partner on Sunday. I'm alone.

The concierge has finally left. It's dark now. I eat cold soup and look again at Iain McIvor's IMDb page. His thin CV, some trivia. Talent and People asked if they could 'share my CV' with KR on my first day. She'd requested it, on the quiet, or so she thought. Yeah, go ahead, I said, knowing full well it wouldn't tell her whatever she thinks she wants to know about me. What she'll get is a curated version of my life on paper, but we all know CVs are total constructs. There's always about as much you leave out of your life story, chunked under those usual headings, as you leave in. I know for a fact KR's will have an early gap she'll struggle to explain when she has to start hawking herself round recruitment agencies.

Of course, she'd google me, try to find me on social, but she won't find this Lily Lunt in any of the usual places.

With the racist corker on day two and giving me all that disgusting detail on her and her partner in the pub, she's making this too easy. It could be over soon if I wanted it to be.

But I don't want this to be too easy.

I want my plan to be painfully drawn-out. They say revenge is a dish best served cold, but it also tastes the sweetest when it's cooked slow.

CHAPTER 5

Katherine

Each year, I interview the next round of enterprising big shots at a photoshoot for the awards edition of the magazine we publish every spring: *Rising Stars of Tomorrow*. The first few years were mildly intimidating as I was finding my feet as editor, the next few, moderately inspiring, and I got a good few shags along the way. Then, the subjects started to seem so much younger than me, their tech-driven businesses less knowable, and me far less shaggable to them. Those years seemed to blur into one until I met Asif.

He was finishing up interning with some 'augmented reality' guru who was one of our 'stars'. I got chatting with him. In fact, he was the only one who seemed to actively want to talk to me at that shoot. He was smart enough, enthusiastic. I knew I'd be able to use him at work, so invited him out for a drink that night to discuss what he wanted from his future. He became my intern a week later. Happier days.

That was four years ago, and as I prepared to do it all over again, I wondered how anyone manages to live their life well and happy when they feel their best years are behind them. And how much worse does it all feel when, like me, you're forced to meet the banks of sharp young things stacking up behind you, like rows of teeth in a shark's mouth.

By Friday, the final day of the shoot, I couldn't even be bothered taking notes. I needed to produce the piece with the minimum amount of emotional energy, so simply recorded foreshortened interviews and decided to present everything as an unfiltered Q&A, rather than the extended profile pieces we'd normally do. There was once a time I prided myself on the quality of my questioning, my investigative probing that created the standout news and features I was known and promoted for. How incurious I was now, the one thing a journalist can't afford to be.

I was bone-tired when I got the text from you:

Just checking – r we still good for Sunday?

I sent back:

Sure. KR

And I got back this:

😊 😊 😊

Ridiculous.

That weekend, when I returned from my normal Sunday run, I found I wanted to dig out my old leather skater skirt from one of a dozen vacuum-sealed bags I'd packed into the tiny attic space above the airing cupboard, the skirt just like yours. I held it in front of my legs after my shower. I could still get away with it, couldn't I?

My mother would have killed me if she'd ever seen the skirt. Firstly, for wearing something so hard and dangerous-looking and, secondly, for spending so much on a single item of clothing. The frivolity. The indulgence. But she was three years cold by the time I'd seen the skirt in Liberty's. She died pinned under a quad bike on our land shortly after my eighteenth birthday. See, you don't have the monopoly on fucked-up childhoods.

Her death had, in fact, been the first time I ever met a journalist. I'd always been interested in writing, I kept notes, even as a young child, all of which went into my first manuscript. I didn't know what I was going to do with my life, but the idea suggested itself to me when a reporter from the *Matlock Mercury* came to the farm, supposedly to get the inside track on the 'tragedy' of my mother's death. As an emotionally stunted only child of a dysfunctional parent, I observed the passably attractive journalist's ability to disconnect from normal human niceties, to be able to doorstep a vulnerable teenager and try to extract her tears. I thought, *Maybe I could do that.*

The reporter wanted his photographer to get an image for the front page to support his narrative: a beautiful, fragile teenager left behind with no family and a farm in catastrophic debt. After the funeral, I asked to meet the reporter 'off the record', enjoying the feeling of such distinctly metropolitan vocabulary on my lips.

He was in his late twenties, which seemed almost impossibly old to me then. I wanted to find out how to get into journalism.

He'd given me the big talk, chest puffed out, trying to blow me away with his incredible tales of reporting on house fires and localised job losses. But I actually felt sorry for him. He was stuck living in the arse-end of nowhere, just like me, but worse, out of choice. His job was to report on boring provincial lives, like mine. I was going to London. To become a journalist. Even then, I knew that no matter what got in my way, I would have the life I deserved, not the one given to me.

I looked again at the skater skirt. I knew it would risk me looking like the teachers you see in their dated casuals on the weekend, so deeply embarrassing, but I wanted to somehow make you think I was cooler than I was. It seemed my partner too cared greatly what he looked like. As I walked back into our bedroom, I caught Iain pinching the gathering roll around his middle through the ancient, half-perished Sonic Youth T-shirt he was wearing.

'Hey, did I always have this?'

'I don't know – did I always have these?' I sidled up to him, winking hard so he could see my crow's feet in all their glory.

'You look gorgeous. Haven't seen that in a while.'

'I know. I think I'm having a mid-life crisis.' I'd put the skirt on.

'Fuck me, we've had more of them than hot dinners in this house!' he laughed, pulling me in for a hug. 'So, what's the plan then? What can I find out for you? What shouldn't we be talking about?'

'God, I don't even know. Get her talking about herself. She doesn't like swearing. Or drinking. Or anything even slightly off-colour.'

'A proper fucking Snowflake. Well, this'll be fun. I was

going to suggest a quickie, but might as well head now and get the beers in before she shows up by the sounds of it.'

*

It was obvious both Iain and I were nervous as we walked towards the pub. I threw on my weekday black biker to avoid giving you the satisfaction of seeing me in the green leather you'd identified I usually wear on weekends. I tried to get Iain to walk quickly to make sure we got to the pub before you, intending to bagsy my favourite table and settle ourselves in. Neither Iain nor I spoke as we gripped each other's hands on the approach to the pub's main entrance.

I should have known you would get to the pub before me.

There you were. You'd sat yourself at a table big enough for eight in front of the biggest window. It was a grey day, but somehow the clouds parted as we opened the pub doors. You were backlit by the sun when we both caught sight of you, flicking your nails on your pale throat and biting the orange pillows of your lips in anticipation, your hair a red halo.

'Is that her?' Iain asked, letting go of my hand.

'That's her.'

You spotted us and removed yourself from behind the table, revealing your amazing breasts in a tight lavender angora V-neck, your full height, and yes, your own skater skirt which made me deeply regret putting mine on.

'Katherine.' You planted a kiss on the air near my ear. 'And you must be Iain? It's so good to meet you, I've heard so much about you.' You kissed him on the cheek, pressing yourself full against him as you brought him in for a hug, in a way which made me sense the blood rushing to his dick. I

110

wished I'd pushed for a quick shag before we'd left the house. Suddenly, I wanted to go. Right now. Iain looked so flushed. Younger. It was as amazing to watch my partner's greyed features bloom into life as it was dreadful. He'd shuffled his way round to the bench on your side of the table, forcing me to remain opposite you both. I may as well have given up there and then.

Throughout lunch, information flew out of you and it all sounded largely plausible; your itinerate London life with your mother (very Bohemian), boarding schools (as I knew already from your CV) paid for by Gemma (I could have guessed that), your father leaving when you were small (me too, though less out of choice than yours), you being caught in the middle of 'two warring mums'; how you've 'sometimes struggled to make friends', but you've found solace in writing your blog about the 'challenges of millennial life' and 'the whole *Leadership* project'. My magazine, your 'project'. You saw me bristling and switched back to talking about your blog.

'So, I guess it's an attempt to chronicle the difficulties around establishing your identity today. To become financially independent; to somehow put together a proper life?' you told Iain, chucking a token glance over to me. Of course, your missives were targeted at people like you in their early twenties, but I found myself thinking, *These are my struggles too.*

'Get many trolls on your blog? What's it called again?' This came out more aggressively than I'd meant, but I was already a bit pissed and unhappy at how confessional you were being with Iain there, when I'd got nothing from you on my own at The George.

'I used to get rape threats all day, every day.' You said the last bit to Iain.

'Fuck, Lil, that's fucking terrible. How'd you cope?'

'I shut down comments and came off social. It just got *way* too much,' you told him and him alone.

'So how do I find your blog, *Lil*?' I asked.

'I was thinking it's probably best I keep that under wraps? I don't want to get caught up in the new sign-off structure. I'd never get anything written otherwise,' you said the last bit privately to Iain too.

'And it's hard enough to get anything done at the best of times, eh?' he said.

'Christ, it is,' you replied. *Christ?*

You and he were getting louder and closer together on the bench opposite. I tried, and most likely failed, to look as if this didn't bother me in the slightest, but as your body seemed to inch closer to his, my blood pressure began to soar. So many questions for Iain. About him, about his writing. I started to talk, but each time, I was drowned out. The table you'd chosen was so wide, I couldn't even kick him underneath it without being completely obvious. He barely looked my way. He wasn't interested in what I had to say, and I could understand why: you radiated pure, vital energy as your vegan 'roast' cooled, and you and my partner explored another conversational tributary wide enough only for two. I started to feel small and stupid in my tiny leather skirt. I ended up acting as barmaid and glass collector. When I took myself to the bar to attempt to flirt with the familiar barmen, I could see that Iain seemed to burst open, and I watched as words spilled out of him, pouring freely into you. Did I look as sweaty that night at The George as Iain did that Sunday?

And you'd discovered a new thirst from somewhere. You matched Iain drink for drink. Impossibly, you knew about The Film.

When I got back to the table, you were gushing, 'OK, this is really weird. Oh my gosh, of *course*. Iain McIvor. *That* Iain McIvor. I've seen it. God, three times at least. I thought it was great. I mean, a bit of a rough diamond, but the writing was really strong.'

'How is it you've seen the film?' Iain asked.

'Oh God, I don't know. Bootleg DVD? YouTube? Anyway, it was my mate who put me onto it. He's a real film buff. We bonded over Béla Tarr.'

And it's then I thought I really saw him drop his toe on your side of the grass: the greener side. But I knew, I desperately hoped, he had to be thinking deep down inside, something didn't smell right. We'd been around the block too many times not to know when something or somebody seemed too good to be true. But like any good scam, you'd made it so appealing that he seemed to want to ignore those voices of sense telling you to go slow, proceed with care. Iain was so ready to hear your flattery even though your interest and fandom were ridiculous. He went to say something to you again, when I finally made a comment that was heard.

'When did you see me in my green biker?'

'Sorry?' You'd had two gin and tonics and at least three large glasses of wine – I'd been watching you swallow them this time – to wash down your fucking pretend roast. You were almost slurring. 'Sorry, Katherine, I missed that?' And your lips had their natural colour now, an indecently youthful pink under the orange lipstick left on the many glasses I'd taken back to the bar. In that moment, I experienced actual hate for you for the first time.

'When did you see me wearing my green jacket?' I said, flicking my eyes to Iain quickly to see he was giving me a *What the fuck?* glance.

'I don't know. A week ago maybe?'

'Where?'

'I'm really sorry, Katherine, I can't remember.' You sent a concerned glance to Iain who'd now directed his eyes from me and to the floor, ashamed. 'Must have been somewhere round here though. Green Lanes? Yes. I think it was Green Lanes.'

'Green Lanes was it? Pretty long road. You follow me down it?'

You didn't say anything to this.

'Kathy. *Love*,' said Iain, increasingly desperate to stop me killing his buzz.

'I'm sorry. I didn't mean to worry you. I'd never want to do that,' you told me. Iain's vision stayed on his shoes, but you held my gaze and took a long slug of your wine. 'I'm just trying to get along, trying to be the most supportive person I can. It's like copy camp. It's nothing major, just a way to help out, but then, I'm sure it'll be a case of, what might you say? *Teaching an old dog new tricks*?' You tilted your chin towards me and then, 'Excuse me.' You smiled, mischief playing on your fleshy lips as you left for the bathroom.

'Old dog,' I nodded and drained my glass.

When you were out of sight, Iain turned to me, 'What the fuck?'

'Yeah, what the fuck, Iain. I'm going. You can do what you want, but I am *not* signing off on her if that's what you're thinking.'

'I wasn't going to ask.'

'She works for me.'

'I know … well, she works for your boss.'

'You're incredible.'

'She seems to think *you're* fucking incredible. That's what she's been going on about. You should give her a proper chance. You don't need to be so bitter, you know?'

I knew Iain well enough to know he'd said the word I'd long used to describe my mother accidentally on purpose. I grabbed my jacket.

'Sorry, sorry. That was stupid. Wait, let me get one more, then I'll come home with you.' He gulped down half a glass of wine in one.

'Do what you want, Iain. You generally do.'

I walked out of the pub alone and into the shop next door to buy some Sunday papers I was probably too pissed and 'bitter' to concentrate on.

When I started up the hill back to my flat, someone grabbed my arm.

I turned and we were suddenly facing each other.

You looked straight into my eyes in that way you do and my heart leapt.

That's when I worked it out. I wasn't just jealous of you. I was jealous of Iain. I didn't like how you seemed to be shining your light on him, not me. I wanted to grab you and go somewhere else, so *we* could talk, so *we* could explore new avenues of thoughts and feelings and hopes.

'I'm sorry about Iain,' you said, and I was so instinctively pleased to see you'd made the effort to catch up with me, I didn't even register the outrage of you apologising for my partner's behaviour.

'What's he doing now?'

'Having his one last drink.' And the way you said it made me believe you saw him for what he was, and even if I were to rubber-stamp you for him, you'd never take him up on the offer. It was madness, but for a moment, I wanted to say something to recommend him to you, to make my choice of partner seem more defendable in your eyes. I hoped Iain wasn't making too much of a fool of himself.

'I'm leaving soon too, but I wanted to give you this,' you handed over a neat card with your prim handwriting on it. 'It's my blog. *Please* don't judge the writing. It's just something I do for me.' You pressed the card into my palm. 'And please, don't tell Gem you know about it. She wants me to keep my private writing and work life, like, totally separate. But, you'll know what it's like. When you're a writer, there's no such thing as clear boundaries is there?'

At that you hugged me quickly before disappearing back into the pub to re-join my partner. And instead of thinking about the horror of the two of you alone together, I was striding up the road to my flat as quickly as I could without breaking into a run. I couldn't wait to see inside your head.

CHAPTER 6

Katherine

A few pictures of you looking stunning. A bit of blurb. A good number of posts entitled things like '10 reasons why interns should get paid' and 'Why does everyone past 30 hate everyone under?' and 'Sex for rent – a millennial housing reality', none of which, of course, I bothered reading, especially once I'd seen the headline for your most recent post: 'You feeling lucky? What I learnt from a puncture and the bus that never came.'

My heart thumped in my chest. I knew it was going to be about me.

A sudden dread hit me. What would you say? Would you be kind or cutting? Would you let me get closer to the truth of you, or give me more riddles about how you came into my life? I left my laptop on the sofa and ran to the kitchen to find some booze. I poured neat gin urgently into a tumbler as I watched the screen from the other side of the room like a burglar I'd just invited into my house.

The most recent post on www.llllll.wordpress.com – tagline: *Life, love, lessons and learnings with London Lily* – was waiting for me. I made myself walk towards it and read it.

Hello, Taxi-Saviour Lady!
(posted 5th March, 10.16 p.m.)

Typical.

On the first day of my new job, sorry, internship (heaven forbid anyone my age actually gets paid for their work, Good Lord, what do you want to do, bankrupt the country even without Brexit? Next, you'll be wanting rent caps and a limit to how many properties anyone over forty can own. Scandalous).

What is wrong with this town when twenty minutes can pass on one of North London's major arteries without a bus? How, exactly, do we plan to compete when the EU is nothing but a warm memory?

Turns out, despite the early signs, it was actually my lucky, lucky day. It left me wondering if we should knock those ladder-retrieving over-forties quite so much, because one of them was kind enough to let me into their cab. An expenses job, obviously (and let's try not to think about how long I could make the £60-odd quid she ended up spending last), but nevertheless, I got into work gratis and almost, nearly on time.

The lesson? Don't judge a book by its cover? Sort of, but not quite. As the cover/appearance, whatever, of this book is pretty impressive.

I'd already seen Taxi-Saviour Lady with her man around and about a few times since I moved here and it turns out our lives were already destined to crash into each other's anyway.

I've seen them as they sipped coffee, walking through

Clissold Park like there's nothing to worry about in the world. I've seen her from my window, striding down her street to cross the road to the bus stop at the foot of my high-rise.

She leaves just after 8 (8.02/8.04 a.m.) every day.

It's funny how you see so many faces, the diverse peoples of London, sometimes it just feels so noisy and your brain isn't actually registering anyone or anything it absolutely doesn't have to. The second your eyes snatch their image from the air, it's just dropped straight away, passes through your mind and out again like a ghost.

But every now and then by some miracle you come across an individual that, for whatever reason, your brain decides to push through the 'background noise' and into the 'actually seeing' bit.

I saw her. She caught my eye, my imagination, which meant I'd been seeing her doing things in her world for a while.

I spotted her in fact, only yesterday on Church Street. I threw away the coffee I'd just bought (I know, £2.80 I won't see again) just so I could follow her into the boutique she turned into. Like so many shops on Church Street, it's a horrifically overpriced joint. I don't want to sound unsisterly here, but I have to be truthful, it's the kind of shop where women of a certain vintage buy oddly cut skirts and shirts that confuse the eye: a visible seam sends your sight one way, but a billow of fabric at the shoulder or hip confuses the direction of travel.

Anyway, back to the lesson. Rather than books and

covers, I think what 'unlucky-puncture-no-bus-Monday'
told me was that sometimes when you feel you're having
a terrible run, you're actually in the middle of a lucky run.

The woman is Katherine Ross, my new boss and I
think she likes me.

She's actually one of those women who are a brilliant
combination of super-confident and really vulnerable
(aren't we all?). She seemed really nervous going to
meet her new boss this morning (OK, full disclosure: also
my aunt and my big boss too and it turns out she's the
Katherine Ross whose pieces I've been reading in the
run-up to moving to London and starting my internship.
Go figure!), but, hey, I took a chance and told her just
to be herself (I know my aunt, she can't stand fakers!)
and she'd be fine. She seemed to respond to that, that
and the fact I was cracking on with some copy within
my first hour of being in the building (Just give me a
second while I shine my halo). I just know she's going
to be a really important figure in my life. I knew before
I'd ever even spoken to her!

Katherine, if you ever read this, let me tell you your
picture byline does not do you justice and please, don't
freak out! I'm actually really normal!

My hands were shaking. I took a long draw on my drink to calm myself.

Since day one I'd had an idea there was something wrong about you and now I knew I was right. But there was zero satisfaction in it, no peace, only panic. How could I have let myself be that vulnerable? That stupid? I'd let you into my life, but you weren't normal, you weren't real. Was there anything you'd told me I could believe? At least now I knew I wasn't going completely mad.

Because you *had* been watching me. Following me. Tracking my movements. I'd 'caught your eye'. Really? You'd been reading my work, but somehow didn't recognise me from my picture byline? You'd followed me into my favourite shop. You said you'd watched my partner's film.

No.

These were not coincidences, or passing admiration. They were part of something deliberate, something sinister.

Pacing about my living room, waiting for you to release my partner, a question hammered through my stricken state over and over. Who are you, Lily Lunt, and what the hell do you want from me?

Iain stayed out at the pub with you for another three hours. *Three hours.* I thought of texting or calling him back to me like some old fishwife who wants 'im indoors where she can keep an eye on him. I thought of calling you and telling you, in no uncertain terms, to back the fuck away from me, my life and my partner. I quickly moved onto considering going back down there to make like everything was just fine, that I wasn't at all phased by your blog, then somehow making Iain come home with me immediately. It wouldn't wash. I wouldn't be able to keep my true horror hidden from you right now. That meant the only course of action was sitting on my hands and waiting for Iain.

I suddenly felt exactly like my mother. Face sour with disappointment, disapproval and abandonment. Bitter. I hated both of you for doing this to me. I don't think I've ever felt as old and 'un-me' as I did that first afternoon you spent with Iain. Every minute felt like an hour and each hour dragged me deeper into a dark blend of swirling anxiety, low-self-worth and blind rage as I read and re-read your blog, knowing all the while he'd be having the time of his life with you; alone, gazing into those black eyes for a second or five too long again and again, as he indulged your surely 100 per cent fake interest in his 'work'.

'It's only me,' Iain boomed from the door when he finally returned. Thank God. It was time to make him scared of you, as I was.

'Nice of you to make it.'

'Sorry, sorry, sorry. I didn't mean to stay so long. She kept wanting one more. I think your girl's a bit lonely, if I'm honest.'

'Well, it was very charitable of you to help her while away the afternoon.'

'What's that supposed to mean?'

'She's got you wrapped around her little finger and you don't even know what you're dealing with. You don't even know what she is.'

'*What* she is? You make her sound like some kind of … fiend.'

'I don't know *what* she is. And neither do you. Here, what do you think of this.'

'What's this?'

'Just *read* it,' I said, turning my laptop to him.

'OK, OK. Let me get a drink and I'll take a look.'

He poured us both huge glasses of red from the box he'd bought home and started to read.

Over the minutes, I watched his face for signs of horror, disturbance, expecting him to stop reading at any minute and say what I needed to hear: *This is messed up. Is she a mate of someone you've pissed off? What the fuck is this girl playing at?* But what I saw instead was him smiling fondly, letting the odd whimsical sigh escape.

'What is it I'm supposed to be seeing here?'

'That's she's possibly a stalker, or at the least, really fucking strange. She's been following me!'

'She just bumped into you on Church Street. Saw you about.'

'You can't tell me you think this is in the realm of normal fucking behaviour?!'

He laughed, shrugged his shoulders. I was starting to feel like the mad woman. How did you manage that? 'And what about the fact she's seen the film?'

'Quite a few have.'

'Oh yeah, how?'

'Youngsters, you know they have a way finding and seeing all sorts of stuff. I think someone's probably uploaded it online or something. It happens. Things become cult, years after. Anyway, that's not important, but you know what is? Do you want to know what I see here?' He was over-emoting now, over-loud, properly pissed.

'Do enlighten me.'

'I see a young girl who's a bit of a loner. Bit of a loner who's a bit … crazy about you. Like I said.'

'You have been *blinded*. One flash of those perfect teeth and tits and you've gone. You've got to think there's something not quite right about her? All the "coincidences". She's been practically stalking me, for Christ's sake. It was her idea to make her aunt buy the magazine. She's … She's got an unhealthy interest in my life. She's trying to take over the awards; everything I do at work, she tries to undo, tries to undermine me. She invited me out for a drink, got me to spill my guts, all the while telling me absolutely nothing about her *and* pretending she's getting pissed too. Then she manufactures the invite for lunch today with you. It's like she's forcing her way into us. Why? Why, would she do that?'

'Look, we've been around long enough to know life's full of weird coincidences. These things happen and, you know, sometimes, they happen for a reason. With the work stuff, I think you've just been feeling, like, really insecure for a while now, and that's not her fault, but you're coming out fighting and you'll be back on top again. And anyway, do you have to be "strange," or whatever to be interested in you? To think you're amazing? Come here, love.' He meant it all; he still really meant it then, he was still mine. So, I let myself be pulled towards him and sink into him. I allowed myself to feel safe again.

'It's still weird. *She's* weird. I'm not making it up. You think I am, but I'm telling you, this isn't in my head. We need to be very careful around her.'

'Young people. They're all weird. I honestly don't think we've anything to worry about.'

'Do I not need to worry about you then?'

'No. *No.* She's a lovely wee girl, but she's just a girl. It's not like that.'

'Good, because I don't think I could cope with you, or

me, doing anything with anyone else. Not yet. I don't mean forever, just not now and definitely not with her. OK?'

He came to hug me and we stayed like that for a moment.

'You know, for what it's worth, I think she could be a good influence on us.' He said above my head. 'You should keep an open mind about this copy camp thing. I might even let her kick-start my writing again. She goes to this creative writing group. It's on our doorstep, just over the park at The Rose and Crown. It's an open session type thing, loads of different people.' Iain let go of me to get himself a glass of water, something he never normally did unless I nagged him to. His back was turned to me as he kept talking. 'She's invited me along. I was thinking about getting my arse down there next time. It could be just thing I need, but I won't go if we've got plans.'

Of course, we had no 'plans' and he knew it.

I hated the idea of you two doing something together, texting beforehand, swapping encouraging messages afterwards; you looking at my Iain across the table as you read something brilliant you'd written to him and a group of people as annoyingly young and as confident in their creativity as you. My heart began to blacken at the idea of it being you who was so obviously reigniting him, not me.

But if I said no, put a stop to Iain going to your group without a decent excuse, what would that say to you? I risked you backing off him and me too. There might be a chance I wouldn't get to spend any time with you again.

And that's exactly what I needed to do.

If I was going to investigate how and why you'd come into my life, I needed to stay close. 'You're like a dog with a bone,' one of the old directors at *Leadership* used to say to me, when I was on to something, when there was an angle I knew I needed to work until I'd got to the real story. So yes, while you'd made it so I was beginning to be afraid of you, you'd also done something else: re-awoken my curiosity, my need to know. Like blood returning to cold, numb fingers. Sensation again.

'You should go.'

Lily

11th March – Sunday Lunch

The Partner is such a sweet, sad man. I planned to show a little of who I was today, and, thankfully, he's easy to talk to, so it didn't feel too much like hard work. He's also even simpler to read than KR. In some ways he could be the easiest thing about this – it won't be like being with the concierge or anything, that much I can tell. But I can also tell I shouldn't be too obvious yet. Him and her, they are set fast in their co-dependence. It won't be completely straightforward, chiselling him out of it.

So, I talk plenty about her, to avoid looking too on the nose. But I make sure I use the little bit on 'Hungarian new wave cinema' from his IMDb as best I can. I also make sure my leg touches his. At first, he moves his knee, suspects it's accidental. Eventually he stops creeping away from me.

She sees something happening, or she thinks she does, until I follow her out of the pub. Because it's time to let her see my blog. See what reading the post I wrote just for KR does to her.

Once she's gone, I turn on 'Lily the wasted firecracker,' the one with shades of KR. It's the version of me I know Iain will like more than any of the others.

'Do you know what, Iain, I think Sunday is my favourite day to get wasted.'

'I thought most people your age didn't get pissed?'

'I think you'll find I'm not most people.'

'I think you're probably right there.'

'Like, I fucking love where my thoughts go when I'm pissed. It's not just about losing your inhibitions with other people, it's about losing them with yourself. That's why I've always made sure my little group of writers meets in a pub and we never get started properly until we're at least two drinks down. Makes sense, right?'

'Makes a whole lot of sense to me.'

'Here, let me get two more of these.' I stand and squeeze past him, facing him, my body in his space and I know he has to pretty much sit on his hands to stop them reaching for me. I can feel it. When I come back with the drinks, I sit where KR sat. I can tell I'm leaving him with a hunger he won't be able to place yet.

'So, who goes to your writing group, then? Just young 'uns like you, is it?'

'Not necessarily. It can be pretty diverse. Members come and go all the time as well. I'm very flexible.'

Ask me, Iain.

'And what kind of experience would someone need to get involved?'

Just ask. Ask so it doesn't look like it's my idea.

'I run a pretty broad church. I'm easy. Except on the two-drinks rule of course.'

Go on, Iain.

'So, do you think that maybe, I could come along one time? I've been meaning to get back on the horse for ages.'

Gotcha.

'Sure. If you make your way to The Rose and Crown at seven this Friday, I'll be there. Give me your email, I'll send you something to critique and you reply with something you're working on. Got it?'

'Got it. Yeah …Thanks, Lil. I'll be there.'

Of course you will. You'd do anything just to sit next to me again.

I call it a day when I realise I've let myself drink way too much. When I get to my building, I'm so thankful the concierge isn't there. But having been in the company of KR and Iain for a couple of hours in a hot pub, I suddenly feel cold and alone. The alcohol in my brain is swilling out memories, panning for heavy stuff I don't want to see again. I've tried to write all over them, but my drunk mind keeps going back to places I don't want it to.

Ruth.

When everything started to go wrong.

But being around KR and Iain all afternoon like that, hearing about their long-past failed attempts to make a better life, I can understand why so many people their age think they need to get bombed the whole time. They never learn it doesn't make anything better. I've already worked that out. And unlike them, there's still time for me to put right what I need to.

CHAPTER 7

Katherine

When I left the house for work on Monday, I was entering a changed world, unarmed. I was mortally hungover. It would definitely be a dial-it-in day. I needed to keep my distance from you, somehow, while I thought about my next move. I wanted desperately to ask Iain more about what he'd found out about you that afternoon, but hadn't been able to bear bringing you up in conversation. The last thing I needed was to show Iain how much I hated it when he said your name.

As I walked down the steps into my road, I wondered how many times you'd watched me doing just that and what you would have gleaned from your observations. You could have seen every time I'd swallowed down my anxiety, breathing it in, pressing it deep into my chest as I walked towards the bus stop. Were you watching me right then, in that moment, from your dark modern high-rise looming over my subsiding Victorian home? From there would you be able to detect the boozy flush of my face, read my nervous habit of checking and re-checking that I had my phone on me before leaving my front step. You may have seen all the times I'd sighed, straightened myself up and summoned a voice in my head to tell me, *Today is a good day*. Before I'd even left my home, you would see you were already winning.

When I got to my desk, you were already at yours. A coffee from you waited for me.

'Good morning. How are you today?' There was some guilt in your voice, some expectation, something intimate and private – we'd seen each other socially and I'd read your blog post. I knew you'd been reaching into my life since well before that day in the cab. You wanted to know what this had done to me. I planned to outmanoeuvre you by showing it had left me wholly unmoved.

'Thanks for this.' I moved the coffee to one side. You weren't going to mess with me that way again.

'How was the rest of your Sunday?'

'The usual.'

'I just wanted to say, I had *such* a lovely time with you both. Thanks so much again for letting me tag along. I didn't mean to stay out as long as I did, but we were just talking about writing and, well, writing mostly.' You seemed like you were on the back foot, where I liked you. But how did you look so amazing after a skinful of booze? Your hair like a new conker, clear eyes, and the general demeanour of the teetotaller you'd let me believe you were. Were you just pretending to drink? I wouldn't put it past you to know how to fool me in some impossible way. I let you go on. 'You guys are soooo lucky, you're totally the sweetest couple.'

'That's a kind thing to say.' I stared at my screen to maintain my unruffled demeanour. But you wouldn't have it, because there you were, shining at me again in my peripheral vision. It was impossible for me not to turn and look at you directly.

And when I did, I saw your orange lips part as you smiled so broadly; such affection you displayed, as if you were basking in the glow of my relationship. I felt the cold and fear over you leave me, warmth seeping in again. Incredible.

'Your blog was very … Interesting. It wasn't what I was expecting at all … Lily, that day in the taxi, you didn't mention anything about you seeing me already? Knowing exactly who I was, about you reading up on *Leadership*, my pieces? You knew who I was, but you didn't say. Another person might have been somewhat surprised. Shocked, even.' *Not me, of course.*

'I'm so sorry. You did seem familiar, but I couldn't place your face at first. Have you not ever done that, Katherine, looked at someone somewhere and thought you knew who they were, but your brain just can't make the connection, or maybe your subconscious is thinking that person is someone you *should* know? I've been trying to find a way of saying it, rehearsing what I could say to not completely freak you out: *I'm a bored weirdo with no friends and a total over-interest in people-watching and middle market trade titles?* Are you angry? Do you think I'm completely crazy?' Your dark eyes begged me to understand you, a hand reaching across the desk and towards mine. And I was disarmed by you again.

'Maybe no more than the rest of us,' I said, before I could help myself. Smiling back at you, your shoulders seemed to fall a notch; mine followed. 'I'd better get on with some work.'

I looked at the coffee, and with a tiny shake of the head at my own craziness, took a sip. Bitter. So disgusting my mouth puckered in protest. Was there a way I could put my mind at rest? 'Hey, Lily. What do you have there?' I said, pointing at your hot drink.

'Hot lemon with a little manuka honey. Why?'

'Don't suppose we could swap. Coffee isn't doing it for me today, but I'm completely parched for something wet and warm. I've only taken a little sip. Would you mind?' I said, holding out my cup to you.

'I'm not much of a coffee drinker really.'

'Please. For me?'

You looked at me quizzically. 'Of course. Here.'

We swapped cups, you watching me all the while.

I took a sip of your infusion. It was possibly fouler than the coffee you'd got me. I noticed you put my cup on the desk next to you. You had no intention of drinking it, but the reasons why were inconclusive.

'Hey, Lily. Congrats on the shout out. Nice work.' Asif had appeared over your shoulder, as had become his way.

'God. Thanks. Embarrassing really.'

'Nah, you're a natural. Own it.'

'Thank you, Asif, that's really so sweet of you to say.' You returned to your typing, before shooting me a demure tick of a smile. Asif may as well have ripped out his heart, and his balls, and presented them to you on a plate. So smitten, he hadn't even asked me how my weekend was.

It didn't take me more than a second to discover that one of the first stories you'd filed had been selected by Tradeweek.co.uk as one of the best pieces from all UK trade titles in the past seven days. The write-up praised your 'lively style' and 'refreshing take on well-trodden paths'. Next, I checked out Leadership.co.uk's 'Most read'. The top ten were all yours, save for the tenth. That was mine. It languished at the bottom, but it was there alright. I re-read it. It was neither particularly interesting nor well-written, but it had sparked a conversation among our readers which was keeping it in the rankings. The comments posted on it included the following:

This piece is so tired. What's the point of having new owners and a revamp if they don't change up the content too?

Totally agree. I think it's time for a new direction. New editor. I think it's time for Katherine Ross to hang up her leather, or whatever lady hacks of a certain age do when it's time to call it a day.

With you there. If things don't improve, I think you'll find subscriptions sinking even lower, IMHO.

And on it went. The sickening truth: my readers were clicking on my story not to engage with the insight, the voice of experience, but to rubberneck at my being pilloried by people who may once have feared me.

That afternoon, I received this message:

To: k.ross@leadership.uk; l.lunt@leadership.uk
From: g.lunt@leadership.uk

Subject: Copy camp

Lily and Katherine,
Your copy camp is scheduled for Thursday. I've booked some space for you at the Rosewood. You'll have a

meeting room, lunch included. Lily, we've discussed the objectives of the day. Katherine, Lily will have prepared a day of exercises and workshops for you.

I think you'll both get a lot out of it.

Best,
GL

On reading this, it was all I could do to grab my phone, leave the office to go sit in the yard of St George's and gaze into the air in front of me. I'd been earning money from the written word since you were in nappies, now I was going to have to sit and be lectured by you on how to do it properly.

I couldn't do my job anymore, not Gemma's way, not your way. Irrelevance. Humiliation. Aged forty-one, with the phrase 'on the scrap heap' hanging around me. And when I got back to my desk, this was waiting for me:

To: g.lunt@leadership.uk
Cc: k.ross@leadership.uk
From: acceptableinthenoughties@gmail.com

Subject: Fit for work?

Does *Leadership's* new code of conduct mean anything, or is it as much puff and nonsense as a typical Katherine Ross editorial? Shouldn't you be under the limit when you show up for work? No wonder everything she writes reads like it's been phoned in. Just sayin'. I share in the opinion

it's time to put Ms Ross out to pasture, give *Leadership* a
chance of being followed again.

I could see through her office walls that Gemma had opened
the message at the same time I did. She shook her head and
looked through the glass in a way that said, *Don't give it
another thought.* You kept typing, but gave me the most
beatific smile when you caught me staring at you.

I emailed Gemma telling her the email had sent me off
kilter. I still didn't want to investigate, but would it be alright
if I went home for the day? She emailed back:

Absolutely. Do whatever you need to do.

When I got home, Iain was buzzing. He was only just pouring
his first drink of the day. He was revisiting something he'd
written a few years ago. This is what you'd done to him. It
meant I couldn't bring myself to tell him about what had
landed in my inbox that day, or all the shitty comments on
my story, thus associating myself with a problem, with being
old and needy. 'Past it' to your 'Making it'.

CHAPTER 8

Katherine

The night before our copy camp I'd ended up matching Iain gin-for-gin. I'd woken up parched in the small hours, fallen back asleep and had the horrific dream which must have somehow made me sleep through my alarm. When I woke again, Iain's absence and the light bleeding around my curtains told me it was late. This sort of thing used to happen a lot when I got sick. Sleep became perverted. Sometimes I'd be so tired the only place I could be was in bed, but once there, I wouldn't drop off. I'd lie for hours, my body like lead, my mind wired with stress hormones that only became more concentrated as I begged it to switch off and let me have my oblivion, shave another few hours off my life. And when sleep finally came, it did so vengefully, plunging me deep enough into the darkness so I couldn't hear my phone trying to summon me to a new day.

I found Iain in the living room looking at something on my laptop.

'Hi?'

'Good morning!' he jumped up and snapped my computer shut.

'What you up to there?'

'It was making a weird noise. Here, does it feel a bit warm to you?'

I went over to him. He was quivering. He was often a bit shaky in the morning, but this seemed different. 'No, seems fine. You OK?'

'I'm great, love.' He handed me the tea he'd been drinking. 'You're a bit late today. Trying to dodge the old copy bullet?'

'It's coming for me whatever I do. Better get on.'

'You do that, love. Eggs?'

'No thanks, I'm late already.' I turned to leave. 'May as well pack that now.'

'What?'

'My laptop?'

'Sure. Here you go.'

He gave me my computer and I handed back his tea. It felt awkward. It wasn't like us. I put my computer in my bag, the tea back on the coffee table.

I went back to our bedroom, closed the door. I checked he'd not tried to access my emails. No. I viewed the browsing history to find it was just as it should be.

But I had forgotten about a file that lived in what I thought was a hidden zone; a folder within a folder within a folder in My Documents, one I kept quietly and only for myself. I should have hidden it deeper.

No time for makeup, even after the quickest of showers. I grabbed my black biker and went back to the living room to say goodbye to Iain. He was in the kitchen, rendering or tempering some foodstuff or other that would become our dinner, some kind of time-consuming and pointless culinary process that would end up down the toilet just as soon as I'd consumed it. But how could I tell him I didn't need him to do his one job in the world? Iain put down whatever utensils he was using, turned off the gas, wiped his hands and brought me towards him for a hug. He held me tight and close. I breathed him in. We kissed. I felt as if I was safe again.

But I wasn't.

And neither was he.

I texted you from the cab before you could let Gemma know I was late. I didn't even bother with an excuse, just told you I was running thirty minutes behind schedule. So exhausted, I just wanted to get through the day.

I got to the Rosewood and scanned the lobby before checking in. I'd been there or somewhere like it before. Coming to hotels like this every week with some of my favourite male contacts was another lifetime ago. It was the time you could still feel kind of sorry for 'online reporters', the era just before the door finally closed on the long lunch. Back then, I still believed London would deliver, that my writing would elevate me. I used to love being wined and dined by my contacts, but to me, I was only filling time; getting leathered on the corporate shilling, as I passed through to my real destiny. That day, the Edwardian grandeur and vivacious, groomed women stalking the lobby seemed to mock the old me. They were rubbing it all in my face; *Look at the lives we have, look at the lives we still have ahead of us.* Anyone would tell you the Rosewood is beautiful. That day, it looked beige. Everything was beige, including me.

Then there was you.

'Want to know a secret?' you came up behind me.

I gasped, 'Christ, Lily. Did you want to—' the words *Try to kill me* suddenly came into my head. 'Did you want to give me a heart attack?'

'Sorry, sorry. I couldn't resist. You looked like you were in a dream world. Everything alright?'

'Yes?'

You held my gaze with shining eyes, 'So wanna know a secret?' You slipped your arm under mine as you led me away in the opposite direction of the business centre.

'OK.'

'But you have to say yes first.'

'I can't just—'

'Oh *please*. You won't regret it,' you said, linking my arm, blasting the air around me with your youthful scent.

'What have you done, Lily?'

'If you come in on this with me you're going to have *such* a better day.'

'Just tell me what you've done.'

'Only found a great way we can get out of copy camp.' You stopped and looked me in the face with mischievous glee. 'So, I cancelled the room and the lunch and swapped them out for some massages!'

'Did Gemma OK that?'

'Oh please, I can handle Aunty Gem, don't you worry about that. Come on, what do you say?'

'I don't know, Lily.'

'How about, yes? Come on, we know I can square things with Gem. We've seen me do it before, right? Why don't you just let me make a good day for us?'

We.

Us.

I couldn't help it. I still liked how that sounded. And I preferred the idea of a massage over the nightmare of you telling me everything the modern reader would find wrong with my writing, especially given my hangover and the strangeness of my morning with Iain. And how much trouble could I possibly get into with Lily dearest, the apple of 'Gem's' eye anyway?

'Go on then.'

'OK, as long as you're absolutely sure.' You sought my consent again.

'Sure.' Of course I wasn't, but the alternative was too awful to contemplate and you knew it.

'OK, great! So, because Gem's made the booking under your name, we just need your scribble here and here to amend it,' you whipped out a suede clipboard and pushed it into one hand, a heavy silver ballpoint pen into the other.

'What's this? Do I really have to sign something? No, I'm not so sure. You sign it.'

'I would if I could, but they've made it so I can't. But if you don't want to, I completely get it. I'll rip this up. Sorry, let's just get on with the copy stuff.'

The very thought of it turned my stomach. I imagined you in front of a flip chart, puncturing the air with a chunky red marker every time you wanted to really drive a point into my rotting brain.

'Give me that.' I signed my name against two 'x' on the form. 'You'd better be able to square this.'

'Trust me, there's nothing I can't get away with,' you said, lips separating to show me those teeth of yours, eyes so bright, and it was so deeply plausible. You were too convincing for us all: Me, Iain, Gemma, Asif.

'Come on. Let's do this.' You nestled into my side and I let you lead me towards a dark corridor.

We entered the quiet dim of the spa together. You winked at the receptionist, who pointed you towards a row of plush chairs. We sat next to each other. I didn't feel I had anything to say to you; to say to anyone.

'How's Iain doing?'

'Fine. Why do you ask?'

'No reason. God, you're tightly wound today! You definitely need some TLC.'

Zeroing in on us, on him, on me. I was starting to see it all, Lily. I felt you studying me, then, the oddest thing: some unquestionable real-life genuine warmth coming off you.

'Hey, how about this: we just pretend like you and I just happened to meet in a cab that morning and we ended up being friends? For this next hour, we're not colleagues. You're not my boss, I'm not your boss's niece, we're not here for "copy camp", we're just girlfriends. That's what we are, really, at the heart of it, aren't we? That's what we would be, in another universe? That's what I think anyway. And if you don't agree then I've, like, completely embarrassed myself.'

Oh, Lily, you were so good when you wanted to be. You knew exactly what to offer me on a plate. Knowing how obvious my desperate need for a new friend was, was probably one of the most degrading elements of what happened between us. You see, there's a specific humiliation that develops when you are lonely. Shame collects in every crevice of your character; pretending you haven't gone another weekend where the only person you spoke to was your partner; fake nonchalance after crashing and burning when you've tried to start a conversation with the woman on the next treadmill at the gym; masking the temporary jolt of joy you feel when the phone rings before realising it's another spam call. Carrying myself in the world like a person who wasn't really lonely took a particular toll on me. My solitude had eroded the confidence that had once made me popular. The promise of restoring it with you was tantalising. 'I suppose it's possible.' Maybe you *could* fill the gaping friend-shaped void in my life. There was no one else lining up to accept the post.

The door on the treatment room opened suddenly, making me jump.

'Katherine and Lily?' A masseuse poked her head out of the door.

'That'll be us!' you told her.

'Would you like to come with me?'

'You can go first. I don't mind waiting out here,' I said.

'We're going in at the same time?'

'What?'

'Yeah, I thought it would be fun. Bonding?' I saw that mischief flutter just below the surface of your smile again, a knowingness. I went to say that simultaneous massage with female interns I've known for five minutes wasn't really my cup of tea, but how old, how prudish would that make me sound? I'm neither of those things.

I mumbled 'OK,' rose from my chair and went into the room obediently, a vision of Iain messing around with my laptop flashing into my eyes from nowhere. What had he been doing? Wandering into that black room, I didn't understand why everything in the entire world was changing. Except me.

The woman led us into a velveteen den with two massage beds. At the foot of one, another masseuse waited for us. They introduced themselves and then stepped outside while we got ourselves ready.

You immediately kicked off your ankle boots and lifted your pink cashmere sweater off your white ribs. Your bra surprised me in how plain it was. It was the lingerie equivalent of a humblebrag because your perfect tits didn't need anything more than plain white cotton. My own breasts aren't bad now. They used to be amazing, before twenty-five years of running and two-odd years of barely eating emptied them. I snatched glances of you as I took off my skinny grey jeans and unbuttoned my shirt. Your stomach wasn't naturally hard like mine, but soft and rounded. Each bit of you glowed in the muted light. Then, you were just there in your very sensible, mismatched knickers.

'Cool bra,' you said. And it was. A melon and mint number from Agent Provocateur. I used to spend a lot of money on my underwear. But like my disposable income and the brand, this bra had faded, having had its real moment in the sun in the noughties. Thank God it was dark in there, you couldn't see how sad my once-flash bra was; how, like me, up-close it was just another shade of grey.

Fuck you. Fuck you for bringing me here. Fuck you for grinding me down like this. Screw your incredible tits, pointing right at me as you went to fold your clothes and place them carefully onto a stool.

I hitched down my matching, discoloured thong that had

cost me £65 ten years ago, and tossed it next to my pile of other fading things. You looked shocked at my full nakedness, but immediately tried to mask it, 'Katherine! You're such a free spirit.'

'Is that what I am?'

'Yes. You've got that, I don't know, that *confidence*.'

'And you don't?'

'No. Not like you.'

A knock at the door and we both climbed onto our tables, towels draped awkwardly across our arses.

The masseuses slid around the tables in sync, drenching our backs, our shoulders, our legs and feet with essential oils. Your head was angled towards me, but I turned away from you and let myself drift off.

I don't know how long I was asleep before the dream with desperate child me came. This time, it played out at slow motion, my dirty toes teetering on the edge of every crevice I needed to clear in order to reach the gate. But this time, I was closer than ever, my fingers in the air above the familiar splintered wood. My unseen mother's eyes burning fury onto me for my show of strength. I placed both palms on the gate, ready to drag it towards me. Wetness suddenly. Blood gushes from my hands.

A moan. A noise, from my core, something primal, woke me.

I found myself somewhere dark, hot, not remembering where I was or how I got there. For a moment, I really felt I was at my mother's farm, in that black place, so utterly alone.

I clambered to get myself upright. My skin boiled, my hair drenched in sweat. I panted. I looked about and I saw you, watching me with probably the worst sentiment of all you could send my way: pity.

I managed to get the towel around me. One of the masseuses handed me a tiny cone of warmish water, but didn't look me in the face.

'Sorry, I had a dream … A nightmare. Sorry.'

My words fuddled out of me in a way I could hardly hear. I didn't know if anyone else would hear me either. Under a dull tide. Alone. Drowning.

'It's OK, you're safe. Just a bad dream,' I heard your voice through the fug.

'Such a bad dream,' I whispered, viewing my veiny hands as if I was seeing them for the first time. Hands that didn't belong to me. My mother's hands. Rough, ugly, broad palms, with short fingers. Built for labour, not for tapping elegantly at a keyboard to fill a clean white screen with words; not for artistic gesticulation; my mother's hands, created only to grind away bitterly.

'Why don't you tell me all about it over coffee?' You reached over from your table, took my shoulder in your hand and then let your fingers run down my oiled bicep, sweeping all the way to my forearm and my wrist. And I felt it again, and, I know, so did you: iron filings to a magnet.

'Can you leave her alone for a minute please?' you told the masseuses.

'Thank you, Lily.' This simple kindness, you protecting me, and that feeling again too: you liked me even though you didn't want to.

I took myself away for a cold shower, trying to wash away the dream and the blood and the sense of my mother. I viewed my flushed face in the mirror. I could see lines suddenly so deep in my forehead, great crevices I'd hadn't registered until that point. I saw my crow's feet. I noticed two curving channels running like a pair of brackets around my thinning mouth. My voice in brackets. A body, a life now in parentheses. I looked hard at myself. I re-applied my makeup, slicking on the MAC Russian Red lipstick I usually saved for after-dark. You texted me to say you were in the Mirror Room.

I joined you at a table in front of a wall of fragmented reflections of you.

You looked breathtaking. No makeup besides your orange lips; that and an ostentatiously healthy, post-massage flush. The whole room seemed rigged to make you look stunning.

'How you doing? I think you look … rejuvenated,' you said.

'What time is it?'

'I don't know. Eleven, I guess?'

Screw it, I thought, and grabbed a passing waiter. 'Hi, can we get a bottle of champagne and two glasses please.' I viewed the disorientating room around us again. 'Fuck, I wish I still smoked. I wish you could still smoke in bars. Have you ever smoked?' You went to speak, 'Don't bother answering that.' You were taken aback. You weren't expecting me to come out of that room match-fit. You'd expected I would come to you tenderised, all softened up for the mind games you'd planned, hadn't you?

'I have actually. I smoked something like twenty a day?'

'As many as that.'

'A pack a day's loads.'

'Depends how long your day is. Fuck, I need a drink.

Here we go.' The waiter appeared with a bottle. 'It's alright, I've got this,' I said, grabbing it and popping the cork myself. I poured a tall measure for me and decided at the last second to pour less than an inch in your glass. I know you noticed and that you'd also decided not to rise to the bait.

'When I was your age, I'd chug through forty, sixty maybe between Friday night and Saturday morning.'

'Right.'

'I'm not saying that's the greatest thing, I'm just giving you a bit of context.' I sipped. 'What made you give up, then?'

'It was easy. I hated it. I smoked twenty-a-day for a week for my student newspaper.'

'Get many bylines?'

'I guess. For a while.'

'What happened then? Fell out with the editor? Had a few too many bright ideas?'

'Oh, you know. I might tell you after a few of these.' You finished your drip of bubbles.

'Thought you hardly drank?'

'People change?' Voice sweeping up like a question.

'Do they?' I topped up your glass to brim-level, unseemly anywhere, but especially at the Rosewood. You looked at me and breathed, smiling as if to say, *Oh, Katherine*, without actually saying it.

'I was worried about you back there.' You smiled at me, pity scratching under the surface of your expression again.

'Don't you worry about me.'

'Why shouldn't I?' You sat forward. 'Because we do have a connection, don't we?'

'What kind of connection is that then, Lily? Really, what do you think it is?'

You went to say something when a waiter swooped in and placed two small square cakes on delicate white plates in front of us. They were white with multi-coloured discs. You sat back into your velvet chair before looking at me hopefully.

'I think you mentioned you liked Damien Hirst?'

'Is that what this is supposed to be?'

'Yeah, like a tribute, I guess?'

'Fuck me,' I pushed the plate away and took a glug from my flute instead.

'What's wrong?'

'*This*. This is wrong.'

'I thought you'd like it,' you said calmly.

'But why? Hirst's dot paintings, they're like the nineties on a page. Hirst said they were about pinning down the joy of colour. But *this* is what they do now. Take away the joy of colour, the joy of my youth. They think you can reduce what we were to a fucking cupcake.'

You checked the room to see if anyone had heard me dressing you down, before rearranging yourself into a soft defiance.

'Katherine, all I was trying to do was—'

'To what?'

'To put a smile on your face,' you said without smiling.

'Why? Why were you following me? Why are you buying me Damien Hirst fucking cakes? Coffee. *Weird* coffee that's got something wrong with it.'

'I always choose organic Fairtrade blends. You might find it's a stronger—' you began to answer, quietly, before I cut you off.

'And how do you know I like Damien Hirst anyway? Can you see into my flat? Are you still watching me? Are you still doing it now? Monitoring me when I'm leaving my house each and every day?'

'No! No. You've told me all sorts of things you like and you don't like when we've been talking. You just … I don't know …'

'Know *what*?'

'Ever since you've come into my life, I've asked myself, *I wonder if this person could be important to me*?'

'Come into your life? No, Lily. You've put yourself slap bang in the middle of mine.'

'I think it's probably one and the same, but that doesn't matter, I guess, I'd just like us to get on, despite Gem making us do days like today.'

I sighed and shook my head, not looking at you. You sensed my exhaustion.

'How about we drink to being two friendless fuckers drinking the morning away? Katherine?'

I knocked mine back while looking you in the eye. You fixed me right back.

And there it was.

A silent understanding we were playing a game.

We would be friends, but only under conditions that would ask more of me than I wanted to give. We could play together, but in the way that the cat plays with the mouse.

'*And* you've started to swear.'

You took the bottle and poured me a glass, before saying again in a voice that remained perfectly level, 'People change.'

Lily

16th March – Copy Camp Day

Over the years I've learnt all it takes sometimes is to paint someone an outline of what they can already see in front of their eyes. That's really all I've ever done, splotch out the dots for people to make the connections and let them see clearly for themselves what they already know in their hearts to be true. I've seen it so many times. You can give someone a way in, or a way back to the truth, then they do the rest themselves.

Taking control, shaping and melding a situation to come out winning, is something that's hard-coded into me. I had to get very good at it very quickly. What I learnt from trying to stay alive between Mum and Gem is the most powerful weapon is truth.

Take someone like Meg back in school number four. All it took for her was a few hints. She did the rest all on her own. Meg, bless her, had realised her weight issues were getting out of control so spent the summer holiday between years eight and nine eating an apple a day, nothing else. That was the rumour. When I saw her that first day back at school, you could see she wanted everyone to think she'd nailed it. In control on the outside, in control on the inside. But I knew better than that. I also knew it wasn't the natural order of things for her to be getting more attention than me. Everyone was so *wowed*. Girls wanted to hang out with her, boys suddenly couldn't get enough of her. Six weeks of starvation and there was a new pretty girl in town. That used to be me, but for real. In the last term of year eight, I was genuinely new and genuinely pretty. That was *my* thing. Meg had changed, temporarily, on the outside, but inside she was still the old her. I had to put her back where she should be. Me above her, my rightful position as someone who is fundamentally way hotter and far more interesting.

After the summer, no one called her Fat Meg anymore, no one *thought* she was Fat Meg anymore, except for Meg. That's why all it took was a hint and a nudge and a bit of temptation for her to destroy the new fake her and get back to who she really was. Thinking about it, all I ever probably said was something like, 'You look pretty much the same', 'They say you're still fat? Who cares?' and 'If you'll always be "Fat Meg", maybe you should just *be* Fat Meg'. I mean, it's no more than twenty-six words, said maybe three or four times, that and the gifting of my lunch every day to a friend in need. Twenty-six words and *I'm* the one who gets excluded. Again.

Meg did it to herself, and she needed to be put in her place. Just like KR.

All it takes to get to her at the Rosewood is the odd whisper in her ear, a hint here and there that her world isn't what she thinks it is. Add to this the idea she can get close to another human being who isn't her partner. But the rest is all down to her and the life she's already had. All the times she's taken something that didn't belong to her. It's backing up behind her, catching up with her, like a massive black wave, one I'm leading to the shore to finally break.

CHAPTER 9

Katherine

We'd nearly finished the first bottle of champagne when you said, 'Tell me what you were dreaming about. You seemed super-upset.'

Of course I knew you didn't deserve to know, that telling you would expose me again, but there was that pull once more. Lily, I was lost at sea, dehydrated, dying. You were the saltwater that desperation makes you drink.

For the time being I managed to say nothing and looked at my almost-empty glass.

'You might feel better if you talked about it. How about if you tell me, I'll tell you something secret about me.'

I looked up at you. 'Would that secret be my choice, my question?'

'Sure. Shoot. What could I have to hide from you?' Mischief dancing around the muscles in your mouth.

'Fuck it. OK, tell me, go on, I dare you, tell me now, did you honestly come into my magazine, my cab, my life completely by coincidence?' One last shot at a direct question.

'Katherine, why would you possibly think anything else? I mean, that's completely insane.' You shook your head and almost laughed, as if I'd said the most absurd thing you ever heard, then added, 'Sorry, I wasn't in any way referring to what happened to you last year. You being sick.'

'I didn't think you were. I asked you a question.'

'I gave you an answer.'

'Did you?'

'OK, if I didn't end up here by fate, coincidence, what else is happening here?'

'How am I supposed to fucking know? You tell me!' You looked at me as if you really didn't have a clue what I was on about. Great liar, not a bad actor either. I was on the spot again, like the crazy one out of the two of us again. 'Oh God, Lily … I don't know … What's going on with me,' I mumbled, feeling like a trainee reporter who'd choked on their killer question.

'Please, tell me about what happened to you in there. I want to hear it. I want to know and I think you'd like to tell someone.' Your hand reached over to mine and you gave me a little squeeze. So warm, so precision-engineered to make me put the saltwater to my lips.

I spoke with my eyes closed. 'Every night since last Monday, in fact every time I close my eyes to sleep, I see myself as a child. Alone, walking through a terrifying version of my childhood. My dad's gone and my mother watches me from on high, but she doesn't help. She wants to watch me struggle. She should be protecting me, but she isn't. She wants me to hurt. I'm on my own, bleeding, about to fall down a black hole. The only way I can save myself is by proving her wrong and reaching this old gate on the farm I was brought up on. I reached it today, for the first time, but all it did was make me bleed more.'

Your breath was suddenly audible. Then you were silent for a moment before asking quietly, 'Shall we get another bottle?'

'If you'd like to, Lily.' Had I actually got somewhere with my little confession, stirred something real in you, a revelation that might unlock the reasons for you coming into my life?

You summoned a waiter, ordered more champagne, then turned back to me. 'How about we do a bit of an exercise? It'll be good for you and it means I don't have to completely lie to Gem tomorrow about us doing any work today.'

'Really?'

'Yeah, it'll be like drunk writing therapy.'

'Come on, we can just make shit up about what we did today. Or you can tell me everything you know about great writing tomorrow. I think I've got a five-minute window somewhere.'

'Very funny,' you said without laughing. 'I'm serious. Get out your laptop.'

I rolled my eyes but complied. What did you think you could do to me next? You retrieved your laptop from your yellow case and I opened mine. 'Alright then, what are we doing?'

'I want you to write about the worst day of your life. You have five minutes. No talking, no thinking time, just do it. I'll do it too. We'll read each other's work and discuss. Go on. Do it. Katherine, I want you to put something of yourself into it. I will if you will.'

Such sudden intensity. Intoxicating. 'OK.'

And it came to me immediately, like a black arrow shooting from the past into the back of my brain. It startled me how ready this day was to come to the surface. I hesitated for a second. Why tell you about it? I looked over to you and saw you peer penetratingly into your laptop. You did seem to be pouring yourself into the task. I began to type, timidly at first, then, wanting to match your apparent effort, I let the once-familiar thrill of writing for myself take me over:

So this was it. The thing I'd been made to wait for. The thing I'd expected to escort me to another plane. The thing my mother told me never to do.

I'd decided exactly how I'd wanted to do it. He knew I'd never done it before and was surprised when I began to command him: Sit against this wall and let me do it to you. And don't speak. I kept my clothes on, guided him into me and waited to feel that feeling; to escape the farm, to transform, to become the woman my mother had never wanted me to be. I prepared for my metamorphosis.

Seconds later, I'm looking at his bowed head and I have to stop myself from bashing it against the wall behind him. I imagined the blank thud of his skull

'Right, time's up.'

'God, that went quick. I really enjoyed that. I've not written anything that wasn't for work for ages.'

I handed over my laptop and as you readied yourself to read my little vignette from my darkest ages you said, 'You should start a fiction blog or something, get writing, get noticed while you write, you know, *share* stuff?'

Good God, this is what all you millennials think, isn't it? Something's only worth a damn if it's 'shared', observed by someone else? You lot can be so holier-than-thou about everything: your diets, your over-complicated and curated 'identities', your 'triggers', your overwrought moral codes, your widespread resistance to booze, but show such terrific lack of discipline when it comes to private thought.

'You shouldn't worry if your writing's a little ragged. We only get better by sharing and learning from each other.' You smiled sweetly, but danger was dancing just below the surface.

'I'm not worried in the slightest.' I thought at the time about what an incredible cocky madam you were, to consider that I'd assume my writing would be in some way inferior. 'Go on, hand it over. Let's see what you've got,' I said.

I half-snatched your laptop off you and started to read.

I don't know what's wrong with me. Why they don't want me. They're sending me away again. It always feels like someone wants to send me away, just for being me. My soul is thinking, Here we go again. Being sent away is the only thing it really knows.

I didn't mean to hurt anyone. I was hurt first. That's where it started. I've been made this way and it isn't all my fault anyway. I can't help it if other people are weaker than me. But they don't see it like that. So here I am, with a red trunk that looks like it belongs to someone else, but it's got my name on it. My mum and my aunt are packing me off 'for my own good', but I hate them for what they're doing to me. Today is the worst day, but it's only a clone of all other ones I've had so far and all those other worst days I know will come.

We finished at the same time. So, this was who you really were. A lonely child whose carer treated you like a burden. My struggle too.

You were back inside your head again when the waiter showed up with the next bottle and started to remove the foil. My words seemed to have affected you.

'No don't take that off. I think we should take this to go. Katherine, I'd like to go somewhere and keep writing. Would you?'

'Yes, I really would,' I told you.

'The bill please.'

And I was as thrilled as I was scared. I was scared of who you were and what you wanted from my life, but exhilarated at the idea of being alone with you. You'd started to free-up Iain's creativity, now you were liberating mine. This is how you got away with it all. Probably the greatest of all your gifts.

I started to pack my things.

'So who was he then?' you asked.

'The guy? No one.'

'You didn't keep in touch at all?'

'Nope. He kept coming by. I stopped letting him in. Don't look at me like that! It was the most disappointing experience of my life. He was a grown man and I was just a girl who had a farm to sell. My mother had just died, I was about to go bankrupt. I knew I had to get out, I knew I had to get away to London or I'd die. I couldn't have anyone holding me back. What, did you want to marry the first guy you shagged?'

I didn't wait for an answer and headed to the bathroom. By the time I'd come back, you'd paid our bill.

'I thought all people your age were broke?'

'Some of us are just broken,' I thought I heard you say, quietly and to yourself.

We left the lobby and I was too pissed for public transport, so climbed into one of the black cabs waiting outside. You followed.

'Just like old times,' you said, bending to get in while I slid over to the far side. I went to inhale the freshness of you, like that first morning I met you. The memory made me try to drag you towards the truth again with a question. 'Just how freaked out must you have been when you saw me that day, given you'd been trailing me?'

'Katherine, really. You make me sound terrible.'

'And aren't you?'

'No. No, not really,' you said, but your intensity, the way you deliberately left your eyes on mine before looking out of your window, made me gaze out of mine to consider my next move. Cat and mouse. I didn't want to bother starting another big conversation there and then, I wanted to get to your place, pour us a glass and try to circle the truth until it had nowhere to go but out of you. But you had other ideas.

'So, do you know what ever happened to him then?'

'Who?'

'The guy from your worst day?'

We were at Gray's Inn Road. I used to go there all the time when I first moved to London. There were pubs where you could pick up bicycle couriers, wiry and hard, just like me. I wondered how many times in my life, like then, had I wished it was the nineties again.

'No. It was a lifetime ago now, and I'm not the type of person who likes to look back to the bad times. Difficult pasts exist for people like me to break away from.' I thought about your patchwork education and your written confessional on the loneliness of the unloved boarder. 'Maybe for people like you too?'

You went to speak, then got flustered and stopped yourself. I'd struck a nerve. Whatever you'd done in your past, it had fucked you up too.

We reached Manor House and I kept looking around to make sure we didn't run into Iain, in case he wanted me to come home, or ask to join our writing session. I couldn't have either.

But in the end, we didn't end up seeing Iain, or writing.

I followed you as you scampered into your building like you didn't want to be seen with me. Perhaps I was too old, too uncool. You made us walk to the tenth floor using the service stairs. You said it made you a better cyclist, but this sounded like another lie I could only fill the gaps around.

As soon as we got inside, you pulled out a bottle of Rioja, poured it into two stemless glasses. You'd come round to my taste in wine. You played around with your phone for a second and put some music on. You watched me as you waited for the first chord to resonate around your huge apartment. It reverberated off the floor-to-ceiling windows and went straight into my heart. The opening jangle of 'Panic' by The Smiths.

You liked the same music I did.

I had no idea people like you liked Morrissey and The Smiths. You started to dance towards me. You took my hands and I danced too.

You made me remember how good it felt to jump and smile and sweat and sing. I felt the years leave me, dancing with you, our bodies blurring together, laughing and panting in the pauses between songs. My pissed mind drifted towards what all my old lot were doing now. You'd given me a shot at pride again, perhaps even arrogance, because I remember thinking, as I took your hand and spun you around, *I bet they aren't dancing with cool young people on a Thursday afternoon. I wonder if they still have any reason to dance at all.*

For the first time in years I felt I could have a friend, and when I did, it was like coming up on a really good pill. Incredible. You made me feel young, until you made me feel so old. A sudden twinge in my back. An old running injury in my groin making itself known, meanwhile your body, so lithe, so perfect, silhouetted against the sun shining off the reservoir ten floors down seemed to mock mine.

I loved your place. I wished your place and your life were mine. I wanted what you had: a blank canvass for you to paint your fresh, hopeful life on. Lucky you. Amazing you.

We danced some more, jumping around, then performing together for an imaginary crowd on the path by the reservoir below, laughing at the rest of the world, together. I saw how you could indeed see my place from a window on the opposite side of the flat that faced out over Green Lanes. How small my slice of the building looked from there. I turned my back on it all to dance with you again.

I think it was after 'Sheila Take a Bow' that we ended up holding each other. The next song was 'Please, Please, Please, Let Me Get What I Want', and we started to sway together, in time to our pulses.

The room started to spin.

'Katherine,' you murmured.

The warm, fresh smell of your hair as I rested my head

against yours and the intoxicating feeling we were going to be friends filled me as I slipped into sleep.

It was dark outside when I woke. No lights on in your flat. We were at opposite ends of a sofa. You'd changed into a vest and jogging pants and were still asleep. I got up as quietly as I could, felt the rush of the booze in my mouth and tried to straighten myself without gagging. You breathed deeply and I watched you for a moment. You looked so sweet and innocent. How could I have ever let myself be afraid of you?

I reached your door. Something red caught the corner of my eye. The trunk you'd written about. It was pushed up into a deep alcove by the door. I stepped towards it. It was beaten up from being dragged back and forth from boarding school again and again. You hated that trunk and yet it had become something you just couldn't let go of, through sheer familiarity. It exuded loneliness. Did that trunk, which you packed and unpacked your little life into, feel like your one constant?

I let myself touch one of the worn corners. Something glinted: your initials, in gilt on the face of the trunk, between the buckles. A wave of nausea.

LF.

Not *LL.*

I *knew* you were a liar from the moment I met you.

Lily

16th March – Copy Camp Day, continued

When I see her at the hotel she looks beaten already. Why? I've hardly even started yet. What, exactly, is so very wrong with her life that she hates it so much? Why is she so totally ungrateful? She's always feeling sorry for herself when her life has been so-far free of consequences for the things she's done. Let's look at the evidence.

Like so many people her age, she owns her own place. She has a job that pays real-life, actual, cash-money. She has a partner who loves her and she's been able to maintain a supportive relationship and a home together for a big part of her adult life. What KR can't see yet is that she has things she doesn't deserve. What has she got to be depressed about? She gets a new boss? Boo-the-freak-hoo. She thinks she's poor (she's completely obsessed by money), trust me, she has no idea. She's getting on a bit – really? Women like me should be learning from women like her: child-free by choice, professional, in control of her own destiny. She probably thinks she's a feminist, but I just know she wouldn't want to take me under her wing and help me learn from her. Just like the rest of her generation, she's so ready to put her energy into hating me, pulling the ladder up behind her to stop me from ever reaching higher. It makes me wonder again what Ruth would make of KR. So many of the things Ruth said she wanted to change about the world come together in KR. It's so obvious: Katherine Ross *has* to be changed or be stopped.

She got herself naked like she was rebelling against me, like I'm the adult and she's the defiant child. On the table, she closes her eyes and falls asleep. I watch her dreaming. She seems soft. Innocent. Then, from nowhere, she sits up, panting like a dog, groaning, totally, genuinely freaked out. She's naked and confused and old, like she has no idea where she is. The masseuses are massively shocked. They look at each other like they just want her out of there as quickly as possible. One rolls their eyes behind her back. Guess what? I didn't like it. For some reason, I didn't want to see her fall. Again. See, despite what they say, I am not naturally bad. I think there was once a chance for me to be good, but somewhere between my mum and Gem, it got lost.

When she comes to find me in the Mirror Room, she's stomping and striding again. The vulnerable older lady has gone and it's pure KR. She's banging on at me about how much better the old days were, humiliating me for not being a hardened smoker. When the little YBA cakes I ordered for her arrive, her sneering was laughably predictable. (That was too much to resist. I knew it would get a rise out of her.)

She asks me about my college newspaper. I've not spoken about that time with anyone else who wasn't my solicitor, Gem or Mum, and none of those conversations were with people who were properly on my side. It would have been nice to be able to share it with someone who'd get why I did

164

what I did, because I think KR would. She knows what it is to try to do something, be something for yourself. She knows how it feels when you've found something you think might be capable of changing you, separating you from the messed-up child you were and don't want to be anymore.

I do want to share with her every gory detail of the nightmare that happened to me there, no edits, nothing left out. My life, wrecked all over again. The injustice. After the thousands of micro-assaults I've endured over the years, the rape by eye every time I walk down the street, it's me who ends up on trial. I wish I could tell my story to Katherine Ross, my older patron, my sexually empowered, bad-ass editor. She'd get angry with me, for me. I'd feel like there was someone else who got it. Got me.

But that's not going to happen, because she's onto me, properly suspicious. She asks me outright what I'm doing, like I'm going to tell her! Right then, I'm thinking, we're no way there yet, because she's learnt nothing. Then, I ask her about her little meltdown back on the massage table and when she tells me, something hits me: Am I actually making a massive mistake?

The thing is, what she's been a victim of, I have too. I *knew* it couldn't be just me. That's why this feels harder than it should. That's why I sometimes have to block myself from oversharing, reaching out, taking her hand.

Could I have played this differently? Can I *still* play this completely differently? We could be there for each other. Maybe we're two sides of the same coin. Maybe I don't have to detonate the years of pain in her face. It could be kinder than that. I can restart things on the right foot. People change, right!?

At this point, I'm seriously thinking about coming clean about what this really is, but I want to go a little deeper before I do, see if I can't get some honesty from her about her past first. I feel happy to share something true about me too. The pain of *my* childhood.

What I learn is that she sees her past as a blip, something to skip over on the way to something better.

No, Katherine Ross, it does *not* work that way. You should know that. You should have been living this truth for a long time by now, but you haven't. You've breezed right past it.

The past lives with me every day. That's not a choice I can make. There's no way I can bring Ruth back to me.

Why should she be able to pretend she's never made a mistake, never wronged another person? Her whole life is built on walking away from the hurt she's created without even realising.

Afterwards, when she talks about the man she used and threw away, she asks me, 'What, did you want to marry the first guy you shagged?' Yes, part of me did, but he ended up having a breakdown, the silly boy, so that was the end of that.

Charlie.

He was completely obsessed with me from the minute he saw me, just after I'd started at my fifth and final boarding school. Charlie's family were very, very rich. Gem loved him, my mum said I'd 'landed on my feet'. He said we could be together forever and I thought, *Alright, that could work*. Who needed to be 'in love' if I could get a nice house with him and never have to worry about money or living with Mum and Gem again.

He was encouraged to apply for a place at Oxford, but with all my moving schools and disruption, my expected results meant I was not. The way I saw it, he would have to apply to the same places I did and we'd pick somewhere together.

But he refused to ditch the Oxford application. He wouldn't do that for me. All the love he'd professed was a lie. Then, when he got in and I knew I was heading to Leeds, he told me we could still be together, but I knew better. If I was hundreds of miles away, he'd move on. People do that. My dreams of an easier life were gone. No, it's not right that he, the weaker party, gets all the power. I had to do something to put everything back in its right place.

In the end, I didn't do much at all to punish him. All I did was draw the dots for him to join. It went something like this: No, I didn't mind he was definitely smaller than the average 'down there' (he was my first, so I actually hadn't a clue!). No, it doesn't feel less. *You* don't feel less. You feel perfect for me. Let me take some pictures of you, something to really remember you by when I'm alone at night.

I didn't actually *do* anything. I just left the consequences of me having the pictures hanging over him, and, of course, waiting in a draft message to the whole year's WhatsApp group. His insecurity did the rest. I told him, 'I'm not like the girls you'll meet at Oxford. You're more than enough for me, no matter what anyone else in the school or the rest of the world would say. I'm so proud to be your girlfriend, I want to show everyone exactly who you are. It's not too late to say no to Oxford and come to Leeds.' Such a sensitive boy.

My therapist said the way I'd 'pushed Charlie away' just before his breakdown was 'a classic act of self-sabotage, most likely a symptom of my deep-seated attachment issues'. The housemistress, Mrs Farnaby, however, saw it differently. 'Your niece has cost a decent young man a place at Oxford and his mental wellbeing. I believe she is a danger to others. I would like you to remove her from this school at the earliest opportunity,' she told Gem in a phone call I wasn't supposed to hear.

But I believe my therapist's version of events. I didn't break him, he did it to himself. Still, I do think of Charlie and all of the others who've made me punish them over the years. He did make it to Oxford in the end, only a year later than planned.

When I saw that on social, I was glad that, in the end, no real harm was done. Being happy for Charlie was a good feeling because it seemed like progress, like there was still a chance for me to be the type of person my mum thought I should be.

But KR didn't think about the man she humiliated once. She didn't think about him ever again, just redirected her life to escaping to London. So cold. No thought for the consequences. Who does that? Not even me. I think about what I've done all the time to try and work on myself. At least I *know* I need to regret Sonnet Samira, Fat Meg, Charlie. I know that's what any normal person would expect. She has no idea what 'normal' is. No true morality.

So, I stick to my original plan.

Back in a black cab to Manor House. *Just like the old days*, I say, like there's a story of us. She's so drunk and malleable, I go back to classic Lily Lunt, the one she can't resist; I listen, I push her out, I reel her in all over again.

I get us both into the flat and put on the music I know she loves and pretend it's my own. She believes me. Of course she does. They always do. Daub the brushstrokes, let them fill in the sky with their brightest wishes, or their worst fears.

She looks so happy she could cry. She feels so sorry for herself and so alone, more alone than me, although she's got Iain. She turns the music up and starts to dance, unsure at first, but then she finds her rhythm. She laughs at herself, takes my hands, gets me up to dance with her. I hold back at first, but before I can stop it, I'm dancing like my life depends on it, and maybe it looks to the people below like we could be something to each other.

We end up holding each other again. We watch the sun go down on the reservoir. She ends up passing out right there in my arms. She weighs so little, it's not too hard for me to get her down to the sofa. I watch her, fast asleep. I lean down and kiss her cheek, because I can. Because I want to. Because of how much she reminds me of Ruth in that moment.

I put my pyjamas on and settle at the other end of the sofa to let the drunkenness take me to sleep, and find myself thinking of the sound of Ruth's duvet swishing against the shared thin wall of our old house as she turned in her sleep, before she turned her back on me to rest. Before I let myself fall asleep, I watch KR breathing softly. She sleeps so peacefully. Seems ignorance *is* bliss. Ignoring the things staring her in the face is how she lives, how she sleeps at night.

When I wake, she's already let herself out.

Asif's been texting me all day. He's so desperate, but I'm too hungover to go out with him as I'd promised. I tell him to come over instead.

Picking off KR's lieutenant: tick.

CHAPTER 10

Katherine

I flew down the service stairs and barely dodged the traffic as I ran desperately to my side of Green Lanes. Once on my street, the panic began to subside. I watched the river of traffic now separating us, calming down a little more. As I turned away and walked up the road to my flat, I vowed there and then that no matter what spell you put on me, I would never let myself invite you into my home.

'Hey, love,' Iain shouted from the kitchen when I got in, a sickening waft of rich, meaty fumes hitting me.

'One minute!' I shouted, shooting into the bathroom.

I hovered over the loo and made the vomit come.

'I was wondering where you'd got to…You OK?' he called from behind the door.

'I will be in a minute.' I used the back of my hand to move my hair from my eyes.

When I looked in the mirror, I was a disgrace. My skin was grey again, my eyes, slits in a bland, creased triangle of a face, sick on my chin and something else.

Orange lipstick.

Next to a smear of sick, your orange on the side of my mouth.

What had you done to me?

'Can I get you anything?'

'I might just have a shower and go to bed. Don't bother cooking me anything. Just sort yourself out.'

'Oh, OK love.'

I took off my shirt, remembering the undone buttons. I checked my neck and my chest for lipstick. I didn't think I saw anything, but I couldn't be sure. I got into the shower and tried to let the water blast any trace of you off me. I felt skinless again. Exposed by you. I wished I could turn back time to ten that morning. I would have said no to your massages, to your 'writing exercise', to going to your flat. We should have gone to the business centre at the Rosewood and you should have been the excruciating work-Snowflake version of you, all 'fair challenges' and 'I hear yous' and 'Yeah sures' and dumb inflections. You'd lied about your name, what else had you lied about?

When I got to the kitchen, Iain was spooning the dark brown contents of a large pan into a tub. 'I'm really sorry. That looks so good.'

'Don't be sorry. It'll keep. What happened to you? What did she do to you?!'

What to tell him. I didn't know what he could already see, or what he was choosing to ignore about you. I needed to keep him on my side and avoid anything that would make him worry I was getting properly ill again.

'We ended up blowing out copy camp, her idea of course, getting a massage and then getting hideously pissed. I think I blacked out at hers, or I slept, at least. I think I actually feel worse for it.'

'You seem a bit rattled? You OK?'

'I'm fine, really. A bit drunk-slash-hungover. I suppose we did do a bit of writing. Maybe that's it too.'

'That sounds positive.'

'We were already three sheets and she suddenly decides we should write about the worst day of our lives for five minutes. I ended up writing about something I'd not thought about forever. I don't know why. I think she's some kind of witch. She just keeps on getting stuff out of me.'

He peered at me, intrigued, suddenly coming alive through his usual evening pissedness. 'I felt something like it too. In the pub. I felt like she'd made me spill my guts out. I don't even know if that's a good or bad thing.' He laughed without mirth. 'I keep thinking about it. It's like she stirs up the sediment in my head, these old, compacted feelings. Deep down stuff.' He was staring into the middle distance, probably conjuring your face, then finally looked at me as if he was surprised I was still there.

'Me too,' I said, because it was true.

'You remember it's her creative writing thing tomorrow. I was still planning on going. Would that be alright?'

The vomit rose into my gullet again.

I wanted desperately to tell him that Lunt wasn't your real name, I wanted to extract him from your gravitational pull. But I knew I needed to build the case against you first. I had to stand up my story, or risk sounding paranoid or worse to Iain. I needed to look strong to him. The real me.

'Sure. Why wouldn't it be?'

The next morning, Gemma summoned you and me to her office for a copy camp debrief. I was late again, so had to walk straight in there with my jacket on. I regretted not calling you the night before to get our story straight about what we'd done at the Rosewood. But I couldn't face it.

'So, you two, how do you think it went yesterday?' Gemma asked.

'I actually think I learnt a lot,' I told her, hoping you'd take your cue.

'Yeah, me too. I think Katherine had some really fair challenges, but I think we reached some consensus on where we need to be going forward?'

Bravo, Lily. A lie with just enough credible features, but very high level and with 'going forward' you'd appealed to Gemma's love of corporate guff. You'd done that before, hadn't you? I always suspected you were a great liar. You kept proving me right.

'That's excellent, exactly what we need. I look forward to reading your next outputs, Katherine.' (*Outputs. Outputs?* How about, oh, I don't know, *articles?*) 'Lily, you can go. Katherine, thought we might have a think about your awards speech while the iron's hot.'

'Sure.' I swallowed the taste of my own vile mouth and clawed around my barren brain for any ideas on what I was planning to say. It wasn't long now and the draft document I'd opened two weeks ago was stubbornly empty. The idea of getting up in front of those people, having them judge every bit of me as I made my grand return, especially after the shitty below-the-line comments readers kept leaving, turned my stomach. 'I've had some ideas on themes I wanted to discuss with you, actually, but what's in *your* head?'

'My one hope is that it will be truly inspiring: a statement of intent, a clear departure from the past. I think that's a theme that works for you, personally, given you had to stay away from the awards last year, I'm correct in thinking?'

'Yes. That's right. I had to stay away,' I said quietly, repeating her phrasing which made it sound like I'd been carrying some kind of contagion that forced me to quarantine myself out of public-spiritedness.

'I know you'll want to make your comeback really strong. So, let's hear those thoughts on how you'll open.'

It's my dearest wish to get through the first thirty seconds without falling over. 'I should think I'll probably begin with some niceties before launching into the main speech, you know: *Ladies and gentlemen, I want to start proceedings by paying tribute to the new management, ably headed by Gemma Lunt.*' Gemma seemed to tighten. Her face went rigid and she tried to smile over how deeply unimpressed she clearly was. Your aunt was looking for my 'best self' and I didn't have one to give her. It was time for a new tactic to get out of there unscathed.

'Lunt. Now I say it out loud, it's an unusual name isn't it? Did your sister want to keep her maiden name? Pass it on?'

'I'm sorry?'

'Well, *Lunt*, it's obviously the maternal name, so that must mean your sister decided to keep it and give it to Lily, otherwise she'd be—' I said, but Gemma shut me down. She was in on the lie about your name at least. She'd have to be.

'Well, we're a very female-centric family.' Lips pursing, shifting towards the left of her face. 'Now, I wouldn't necessarily start on the new management. Start on your vision for *Leadership*. Where are we taking readers next? Play in all that great stuff you picked up from your hard work with Lily yesterday, that's sure to make things really pop.'

'I'm sure you're right.' Gemma knew your real surname, but she didn't really know you at all, did she?

When I returned to my desk, there you were, typing away, smug as usual and distinctly sober-looking. You didn't look like someone who'd crossed the line with her boss. The other interns were going for coffee. I asked them to get me one too. (Why didn't the little shits ask me? I was their fucking boss. They should have been asking *me* what I wanted every day, twice a day. I should not have to get them to turn around just as they were about to leave each and every day to take my order and my pound coins when I had them.) I could see Asif was now in with Gemma. We were almost alone. Time to press your buttons.

'Did you actually drink anything yesterday?'

'I was completely hammered. You couldn't tell?'

I shook my head vaguely. 'I don't even remember crashing.'

'That's OK. I think you were really tired.'

Patronising comment followed by serene typing. Classic you.

'When I got home, I was really sick, but I could have sworn … did I borrow your lipstick or something? I had orange on my …' I touched my face.

You shook your head. 'Not unless you snuck it out of my bag when I was out of the room.' Pushing your chin out to me, you smiled and blinked slowly. *Alright then.*

'I've been thinking about what you wrote. Was it about being sent to boarding school, you were a boarder weren't you?'

'Yes. I think you already knew that?' You cocked your head a little to the other side. Cat turned mouse.

'Did you have to lug that trunk I saw back and forth everywhere to – where did you say you'd gone to school?' Your CV. Of course. There it was, in my inbox already. Waiting silently for me to look again when I'd started to put the other pieces of the jigsaw together.

'I don't think we talked about it,' you were flustered. 'My trunk? You saw that?'

'It was there, in your hallway. I passed it on my way out.'

'I should really throw that thing out. Don't know why I can't.' You tried to laugh, but I was getting somewhere now. Or perhaps I would let you go for the sport of it.

'It's not always easy to let go of our pasts, even when they really hurt us.' I sent a sympathetic expression your way, squishing my mouth to a line and tilting my head in the pastiche of maternal concern Gemma had perfected. You knew I was faking it too, just like Gemma.

'Sure … Well, I guess I'd better head. I'm due at The Dorchester. Gem's made me the lead co-ordinator on awards night?'

You couldn't pack away your laptop into that silly yellow case quick enough. You all but sprinted to the door to escape the conversation. I was on to you and you knew it.

It was barely five when the office cleared. Gemma left early for 'the Norfolk house' and the interns excused themselves shortly after, confirming my suspicions they were wholly unafraid of me. I wanted to get out of there quickly too, I *had* to shag Iain before he saw you in a pub this time round. But once the coast was clear, I couldn't resist reopening your CV again, then googling one of your old schools, then another and another, cutting and pasting the years you'd attended and the contact numbers into an email I sent to my personal address.

I didn't hear Asif come up behind me.

'K? I've been meaning to talk to you,' he said. 'How are things going?'

'It's not been the greatest week.'

'Oh yeah? I mean, do you want to tell me about it?'

He was using what used to be our old code for spending some time with each other. It always started with some innocent comment, and a brief chat over a bottle of beer or whatever other booze was hanging around in the kitchen's fridge. 'I really shouldn't … Oh fuck it, go on then. Hit me up, then. Go on.'

'Oh, OK. I'll see what I can find.'

He disappeared into the kitchen corner and returned with an opened screw-top bottle of white and two cloudy tumblers. He poured quickly, splashing drops all over my desk. 'So, what's going on with you?'

'Well, you would have seen me being trotted in and out of Gemma's. In and out constantly. Then, of course, there's Lily.'

He sat up straighter. 'What about Lily?'

'She's always watching me, trying to trip me up. You know we were out at this copy camp thing yesterday? She derailed the whole thing. And you know she got Gemma to buy this place? But do you also know she'd been stalking me round my neighbourhood before she'd even started? Watching me leave my flat every day, following me. Writing some creepy blog about seeing me. Then, I also have this troll that sounds a whole lot like her. It's all too weird, isn't it?'

'Why did Lily say she was following you?'

'She said I'd *caught her eye* or something. I mean, she's weird, isn't she?'

'I don't know, I think she's really great, I guess. But if you're worried about something, why not just talk to her? She's really easy to talk to.'

He put his hand on my arm and I felt a familiar but almost forgotten jolt of desire move between us.

'This is very bad, Asif.'

'What is?'

And before I really knew what was happened, he was roughly grabbing my breast, and I suddenly realised how I'd missed that sort of thing. Iain had become so tender, so caring, so tentative since I'd got sick, it was kind of getting on my nerves. Asif and I kissed with force, with urgency, and fuck, it felt so good. I went to free myself from my shirt and it felt like the last two years hadn't happened. I'd missed this; I'd missed feeling like myself. I had a taste of the old me and I liked it. Everything felt so good.

Right up until the point I saw you.

Inside the security double doors, peering into the office. Come back to check on me, had you? I suppose I mustn't have disappointed, because on seeing me with half my tits hanging out with Asif, you doubled back on yourself. A fluster of initial shock, then a ripple of determination, right before you turned to leave, heading north to get yourself ready to meet my partner with a fresh new angle on me.

'Her. Again.'

'Who?'

'*Lily.*' I pointed to the doors behind us. Asif turned, but by the time he was facing the door, you'd disappeared.

'Where?'

'She was just there!'

'Shit. Are you sure? I really don't think there's anyone there.'

'She *was* … Anyway, Asif, sorry, I'm late. I've got to go.'

I buttoned myself up again, thinking it was around the same time the day before when I'd been doing the exact same thing after you. I switched my machine off with one hand and wrestled my jacket on with the other. You could be over the bridge by now. I needed to move.

'What was it you needed to say to me? You wanted to tell me something?' I hitched my bag roughly onto my shoulder.

'Well, it could be nothing, but I overheard Lunt Senior mention something or other about a questionable expenses case you'd put in? Something about a £66 cab fare on expenses? Just thought I'd give you the heads-up.'

'Fine. I'll add it to the list.'

'I'm only the messenger, Katherine.'

'Sorry. Look, I've got to go. Talk to you next week, alright?'

'Sure.'

As I hurled myself down the steps and out of the door, towards a bus I would will with all my might to get me home in time to have sex with my partner before he laid eyes on you again, I swear I could still smell your scalp in the stairwell.

I sat, as usual, towards the front of the top deck. I glanced out of the window, noticed my jaw tightening in the glass, before turning my gaze to the roads below.

And there you were on your bicycle, sneaking into the sliver of air between my bus and the kerb, racing north ahead of me to meet Iain. Viewing you from on high, I couldn't see your blinding smile or your dark eyes, but only a young woman who was certainly out to take something from me. I dared the bus to inch too close to the pavement, towards you.

I watched open-mouthed as you peeled away from me, turning west down London Wall towards Barbican.

Not you, but someone just like you. From where I was sitting, you lot all looked the same.

When I put my key in the front door, I could hear music, Iain's music, Jesus and Mary Chain, vibrating through the shared hallway. Iain never played music in the evening. Not normally.

When I got inside, I caught him prodding his midriff again. He'd had a shave. He never did that in the evening either. His bomber jacket was already on; I was too late.

'Hey, where've you been? Thought I was going to miss you.'

'You look good. Time for a quick one before you go?'

'Ah, love, no. I don't want to be late from the off. The old man wants to make a good first impression with the whippersnappers!'

'OK. When you come back, then.'

I nearly told him I'd wait up, before realising how pathetic I'd sound. That wasn't me.

'Definitely.' He kissed me and went to meet you and your cronies with what could only be described as a spring in his step.

'Wish me luck!' he shouted back up to me as he descended the communal stairs.

Don't go, please, don't go. I'm begging you, Iain, know you need to turn around right now and stay here, with me.

'Good luck,' I whispered. How he'd need it with you. Poor Iain didn't have a chance.

I went to the living room and switched on my laptop. When I heard the front door close, and it was just me and my computer, I had the overwhelming sense this was my future.

CHAPTER 11

Katherine

Home alone on a Friday night I was sat staring at boarding schools' websites; pictures of gleaming children, and no hint of their inevitable inner turmoil. There were somewhat sickening 'visions' and 'mission statements' like: *To develop the individual's full potential through the pursuit of the exceptional … To nurture independence of spirit in preparation for adult life*; and much harder to find details on fees.

I finished one of Iain's bags of wine and called the one you must have gone to when you were sixteen or seventeen. I got through to the switchboard and rang the extension for one of the girls' dorms. It rang for a long time until someone picked up, a housemistress, I suppose.

'Mrs Farnaby speaking, how may I help you?' came a foggy voice.

'I'm trying to track down an acquaintance. I have some important information for her. She was with you a few years ago, when she was sixteen, seventeen. Her name is Lily.'

'Lily.'

'Yes. I'm afraid I – she won't reveal her second name.'

'Who are you? Could you possibly call back in office hours?'

'I'm afraid it's urgent.'

A long pause.

'By any chance are you some kind of health professional?'

'I'm not able to say.'

'Well, regardless, we wouldn't give out personal information about a former pupil. We have to guard their privacy, no matter who they are, or what they may have done. If you were to approach us in writing, we could pass your details on, but otherwise, we can't take this any further. It goes without saying that if someone is in any immediate danger, you should hang up and dial 999. Goodnight.'

The phone deadened.

Health professional. You'd been to a lot of schools. You seemed to last no more than a year, two years tops at each. Your mother and Gemma had shipped you off all over the place: Sussex, Norfolk, Dorset, even my own Derbyshire. No wonder you were screwed, but what was wrong with you to deserve being moved around like that?

I thought I could hear someone coming up the front steps and checked the time. Nearly eleven. My partner had been out with you and your creative coterie for almost four hours. I imagined the rest of them would have left by now, leaving just you and him. I was thinking about texting to say I was taking a night stroll and joining you for last orders in The Rose and Crown when I got a text from Iain:

Havin one mor, thn be home. xxxc

So he was pissed and would be back to me soon. The Iain I knew. All was well-ish in the world, then. One of the many things my partner loved about me was my ability to accept exactly who he was and my apparent absence of jealousy. That sort of thing was for lesser women; the closed-minded, the habitually monogamous, the provincially-persuaded. We were far too cool for that. If anything, our affairs in the past powered us higher and closer. But that was then. We were different. I was different, more alive. Now you were the one full of life, so much life it had the potential to destroy us.

By midnight Iain still wasn't home. I tried to nap on the sofa, couldn't, so texted Asif:

Hey there. You in bed? Xxx

This used to be the cue to start sexting, but I didn't get an answer for twenty minutes. Eventually, he sent this:

Hi. Bit knackered. Started dating someone this week. You ok? xxx

I didn't bother texting back.

When Iain finally came home that night, two and half hours after his last text, he spent a long time in the bathroom with the tap running. I pretended to be asleep and dared not ask why.

People change.

The next morning, I was awake before Iain. I checked my phone while I was still in bed. Acceptableinthenoughties had sent another message to Gemma and me:

Subject: Katherine Ross: an urgent appeal for change

You either need to put the old girl out to pasture, or do something about her writing, because I don't know what I'll do if I have to read another fucking turgid piece of so-called 'insight'.

I emailed Gemma:

This is putting me under a lot of pressure and distress. I think I can ride it out, but what do you think we should do? KR

She texted me from her personal number:

I'll do whatever you would like me to do. Let's discuss on Monday if you still need to. Any further thoughts on who this might be, out of interest? GL

I drafted a message back:

No. You?

Then deleted the 'You?' It didn't feel like quite the right time to push it, yet.

But I knew her game – she was trying to avoid an email trail on this. This could only mean she was very worried it was you, as any right-minded person would be. The major difference being, she was out to protect you by managing your mischief, when it was my mission to remove every layer of your pretences so we could all see who you really were.

I turned to Iain. He was fast asleep/unconscious, so I ended up getting out of bed first. This virtually never happened and I wasn't sure how to fill the minutes before he joined me. They dragged and dragged. You'd made me feel like a waiting fishwife again; primed, ready to unleash on my partner, arms crossed over my wizened chest.

Eventually, he ambled into the kitchen where I was attempting to make waffles.

'Morning. How's you? You were in late,' I tried to keep my voice as neutral and non-pathetic as possible, suggesting that me 'rustling up breakfast' was totally normal, as if I knew exactly what I was doing underneath the clouds of flour and spills of milk, as if it was not a desperate attempt to pass time and appear cool and in control of my paranoia.

'I know. I don't know where the time went. Sorry.'

'Don't apologise. I'm glad you enjoyed yourself. How was it then? What were they like?'

'Oh, as you'd expect.'

'So ...'

'So?'

'Tell me stuff!'

'It was faintly excruciating, but essentially liberating.'

'Liberating?'

'Yeah, after all these years, talking about my stuff, my ideas. It's been a while.'

'And do you feel *inspired*? Are you going to keep at it? What did you take? What are you working on?'

'I've kind of revived an old script.'

'Right. You didn't say exactly what you'd taken.'

'Well, you didn't exactly ask. Here, let me do that,' he

relieved me of the stupid waffle iron I was ham-fistedly trying to oil.

'I'm sorry,' I said. He shook his head faintly as I spoke. I went on, not knowing what else to do. 'I know I've been really wrapped up in work. Gemma. *Lily*, for God's sake. What do you make of her, really? What was she like in her natural habitat?'

There was a stillness to his face as he worked some greasy kitchen roll into the dimples of the iron, a studied unstudiedness, wholly unnatural; Iain shutting me out.

'I think she's just a young woman, trying her best to get along … Are you having one, or were you just doing them for me?'

'For you.'

'Alright, well some of this might end up in the bin. I can't eat all this.' He viewed the gloppy batter I'd cobbled together with unhidden disgust.

'I thought you'd be hungry.'

'I am, I just can't be eating so much.'

He was self-improving. Not because of me, because of you. I knew that.

Later on we shagged and it was good. It wasn't an absent-minded Saturday shag, it was focused. Iain did everything I liked and more. It felt like how we used to be. But I couldn't help but worry, was he thinking about you? Worse: was he practicing his best performance, building up his confidence to be with you?

Afterwards, in bed, he told me you'd invited us to a party the next weekend somewhere in Sussex.

'Could be fun. Get out of town for once. We've not been to

a decent house party in donkey's. Let's show the Snowflakes what us old ravers are made of.' And he sounded like him. Me and him Iain, *Back to ours* Iain. But it wasn't this that made me say yes.

Because this could be a chance to really probe who you were, to investigate you, grill your friends. You hadn't come out of nowhere to bring me down. If I asked the right people the right questions, I could tap the truth at its source. I wouldn't fluff my questions this time. And then there was that other, lonelier voice calling out of me, *Maybe I'll get to dance with Lily again. Maybe it was all in my head. Maybe everything will be alright.* This was how low-hanging my life was, overripe fruit, waiting for you to take it down with ease.

'Sure. Why not? Maybe we could get a nice B&B. Make a weekend of it?' I said.

'The Ross-McIvors are ready to party!'

'Apparently so.' I kissed him and lay myself down.

'Why don't we get something in? A couple of Gs?' Iain asked me.

'Fuck, did I wake up in 1990-something?!'

'Come on. We remember how to party don't we?' He wanted to feel young again. He wanted to *be* young again, for you. 'Let's have a look-see if I've still got a dealer's number.' He went to scroll through the contacts on his phone, but then turned away slightly, so I couldn't see the screen. Small things that speak of the disturbance below. 'There he is. Still there. What do you reckon, two?'

'You *do* know millennials can't afford coke? We'd better get more in if we're going to do this. Maybe we could sell a bit on.' *I can be young again too, Iain.*

He started texting. 'You're a funny girl.'

'Well either we do that, or they hoover up all our drugs for nothing.'

'OK, you know best. Here we go. I'm writing the text, *4 pls mate*, I'm doing it, I'm going to do it. You gonna stop me?'

'Just do it!'

He thumbed his phone. 'And it's done!'

'And you're a funny boy.' I kissed him and stroked his hair back off his forehead, his sweet, boozy scent my one true home.

'You know I love you,' he told me and I sensed an unspoken 'but'; a 'but' waiting in the wings for me. *I love him so. Please don't leave me. Not for you, Lily. Not for anyone. We need each other.*

'And I love you.'

And we shagged again, but this time I believed it was all for me. He'd not gone yet, but there was more I could do.

It had started as an idle thought perhaps a week earlier. A small notion, one I'd chosen not to look in the face. But with the creeping sense of my partner slipping away from me, I decided to nourish it, force-grow it to its fullest scale. My head on Iain's chest after sex, as it had been ten thousand times before, I said to him, 'Iain, I have something to tell you.'

'Go on.'

'For the past couple of weeks, I've been having this really sad, awful, recurring dream. There's me, twelve-year-old me, at the farm, trying to reach this gate. I go to open it. I don't know why, but I can't. Something always stops me. This dream … I wonder if it's trying to tell me I've made some … some choices I should have approached differently.'

'What kind of choices?' I felt his chest heat below me, his blood quicken.

'Really big ones.'

'Such as?'

I brought my head up to look at him square in the face. 'I think I was wrong about us not trying to have a family. I was thinking maybe, we should start thinking about it.'

Stillness at first, then he sat up in a way that meant I had to parry out of his way or get an elbow in the face. 'Fuck me. Fuck me, Kathy. Why? Why now?'

'I don't know. The dream; this dream that's tormenting me every time I close my eyes. I want us to have a family. I think that's what I need to make me deep-down happy. To make us deep-down happy. I mean it's kind of obvious, really.'

'Obvious, is it? Well, it wasn't fucking obvious ten years ago when we might have had a chance with all that.'

'Hey! I'm only forty-one! I could still do this.'

'Are you serious?'

'I don't know … Do you want me to be?'

'Fuck, Kathy. I don't know. You have a fucked-up dream and suddenly you want a baby? A kid?'

He hadn't been looking at me, but at the last sentence he turned to stare me in the face and I felt the full power of his resentment, like a heat lamp burning down on me. I thought he'd fallen in love with me because I wasn't like women his age, soft and needy, ragging for children and 'normality' and to straighten him out for sobriety and fatherhood. I let him be him by being me. I facilitated the life I believed he wanted and that I wanted too. Laughter. Sex. Lots of sex and with other people from time to time. But we were older now. I was still me, but now that wasn't enough anymore. Another middle-aged woman whose man was going off her. Me, finally getting all caught up with my feminine archetypes after all those years of fighting them.

'What do you mean? I've made mistakes in the past about our life and now I'm being honest. It's taken a long time to unpick my childhood. You'd be terrified about what kind of parent you could be if you had a mother like mine. But not anymore. I want to think about the future now.'

He said nothing, closing his eyes as I spoke.

'I can't believe this. I just … can't quite believe it,' he said eventually.

'Why would I lie to you about something like this?' My tears finally came.

'I don't know!' he shouted. 'I don't know,' he said quietly, turning to me and moving my flop of hair away from my eyes. 'Fuck me, you know how to keep surprising me. Is this for real?'

'Yes. It is real.'

He sighed. 'This is big. Let's just let this sit with us a while. OK?'

We were quiet for a minute while the explosion settled. We laid on our backs, the white ceiling looming over us, not touching. After a while, he reached out and found my hand. 'Come on, let's go for a walk.'

We ambled over the park, hand-in-hand, passing through a row of cherry blossom trees. A sudden gust of wind stripped them near-bare of their toilet-roll coloured blooms. I laughed like you would in a film, a love story. But it was a little too loud, and the way I shook the petals from my hair and brushed them off his shoulders, the corniness of it all took me over. I was suddenly embarrassed by the whole scene. But I still wanted my love story. I wanted to believe it was all real and everything was as it should be. Iain kissed me long and tenderly. But what I felt in the love of that kiss was a kind of sympathy.

We stopped, he held my head in his hands and kissed me again and pulled me into a hug.

'I love you so much, Katherine. Despite—' he let it hang.

'Despite what?'

'Nothing … Nothing.'

And we looked at each other for a second. He searched my eyes, looking for something we were losing, or maybe something I alone had lost all by myself.

'Come on, where do you want to drink then?' I asked him.

'Thought I might head back to The Rose and Crown. I'd forgotten how much I like that place.'

'Wherever you like.'

I spent the rest of the day trying to be cool Katherine; perfectly ripe me. I enabled him in drinking more, though he seemed less bothered than he would be normally. I talked up the fun we'd have at your party. I kept talking about you, bringing the conversation round to what the party house would be like, how posh it would be, how snowflakey and entitled your friends would be, how mad we were going to make it all.

'We've still got it, me and you, haven't we? No matter what we decide on what happens next.'

'That we do.' He squeezed my hand across a tiny table in the corner of the pub.

*

The next morning, as I headed out for my normal Sunday run, who did I see strolling in through the Green Lanes gate?

You.

You with Asif.

I made it to a nearby clump of trees to watch you. Hand-in-hand, walking slowly, steam rising from your organic, Fairtrade, caffeine-free, fucking weird non-coffee. I'd guessed Asif had succumbed to you too, now I knew for sure you were the one he'd 'started dating'. I could see clearly he was well and truly suckered. I don't remember him ever looking at me the way he was looking at you. It was obvious he was yours to do whatever you wanted with. You'd successfully removed my only ally at work. Now I really was alone there. What were you planning to steal from me next? I had to get to that party and be the reporter; discover the who, when, why, what of you. If I didn't get one step ahead of you now, everything I cared about could be yours for the taking.

Lily

17th March – Creative Writing Night

I'd been wondering if she'd be able to resist muscling in on my 'writing group' with Iain after Thursday. In fact, I was seriously worried. I was already on the edge after she said she'd seen my trunk. She would have seen my real initials. But watching her going at Asif like that, I couldn't have planned it better myself.

'This is very bad, Asif,' she says, practically rubbing herself on him.

'What is?' the poor clueless boy says back.

Suddenly, she grabs his hand and puts it onto her, starts moving it around and kisses him full-on like a horny teenager. He looks like he didn't know what hit him.

She sees me at the door mid-move. Asif looks down, trying to catch his breath. The look in her eyes – I knew she'd definitely leave me and Iain alone tonight.

Asif calls me five minutes later.

'I don't know if you saw anything just now? With Katherine?'

'More than I wanted to.'

'I didn't want to do it. I didn't want to do anything with her. I guess I'm still a bit flirty, that's what she likes, but it's not like that, not anymore.'

'Asif, please don't worry. I completely understand what it's like for you with her. Want to catch up over the weekend? Come to Stoke Newington on Sunday?'

When Iain gets to the pub, he looks anxious. He's cleaned himself up. He doesn't look half bad, I guess. I'm waiting for him on a bar stool.

'Hi, Lily. Where are we then?' He's very nervous. He should be.

'This *is* "we", I'm afraid, everyone else cried off. Sorry, you'll have to put up with just me. I bought you a double Grey Goose to say sorry.' I hand him a drink.

'You dancer,' he says and takes a huge gulp. 'It's probably for the best it's just you and I. I've not let anyone read my stuff for so long. I've been bricking myself if I'm honest, Lil.'

'What do you need to be nervous for?' I turn my body to him and tuck a strand of hair behind my ears, gazing at him while he speaks. He blushes.

I lead him to a tiny table in the corner that no one ever wants because you have to practically sit in the other person's lap to fit round it. Our legs will be touching from the off.

He was insanely complimentary about the bit of rubbish I sent his way ahead of our meet. An abstract short story about drowning I'd written during my exile after they kicked me out of Leeds. Iain's stuff was so-so, I guess. A bit shallow. He'd showed me the start of a script for a piece of comedy theatre. It was funny in parts, but I wanted to know: What is he trying to say? What's the message? He doesn't know.

'Do you know, Lil, I haven't really thought about it.' He looks stung by this bit of self-awareness. Softening up nicely.

'But there's so much warmth to it. This comes from such a generous place. It really makes you want to get closer to the material.' I blink at him.

'Really? Well, that's something, then. Funny, Kathy always used to say something like that. The way I used to write copy, in my agency days, always brought people in. She said she didn't know how to do what I do.'

'Wow. That's really … sweet.'

'Can I tell you something?'

'Anything.' I draw my chair in, so he's practically touching my sweater with the back of the hand that's wrapped around his tumbler. I'm thinking I could probably turn the night right there and then, but then he dips down and starts rifling through his backpack.

'I tried to dig out the last thing Kathy wrote. Couldn't find it, but I did find her first manuscript. She'd kill me if she knew, she's never even let me read this one. But you seem to have made quite the impression on my girl, got under her skin, for want of a better expression, and you seem to know your stuff when it comes to writing. Would you maybe have a little look and see what you think? Maybe we can think about how to get her going on her own stuff too? It might really help her feel like herself again.'

He handed me her manuscript. Just like that. A portal to her inner thoughts in the palm of my hands.

'I don't know what to say.'

'Just say you'll have a little read, have a little think. Maybe we could compare notes next time? Try to help her? Right, I'm off to get us another pair of these,' he says, scooping up our glasses.

'OK, I'll make a start now.'

Creep Feeder
By Katherine Ross

'THE animals eat before you,' her mother tells her over and over. Every day, when she's rocked awake at 4.30 in the morning. It's hard in the summer, heart-stopping in the winter. She asks for food, a bit of bread to stop her stomach from attacking her. Every morning, she's told the same thing: she's at the bottom of the pile, ahead of her are 500-odd ewes roaming clueless on the poor soil her mother refuses to feed too.

There was a time when the girl wanted to know why her mother puts the minimum food into her own body, why she goes to bed before the sun goes down, why she provides only minimal care for the sheep, the land and the daughter. But the girl has decided her mother doesn't deserve these enquiries. When the mother is so disinterested in the girl, why should the girl bother?

The land was starving, that's what the shearers said.

With her father gone, the farm was dying and so was the girl. Something had to change. The shearers said that too.

Sometimes the girl wished the very air would change. Sometimes it seemed too clean. On a clear spring morning, the kind of day that dickhead ramblers would flurry over the footpath at the edge of the far paddock, the air was so pure, it made her nostrils burn. 150 years her mother's family had worked this land, this air, but it seemed to oppose the girl's flesh and bones. That clean air was no good for the girl at all.

He was back already. Part of me was gutted, but also glad, I didn't want to rush reading it, though I was *so* tempted. I wanted to suck the nutrients out of every word, extract every drop of meaning. It was like seeing across time and into her soul.

'This is really something,' I said and I meant it.

'You think? That's great.'

'Can I take this copy home?'

'I was thinking, how's about you read what you can now and let's meet up again really soon so we can talk about it together? I reckon if the two of us told her that her writing was maybe worth something she'd properly get on the mend again. I mean, she's doing OK now, but I know Kathy, she's doing her best, but she's not there yet. I think if she's going to get past it, she needs to go back to the start, remember what she wanted to be and try again. It's not too late for her.'

I nod. 'Is she … I don't know how to put it in the right way, obviously she's back at work now, but I agree with you, she still she seems pretty… troubled.'

He rubs his forehead, 'I think it's fair to say, you've probably not seen the best of Kathy. This past while's been really rough on her. How it all went to shite at the magazine. She didn't really see how bad it was getting until it was probably too late and by then, your aunt's lot came in. Nearly twenty years of her life, about to go down the drain. Sometimes you're up, sometimes you're down. She's been more down than up in the past few years, but she's a tough girl. I should think you'll know that, working for her!'

'I've heard she can be pretty hard on some of the interns, probably because they're not pulling their weight? But she's kind of left me alone in that respect. I really think we'd be really good friends if we didn't have to work together.'

He believes me, of course.

'Well, you had her pretty hammered yesterday. Did she seem OK when she left yours?'

'I'd actually fallen asleep by then. I thought we had a great time. Did she tell you? I'm a massive Smiths and Morrissey fan too?'

'Well I never.'

'We were tooling about my place like no one's business.'

'I would have liked to see that.' Here's a decent segue.

'Hey, do you guys fancy getting out of town? I've got this party next week, some old school friends, just outside of Haywards Heath. Wanna come? Come on, I'll make sure there's plenty of Smiths on the playlist.'

He laughs. 'Why in heaven and hell would you want old farts like us hanging about, cramping your style.'

'You're not old. Listen, do you guys know how sexy you are?'

'Sexy?' he laughs, blushes again. He pulls his T-shirt off his torso and looks around. He wants to hear more. He wants to believe it's really true.

'For sure. You've both still got it. Katherine's cool as fuck, and you …' I start, and he grins at me, but I say nothing.

Go on, meet me in the middle, Iain.

'And me what?' he says after a second.

'Well, you must have had more than your fair share of admirers?'

'I may have, from time to time, but not for a while.'

'Is that so?'

'Well, it's no real secret to say Kathy and me, we've technically had what other people might term an "open relationship," but, you know, with her being ill and all, it's not really been on the menu, so to speak.'

'Oh, OK,' I say, making a show of shaking off some visible doubt that's made me uncomfortable, then trying to pretend everything's just fine. It works. He looks at me, waiting for more. 'Nothing. I'm sure it's nothing at all. Sorry. I didn't mean to make things awkward.'

'Lily?'

He has an idea who Katherine Ross is. I breathe first before saying, 'It was some of the interns, talking some shit the other day.'

'Talking about what?'

'About Katherine. And Asif.'

'Well that happened, a while back. He was getting a bit much, so we put the kibosh on it.'

I nod, before quickly changing the subject. 'These are going down great. Another?' He finishes his drink before putting his glass down on the table. I watch him from the other side of the bar. His doubt in 'Kathy' seems to be growing. He looks uncomfortable, but he doesn't look susceptible yet.

We talk some more, mostly about all the things he's been thinking about writing, which I respond to accordingly. 'Wow, that's so creative. It's rare to come across someone with such originality. Special.' And, 'An agent would be a fool not to snap you up. If I were them, that's what I'd do, I'd claim you as soon as I could.' But he's not biting yet. Suddenly, it's getting late and I'm running out of time. He pulls out his phone and starts texting, her, inevitably. **Be home soon, babe xxx** or something totally co-dependent like that. If I can't get to him tonight, I might not have enough time before she works everything out, because she will. Secrets always ooze out eventually, no matter what people wrap around the truth.

I try another tack. 'Iain, if there's one thing I want you to take away from our night together, it's that you've got great writing in you. So, next time, I want to read something that's really you, right from here.' I place a finger on his chest, his heart.

'Christ, I'll have to see if I know how!'

'Course you do, you could do it now if you wanted to. In fact, I've got it … I want you to tell me the one thing you've always really wanted but never had. It has to be something that can't be changed, something you have to live with forever.'

'So, I can't say not winning a BAFTA for best screenplay, because that could still happen, right?'

'Totally. It has to be something you can't change, but you would if you could.'

'Right. Shit. Can I have a bit of a think?'

'What, you don't know it straight away? I wonder if some-one really needs to think about this question, maybe they've been supressing something? Perhaps you've been blocking lots of things you've wanted deep down?'

He swallows. His eyes fill. He puffs out his cheeks and looks at the ceiling. Jackpot.

'Christ … Fuck … I've— I've not really thought about it. No one's really asked me. Fuck.' My only true talent. Being who they need me to be. He takes a couple of big sips of his vodka.

'Go on. I want you to talk about this and write it up for next week. Honestly, it's the sort of thing that's going to really free your writing, your voice.'

201

'My voice.'

'Yeah, let you hear your own voice again. Maybe let someone else hear it too.' I decide it's time to turn the night. I reach out and hold his hand. I stroke the base of his thumb with the tip of mine. I feel the small muscles in his hands pulse, a twitch of surprise before he holds himself still a few seconds before moving his hand to his face, taking a deep breath.

'I love my girl. I love her more than anything or anyone in the whole world. She *is* my world. She's stood by me thick and thin. She gets me. We get each other.'

'Go on.' *Go on, Iain, tell me everything. Give me all of it.*

'And there are some things I've had to let go. Things I don't know if we can reverse … God. This is hard.' He takes another sip, wipes his mouth with the back of his hand. 'Kathy and me, well, you might have wondered, *why don't they have kids?* I mean she told me early bells she didn't want kids. Mother issues and then some. She told me our lives would be shite with kids. We'd never get anything done, you know, "pram in the hallway is the enemy of art" or whatever. I brought it up, or tried to, early on. "Are you sure it wouldn't be nice to have a wee Iain or Kathy running around?" And she'd be like, "No. Why would we want to fuck up our lives and that poor kid by being its parents?" I'd try again and she'd be like, "You want a kid? What comes next? A fucking savings plan for their education we can't afford, barely getting pissed or going out ever again … The flat'll be too small, so we sell up and move to fucking Enfield?" And I'm thinking, "That doesn't sound half bad," but she sticks to her guns, says it's for the two of us to have a great life together, no one else, and that's going to be enough.'

I make a sympathetic face. 'It was the right thing for her, but it wasn't the right thing for you, was it? You wanted her to try harder for something you really wanted and now you feel you can't have?'

He nods, looks down at his drink. 'Sorry, I can't believe I've said all that. I need another. You?'

'Please.'

When he goes to the bar, I can tell he's angry. I watch him down a couple of shots while he waits on the vodka tonics, before turning back to her manuscript. I need to get through as much as I can before it gets taken off me.

The mother cannot hide her disgust when the girl's breasts begin to show. She does not acknowledge the girl's puberty by buying a bra for the child. As she grows, the girl is forced to improvise, tying a musty silk scarf she finds in her attic, binding her chest with a great cloth 'X'. It's when she does this, she realises she's gaining on her mother.

There is power in this.

The girl can choose to feel no shame, only intrigue over what she might be able to do with something of which her mother seems so petrified.

This gives the girl some comfort, while her lungs burn as she loads the creep feeder, seeing the perfect opposite of her life for the thousandth time. Shaking the grain from bucket after bucket, the lambs crowd through the narrow bars that block the ewes from eating their children's feed. Here, the young eat first. The proper natural order.

They're protected from their mothers' needs. That's how it should be, she thinks, her stomach growling angrily as

she watches the creatures fill themselves. If her own mother
wouldn't put her first, she'd have to find some way of doing
it herself.

Protected from her mother's needs.

Yes. I get that.

'There you go,' Iain says, plonking the drinks down.

'In the nicest possible way, is this a thinly-veiled auto-
biography?'

'I'm not sure, I'm not too far through it yet.'

I nod, wait a second before I ask him, 'Iain, I want to hear,
I want to understand how much not having a family has hurt
you. I think it's something you need to explore for you and
for your writing too.'

'It's hurt plenty.'

'And *how* does it hurt you, Iain?'

'Let me count the ways. Walking through the park's hard
some days, when I see the dads with their lads, or in the pub
with a little one in one arm, pint in the other, I think, I could
see myself doing that. That could be me. And—' He's really
choked-up now.

'And?' I squeeze his hand again.

Give in, Iain, give in to yourself.

'And when I wake up of a morning, and think about the
future, and do you know what I can see?'

Give in, Iain. Give in to me, Iain.

'Tell me.'

'Nothing. I can't see shite. It's just blank. Just another day,
another hangover, another night in. I start the day and don't
know if I'm going to get through another; how we're going to

keep doing what we're doing, the same thing over and over; no change, no growth, no fucking joy.'

He looks at me, hard.

Gotcha.

Almost.

'Christ, look at me, gnashing on about all this sad shite. I'm sorry.' He wipes his eyes with the heels of both his hands.

'It's OK to hurt. It's OK to want more from your life. I get it. I hear you.' I get off my seat and open my arms. He blinks, gets up slowly and lets me hug him across the table. 'I hear you,' I whisper again, my lips brushing his ear. He turns his head for more. I don't give it to him, but we stay like this for a few moments. I angle my head a little closer, then I let my fingers run down his neck before slowly sitting down again. Our knees are still touching under the table.

'You hear me,' he says, softly, not moving his knees either.

'Yes … Do you want to know what I've always fantasised over, Iain? Would you like me to tell you the thing I ache for more than anything else?'

He nods, I open my legs a little further. 'Tell me,' he says.

'Fucking the life out of someone amazing. Having their baby.'

His eyes spark and his jaw slackens with disbelief before he gets himself together again enough to speak. 'Is that so? And what is it, exactly, that would make "someone amazing"?'

'It would have to be someone who wanted it deep down, and who really wanted me.'

I wait a second before leaning forward again and, under the table, move my hand up his thigh to where his hardening cock waits for me. He doesn't move. I've almost won.

We finish our drinks quickly, looking right into each other. Anyone watching us would know exactly what he wants to do to me. I don't know if it's the booze or the fact I feel quite sorry for him, but as he walks me across the road to the churchyard of the old St Mary's, I'm not repulsed. I'm curious.

Then, when he kisses me, I like it. I actually really like it. Hands everywhere, he reaches down the front of my skirt and between my legs and moans when he feels me. He feels my youth, my readiness. Suddenly, he can see a future, a startlingly exciting future and I feel a surge of power. I feel completely adored. It has been a while and I find myself almost giving him everything he wants in that dark alley, surrounded by fallen grave stones. But I can't let him have it all, yet. I know how to play this game.

'Iain, we can't do this. We can't do this to Katherine.'

He pulls away from me and I can see saying her name has punched through his drunkenness.

'Fuck. Fuck! What am I doing!'

'Iain, Iain. No, please, it's my fault. This is all on me.'

'No, it's me. It's me. I've not stopped thinking about you since Sunday. I feel like I've known you forever. Christ, I've never had a longer week.'

He looks at his shoes, then asks me, 'Was there ever anyone else coming tonight?'

'What will you do to me if I told you, no?' And at that he pushes me back against a tree and manages to get his hand under my bra. It is quite delicious how desperate he is. I was right: this bit was going to be by far the easiest part of my plan. I think I could enjoy him.

But he can't see my grand design yet. I have to look as if I'm resisting what I really want to do, for the sake of his partner, my new best friend. I know he feels like someone's heard him for the first time in years, and not just anybody, but a young, hot someone. I'll have to push him away first, maybe a couple of times. I make him stop, then take his hands and say, 'I can't believe this is happening.'

'I know. I *know*. What are we going to do?'

'I really don't know. I don't think I can do this to Katherine. She's not only my boss, but I also think she's a really special person. I don't think *you* can do this either. Not really. You love her too much. I know that's why you were trying to put her, her work, between us. You were trying to stop yourself. You don't have to feel guilty.'

Some people really are just too easy.

'God, you're right. I think you're right.' He stares into the middle distance. Mystified by himself.

I kiss him on the forehead. 'Walk me home?'

We jump the fences to the park and it turns out I can't resist letting him stop me in my tracks a couple of times to kiss me deep in the darkness. When we climb over the Green Lanes gates on the other side, he makes a joke of walking off his erection and we laugh. People would think we're together. I can tell from the way he says, 'Goodnight, Lily', he already thinks he's in love.

18th March – A Walk in the Park

We text each other on and off all morning. He knows it's totally wrong, but he'd kill to hold me for just a minute. *Me too, Iain.* He can't help it, but he can smell me everywhere.

So, it's not just me, then? He wants to know my pain. *I want to hear your stories.* He wants to see me shine. *Perhaps we could make each other shine, Iain? xx*

I know KR. She's too cool to be a phone checker. She's not there yet, but I'll bet we're not far off it now. She'll start to notice things are moving soon enough.

I watch them leave for the park from my window on the world. She comes out onto the front steps of their building first. Pretends to look around. Lets her eyes travel right up to my window.

He locks up after her. While she spoons about her handbag looking for something she can't seem to find, he turns the key and sneaks a little look up to my high-rise as well. Longingly, painfully. His body is with her, but the rest of him is up here with me. I can see it all. They walk out of their road and onto Green Lanes. I get my coat and slip out of my building. Something tells me I need to stretch my legs too.

Such a sunny afternoon, perfect for a lovers' stroll. Spring is really here. The wind feels urgent. It wants to blow in a new season. So do I.

They trot along like nothing's changed in their world. Like they haven't a care. They walk through an avenue of pink trees and all the blossom blows down onto them. I'm quite close now. I hear her laugh. She looks quite beautiful as she shakes the petals off her. She brushes some off him too. He holds her close and they kiss for a really long time, then kiss again. I can sense the years moving between them. Like a kind of magic. She's glowing, shy like a school girl. He looks into her face for a long time before they start walking again. Anyone would think they're in love. But for how long?

I start texting.

I thought you might like to know what I'm doing right now. I'm thinking of your hands on my skin, how wet you made me, how much I'd like to slip myself onto your hard cock. I know it's so bad, but I can't help it. Am I bad? What should I do to myself next? Your Lil xxxxxxxxxxxxxxxxxxxxxxxxxx xxxxxxxxx

He fishes his phone from his pocket, holds it just out of her sight by his outer leg and reads it without her noticing. Straightens his jeans. Keeps walking, though he looks over his shoulder guiltily. But he doesn't see me. He leads them towards The Rose and Crown. If he can't have me now, the only other place he wants to be is the scene of the crime. Good sign, but I don't think I can turn him properly with sex alone. I need to provide him with some continuity, or the illusion of it. A link to her. A signal. A chance at replaying the past he thought was lost. The possibility of a future he could still have. I walk past the pub. They don't see me heading to a designer boutique on Church Street.

I try on another oversized shirt, leather jacket and an asymmetrical black dress for the awards. It's so very KR, just the sort of thing she'd choose for her return to centre stage. Sometimes I feel like I know her better than she knows herself. After I've paid, I get a text:

I have to see you again, even if it's just from afar. Ix

CHAPTER 12

Katherine

Awards night used to be one of my favourite of the year. A chance to dress up, flirt with hundreds of people, be centre stage, look great and get laid in glamorous surrounds. But this was my twentieth *Leadership* awards, which of course didn't include last year's. This year, I was 'fighting fit' despite the fact that I'd been summoned to the headmistress's office on Monday morning to have the speech I managed to stitch together pulled apart, while I gazed out the window thinking how much I'd rather be running the 'How was your weekend' gauntlet than being told how to write by your aunt.

She'd used one of your tricks at the top of the show, asked if I was OK, checked again, that I was sure I was, indeed, 'fighting fit,' before launching into a line-by-line takedown of my first cut. My total humiliation almost complete. I walked out with what looked like a highly classified document, heavily redacted. Whole sections scrubbed out to protect the world from my lazy writing. You saw it too, of course. I knew it wasn't incredible, but I don't know what she was expecting from me. She was more than happy to position you as the white knight who would save the awards day from my leathery clutches: 'Katherine, Lily's got *slightly* ahead of the game. She got the impression you might be struggling, so went ahead and drafted something to be delivered on the night, by you, of course, but in all truth, and this may be hard to hear, it's her voice that's really capturing where *Leadership* is and where we really need to be.'

'I've already specifically asked Lily to stand down on redrafting for me. With the greatest respect, her voice is not *my* voice. I can't see this working,' I told her, my anger rising. I'd seen this sort of behaviour a thousand times in interns those last few years. You tell them not to bother doing something, they go off and do it anyway and then proudly present the fruits of their labour like a tabby cat with a dead bluetit. When I'd turned them down in the past, they'd go above my head to moan but would be turned away by my old directors. In this new world, all their complaints and ambitions were met with open ears. Your lot were getting it all now: the indulgent parenting transferred workplaces where management let the thinness of your collective skin define the atmosphere.

'Please, I'd like you to take a look. Read it through. Make it your own.'

'I'll see what I can do.'

I returned to my desk and tried to tune out the sound of the interns flogging eleventh hour tables for the awards. The ceremony, pegged in your re-draft as 'an inspiring celebration of true excellence in management', was just another revenue stream; a means of separating subscribers from their budgets. The 'shortlists' were shameless this year. Up to a dozen nobodies for each category, all with the aim of lengthening the interns' call lists and deepening *Leadership*'s ailing profits. The horror of what they were turning my magazine into.

I tried to think of reasons not to walk out of there. But my flat was already starting to feel less like home. Iain and I had a good enough weekend on the surface, but those small, devastating things kept happening. When we walked to the shop, he kept turning around, looking back over his shoulder. He seemed to go to a private place in his head when we watched a film. He even held back on his drinking. He ate less. Nothing you could point to as evidence specifically, but very small things told me something was shifting. I felt more alone than ever.

I knew you were due in from a sponsors' meeting soon, but I couldn't let you see me this down. So, off I went to St George's, turned my back to the office building to find a way of levelling myself out. From, *I can't do it anymore*, to, *I have to take it,* to, *Find a way to make today a good day*, all the way to, *Today is a good day.*

I left the graveyard on a superficially even keel, but you were about to rock me off my guard in a way I couldn't have imagined.

When I got back to my desk, I was considering some kind of move on the offensive. I was going to allude to the fact I couldn't give a shit if you'd seen me with Asif, or that I'd seen you with him in the park, and all my moment with him had done was warm me up for a hot weekend with my partner. *My* partner. I'd held my own happily against the other women Iain had been with while he was with me. This was me. This was us. I *could* do it again, stand firm, particularly because I knew, I always knew, it was me you were really trying to get the attention of. What happened next only served to confirm this, albeit in the most disturbing way possible.

You'd taken whatever you thought you were doing to me to a whole new level. You were shameless now. How intimately had you been studying me, unpacking every detail of my appearance, the way I move through the world? It chilled me to the core.

Because through the double doors that morning, in blasted my past; a sickly-dazzling reminder of me at the height of my powers, the days gone by that I'll never get back. The days that now belonged to you.

At first I couldn't process what I was seeing, as if I didn't want to confront this new act of war, this blatant move to take yet another pillar of my identity away. *Had I actually met you before we shared that cab?* I thought for a split-second. Was that why you looked suddenly so familiar, like someone I once knew but just couldn't place?

No. There was nothing coincidental or accidental about what you'd done.

Because into my office entered a clone of me, a back-to-the-future doppelganger. You'd altered your appearance, with your hair slicked back – a wave of red striking out off the left side of your temple, selling the full teardrops of your cheeks and the black mystery of your eyes more strongly than ever. You'd even altered your movements. You strode through the doors exactly as I did, throwing them open with a slap on each door, then walking through the dead centre. This, instead of your usual, ever-so-humble creeping in through the single door on the left side. And you'd ditched the pastel, tit-clinging cashmere V-necks for an oversized cotton shirt, acid yellow, tucking it decisively into a grey ankle-length pencil skirt split to the thigh. You topped the whole look off with a black leather biker exactly like mine.

Your impersonation was as shocking to me as it was mesmerising to everybody else. They gawped on as you took your seat, flicking your hair out of your eyes with a tick of the head, not with a twee little tuck of the fingers behind the ears as normal; your reimagining of Katherine-Ross-in-the office fully considered and complete.

Inhabiting my style and movement had propelled your beauty to another level. An exquisite meeting of the soft and young with the hard and worldly. You wanted to show me you could be me and more, didn't you?

'Everything OK?' You flashed me those blinding, brilliant teeth, gleaming out from Russian Red lips.

I tried to mask how disturbing I found your scaled-up mind games. I was initially grateful when Gemma summoned me away from my desk and back to her office with a gesture of her arm. When she noticed you, her expression was one of shock that quickly darkened to something else before she gave a small shake of her head. She didn't really know what you were either, did she? Perhaps she never did.

'Sorry to call you back in here again, Katherine, but I have a couple of things I need to discuss with you.'

'What is it?'

'I'm afraid Acceptableinthenoughties has been in touch again.'

'And what are they saying this time?'

'Well, the email itself doesn't make any specific allegation.'

'Can I see it?'

'There's no need.'

I knew full well she was hiding something. 'I think I'd really like to see it.'

'You don't need to worry about what the troll wrote specifically.' *Liar.* 'But I did actually need to catch up with you about something else.'

'Right …' *What have I done now?*

'Katherine, you need to know, things are different now to how they were. They have to be, if we're going to make it.'

'Different how?'

'I was prepared to hang fire on the ridiculous cab journey to work you'd put on expenses.' I opened my mouth to defend myself, but she kept going. 'But really, you can't have thought what you did at the Rosewood was OK and that I wouldn't find out? I'd sent you and Lily there for a very specific purpose. Lily is young and impressionable, but I would have expected more from you. I'm sorry to say I've had to let Talent and People know. You need to consider this your second strike, Katherine. Because of this, I couldn't *not* take account of the cab incident. This is a pattern. It needs to stop.'

'Gemma, surely Lily filled you in?'

'Filled me in on what? That you're leading by spending my training budget on a massage?'

I went to speak again, but stopped. I knew she'd never believe ditching copy camp was her darling Lily's idea. I fumed. I was going to have to watch my back very carefully at work from now on, or face death by a thousand 'HR-logged incidents' because of you.

'I understand.' *I understand perfectly.*

'I don't know that you do. Do you know how many pale, male and stale editors they wanted to ship in when we took over, or just how hard we had to fight to keep you on? You know, Lily, in particular, was absolutely insistent you stay. She said in this day and age we couldn't start the new era showing the world we thought the only way to fix *Leadership* was to get a man in. I petitioned for you on this argument and *that* means it's going to be on *me* if you don't get back to your best and change your attitude to this workplace. So take this as a warning and now let's move forward, let's see you at your very best at the awards. I want you to get yourself down to The Dorchester with Lily this morning. They're doing some final checks before tomorrow. Go. Take some ownership of the space again. Practice your speech. Do whatever it takes, take your awards back, because it was your night, Katherine. That's what everyone says. It can be that way again. The next time I speak to HR about you, I want it to be about a marked change in your performance, not your final caution.'

They must go for some kind of special class in the Human Resources module of whatever course Gemma had paid for to hit those icky soundbites. What made her think she ran this place better than my old bosses? That she could just bus in her niece and run the whole thing like a family empire?

I took a second to breathe. 'I'd like you to speak candidly with me, woman-to-woman: do you really want me to succeed here?'

'What is it you mean, Katherine?'

'Do you still really want me—' It felt that tears would be expected and potentially helpful. Thankfully, they came. 'Do you ... do you really want to see me back on top?'

Gemma pulled out a box of tissues from nowhere. They must teach that on 'the module' too.

'I do. I know it might seem as if I've been a bit hard on you, but that's because I see a powerful woman in her prime. We need to look after each other. I want to see you thrive again. Enjoy a real renaissance.' She said 'renaissance' in a hokey French accent and by now, she'd come to my side of the desk and squeezed my shoulders. One of her tissues found its way into my hands, and this facsimile of kindness helped escort a fresh gush of tears to the surface.

'Oh god, I can't believe I'm crying at work again. I haven't done this for a long time. I'm sorry.' I hadn't actually cried once at work, but I know the rules, Lily: you can't look like you're made of stone in moments like these.

'Don't be sorry, just say you're going to come out and do your best. Because you still have your best in you. I believe your finest hour is yet to come. It had better be, since I lobbied so hard for you with the board!' Superficial, motivational care, spectacularly failing to distract from the distinct sound of thin ice cracking below. I wondered whether this is what she did to you, if perhaps part of your problem was being asked by Gemma for your 'best self' every day, even if you were dying inside. I thought I understood you more than I ever had in that moment. She would drive me mad too, I thought. *Health professional*, the woman at your old school had said. *Mental health professional*, that's what she should have said.

I looked out at you again and my blood ran cold. You'd replaced your saintly at-work smile with my typing frown. It was uncanny. You must have been staring at me when I had no idea, and practising in front of the mirror in your apartment to perfect the imitation.

The truth of what was at stake began to dawn on me.

You were more than devious in your framing of me for crimes you had committed, you were more than ruthless in your daily undermining of me in my workplace of more than twenty years, more than heartless in your pursuit of my partner.

You were dangerous.

I got up to leave Gemma's office, trying to ignore the image of younger me in my peripheral vision. You were twisting around on your chair, gazing up at Asif as I went to the toilets to dry my eyes. Not a mirror, a cracked window to a past just gone; out of reach.

'Leaving in ten, Katherine,' you called just as I got to the double doors out of the office. I slammed both palms against them and wanted to kill you there and then.

Just before I went, I made a discreet call to IT to get Acceptableinthenoughties's email forwarded to me. Gemma clearly wanted to avoid creating an email trail to show all the times the troll had sent threatening messages, and she'd done nothing about it, so I'd create my own.

Subject: Time for action

Dear Publisher,
If you don't do something about Katherine Ross, I will.
She deserves to die before she bores us all to death.

A death threat.

The time was coming for me to ask for my investigation, see where this would leave Gemma.

We were waiting for the train on our way to The Dorchester. You stood in front of me on the edge of the tube platform at

Borough while a party of school children shrieked around us. You, head down, on your phone, speed writing whatever thoughts were in your skull that you felt needed to be captured. Me, up against your back as the children bumped up behind me, the low roar of the approaching train beginning to reverberate around the platform then, as it got closer, in our chests.

'I know you fucked me, Lily,' I shouted into the back of your head. I tried to stay as calm as I could, but I was shaking.

Your head stayed down, but your fingers paused for a heartbeat, then resumed tapping away again.

You turned to speak to me. 'What did you say? It's really loud.'

The train clattered ever-closer, the children becoming very excitable at the sight of it. I was struggling to stay on one spot.

'You fucked me over. At the Rosewood!' I screamed, the train only metres from us.

You turned all the way round to face me, almost nose-to-nose. A child shouldered the back of me, and I could barely stay upright. If I fell, I'd instinctively use your body to steady myself. You would have nowhere to drop but right under the train.

'Sorry,' you just shrugged at me, like it was nothing.

My breath fast, hot with rage. My fingers tingling.

The train skimmed by, just inches behind you and ground to a stop. We boarded.

'I told Gem it was my bad,' you said, going to take a seat opposite me. 'But, the thing is, no matter what I said, she just wouldn't believe it wasn't you.' You smiled, raised your eyebrows, then returned to your phone.

Now, in this moment, I could feel my hate grow; an acorn

with epic potential. It was now or never to wrestle control back, to be on top again.

I thought for a second about the nature of the beige cloud that smothered me last year and had threatened to again. Perhaps it was always coming for me, waiting to envelop me should my life not deliver, if the fixes I'd sought for my horrid childhood didn't work. So where was the beige now? The underlying issues had not gone away. My stagnating career, our patchy finances, our creative disasters, my middle-aged trough, were becoming more entrenched every day and the chance to make good on the losses waning. Perhaps my mother had been right about my life after all: it *was* worthless, I would indeed amount to nothing.

You coming on the scene? It had served to bring all these realities into even sharper relief. But you'd achieved something not even you could have foreseen. I was starting to feel something shifting inside and around me. You were forcing the beige cloud to mutate into something completely different. This new filter made life feel urgent again, rather than deadening it; it demanded I stay awake and alert at all times. It demanded I bring my best fight.

So I ended up writing furiously on that tube journey. I may not have written a published manuscript, but I do know that good writing reaches out to another person, and the only way you can do that is by putting the truth to good use, however difficult. My truth? Illness, failure, loss of purpose. They were nothing to be proud of, but they were all I had to give.

CHAPTER 13

Katherine

At The Dorchester, they'd already started setting up the tables for the awards. It all looked exactly the same as it always did. It could be last year, or ten years ago, or any other year. Purple light, something frothy and timeless about the place. Outside of fashion. Practice bursts of incidental music to accompany the presenters and winners to the stage, pumping from the speakers. The machine-tooled 'rock star' moments the events company engineered for every occasion, whatever the sector, whatever the award. People come to awards to be told they're special. They put on their hired tux and occasionwear, get their hair done; maybe they tell their spouses they 'may as well stay in London' so they can get properly leathered or more, because 'it's a special night'.

But you can't show me any occasion more devoid of prestige and kudos than any corporate awards ceremony, even ours. After *Leadership's* gongs were over, they'd flip the tablecloths, change the display boards and roll in the next set of idiots who put their faith in their industry's 'special night'. Dentists. Teachers. Accountants. Hairdressers. The trade body they give money to, telling them there's a significance it's possible to attach to their job, promising that you could feasibly be recognised as the 'best' in one small subcategory of what you do. To be told, and for the world in that ballroom to hear it: your job matters; you matter. Little wonder so many people, particularly those of us in middle age, are willing to pay to participate.

I watched you swish about from table to table, cooing with some Felix Fucknuts or other. Another slew of kids buzzing around, somehow managing to look and sound exactly the same; that high-register enthusiasm, that waffle you all spout before you get to the point, those Insta-ready facial expressions and the instantaneous alliances you strike up with your own kind.

'Katherine, I think we're ready for you, if you'd like to do your run through?' you said, from behind a clipboard. You handed it to one of the other intern-types and walked up to me with an iPad.

'I loaded the new draft speech on to this, in case you couldn't print off yours. Paper-free Wednesday and all that.'

'That's very kind of you, Lily, but I'm not using that. I've got something of my own.'

'But Gem—'

I stopped for a moment, about to falter around my reasoning for not towing the line, before something occurred to me. 'But you can handle Gem if we change things up, can't you? I think I remember you telling me that.' I walked past you, trying to steady my breath in light of both what I'd just said to you and all I was about to say to all those people who were currently fussing about the ballroom. They would surely stop in their tracks when they realised what I was saying. And when they did, they might laugh at me. They might pull out their phones and record me, then share the video on social media, the caption: Check out this mid-life meltdown! It might go viral. My life could be over.

I reached the stage. Walking slowly and deliberately towards the podium, I listened to the blood in my ears, thought about making my excuses and coming back to try again later, before timidly adjusting the mic to the level of my mouth.

'Hello … Hi? Could someone possibly work with me for a quick sound check?' I called out to whoever's job it was to care, stalling for time.

All but one of the young people ignored me. It struck me: they already thought the very worst of me, they already had me pegged as a sad case, a has-been. I didn't have anything to lose. *Go on, girl, show 'em Kathy's back*, I could hear Iain say.

So, in my flattest, most comically middle-aged voice, I said, 'Good evening, Mayfair. How you feelin'?'

And the little cunts laughed. I had their attention. OK. It was time for me to go for broke and see what I could make from the pieces of me.

I breathed. Swallowed. Breathed again, then began for real.

'My name is Katherine Ross, I am the editor of *Leadership*. I'm also someone's partner. A daughter. And I'm a failed writer of novels with mental health issues.'

Stunned silence.

And I would have liked, in that moment, for everything and everyone to go away, for me to disappear, to be wiped off the face of the earth. But I'd started now. I was saying the unsayable about me, or rather the things everyone else was saying about me behind my back. I couldn't turn around now.

'Who are you? Who are we?'

The whole room seemed to stop. It felt like the only person breathing was me.

'If you're recognised as this year's Rising Star, will you still worry you could be doing better?

'If you win Consultancy of Year, will you immediately wonder who will win next year?

'Maybe, if you're recognised here tonight as Senior Manager of Year, you'll hear a voice in your head telling you, *You don't deserve this.*

'The raw fact that we may sometimes sidestep is how leadership is as much about weakness as it is strength.

'It's only by knowing our weakness we find the power to become stronger.

'It's only by showing and sharing our authentic selves, which include those doubts, those areas of our characters and our work where we know we could make more headway, that takes us to Truly … Great … Leadership.'

I looked around, young faces peering at me and me alone, absorbed in my words. In pity or admiration, I wasn't sure yet, but whatever they were hearing in my speech, they felt its power. I continued, my confidence beginning to grow.

'So tonight, as we celebrate just that, I want to ask us all to celebrate our own and each other's weaknesses. Can we do that? Together? With a new spirit of authenticity and togetherness based on more than circumstance, chance, economics. Bonds based on truth.

'Emotional truth. And personally investing in ourselves and each other.

'Because it's the right thing to do? Yes. And because it's good business.

'So, see weakness. Walk towards it. Make friends with your own Achilles heels and see the opportunities. That's what Gemma Lunt and the buyout team are doing with *Leadership*, and also with me.'

And now, for the big set piece, the darkest, juiciest morsel for them all to pick apart. One more breath before I went for broke. 'This time last year I was suffering from a debilitating bout of what some of you would describe as depression.

'I was an editor who could barely write. I felt worthless. I could barely get out of bed. And *Leadership*? Financially, we were on our knees and, I'll admit it, we'd lost our mission. So had I.

'But standing here before you, tonight, I am here to tell you:

'I found myself again and at *Leadership*, we have come together and we have worked with perceived weaknesses and we have turned them into our greatest strengths.

'So, I say to you tonight:

'Let none of us walk away from our flaws. Let none of us leave behind the colleague who asks you for more.

'Because it's in these so called "weaknesses" we'll discover our greatest potential.

'I would like us to come together and make a toast … a toast to all tonight's winners. And especially to all tonight's losers. You are many. We are many.

'And to all of us, whether we're wading in the darkness of self-doubt, or soaring in the heights of being recognised here tonight, to you and your –' I raised an imaginary flute into the air ' – greatest failing. Think of them afresh with your peers and colleagues, and with the new *Leadership* as your manual …

'Your greatest opportunity.'

A pause.

Then the applause erupted. Loud, heart-felt, rapturous applause.

At first, I was worried you and they were all taking the piss out of me. I stepped down and walked back to the table near you. My knees soft with adrenaline, all I wanted to do was get my bag and leave the main hall for the painted reception room and then out to the real world. But the applause went on. And on. I looked about for you, I wanted to see the look on your face, but the continuing applause must have been too much for you because you'd already disappeared. A young lad, nice-looking thing, approached me with tears in his eyes. 'I just wanted to say, I suffer from crippling social anxiety. I totally hear you. That was the bravest speech I've ever heard. It was … amazing.'

I'd done it. Scooped out something from inside me and put it into words that were truly meaningful to other people. So, maybe I wasn't an irrevocably bad writer after all. I wasn't actually a loser. I wasn't someone to be pitied, or to avoid, or to simply not even register as existing. I was fit to be admired, to be rewarded and recognised.

'That's so kind of you to say. Could I trouble you to type this up and make sure the team gets it on the autocue tomorrow night,' I told the sweet boy with social anxiety.

'You got it.'

'Thanks so much. And thanks for all your hard work, you guys,' I acknowledged the bubble of the young and unpaid that had gathered around me. You were still notably absent. 'We don't say it enough, but it's because of you that nights like the *Leadership* Awards can happen.' I made eye contact with as many of them as I could. 'Why it's going to be completely awesome.'

As I walked towards the exit, the interns' 'whoops' ringing in my ears, I passed you. You seemed as blown away as everyone else, but not because of what I'd said, more that I'd been able to put something of my truth into the written word and other people had been moved. And I felt, for one moment, like I'd shown you what I was capable of. I had it in me to be better than you. I think I was even laughing to myself as I reached the main road. Victory felt possible.

Stood by the road, sun shining down on me, I thought about crossing into Hyde Park for a stroll before going back to the office. But first, I wanted to savour the moment, lose myself in my success. I closed my eyes and let the sun warm my face, breathing in the fumes and trying to imagine it was fresh spring air, just for me.

For the first time in the longest time I'd made myself visible. I'd ensured I was seen on my terms and in the best possible way I could imagine; through my writing, through the talent everyone had forgotten about, including me. I felt a great weight lifting, moving off me and into the warm sky above. I felt, for one short moment, as if I was floating.

Suddenly, there was something at my arm. It shocked me back to reality, dragging me out of my moment and making me stagger.

Before I could stop myself, I was falling off the kerb. My foot coiled under me, propelling my body into the road.

A flash of instantly-familiar acid yellow cleaving through

the haze in the corner of my vision as I slammed onto the tarmac.

The noise down there you could never imagine. So loud it brought my heart high into my chest.

I froze. Alone and helpless as cars raced towards me.

The growl of the traffic filled me. I couldn't make my body move.

This was it.

An image flashed behind my eyelids.

Not Iain, the last thing I would see before my death.

Not my mother.

The selfie you'd taken of us.

You and me looking great. You and me looking like friends, as if we were on the same side.

The angry whine of brakes.

A black cab screeching to a halt.

I can hear my breath again. I'm alive.

Grit in my knees, pain rocketing from my ankle; voices raging as a bottleneck formed around the lane I was blocking.

'I'm sorry,' I squeaked to no one, before ungraciously managing to get to my knees, stifling a yelp in my agony.

'Katherine, here, let me help you.'

You.

You were why I was in mortal danger.

'Don't touch me.'

You stood between me and the pavement. I went to pull myself upright. You reached out to me.

'Please, get out of my way.'

I tried to walk, leaning against the cab for support, the raw flaps of skin on my hand pressing painfully on the warm metal bonnet. Finally, the driver came out and signalled for the motorists streaming around his vehicle to calm down while he helped me out of the way.

You continued to watch, an implacable expression on your face.

'Could you take me to Borough please? No wait, I want to go home. Manor House,' I said, and he walked me to the passenger side and opened the door.

When the taxi was finally on the move, I flipped down the seat opposite to hoist my rapidly-swelling foot onto it before opening the window, leaning towards the open air with eyes half-closed as I tried to level my breath.

You were stood squarely on the edge of the kerb, exactly on the spot I had been.

I strained to turn my body to look at you properly, but by the time I'd hoisted myself around you'd turned to unchain your bike from the railings behind. I had so wanted to fix you right in the eyes to show I wasn't scared of you, but by now, I really was.

'Hello?' I called out to Iain when I got back to the flat.

Nothing.

I went to the kitchen/living room where, by this time in the day, I assumed Iain would be butchering, peeling or kneading something with his box of wine by his side. No.

Perhaps he was having a nap. I knew he did that sometimes in the afternoon, but there was no one in our room.

Then, I heard him.

Panting from the spare room; rhythmic, determined exhalations.

Him with you. How could you have beaten me home?

I waited outside the door. Dizzy. Petrified. Listening to Iain grunting, thinking of the pristine curves of your body under his. He sounded like he used to sound when he fucked me. Forceful, not worried I might break. I pushed open the door.

There was Iain on the floor, sodden with sweat. He was in his boxers and an old T-shirt, earphones in, his music loud and insistent. He hoisted himself into another hard-fought sit up and his pant turned into a high-pitched gasp. He laughed at himself as he took out his earbuds.

'Hey! Wasn't expecting you back yet.'

'Evidently. What are you doing?'

'What does it look like? I'm doing something about this.' He grabbed the layer of fat on his stomach. 'Before it's too late.'

'Too late for what?'

'I don't know. I've just been feeling a bit old, bit on the creaky side. You know I've been saying for a while I was going to do something, well, today's the day.'

'Well, I'd better leave you to it.' I turned to hobble away.

'Hey, what's happened to you?'

'I … I'd just done this amazing speech at the awards rehearsal.'

'Go on.'

'And … I think I fell into the traffic afterwards. Or—'

'Or what, love?'

'Lily. She was right behind me. I …' I let a little whimper out 'I can't say for sure if she didn't actually push me. I think she pushed me and I was nearly killed. The traffic, a cab, it only just stopped … right by my head … it was this close. I could have died. And do you know why? Why she'd want to hurt me, or at the very least, give me one *hell* of a scare today? She can't let me have anything good. If she sees me doing or having something worth anything at all, she has to take it away. I'm telling you that's what this whole thing is about.'

At this, he was up on his feet. 'Hey, now,' he began moving me back towards the living room. 'Come on, calm down, love. I think you're in shock and when people are in shock, they can't always think straight. Sounds to me like you've had something horrible happen and Lily just happened to be there.'

Iain, on your side again, even when I was all but sure you'd shoved me into oncoming traffic. He'd come to hold me, but I pushed him off me.

'Why don't you hear me when I talk? When is it you'll actually hear me when I tell you something? There have been too many times when something bad happens and she just *happens* to be there.'

He was looking at me like he didn't know me. Like I was mad. He managed to say, calmly and clearly, 'I think … I think you're exhausted and you've been nearly run over. So, come on, let's get you sat down, get some ice on that ankle.'

And my partner walked me to our living room and helped me onto our sofa. He raised my foot, placed it down on a bed of towelled ice. He massaged my shoulders and listened to every word I said and told me he loved me. I was starting to calm down, but there was more I could do and this felt the right time to do it.

'I didn't tell you, did I? Guess who I saw getting up close and personal at the park the other day?'

'Who was that then?'

'Lily and Asif. They seemed really into each other.'

A pause.

'Oh, yeah? Going for women his own age now is he?'

'Thanks?'

'You know what I mean,' he said quietly.

I watched him from the corner of my eye. He took a thoughtful slug of his drink and didn't say anything for a while.

'So, how you feeling about awards night now?'

'I don't know. This isn't great,' I pointed to my swollen ankle. 'But, my god, Iain, the reaction to my speech. It was incredible. I think it could really put me back on track with the new guard and Gemma, with everyone, maybe even my team.'

'That's fantastic. Hey, why don't I come along this time? Be your bag man. Let me see your moment of glory.'

'If you think you could stand it, I'd love it if you'd come.'

'You couldn't keep me away.'

He was there for me. It *was* real. That's what I told myself.

After a day at home letting Iain fuss over me, I could almost convince myself I was on solid ground. On the night of the awards, I hid my support bandage under a killer black dress, a one-shoulder, to-the-floor, cut-price bargain from Mugler via express delivery on Net-a-Porter. We were bouncing along the edge of our overdraft limit ahead of time that month, but I knew I wanted to look as good as my speech sounded. This was going to be my comeback special and that demanded a special dress.

I couldn't wait to give my speech. They would all see me for who I was, a woman with her very best to give, with promise still untapped, someone who demanded attention and respect. Iain would see me looking and being my best too.

Iain. At my side. Holding the cab door open when we pulled up to The Dorchester's entrance, happy in the shadows once inside, unobtrusively supporting me as I worked the room. Gemma caught my eye from time-to-time, approvingly. Asif watched too, though gave Iain and me a respectfully-wide berth.

I'd seen you, lurking in the shadows with your clipboard and headset, giving the impression the whole thing would fall apart without you. I couldn't bear it. I wanted you as far away from me, and Iain, as possible. You were still trying to work out how to get my hairstyle right without actually cutting it, but you too had managed to get yourself a black sharply-cut off the shoulder floor length evening dress, that made Gemma pass some stupid 'Mini-me' comment, as if these gestures were simple flattery, not the result of studying me so closely you were able to guess exactly what I'd choose for my comeback night.

But you couldn't undo me that night, not when I already knew the power of speech. When the time came. I was calm, I was ready.

Loud applause enveloped me as I slowly climbed the steps. I felt the support, the affection, the respect from my audience. They remembered who I was. I did too. They had missed me last year, that's what so many of them had said as I'd greeted them with Iain at my side. Approaching the lectern I let the purple lights warm my blood and swell my heart. Blinking in the startling heat, I *was* fighting fit, genuinely this time. They were still my crowd, still my people. This was still my time.

By the time I'd got behind the lectern, I felt like some kind of venerable professor about to address an adoring collegiate community. There was no chance I was going to fluff my lines. I beamed out and soaked up the applause for one last moment before getting ready to throw myself over the cliff edge of raw honesty and soar on the appreciation I knew would follow.

I looked to the autocue.

Swallowed.

Started to panic.

Because what was on there wasn't my redraft, it wasn't your redraft, it was the very first piece of rubbish I'd written that Gemma had taken to pieces. Dull. Perfunctory. Beige.

It was now all I had to work with.

You. A new low.

It was suddenly so hot and so quiet. I felt very, very alone. I searched for Iain, but the lights in my eyes meant all I could see were hundreds of black silhouettes watching my every move. I tried to somehow remember what I really wanted to say.

'I'm Katherine Ross … I edit *Leadership*.

'I'm a failed writer with mental health issues.

'This time last year … I … I couldn't get out of bed. I was very, very down.'

Not good. Not good at all.

'I … I got myself into a very dark space.'

The words creaked out of my arid throat.

'I mean, don't we all sometimes? Find ourselves, swimming in blackness?' The whole room stopped. 'Even all the winners tonight. They all have their weaknesses. I'm pretty sure about that … Aren't you?' My voice cracked. 'And if they think they don't deserve their recognition, well, if we're being honest, they're probably right … Because leadership … it's all about weakness really, isn't it?

Confusion. Hands cupping around the ear of the next person to whisper. *What's wrong with her? Is she alright?* I ploughed on, trying with everything I had to retrieve my brilliant speech from somewhere in my soul, because that's where it had come from. But it was lost. All was lost now. I was back to the Katherine Ross they already knew. Floundering. Useless.

'The new management saw weakness. And an opportunity,' I looked around for the champagne flute that was supposed to be there. It wasn't. Was that your handiwork too? 'So why don't we all put our doubts to one side and raise our glasses to being weak?

'After all. Weakness … It's good business.'

Silence.

Then, the light shifted. I could see them all: some in gape-mouthed mortification, some cackling into their glasses, a shake of a head, a rub of the eyes; squirming. I wondered, in that split second, as my heart seemed both to stop and beat uncontrollably at the same time, whether it was physiologically possible to die of embarrassment. Frozen, I didn't know how to get out of the moment. I looked to where I'd sat Iain, but his seat was empty.

Finally, Gemma arrived to move me on, clapping as she mounted the stage to usher me down. A thin applause obediently broke out.

'I think that's enough Katherine,' she said into my ear. 'Why don't you have a bit of time out in the green room. We'll find Iain, let him know where you are.'

She propped me up as I limped slowly through the sickening violet lights, watching my feet to avoid not only the network of cable threatening to trip me, but the pity radiating off the tables of people who once respected me.

I was ushered into a draughty back corridor towards the 'green room', a holding bay for the speakers, presenters and technical team. It was a windowless room that smelt like dirty tablecloths. Somehow, Gemma had retrieved my jacket and it had found its way on to my shoulders as she lowered me into a tatty seat in the centre of the room.

'Gemma, the wrong draft. I'd written something much better. It was really strong. Lily must have—'

'I'm sure Lily is speaking to the person who was managing the autocue right now. They will be reprimanded.'

'But—'

'It's OK, Katherine, try to calm down, have a glass of water, and if you think going home is what you need to do, do it.'

She pressed her mouth into that lipless line again, but this time, there was a tension to it, an overplay. My disastrous performance had undermined her reputation too.

A knock at the door and I knew it would be you. You couldn't resist could you? You couldn't walk away from the chance of seeing me laid this low, though I was nowhere near the bottom yet.

You poked your head around the door. 'Katherine, I'm so sorry, I definitely asked for your version to be loaded on.' You looked sympathetically at Gemma who watched you carefully as you came in and pulled up a chair opposite me. She remained there for another moment before nodding to the floor. 'I'll see where your partner's got to.' She looked over her shoulder at us once more before leaving the room. She didn't want to believe you'd screwed me and fucked her

236

in the process, but somewhere, quite close to the surface, I could tell she knew you had.

'I have no idea what happened.'

'Of course you don't.'

'I'm just, like, so, *so* sorry about how it's all played out tonight.'

I was tiring now, running out of ideas on how I was going to get out of that room with any kind of advantage over you. 'Some people are saying you look a lot like me tonight.'

'Really? That's so amazing. I guess I must have been inspired, you know, subconsciously?'

I tipped my head back to the ceiling, exhaustion taking over.

'Please, don't think bad things about me, Katherine. I loved dancing with you the other day. I haven't had that much fun in, well, I can't remember when.' I looked back to you to see your black eyes pleading. 'I'd really like you to come to the party this weekend. It'd be so nice to see you guys away from all this. I think you'll find you'll have the kind of weekend you won't forget in a hurry.'

Strange energy contracting in the tiny muscles around your eyes. This game was starting to feel like one I couldn't, under any circumstances, afford to lose. I would go to the party and I wouldn't be leaving there without some answers. But you didn't need to know I'd be going yet. I would let you sweat.

'We'll see.'

Iain flustered through the door. 'Kathy. You alright? What happened out there?'

'I don't really understand myself.' You and I kept looking right at each other.

'Your girl Gemma's squaring it. You'll be right.' And I saw he tried to get you to look at him, but you remained fixed on me. How could he not realise this was all about me? 'Shall we maybe get going?'

Losing in front of my home crowd. So many people I'd not be able to look in the face again, and yet I had to try. My instinct was to attempt a fight back. 'I think I'm going to get back out there. I need to fix this.'

'You should go. Get home. No one's going to think any less of you,' you said, Iain nodding along with your words like an idiot.

Yes, they *will* think less of me. They already do, because of you, The Princess Regent in the madness of Queen Katherine. My reign coming to an end. And worse. The things that held my life together in their closing chapters, though I couldn't see it yet. I still thought I could win.

'Please, love. Let me take you home. Let's get out of here,' Iain said.

You looked away now. You could see he was mine and always would be. The magic of all our years together that you could never match. But as I buried my head in his jacket as we left The Dorchester, I could have sworn he reeked of you.

Lily

22nd March – Awards Rehearsal Day

Just when I think I know what she's about, she surprises me. Her speech at the rehearsal. The guy next to me actually cried. An inspirational performance to restore her reputation, so insanely brilliant it draws a crowd of adoring interns around her and leaves her skipping out of the rehearsal with a smile on her face. Not on my watch.

I follow her out of the building, working out as quickly as I can what I can say next, something like, 'That really was *amazing*. Before you arrived, everyone was saying they were worried about you, how they were all going to be super-nice to you, so they'd keep you on an even keel, but I know for sure that reaction was 100 per cent genuine. Can you *believe* how moved people were!?'

She's about to cross over. It's so noisy out there, I have to call her name to stop her. She hasn't heard me, so I reach for her arm and just like that, she's on the floor. I didn't even do anything and she's there, fallen to the ground on all fours, about to get flattened by one of her beloved black cabs.

That's when it happens again.

I go to save her when I could have let her get seriously hurt, even though I know she wouldn't do the same for me. She's everything I hate about her generation, exploitation with a side of prejudice. *She is the sins made flesh*. I just know Ruth would agree with me if she knew KR.

But although I want KR down, I don't want her out. Not yet, anyway.

23rd March – Awards Night

Iain arrives at The Dorchester, literally, as his woman's crutch. She limps around at his side looking like the queen. She holds court, introducing her man-in-waiting some of the time, but mostly ignoring him. He scans the room for me as she schmoozes. I stay hidden. Let him wait until he can't stand it anymore.

He drinks away his frustration, chugging down most of his table's allocated bottles of garbage wine. He keeps looking for me, discreetly to begin with, but as the hours tick by, I can see he's getting totally desperate. It's nearly time for her speech.

I move my hair to one side, slather on the Russian Red and text:

You look hot in a tux. I'm right behind you. Come behind the stage curtain at the back. Dare you. xxx

He's up on his feet, checking behind him, not noticing KR staggering her way to the stage. I can barely watch what happens next. Sonnet Samira pops into my head before I can stop her, but thankfully he arrives before I have to think too hard about either of them.

Now he's with me, in a gap behind a velveteen curtain at the back of the ballroom. When he sees me, he has no words. He looks me up and down and I know for sure I've nailed KR's look. He's knocked for six. He can see it: a vision of the future, all the more appealing when it's repackaged as a vision of the past. He kisses me, breaks away for a second to push me against a wall as I start to undo his zip.

Just then, her voice cracks over the PA.

It could have been so perfect. I was seconds from managing to orchestrate her losing Iain *and* what little professional reputation she has left at exactly the same moment, but then he hears her. Her falling apart, his siren call. He lets go of my butt cheek.

'Lil, I'd better get out there. She needs me.'

Of course she does.

'I understand, Iain, but *I* need you in my life. I need you inside me.'

'I ... I can't,' he stammers, and with this goes out to find her.

This is massively annoying, but I can't let myself get too angry. I've still got work to do. I straighten myself and head towards the green room. They *have* to come to the party now.

CHAPTER 14

Katherine

I called in sick on Friday after the awards. I think your aunt was happy I'd be out of her face for the day, so she could soothe the various parties after my speech debacle without me being there. My absence obviously made you very concerned I wasn't going to make your party the following day. You texted me repeatedly, desperately:

> *Can't wait to see you xxx*

And another:

> *There'll be no one there as interesting as you. Please come!*
> *X*

I wonder now whether you'd sent exactly the same messages to Iain, because, thinking back, I remember him emerging from another room a couple of times with a fresh energy and a distant look in his eyes.

Iain too saw me disappear into my own world of thought on Saturday morning, as we waited for the party. We both knew something strange was happening, but we didn't say. I wonder how many long-term couples do this as they stagger towards their obsolescence as a pair.

The odd mood continued when we left London, driving towards Hayward's Heath. We'd decided to make a weekend of it, booking a suite in a boutique B&B in a village a couple of miles from the party. With the spring light fading, a bit of coke and half a bottle of prosecco in me, I rehearsed the lines of enquiries I planned to use on your friends. I knew you hadn't bet on Katherine Ross the hungry reporter stomping on your home turf and that felt good. I'd get the answers I needed to understand your motivations, then I'd engineer getting you on your own, have the deep and meaningful conversation we needed to have so I could circle your endgame until you confessed.

Iain and I got changed twice apiece, laughing at how ridiculous we were being, but both backward glancing at our old arses in the mirror, tugging and pinching bits of our bodies and our faces, seeing which sections bounced back when we didn't want them to, which folds and creases remained when the fingers left them. The coke and drink had already left me flushed. I looked about as old as I'm capable of looking, so put on another layer of foundation, but this only made me look even more dried-out and desperate to mask the truth of my skin. I wanted to wash it off and start again, but our taxi was there. It was time to go.

We sped through country lanes, through picturesque hamlets then into a shabby little enclave of small 1930s semis.

I looked at the address on my phone again, 'Greenings. It's got to be posher than one of these, surely?'

'If it isn't fucking *Brideshead Revisited* territory, I want

243

my money back,' Iain muttered distractedly as he peered at the street outside and its unstylish homes.

The taxi stopped.

I leant forward to speak with the driver. 'Hi there. Is this the right address?'

'According to my satnav it is.'

I looked at Iain for some comradery, some sign he too felt that this was not what we were expecting; any indication we were in this together. But he'd already leapt out of the car and was walking towards the house, neglecting to help me get out the car with my bad ankle. I was left to pay, then hoist myself and our bags of booze out of the taxi unaided.

I clinked and groaned my way up the front garden path, a sarcastic *Thanks for your help, Iain* clawing to get out of my mouth. He was standing in front of the door of the most rundown house on the lane. A nasty white and black plastic sign for 'Greenings,' propped against the side of the door.

Behind net curtains, the front room window dripped with condensation. There was pink light and the low thrum of music, but no smell of cigs. So, this was how Snowflakes partied. Through a gap in the nets, I caught sight of people who looked just like my interns, individuals who saw me as a relic, someone they don't want to shag or socialise with, unless they're using me as a sounding board for tales of how great their lives are. Would any of them even talk to me? Of course not. I didn't belong there with them, not by a long chalk.

'Fuck. I don't think I can go in. Shall we just not go in?' I whispered, suddenly embarrassed by my bulging bag of gin, my cakey makeup, my limp, and every one of my forty-one years.

'What's the matter?'

'Look at it. Look at us! We're at a teenage party in some kind of squat. I think anyone would say we're a bit past it for this. This is a mistake.'

'Calm down, love. Let's get in there, have a drink, couple more lines, see where the land lies. C'mon, we've come all this way.'

'I probably shouldn't really be having any more if we're serious about, you know, trying—' I said, but I was cut off.

'Let's not do that now. *Please*, let's do like we said: enjoy an old-fashioned house party, forget all the other crap going on in our lives. Let our hair down.' He stepped up to a doorbell that was covered by strips of yellowed, dried-out Sellotape.

Crap in our lives, I was thinking of throwing back in his face, just as you peeked from behind the lacey curtains before rushing to come to the front door. I would have to go in now you'd seen us.

I shot Iain a filthy look that he refused to acknowledge and in the seconds before you opened the door, I mentally prepared myself. I was about to go into enemy territory and needed to get my fight on.

You pulled the door near off its hinges in your enthusiasm, you couldn't wait to get us inside, stop us from escaping. Your hair was back to normal, and you were wearing your oversized yellow shirt again. You'd paired it with your black leather skater skirt. Bare legs. Your lips had a rich slick of the usual Flaming June lipstick. The darkness of your eyes punctured the dirty tangerine of the street light. Sensational.

'You guys? You came!' You drew us both towards you for a hug in the hallway, somehow managing to kick the door shut behind me in a way that made me startle. 'I can't believe you're here. Come in, come in, we're all expecting you.'

You led us into that oddly smoke-free house. Clusters of your kind clung to patchy walls and bust-up chairs. Some appeared to be sipping water and all of them, whatever race or gender, seemed to somehow look exactly the same. You called out their names quickly as we ambled past. I tried to retain at least some of them but my senses were insulted by the weird collective energy I could feel, but couldn't quite understand. It wasn't a party buzz, not in the way I remembered it. It was a kind of *doing* energy. Task-based. It seemed they were there to have a reasonable party in a measured way; they may say they're up for staying to the small hours, but they'd more likely be cycling back to their mum's at the back of twelve. And sober. And with some useful information or new connection with someone; some new creative project in the pipeline. As I passed through another bank of good teeth, shining complexions and big hair, I realised I wasn't intimidated or embarrassed, I didn't think any less of myself as I shambled through to that front room.

Instead, I felt another batch of *Fuck yous* coming on. *Fuck you*, with your holier than thou sobriety, your earnest social activism, your fear of difference while signalling to embrace it in Insta-friendly ways, your stupid blogs, your houseplants and cacti, all your show-off 'content' and social media strategies, and really, *Fuck you*.

Iain had already started a conversation with a bunch of lads and was fishing the gin and the plastic tumblers we knew we'd need from a Spar carrier bag. He held them in his fingers like the claw of a fairground grabber, slushed the gin neat into the cups and handed them around. I took one from Iain and necked it. Two of the lads giggled like it was the wildest thing they'd ever seen and shook their heads at first, before one shrugged and downed it. Iain did the same, then the other two. See, we're good for something, us oldies. Maybe some of them would talk to me after all. I felt good enough to practice my questions on the nearest 'Barney'. I was trying but failing to get anywhere with him. I sensed you watching my investigation and sure enough, you sought to obfuscate my efforts.

'Here, I got you a drink.' You passed me a plastic half-pint of red wine. 'You looked like you were dry. You having a good time? I'll come find you again in a minute, just spotted someone I need to catch up with. Ciao!'

'Barney' waved dumbly at the air where you'd been. 'Who did you say she knows here?'

'I didn't. I don't.'

What else could I do but keep starting conversations with new Barneys, asking how they knew you, or opening up with something like, 'Such a nice crowd here, you're all as nice as Lily.' And they'd say something like 'Lily?' or 'I literally met her this second, she's the sweetest.' No one I spoke to had any idea who you were. Sure, your true friends could be out there somewhere, but if they were, they were actively avoiding me.

I didn't buy it.

You'd bought us to a party where you were some kind of social phantom. This meant Iain and I were floating around untethered and vulnerable. I needed to stay close to him, but I had to speak to you alone too if I was going to get close to any kind of answers.

I'd lost you somewhere in that grotty little house. And I'd

lost and found Iain again a couple of times as the place filled and we ending up talking to various young, insipid faces. I kept reaching for Iain. Below the vision of all those people who didn't know you, to me we were holding hands like our love was a beautiful, ancient secret no one could see. It was OK. I was still in control because I was his and he was mine: a warm island of two in a Snowflake sea.

I let his hand leave mine when I finally saw you come back into the room. You'd evaded me, made me wait for you. I know you did this on purpose, to make me so ready for any crumb you'd toss my way. I had so much I wanted to ask you, but I had to stay cool.

'How you enjoying the party, Lily?'

'It's great. You guys having a good time?'

'Sure. Your friends are all lovely.'

'Aren't they.'

'Yeah, you must introduce me to some of your best friends properly.'

'I definitely will, once I manage to get you guys in the same room.' You didn't even pretend to look around for these imaginary people.

'And who is your best friend Lily *Lunt*? Go on, point out your friends, your real, actual friends, from your school, from your actual past. Where are they?'

'They're everywhere. Everyone loves me.' You tossed your head extravagantly then brought your face to mine in defiance. 'Who do you think my best friends are? Who would you pick?' You lost the light in your eyes for a second. I felt close to actually getting somewhere, but with your eyes so dark like that, you started to scare me.

'Right, come on, let's get cracking!' Iain was behind me, trying to plonk himself down on the arm of a faded armchair. He missed the target and would have fallen on his arse, had he not grabbed me on the way down. The extra weight on my ankle made me cry out.

'Fucking hell, Iain.'

'Sorry, babe,' he said, not looking to see if I was alright, instead focusing on the wrap of coke he was fumbling with, which was about to go everywhere. I hadn't seen him that pissed for a while. I suddenly saw him through the young eyes around us. His box-fresh dad T-shirt clung to an undeniable middle-aged roll, paired with jeans he's owned for more than ten years, a smile that lingered too long not to be considered cheesy. Dusty Converse. A faded man.

'Give me that,' I said, then under my breath, 'I'm fine by the way. And you need to slow down.' But he hadn't heard me.

'That's my girl. You know she's a journalist? How can you tell? Look how she racks them up. You see, with most folk, they're vertical, all uneven, but Kathy? She chops hers out horizontal … same length, all spaced out, same size, like lines on a reporter's notepad. Beautiful that, eh?'

Here, he had a point. I'd deftly set out six perfectly horizontal lines of exactly the same width from tip to tip, tidying up the ends so they were all exactly the same size, as was my way. One for me, one for you, one for Iain and one each for the lads still hanging around Iain for free gin.

I did the first line, then went to ask, 'Who wants next dibs?' I was still looking down at my handiwork, but when I raised my head, all I saw was unbidden horror.

From nowhere, the Snowflakes had amassed around me,

looking at me as if I'd just killed someone. The pearl-clutching disgust on their faces; on your face.

'No thank you, Katherine. I don't think we need *that* to have a good time,' you said, and looked to the Breakfast Club around you for supportive 'Yeahs' which they duly supplied.

'I'll take that as a no, shall I?' I handed Iain back his bank card and a rolled tenner.

'Ah well, your loss, kids.' Iain hoovered up three lines, one after the other.

'*Iain,*' I warned.

'Yeah, this is my Gran's house,' 'Dan' piped up from nowhere, 'I don't feel comfortable with you doing that here?' the stupid boy's voice rising at the end as if he was asking a question. I heard another voice, 'God, don't they know how many London kids get slaughtered for that?'

I couldn't bear the disapproval, and worse, I knew whoever made that last comment was right. This kept happening: something from your lot I immediately dismissed as a pile of shit, until I thought about it, and saw it really wasn't.

I was making a bad job of coaxing the powder back into one of the wraps.

'Let's pretend we didn't see it,' you told me, shaking your head, reminding me once more why your kind, even when you're coming from a right-minded position, remain so fucking irritating. I was about to restart our conversation, but you were swallowed for a selfie by a group of girls who only earlier told me they weren't sure who you were.

'Fucking hell, these kids don't like to party much, do they?' Iain slurred in my ear.

'I've got three hundred quid's worth burning a hole in my pocket.'

'Fuck, lighten up. We can still have a toot.'

'I don't want to.' I kept my eyes on you, now dancing with a new group of people to one of those bands I don't know or understand, one that has numbers where there should be letters in their name, consonants where there should be vowels. It seemed as if you had no intention of talking to me, you'd just got me there to throw your youth in my face. Humiliate me again and again. 'I really think we should go.'

'No!' He said it desperately. He heard it too, and added, 'No, I mean, they're not too bad, eh? Come on, let me get us a drink and give it another whirl. We're just getting started.'

'You're pretty far gone already.'

'Well, pardon me for getting pissed up at a party!'

I knew I wasn't going to get him out of the door without a fight. It was already demeaning, having a middle-aged quarrel about drugs in front of your lot. Iain was looking over my shoulder as if he was watching out for someone more interesting to talk to. As if he was looking for you.

'Sorry. You're right … Well, I reckon I'm about ready for another. You?' I took his hand again and led him towards our bag of drinks near the sideboard.

'Sounds good to me.' His eyes kept flicking around. I needed his attention on me.

'Have you noticed, no one here really knows her?'

'Who?'

I rolled my eyes before I could help it, '*Lily*, Iain, *Lily*. It's like, there's a whole load of kids who'll have a debrief over smashed avos in the morning and sit around and say, *That girl? I thought she was with you?* But no one will know where she came from, or where she went. Go on, go and ask someone, anyone, how they know her.'

'You've got a very active imagination. You should try writing fiction.'

'Yeah, and you should put your pen down until you can do better than fucking stupid clichés.' At this, Iain's jaw tightened. 'Sorry, sorry, I didn't mean that ... It's just she doesn't add up. *Again.* I know she's hiding something. I found out her name isn't Lunt, by the way. Also, I've not told you, but someone keeps sending me vile, incriminating emails with stuff in them only she or I could know. What do you think about that?' May as well lay my cards on the table because I could sense something dangerous about Iain. He was focusing too hard on my face, like he had to force his eyes not to be obviously tracking you as you moved around the cramped living room. 'Why are you here, Iain?'

'You know why. Because I can't spend another hundred thousand nights sat at home getting pissed without a bit of a break ... What are *you* doing here?'

'Because ... because I needed to know more about her, but given she's lied about knowing anyone here, I'm hitting dead end after dead end.'

'You are reading way too much into things. *Way* too much. I don't know ... Sometimes, can I be honest for a sec? I just don't know—'

I didn't like where this sentence was heading. I had to put the brakes on it. 'OK, let's forget it. Put it down to another long week. I'm sorry. I don't know what's wrong with me.

It's all me, I know that, really. Come on, let's keep mingling with the Snowflakes. Please. Come with me.'

I found a quiet spot to chop us another few lines and saw him coming back to me again. After we'd refreshed ourselves, I led him out again into the 'party'. The only two high people there, we had a little secret and that made us a team. We somehow got our groove on, producing an old cool couple routine. We talked ourselves up; I offered internships and sage advice, Iain, a sofabed to crash on 'if you're ever in London.' And as Iain became less cogent, I wasn't overly worried, since I'd ended up allowing myself to get peeled off by some not-bad-looking Felix or other. When I went to get another drink, I couldn't see Iain, but given the state he was in, it seemed likely he was slumped in some corner to 'rest his eyes' while awaiting his 'second wind'. This used to happen a lot at our parties, back in the day. Same old, same old. It seemed the right time to focus on finding you and having the conversation we needed to have.

The room was full, but there you were alone, leaning against the wall near the door; me against the opposite wall, viewing you through a group of kids. You didn't look at me, but you knew I was watching you. You were texting someone.

My phone vibrated in pocket.

You were messaging me. My heart leapt like a teenager waiting for their first kiss.

Meet me in the garden in 2 mins. It's time. xxx

You focused on the floor as you tucked your hair behind your ears. You were asking to be observed. You stood up straight, decisively, then turned to leave the room. I took a breath and made myself wait for a minute to pass before letting myself walk as calmly as I could towards my fate.

The pink room swirled about me as I left it. I sensed the truth, hot and pure awaiting me. I headed to the kitchen and then out through the open door into the yard. On I went over the skinny strip of scrub that passed for a garden in that random grandma house, excitement rising. *It's time.*

I could see a love seat towards the end of the 'garden'; a small bench under a ragged apple tree surrounded by sentimental little tea lights in wire-hung mason jars. It faced out to a forest of savagely tall nettles. And there you were in the middle distance, opposite the bench, your face turned towards the stars.

I had to tread carefully, stepping over broken bricks to reach you. I picked my way through the undergrowth, something of the fairy tale in the air as I dipped low to avoid a shooting clump of buddleia at my head and dodged a mess of brambles at my feet.

You began to speak. Someone I couldn't see, until I noticed an elbow poking out from behind the tree. It seemed familiar. One of the lads from before? If he didn't shift, I planned to scare him off, say something to send him back in the house so we could really talk, like you wanted to, like we had to.

I moved forward again, lurking for a moment behind a dead oak. I was close enough to hear you now.

'You're sure? You're absolutely positive you want this?'

Consent and double-consent gained. Making someone firmly agree to something they don't fully understand.

And then he came out of the shadows, his back to me.

Iain.

He sat down and waited for you on the love seat.

You walked towards him, savouring his attention as you approached. He reached for your hands and pulled you towards him, seizing you with an urgency that ripped through my heart.

You straddled him. You kissed him hard.

The moonlight caught your fingernails – the same mimosa colour as your stupid laptop case from that first morning you invaded my life – as you moved my partner's face to your tits. He obliged, tearing open your shirt and pushing up your bra to free you.

Overwhelmed by you, he lifted you away from him for a second so he could tug his old jeans and the boxers I'd bought for him down to his ankles. I could see how much he was dying to get inside you. My stomach dropped to the floor. I saw myself running forward and pulling you off him, throwing you to the floor and kicking you hard in the stomach.

But the physical me could not move an inch. So on I watched, my world disintegrating as he grabbed your arse with both hands underneath your leather skirt while you threw back your head, eyes shut in apparent ecstasy. I felt as if I was about to vomit. I'd seen more than enough. I had to get back to the house without being noticed, preserve what little I had left of my dignity.

But then something changed in you.

You brought your head back and your eyes were open. You looked down to watch Iain on you. Impassive. Once-removed. You then began searching the darkness for something, him still devouring you, unawares.

I drew myself behind the dead oak, but I could still see you through the dry branches.

Your eyes stilled. They'd found what they were looking for. Mine.

You stared right at me.

You didn't move for a second or two. You wanted to make sure I was definitely watching.

Looking at me, you reached between your legs and pulled your prim cotton knickers to one side with your fingers. You made a fake groan as you lowered yourself onto my partner's cock. You held my gaze throughout.

But I couldn't turn away now.

Because if I did that, you would know just how much hearing Iain's moans as he pulled you onto him destroyed me again and again and again. You would know by how much and how hard you were beating me.

So I stared right back at you, Lily.

I made my body stand there, forced myself to watch, didn't let myself so much as flinch the whole time you looked at me as you fucked my partner. I let myself hear him come in you, sounding like he was being strangled as he said your name. Only then did I allow myself to disappear into the night and slide into the darkness of my total isolation.

I ran past the babble of millennial inflections bouncing off the walls, the air a dizzying rose-coloured fuzz, clean hair and faces melting into one. I pushed my way through to the front door and burst onto the empty street.

I found I was bent double. My hands on my knees as if I'd just come home from my Sunday run. A net curtain twitched across the road as I called a taxi, my words arriving between pants that reverberated up and down the sad little street. I didn't belong there. We never should have come.

When I got back to the B&B, I stayed only long enough to gather my things, including my cars keys.

Drunk, I raced through unlit country lanes. I took corners hard, barely braking. Rage taking me over, at Iain, at you, but mostly at me. I should have known.

When I had no idea where I was anymore, I stopped at a passing place. Watching the sun rise from the back seat of my Mini after a scrape of sleep, I had that feeling again: this was another vision of my future.

Lily

25th March – Party Time

I don't have any friends. She knows it. Yes, I'm completely alone, but I guess I'm so used to not having anyone, I can hardly feel it anymore. I had someone once, but not for long. My room in Ruth's house in Headingley was where I finally thought I'd found home. Talking with her for hours and hours, I never felt the need to be in control of her. It was no work at all, because if she was winning, I was winning. I think this means I loved her. These days, I'm struggling to have anything like a meaningful conversation with anyone my own age, in fact with anyone else who isn't Katherine Ross.

Because this thing is taking me over.

Talking to anyone but her is like sucking a sweet with the wrapper on. No flavour. No spice. No danger. No point.

I found out about the party on Twitter. A friend of a friend of an old acquaintance, in the distant galaxies of one of my old lives. This would do. It feels like this is exactly what I need to move things right along. Neither of them can keep away from me, even if they tried. This is the closest I've ever felt to powerful my whole life.

I've started to daydream about pushing the concierge out of my window, viewing the bloody pulp of his body on the gravelled shore of the reservoir below me. But at least I can see he knows he's doing something wrong. The way he shuffles into the apartment, avoids looking into my face, tells me he knows how he's using me isn't fair or right. But Katherine Ross has no moral awareness. She doesn't even know her sins. She thinks she's blameless and given all I know, I believe that's the greatest crime she could commit. I have to punish her.

26th March – The Morning After

Finally, they arrive at the party. Both of them have made an effort and it's so sad to see. She's got too much makeup on and his brand new T clings to his dough-like pecs. I can't help it, I'm hoping the people here will be kind to them. I'm not a monster, you see?

'Who the fuck are they?' I hear someone say when they see them get out of their cab, and I admit there's something a bit ghoulish about the pair of them in the streetlight, her hobbling up the garden path with her bulging bags for life, having some kind of a go at him. Him, all red and obviously drunk already racing to the door to get away from her.

'Oh my god, they're coming in! Don't let them!' another person says, at which point I jump up and say, 'Don't be insane. They're with me.'

Of course, they freak everyone else out. A couple of people complain that 'That old woman keeps asking me weird questions about you'. So that's why she's here. She's looking to solve the puzzle. Of course she is, and of course she assumes she can do it her way. So arrogant, so *her*. So, I egg her on without giving her anything more than I need to keep them there. She needs to come to her own conclusions by herself. That's when this works best.

It's almost painful to watch them, messing about with their grim drugs. I share in everyone's horror, but it's more awful for me because I've vouched for them. They have no idea of how the world works now. It's worse than that. They don't even want to know.

Eventually, I know the moment has come. I feel a surge of nerves, but massive energy too. Power, or something like it.

I send them both the same text, but I tell him to come and meet me now under the apple tree, then ask her to come in a couple of minutes. It works out perfectly.

How she wants to look away. How repulsive she finds seeing me on top of 'her Iain'. What woman wouldn't? But what other woman would try to stare out their rival in the very moment they're doing their partner?

I keep waiting for her to blink first, but she refuses to acknowledge the truth: I am hurting her. *I am winning*. Even as it couldn't get *any* worse for her, with her partner on the verge of coming inside me, she stares on. Totally defiant, like I can't touch her at all, like she could pretend this hasn't changed a thing. But it has and we both know it, despite her refusing to look away.

After I'd done with Iain, she finally steps back where I can't see her anymore. What will she do now? Will she let herself crumble now I can't see her, or will she come after me fighting? The wait is exquisite, especially because I know what Iain plans to ask her when he sees her next. I'm moves ahead of her and I'm going to do everything in my power to make the punishment fit the crime. I'll make it so she *will* blink.

CHAPTER 15

Katherine

By Sunday night I had forty-three missed calls from Iain. You didn't call or text me directly, but I wondered about how much you were shaping Iain's texts. I had a vision of you drafting them together, passing his phone between you in between exquisitely guilt-sodden sex.

This from Iain:

> *Katherine, I don't know how much you saw, but I'm sorry. Things just happened, I'm going to leave you alone this weekend, but we need to talk. x*

Leave me alone? More like not drag himself out of your bed.

I wondered, had you got the first train back to London in the morning together? Had you nestled your head in his chest and dozed as he gazed out of the window, occasionally turning his head to kiss your hair, which he would find startling in its natural vivaciousness, while calling to mind my dried-out, fake black scruff? And when you got off the tube at Manor House, did you run back to yours together, for fear of bumping into me? And when you let him into your flat, did you shower together, fuck and then fall asleep sweetly in your bed? When you came to, did you fuck again, or did he disappear to fish around your flat for something to cook for you? And when you got out of your bed to find your lover, were you just wearing my copycat shirt and nothing else, and did he just have to fuck you again, there and then? Did you let him swim in his morning guilt before leading him to that big window over the reservoir where you knew he'd see gorgeous sunlight and maybe also the possibility of a piercing bright future? Did you fuck again, with your hands pressed against the glass, him behind you?

When I got back to London and unlocked the door to my flat, it felt like going into a museum. A staleness I hadn't noticed before, probably because me and Iain had not been away overnight for nearly two years. The overbearing atmosphere of a monument to times gone.

I closed the door behind me and gazed at The Film poster for the thousandth time. I went to the living room and looked around at all my things. Beautiful things under grey dust.

I dragged a chair and reached up to one of my display mezzanines. On it, three Ashanti masks I'd picked up for peanuts in Ghana. I took the largest in both hands. I let my thumbs stroke its nobbled surface and thought about the cut-off combats I'd worn over the three weeks I'd spent in Africa, without Iain. I was twenty-seven. Life felt real. Vivid. Why doesn't anyone tell you that's It. These are The Days of Your Life. Why do you only realise that was It when It's all over, when It is in your rear-view? Why do you only really see It when it's someone else's turn? When you realise how old you've become because looking at the young makes your blood hot and your heart sink?

I raised the mask above my head and let it drop to the floorboards. It split as if it was divided by the hours on the clock, a dozen or so isosceles shards reaching away from what was once the centre. I retrieved the next one and did the same, and again to the third.

Balinese ceramics: smashed. An art nouveau clock Iain had spotted in a market near Avignon: in pieces. A Victorian child's rocking chair: smithereens. Everything I could reach, I took in my hands and shattered.

When that was done, I walked back to the hall. I lifted The Film poster off its hook. A shift of dust rose at the sides. I coughed and my eyes watered. It was heavy. It wasn't easy for me to get it into the living room. I balanced it on the coffee table for a moment, looked at it one last time before letting it drop onto the hard floor. Stepping over it, I saw the impact had only left a single crack running across its width. If I were to put it back up again, Iain wouldn't even notice it was damaged. I grabbed a thick slice of the largest splintered Ashanti mask, got to my knees, raised it up and over my head and brought it down on the crunching pane. Again and again until my sweat mixed with powdered glass. Words formed between the blows. Iain and you. You and Iain. Not a sideshow. Not a stepping stone? No.

'This … Is … About … Me!'

Even though I'd watched you screw my partner with my own eyes, I still knew I hadn't called you wrong. This *was* all about me. I still believed this. You had zeroed in on me. Watched me. Tried to undermine me at every turn. Except when you weren't. Except when you shone at me. When you smiled. When you touched my hand. When you danced with me. When you shared what I thought were your deepest truths. About your childhood; the pain of neglect. A pain I knew as well as you did. Or was that a lie too?

> *Please Kathy, I need you to talk to me. I need to know you haven't done anything stupid. Just text me one letter. Let me know you're ok. X*

I think the guilt was really getting to Iain here. Was he worried he could have blood on his hands? And wouldn't *that* kill his buzz?

> *Kathy, I'm so sorry. I know I've hurt you. Can we talk? Please? Xxx*

I think he was already missing me by then too. Perhaps you'd said something insipid, taken offence at some off-colour gag he'd made, and maybe he'd realised exactly how young you were, how you were obviously wired completely different to him, and me. He'd also, surely, discovered how you didn't have any detectable sense of humour. That would bother him, if he'd managed to see past the tits, the teeth, the overall nubility. Or perhaps you'd suggested another bottle of wine wasn't a good idea. That at least could have made him pine for me again.

Iain wasn't much, but he was mine.

You stayed away from work that Monday morning. Getting myself to the office wasn't easy, but I intended to stay on the right side of history where Gemma was concerned. I wondered if she knew what you'd done yet.

Clearly, it was a tough start to the week for Asif too. You must have told him you'd been with someone else; maybe even told him it was Iain. His eyes were red and he kept clasping his hand over the lower half of his face. He didn't even look at me when I came in.

And just to keep things interesting, Acceptableinthenoughties emailed both Gemma and me later that morning:

Subject: Appropriate behaviour?

Dear Publisher,
Your esteemed editor is a drug user. I strongly suggest an appropriate and immediate response, otherwise I'll be forced to take more direct action.

Because hundreds of kids are literally slaughtered for her drugs.

Time is running out.

Gemma arrived late and called me straight into her office.

'Take a seat.'

'Mind if I stand?'

'Would you tell me now if you know anything about this.'

'Do you want to be more specific?'

'Do you know who is sending you these messages?'

'I can't be sure, but, this is really difficult for me to say to you …' She sat there waiting for what she must have felt was the inevitable. 'Can I ask you, Gemma, why did Lily say she wasn't coming to work today?'

'She's not well. Sore throat,' she said flatly. She clearly didn't believe it any more than I did.

'A sore throat,' I nodded, dragging out Gemma's agony. 'So nothing to do with the fact my partner and I attended a party with your niece this weekend, but I didn't get to take him home because he was too busy shagging her. So, I wonder now, just *who* could have been sending these unkind messages?'

And I saw that twitch again, the one I'd seen that first time I'd asked her if there was anything I should know about you. Gemma sat forward in her seat and placed her hands flat on the surface in front of her. Her whole demeanour seemed to change from 'Say it isn't so' to 'Let the training kick in'. How many times had she needed to clean up after you?

'I need you to say *nothing* about this to *anyone* before I've had a chance to speak to her. Am I clear?'

'As a bell. Are you going to be investigating now? Has this gone far enough yet?'

'If that's what you expressly want me to do, I will,' she said firmly but I detected a tremble that belied she already knew any enquiry's conclusion.

'I do, Gemma.'

A final purse of the lips. Gemma only knew about the previous crimes, not the current. You were vulnerable, and now I could see she wasn't party to your masterplan, Gemma was at risk too.

I spent the rest of Monday doing no work at all. I ignored the interns, looked up impossibly expensive wellness retreats, called an old contact and got him to take me to lunch on the Southbank, where I stayed until gone 4 p.m.

Like so many things, a lunch with him was so much less fun than it used to be. He was one of my bank of regulars. The older guys I'd go to for free bubbles, a snippet of news, some bit of gossip I might be able to spin up into a feature, and a sure-fire ego boost. I let them drool over me at the restaurants of the moment, occasionally letting them have me, because their gratitude and awe at getting me into bed was something else. But that lunch shattered another illusion. I'd allowed myself to believe they worshipped me, my bravery, my craft, for God's sake! No, they only adored the twenty-nine-years and below version of me. They gave praise at the altar of my young flesh, but their patronage, which I had felt gave me power, did not. It gave me and every woman like me a shelf life.

'You must tell me more about your stunning new recruit,' my old contact said, eyebrows high on a greasy forehead.

'There's not much to tell. She's just a kid. The publisher's niece. You know how it goes. Anyway, tell me what's been keeping you busy.'

'Ah, part of the family business is she? Well, however she got there, she's really got something. She made quite the impression on the great and the good at your awards.'

Of course you had. With me out of the way, the floor was all yours.

And yet even in my rage at you, I could see you and your kind had a point with the movements you'd instigated to put a halt to sex entering the workplace. I'd previously lamented the rise of such puritanism. I'd called it out as the neutering of society. Why couldn't we all do what we wanted without securing written consent first? But now I realised all those times when I felt I was riding high, I was doing so on the most narrowly-defined of patronages. I could now see just how limited, how temporary these endorsements were. They converted three-dimensional women with brains and hearts to ravishing fillies when we're young, then beasts fit only for sympathetic pasture, when we dare to age. Definitely fuck you, I thought that afternoon, but definitely fuck them too. Yet another incident where I'd automatically written off the millennial perspective, then was forced to see you lot had a point after all. Fuck you for being right.

Iain texted to say he was waiting for me at home. Good. Let's see what he had to say. Let him see the mess he'd made. But I wouldn't be rushing back to him. He needed to see the cool, hard me. The devil-may-care me. The strong me. The young me.

Gemma left before five, the interns slunk off indecently soon after.

Asif was still there, forlornly pretending to work. He'd stayed out of my way all day, but he obviously wanted to talk and I wanted to know what you'd told him.

'So. How's it going, Asif? Heard from Lily today?'

Trembling, he told me, 'I … I thought she was perfect, K. It's like she made herself perfect for me. Everything she said … Now—'

'Now you know she's a liar and a cheat.'

'I guess.'

'What did she tell you about this weekend?'

'Not much. She'd already told me to cool down because she was falling for someone. Yesterday, she told me about her and Iain. She didn't want me to hear it from anyone else.'

'From me? And *falling for*? What a crock of shit.'

'She told me exactly the same thing last week,' he rubbed his eyes. 'Sorry. I've not been myself lately, distracted I guess. She's just so ... distracting.'

'Don't worry,' I said, not wanting to look at him. 'We'll save it all up for your next review.'

'Review?'

'Yeah, I've heard whispers ... They'll be making me do a fresh round of job losses. I'd put money on it.'

'Shit. Right.'

'Don't worry, I'm sure you'll be fine. Drink?'

'I'm not really in the mood tonight, to be honest.'

'Your girlfriend's just fucked my partner; my life. Would you please have a drink with me, Asif?'

'OK ... sure. Whatever you need.'

I retrieved the remaining third of the bad wine from the fridge and took it to his desk with two mugs. I chucked down a wrap of coke in front of him, and let it all happen. We got high, decamping to the toilets to screw. And I did feel like me again.

CHAPTER 16

Katherine

There was a sick excitement as I climbed the stairs to my flat. I wondered what Iain could possibly say to me, whether I'd be greeted with contrition or defiance. I considered the narratives he'd choose and how we would all be cast: who would he paint as the hero, the villain, the innocent. Whatever the story, the ultimate ending had to be that he was very, very sorry.

I'd picked up a bottle of wine and a big bag of popcorn, like I was readying myself for the show. I also wanted to give my impatient, coked-up jaw something to do.

I walked into the living room where he was waiting in silence. He stood up from the sofa in a hammy manner that reminded me of a soap opera policeman about to tell the parents the bad news of what's happened to their daughter.

I didn't look at him yet, but went to the kitchen and got a glass for me before sauntering over to a chair across the room from him. I poured myself a drink and opened my popcorn, took a sip, then started spooning fistfuls of food into my face and waited for him to begin.

'Are you off your face?'

'And you'd care, why?'

'Don't start, Kathy. Please.'

'Well, don't tell me how to be.'

'What the fuck happened here then?' He scanned around the broken mess of our home. 'Looks like we've been burgled. What did you do to my poster? It's fucked.'

'What happened here is what happens when you catch your partner *screwing* your intern.'

'OK, OK,' he held his hands up.

'Iain, will you just sit down and get on with it.'

He obeyed and took a breath, 'OK. I made a mistake doing what I did, how I did it on Saturday, big time. It was disrespectful to you and it didn't fully respect Lily.'

'Didn't *fully respect* Lily? Next you'll be telling me about your "triggers". Wow, Iain, you're so fucking woke now it's kind of making me sick.'

'Would you just let me *speak*? The sooner I say what I need to say the better. Please just listen and I'll be out of your hair.'

'What if I don't want you to be out of my hair?' I dropped the popcorn and encouraged tears to come.

'Kathy, please. I need you to listen for a minute.'

'OK,' I swallowed. 'Go on.'

'I've come to realise … I need to change. I want to get sober. I *need* to get sober.'

'So, is that what was happening on Saturday? That was just the booze problem you've suddenly realised you have? Out of the blue. We're going to medicalise this are we?'

'Please. *Please.* This is important. I take full responsibility for what happened on Saturday, but can you remember something? Or maybe it's that you've made a decision to forget. Me in rehab. Me before you and me. My big bro, God rest him, giving me chance after chance. Just before I met you, the last one. He had somewhere booked for me. Then you came into my life. You made it all OK. What did I need rehab for? I was fine, wasn't I? Who says I have a problem? Well, not you. Fantastic. Happy Fucking Christmas, wasn't it? Life was so fucking easy with you, it was so "great". No matter I can't hold down a job. No matter I never made it back to rehab and I never spoke to my brother again. No matter we don't do anything normal couples do.'

'You want to be a normal couple now? Some great timing there, Iain. Did you want to be a normal couple when you were fucking *her* in the *fucking garden*?'

'Please. Please don't. I'm sorry. I've said I'm sorry.'

'What you were saying, it was great, it *is* great because we were great together. After all this time, we still are; we can be again. Even better.'

'I think we've too many secrets.' He shook his head slowly. I shook mine more desperately as he went on, 'You and me. Too many secrets. Too many things we know, deep down but we never say.'

'Like what?'

'Don't make me say them. I don't want to.'

'But Iain, *we* don't have secrets. Not really. That's why we work.'

'You don't know my secrets and I can't make myself think too long about yours.'

He chewed the side of his thumb, then rubbed his palms together. He didn't normally do that.

'I don't know what you think my secrets are, but—'

'Don't. Please. I don't want us to do this now. Maybe never.'

'Tell me, Iain. I deserve to know!' I stood up, shouting.

'Well, I know what you make yourself do in the bathroom after dinner every night, for a start. You think I don't, but I do. Always have. I'm not stupid. I don't know why—'

'Is that all you've got? *This* is how you're justifying what happened on Saturday?'

A pause.

'What else?'

'No. Not today.' He breathed out hard again, as if I was trying his patience. 'The thing I want you to know first and foremost is that I want to stop drinking. Forever.'

'I understand that. It's your decision, but you know you're fine as you are, regardless of whatever *she's* said.'

'It's nothing to do with anything Lily's said, or not said. It's where I'm at. Where I've got to. I can't live like this anymore. This's been building for a while now.' *Where he's at?* Your clean white mitts were all over this little move. 'I need things to change. *I* need to change and I can't do it with us doing what we always do, being who we always are.'

'I'm here. I'm still here for you, Iain. We can change together. Forever.'

'I need to ask you to help me out.'

'Anything.'

'Rehab. It doesn't work for me. I need to do this at home. Here.'

'OK, I'll research it, I'll help you. Whatever it takes.'

'I can't … I can't do it with you. I have to do it without you. I want you to live somewhere else while I get this done. I'm asking you, begging you: can you leave me alone, here? To save my life. Just give me a month or so to do this. Please.'

He seemed sincere, but what he was saying had to be a sick joke. 'So, wait a minute. You fuck her and I'm the one moving out?'

'It wouldn't be like that.'

'What would it be like, then?'

'It would be you, giving me half a chance to save my life.'

'Save your life. Without me. With *her*.'

'This isn't about Lily. What's happened, I think it's just made me realise I need to do something about my life. What happened on Saturday, it shouldn't have happened—'

'But it did and I don't know why I need to move out because of it. No, Iain, no way.'

'Please. I am begging you. I want to change. I need to get better.'

'But you're not even sick!'

'I'm not right. *We're* not right.' I shook my head. 'You. You're not right either. I think you know that, deep, deep down.'

'In case you hadn't noticed, I was doing alright until *she* came along.'

'I don't mean the depression, I'm talking about before; the secrets you've been trying to bury all these years. Even if you won't face up to them, I've started to put some things together. Give me some time and space to get better, and let's see if we can get past them.'

'No. I'm not going to do that. We're going to work through this *together*.'

He went quiet.

'Sometimes I look at you and I wonder: *Does she know what's real anymore?* It's like you live in a parallel universe.

274

Do you know what's true and what's not? You think Lily's the troll? You think she's out to get you? It's not right, despite what I did on Saturday. It's not her fault.'

'Why are you on her side? I'll never understand why you can't be on *my* side. I don't understand why you think she's right, not me.'

'But you haven't been on my side, Katherine. You let me get to this.'

'Wherever you think you are, it is on *you*. My crimes here? To provide for us. To put up with a world of work bullshit for you. For us. And now, you're punishing me for it, going on about "secrets". What the fuck, Iain? No. I am not going anywhere. And neither are you. That is who we are and until she came along, that was fine.'

He looked at me in a way I'd never seen before. Such a darkness in his eyes. He didn't look like Iain anymore. In all our years together I'd never once felt fear. Now I did, and it was raw and hot, pulsating inside me. He seemed to have crossed an invisible threshold into somewhere new and diabolical. I was terrified about what that new version of Iain might say next.

'Nothing to do with you is right.'

'Stop it. I don't like how you're looking at me. I don't know you when you're like this!' I fell to my knees on the carpet next to his feet and put my hands on his thighs, my heart breaking as I sensed him flinch at my touch. Iain, recoiling from me, not opening himself to me. How far he'd gone already, how I wanted to reel him back. 'Please, listen to me, let's just try and put what happened this weekend behind us. I'll help you cut back on the booze. Give up, even. I'll give up with you.

This is me we're talking about. I can do anything I put my mind to, you know that.'

'Oh I do.' He hooked a finger under my chin to bring my face up to meet his. 'Who are you, Katherine Ross? Do you really want me to start talking about what happened the year your mum died, or are you going to get the fuck out of here and let me get my shit together? Your choice.'

His eyes were shadows. I stopped breathing for a second before the breaths came quickly. The truth: a shark's fin of truth, barely under the water line, on the verge of slicing through the still surface. I didn't want him to say the words I thought were in his throat. What he thought he knew.

'I don't know what—'

'*Katherine.*'

Eyes like shadows, the feel of his finger under my chin, a foreign sensation.

'OK,' I shuffled away from him, still on the floor. I looked at my hands. 'You're wrong, but … I'll go tomorrow. I'll go for you.'

He watched me, waited. After a moment, I could see him nodding from the corner of my eye. By the time I made myself look at him again, some normality had trickled back into his face.

'OK … OK, good. Thank you. Where will you go? I don't, you know, want to—'

'Want to put me out on the streets?' I tried to laugh, tried to normalise what had just passed between us. 'No, don't worry about me; there's loads of people I need to reconnect with who'll put me up. Could be like my own social life rehab?' He nodded to himself. He couldn't look at me. He felt sorry for me. Iain of all people and after he'd made me fear him. I wanted to know if there was any bit of my old Iain in there somewhere. 'This is probably just what we need. Could be really good for me, for us. I understand that, I really do.'

He got up and started walking slowly towards the door, leaving me on the floor. I turned to watch him leave. He looked at the empty wall, a grimy rectangular void where the film poster had been, but chose not to say anything.

'Where will you go now? With her? Did you stay with her on Saturday night?' I asked, pulling myself off the ground.

'No ... No. This is about me sorting myself out. She was staying at some posh manor house place. I went back to the B&B. You were gone. I tried to sober up.' He looked right at me. 'Did a bit of reading, as it goes ... Anyway, I'm staying at The Rose and Crown tonight. I'll come back here tomorrow if you're still alright with it.' I went to hold him, but stopped myself. I knew I stunk of sex with someone else.

'Kathy?'

'Yes?'

'We need to not be in contact with each other while I'm doing this. No phone calls. No texts, no emails. Nothing. I have to do this without you.'

'So you can be with her while my back's turned?'

He looked down to the floor. 'Katherine. I have got to get on top of the drink. If we're still talking to each other, I can't trust myself to not reach out to you, to not call us back to where we are now, and I don't want to do that. Do you understand? Just give me four weeks, OK?'

He still loved me. He didn't want me to see him go through

detox, but he couldn't trust himself not to want me back in the flat. 'I totally understand. A month. OK.'

'I'm going to go now.'

'OK. If you think that's the right thing to do.'

'And hey, maybe don't go finishing that on your own.' He gestured back at the bottle of wine on the coffee table. 'Looks like you've had a fair bit already. Who were you with?'

'Just Asif.'

'Asif. Right.' He looked towards the ceiling and nodded. 'I saw the whole thing, you know? Her on you? I saw it all.'

'Lily said she thought she saw you.'

'Thought she saw me? Oh, she saw me alright.'

He pushed his fingers hard into his eyes. 'I'm going to go now.'

He started walking out the door and down the communal stairs; I watched the back of my partner disappearing into the shared hallway below. He'd nearly turned the corner to the next flight when I called out to him, 'Whatever you were going to say…' He stopped without turning around. '…What you were going to say before, about what happened that year, whatever you think I am, or I've done, it isn't what you think.'

He turned and looked up the stairs back at me. 'OK, Katherine.'

And with that, Iain left. I closed the door and put the deadlock on behind him.

I threw my things into my Samsonite, but ended up transferring the whole lot into bin liners, because I'd be able to cram more into my Mini that way. My life. In rubbish bags. If you saw me in that moment, hauling my bulging plastic cargo down the stairs and slinging them into my car, would you have been happy? But I hadn't sunk low enough for you. No. Not yet.

I woke early and, looking around the mess of the flat, decided to get out of there, my boots crunching on smashed possessions as I left, thinking, *Let him clean up. He's made this mess.*

I went to the Town Hall Hotel in Bethnal Green. I could afford to stay there for a couple of weeks maybe, but booked just two nights to start with, hoping against hope Iain would come to his senses. If he didn't, I could see I was going to have to make some hard choices. Driving east that day, it felt like my life had been all about hard choices. Sacrifices. Being backed into a corner. Being forced to come out fighting, fists up, doing things I didn't want to do, being a person I never wanted to be. My life has rarely delivered me the luxury of the happy path.

When I got to Bethnal Green, the first thing I did was go for a swim. In the pool, my mind turned to work. Gemma had to be on the back foot now, surely, with all her niece had done to one of her senior employees. Against all odds, given how weak I should have felt, I found myself powering through the water, earning admiring glances from the only other person in the pool, some City boy type. If you need to know one thing about me, Lily, it's that I dig deep. Resilience. The one thing your lot are widely known to lack in abundance.

Patting myself down with towels I didn't have to wash myself, I felt surprisingly rested; positive, even. Asif had texted me the night before, telling me how much he'd enjoyed himself and asking when was the best time for us to have our review. I would have just stayed with him, if he didn't still live with his mum.

I'd decided to head in late. What was Gemma going to do, sack me? She wouldn't dare.

Just as I was about to board a bus to Borough around ten, my phone rang. Your aunt. 'You're going to get an email shortly. You need to read it and afterwards, do not attempt to contact myself, Lily or anyone else who works at Leadership Media. That's all I can say at this stage.'

Gemma hung up.

I shook as I waited for that email. It was probably less than a minute, but I felt my whole life get sucked into those seconds.

From: g.lunt@leadership.uk
To: k.ross@leadership.uk
Cc: hr@leadership.uk;
correspondence@bainesandlloydlegal.co.uk

Subject: Notice of suspension

Dear Katherine Ross,
We have been in receipt of a number of allegations in relation to your conduct and persistent financial impropriety, including unauthorised spending on your Leadership Media credit card.

These alleged incidents constitute gross misconduct. If any or all are proved this would constitute grounds for instant dismissal. However, we want to ensure you are treated fairly, so will establish the facts by means of an investigation before pursuing any further permanent action.

Without prejudgment, however, take this email as notification of your suspension without pay until further notice as we complete our investigation. This is in line with the refreshed terms of employment you signed under the new ownership of Leadership Media.

You will be contacted in due course. In this period, you are requested to not attempt to contact, solicit or respond to contact from any employee of Leadership Media.

Of course, I called Gemma immediately.

'You have been given very specific instructions not to—'

'This is complete bollocks, Gemma. You haven't even given me that credit card yet. What else are you and her fabricating about me?'

A pause. 'I'm hanging up now. Don't attempt to contact me again.'

I went back to the hotel lobby and thought about calling Iain a thousand times. I wondered if you'd have told him about my dismissal. But why would you? He might feel sorry for me, invite me back home. Eventually, I gave in and dialled his number. He needed to know he'd made me homeless and you'd made me effectively jobless.

But he had blocked me.

The caller was 'not available'. I'm guessing that was your idea. Clever. You knew you'd have to pull out all the stops to keep him away from me. You knew he would always need me because you didn't know how to let Iain be Iain. I, however, did.

Persistent financial impropriety. I knew you must have set me up and I needed to establish my lines of defence, in addition to never even seeing the card I was supposed to have been using for 'unauthorised spending'. A list quickly took shape:

1. Failure to defend me against the distress of an internet troll: they hadn't maintained a safe environment for me.
2. Age discrimination/nepotism: I was being managed out of my role by a younger, cheaper replacement, who happened to be the boss's niece.
3. Unfair treatment in light of my mental health: what decent employer tries to sack someone suffering health issues and offers such little support?

I would not go quietly. Not now I had nothing to lose.

CHAPTER 17

Katherine

No word from Iain. Nothing for four days. I thought about going back to the flat, but I knew that wouldn't do me any good. Too needy. Too dependent. Too not-me. I recognised I'd have to play the longer game and play it by his rules. Fine, I'd give him his month. There was no word from you, though that was much more predictable. Of course I thought about calling you, especially when I'd had a drink. But you would surely be anticipating my call. Not giving in and doing so, that was old me, fighting Katherine, showing you how much stronger I was than your expectations.

And no word from work either since the email. Sliding toward my credit limits, I had no choice but to check out of the hotel after four nights. I needed to start conserving what little I had. I called the mortgage company and asked for a 'payment holiday' (something that sounds jolly and really isn't). Iain paid our bills out of his Holloway rent, so I didn't have to worry about that. My life, out here on my own, it was going to cost if I wasn't careful. I made a new plan. I showered in my gym while I waited for my cancelled membership to expire, and necked sleeping pills and crashed in my car. That's what I'd do for as long as it took for Iain to scratch the itch of sobriety, get bored and start missing me. Wait for the shark to sink back to the deep.

I wonder, did my strength surprise you, Lily? Snowflake, the things I have done in the past, the ways in which I have dug deep you would never believe. As a child, I was half-starved by my mother. Today, you would call it neglect, but back in the seventies and eighties, it was discipline; it was what toughened us up, made us fit for the fight. You lot have absolutely no idea what people my age went through with our parents, even the good ones. Mine was not a good one, but she did make me strong when the going gets tough. I may have been weak those last two years, but I'm at my best in a crisis. I reckoned I could go for weeks like this. And as you know, I did. Living cheap. On the edge of what's tolerable. And in a way you could never understand, this is my comfort zone. I decided I would start to write again. Hard as nails and cool as fuck when the shit hits the fan. That's who he loved. Iain would eventually hear about what I was going through, and he'd see the real me, the old me.

But it was never easy.

Especially not that first night when I drove for two hours, trying to find somewhere both secluded and legal or, failing that, anywhere I'd have a fighting chance of being able to park long enough to get some sleep. It changed my view of familiar streets and neighbourhoods. I settled for a deliveries entrance off Church Street. I got there just as the pills kicked in.

Every piece of me hurt when I woke before the sun rose. I wondered again, why hadn't I tried harder to give Iain what he wanted. Who knows, building a family with him, maybe I would have been happy too. No, in my heart, I knew Iain and I would open new realms of misery were we to start a family. When we got back together, we'd come to our senses together, find a new peace. Maybe even a sober peace. We'd help each other write again; discover the next phase, think about our careers, maybe even think about leaving London if we thought that's what we needed to re-set.

My first manuscript: I would bring that out of the darkness, let him read it, or an abridged version anyway; make him understand my childhood and the choices I'd been forced to make. If I gave him a chance, he would understand.

I tried to maintain some kind of control. In those wilds of sleep deprivation and deep anxiety, I found a rhythm I could live with. I usually woke before five, parked up near the gym and waited for it to open. I cycled, swam, steamed, had a discreet nap, maybe, nursed a coffee in Costa on Stoke Newington High Street (avoiding the family-run places on Church Street where I assumed I'd be more likely to be moved on). Then it would be off to the library if it was raining, or if it was sunny, I'd drive to Highgate for a stroll and a sit in Waterlow Park or somewhere else I knew I'd have little chance of seeing you or Iain while he got whatever he thought he was doing out of his system. Shop sushi eaten while I sat on my jacket. Another nap in my car with my sunglasses on, book in my lap. Another coffee. Drive. Then, it would be time to find a place to park for the night, or get near to it until it was quiet enough to park there. Gin. Bottle of wine in a pub, maybe a salad. Sleeping pills. Car. Sleep. Horrific dream about my mother, blood, the farm. Repeat. I survived this way for three weeks without cracking.

I kept imagining how you'd present your lies to Gemma.

How far you'd go to look blameless. You'd fucked my partner and your aunt knew it. Pieces were starting to not so much fall into place, but drop away; become eliminated from my enquiries. I knew there could never have been a grand plan with Gemma to simply unseat me. If there was, it wouldn't have involved you screwing a forty-nine-year old jobless boozer. That was all your idea. Gemma was not 'in on it'. She wanted to be in the centre of your world, but she was outside of what you really wanted when you asked her to buy out *Leadership,* wasn't she? You were using her life for your own ends too. Using people like that, it's just what you do, your nature.

I thought I was starting to understand your modus operandi. And if I could understand that, I could understand you and if I could do this, then I could win. I'd felt this way before – the time right before my mother died. Seems I'm never calmer than in the darkest hours before the dawn.

Lily

8th April – Days of Justice

One last hurdle to clear.

When I know for sure she's realised she has nothing left in the world, that's when I'll sock it to her. I'll tell her about the universe of pain she's caused, and why it had to be this way.

In the meantime, life is sweet, a pretty warped sweet, I guess, but I have moments in the day when I feel something like OK. Now he's through the worst of the detox, Iain looks after me like no one I've ever been with. It's really no work at all. It feels like the kind of stable, predictable domestic set up I've never had. Like the one I nearly had with Charlie. Iain cooks dinner for me every night and he thinks my 'best self' is whatever one comes home to him. I've stopped trying so hard to play the woman of his dreams. I *am* the woman of his dreams, just by showing up. He doesn't ask anything of me, and what I give, I find I give quite freely. It's feeling rather easy because now I'm here, I've stopped looking for the angles. The relief is overwhelming. I guess I'm ready for what I've found with Iain.

I feel like I'm changing and so is he. He doesn't drink anymore and he says he's finding it easy. He was looking for reasons not to drink, now he has one: me.

She was gone, but he wouldn't let me see him at first. He wanted to become 'the man he knows he can be'. He was drying out and had been prescribed something to make it less awful. Apparently, the first forty-eight hours are the worst, so, after three days, I called him to say the concierge of the building was coming on to me. I didn't feel safe there anymore. He was letting himself into my flat. Was there any way I could crash at his …?

He left me alone on the first night 'out of respect for Her', but by the time the sun was coming up, he was knocking on the door of the spare room, asking if I'd just let him talk to me, explaining how restless nights were a symptom of detoxing, that's all. By the second night, he was asking to sleep in the spare room with me to try and find some 'peace,' an evening which ended with the inevitable.

By the end of the first week, we'd fallen into their bed. I think I could smell her still, on her pillow.

One time, a few days later, just after we'd finished, I had an idea. I shot up out of bed.

'Did you hear that? Keys in the door … It's her.' I grabbed his arm in supposed panic. He froze and we listened a while to the silence while the threat of her finding us sank in to his consciousness, eventually saying, 'I guess we're alright now, but she does still have keys, right? Do you think it would be a better idea, just temporarily, to change the locks while you properly dry out and we work out how to tell her? She can't find out like this. I couldn't do it to her.'

In the morning, a locksmith was called.

By the end of week two, the clothes she'd left were shoved into the corner of the wardrobe. He tipped out the rest of her drawers into the Samsonites they used to drag onto EasyJet flights to the mini-break destinations of Europe. These ended up in the spare room. He'd never felt so alive. Or in love. 'This is the happiest I've ever been,' I tell him because in a strange way, it really is. I'm looked after, I have a secure home, no money issues for the time being, since Gem made me Acting Head of Content. Bigger than that, I know my finale is nearly here. The punishment nearly done, my revenge almost completely executed. Everything is feeling *so* good right now. The breaking of bone. The chance to reset it cleanly.

Things got a bit sticky with Gemma, but not for long. She'd called me into the office to give my testimony.

'Tell me, Lily, honestly, what do you think you're doing with Katherine Ross's partner? I need you to look me in the eye and tell me the truth.'

'The truth is we became friends. We bonded very strongly and very quickly over our shared interest, writing. Then, things just developed.'

'Just developed.'

'These things happen. You remember that? You know what it's like to fall for someone who's already with someone else? At least Iain isn't actually married. No kids either. So that's pretty clean, wouldn't you say?'

As Mum told me on the sly, Gem's Big Love was a married guy with three children. She met him at her golf club in Norfolk. A lot of people got hurt by the affair, especially her when he decided to scuttle back to the wife. I was primed and ready to detonate this little grenade of truth. I'd been practicing where and how I'd drop it. I deployed my reality bomb perfectly. Gem wanted the whole conversation done with quickly.

'We're not talking about me, or mistakes that may have been made in the past … If this is one of your stunts, I need you to put an end to it right now. This looks very bad for me *and* for you. It was you, after all, who insisted we retain Katherine Ross. What's this really about, Lily? Tell me now, say you'll end whatever it is you're doing now, and I promise to help fix whatever needs fixing.'

'Nothing needs fixing, Gem. This is about … life surprising you. You understand that.'

Gem blinks and looks right at me again.

'If I find out there's more to this, there will be consequences. If you value your new role *and* your allowance, you'll tell me if there's more to this *immediately*.'

'I don't know how many other ways I need to tell you. I've fallen for someone I probably shouldn't have. No need to threaten to take away my sweeties.' Too much. At this I get The Face. Teeth gritted, cheeks puffing out. 'Gem, I promise you, there's nothing more to it than what I've said. Obviously, *clearly*, I'm *really* sorry it's causing you so much hassle. I get it. If I tell you that it's serious, that I'm feeling better than I've done since before, you know, would it make a bit more sense to you? It's early days with him, but I think, against all odds, I might actually be in something that could make me happy. That's the truth … We haven't always known if I'd ever get to feel happy again. This is big for me.'

The Face disappears. She's bought in. Of course she is, she doesn't want to believe all of this is 'one of my stunts', because that would mean she is wrong and my mum is right about me being 'wrong in the head'. It also would mean

Gemma Lunt, hard-nosed woman of business, is a sucker. Neither of these are allowed to be possible.

'Well, if that's the case, then … that's that … Just be careful, OK?'

'Always. Thank you, Gem, I knew you'd understand.'

She nods. Looks at me with eyes weighed down with empathy, then, 'I need to ask you about one more thing. Can you shed any light on any of these transactions?' She shows me Katherine's Leadership Media credit card statement. Champagne at the Rosewood, the leather jacket, shirt, pencil skirt and cocktail dress from her favourite boutique in Stoke Newington, the insanely expensive hotel for the night of the party in Sussex. Quite a rap sheet of profligacy. So KR.

'Wow! Not a clue, I'm afraid. Sorry.'

'Lily, Katherine said the card has never been in her possession.'

I could sense Gem preparing to analyse my every next word, every tiny movement of my face, just as she had done every time she'd questioned me over some 'incident' or 'unpleasantness' or 'stunt' I'd ever 'got caught up in'. I could see I needed to go a little further to convince her I knew nothing about the spending. If I didn't play this right, she'd start to wonder how someone unpaid like me could possibly afford my beautiful new leather jacket or my dress for the awards. I know by now you can hide whatever lies you choose in plain sight, as long as they're lies people want to believe and as long as you know when to use the right pieces of the truth.

'That's weird. Sounds like she's trying to cover her tracks? I mean, she never really got how this place isn't her own personal cash machine. I tried to help her see things are different now, but she never listened when she *so* needed to. Like when she used racist language around Asif. I tried to help her. I told her it was wrong. She wouldn't hear it.'

'She did what?'

'Yeah, on day two of me being here. She'd said something, like, *so* offensive to Asif, trying to be cool, I guess. She said she was "down with the brown" or something else about the colour of his skin? I tried to help her understand why it wasn't OK, but she didn't want to change. She didn't think she needed to.'

Gem shakes her head. She's stunned. 'Asif would corroborate this?'

'Yes. I'm sure he would.'

'Well, that's gross misconduct. She's gone. That's it. What a shameful way to end her career.'

'It is. It's a real shame for her and for us. For me. I thought I was doing the right thing, helping to keep her on. I guess I'm still learning too. I'm sorry.'

Gem smiles, squeezes my shoulder.

'You did your best for her. We all did. As long as you keep trying your very best, that's all I've ever wanted from you, you know that.'

'OK, I'd better get back to it, I'm planning forward features for next year. Things are going to change around here, I promise, for the better.'

'That's my girl.'

'Oh, before I go, I'm guessing you'll be clearing her things. Her filing cabinet included?'

'Oh god, yes, it's ghastly.'

'Some of the interns were wondering if it would be possible to use the floorspace for an air purifier? It would make a real difference to their quality of life here. Be good for morale?'

'Great idea. I'll ask Facilities to get onto it today.'

Later that day, the filing cabinet is forced open by security, its paper guts spilling out all over the floor. In amongst the rubbish is the final evidence Gem needs: the maxed-out card KR has never seen and I've been using to turn myself into a younger, better version of her. It's like that hunk of sad grey metal has been watching me from the corner of the office since I got here, like it knew its days were numbered. It's such a total relic, fit to burst with pointless old spiral-bound reporter's notepads and back issues from her heyday. There was almost no room for me to slip the card into the thin gap between the lock and the bottom drawer when I popped into the office on the Sunday after the house party. I couldn't wait to see it gone.

But poor Asif. Though he was getting super-annoying, it wasn't easy having to watch him being marched out of the office by security on the same day KR was suspended. Gem, on the other hand, could hardly hide her delight when she told me he'd both stood by my story about Katherine's racist outburst, and had been shown by IT to be the one sending KR death threats. For Gem, order has been restored. I am completely innocent of all charges. All is well in my world.

I sleep so well in KR's bed. Sometimes I'm dead asleep at 8 p.m. The draw of it. The sleep of the just.

CHAPTER 18

Katherine

It had been nearly three weeks. Any novelty my work-free, car-sleeping existence held had gone. The credit cards were teetering on the brink and the 'investigation' seemed to have ground into the sand. Perhaps their tactic was to let me bleed to death financially while I awaited my fate, then maybe offer me some miserable sum just to make sure I'd go quickly and quietly, once they knew for sure I'd be truly desperate.

I'd given Iain the best part of his month to get his shit together. I'd stayed away mostly, except for the occasional time in the middle of the night, when the pills wouldn't give me rest, when I'd sometimes park up on my road and watch my flat until I fell asleep, waking at dawn to the sound of foxes going through recycling bins.

I'd decided I'd done everything he'd asked of me for long enough, and let myself have a night at The Rose and Crown, confident it would all be over soon. I'd be able to get home, share my partner's money again, rebuild our lives. I knew he'd ultimately be relieved I'd taken the decision as to when we came back together again out of his hands. He always looked for me to lead when it came to us. This would be no different.

On the pub's roof terrace, with a cup of black coffee in my

hands, gazing at the spire of St Mary's, everything felt like it might be right again. My thoughts were clear. What Iain and I were, it had a rich, dark patina that you, Lily, could never replicate or replace. You couldn't provide what I could. I accommodated him, while you would fight his true nature. And your *assault* on Iain (how else could you describe it?) and my career, my best guess at that stage was you did a whole lot of shit just because you were so entitled. You thought yourself so precious, you believed you deserved everything someone like me has worked so hard for. I couldn't get closer to the truth than this, so it was going to have to be enough.

I felt that if I crossed paths with you that morning, before I headed out over the park back to Manor House, I would be very sporting about it all. I would advise you, in a sisterly way, to concentrate your efforts elsewhere and make sure you had something else going for you than great tits and a fuck-me smile because, believe you me, you were going to need it in less than ten years' time.

It wasn't yet eight by the time I'd decided I was ready to head home.

I didn't believe Iain would be sober. Without me there, he'd most likely be coming round about now. I waited for the butchers on Church Street to open and picked up the bacon and black pudding I knew he loved, and stopped by a bakery for a fresh loaf of sourdough (£4.80's worth!). I wouldn't let myself in, I'd press the buzzer, see if he was interested in my thoughtful offering (he would be). I'd put no pressure on him to start with, watch him cook while speaking of all the time I'd had to think, how much better I was feeling, how I'd started to look for a new job, begun writing again (I hadn't yet, even with all those empty hours). He and I would laugh. It would get to lunchtime. He would need a drink. I'd join him. We'd end up back in bed, or just screw on the sofa like the old days. He'd let me in again. I'd given him time and this was how that time was going to end.

So, I set off over the park, my overpriced groceries in my hand, buoyed by a sense of destiny and redemption. The trees bristled with life. I breathed the goodness of the park into me, until I was just approaching the Green Lanes gate. My eyes found themselves on him.

Iain.

That was him, wasn't it? How could I have forgotten my partner's face after just a few weeks? So lean, so young. He was running towards me. He was *running*. He hadn't seen me yet. This wasn't how I planned it, but decided it was a good sign that fate had brought us together.

He saw me. His face fell. He tried to keep jogging, then thought again and started walking towards me. He looked like a stranger. My Iain: a total stranger.

'Fancy seeing you here,' I instinctively went to kiss him on the cheek, like an acquaintance. He accepted the gesture and my heart began to break. He didn't even smell like Iain. No sweet boozy scent.

'Yeah.'

'You look fantastic.'

'You look great too. You always did. You always do.'

I nodded, smiling and blinking into the sunlight behind him. He looked around for words he couldn't find. 'Where've you been staying? You hook up with Donna again, or Debbie whatshername?'

'No, not her. Not them.'

'OK. Well, you look well. Where you off to?'

'To see you.'

'Right.'

'It's time you and I talked, don't you think?' And suddenly, I could tell he was trying not to cry, nodding into the middle distance as tears filled his eyes. 'Can I come round? Can I come home yet, Iain?'

He shook his head. 'Things … Things have changed. I've changed.'

'How? Is it her? *Her?* You know, she won't last the distance. Neither will you.'

'It is her—' he began.

'Oh, for fuck's sake, Iain.'

'It's her, but! But it's mostly me. I'm sober, love, I'm writing again. I feel like I've got some kind of a chance again.'

'That's great! You're dry, you're writing. You've achieved what you set out to do and now it's time to get to a new future. But that's not with her. You *have* to know that.'

Silence for a while. He seemed to be choosing his next words carefully. 'Me and you. I don't want to say it here, but I don't know that I'm good for you and I don't know that you're good for me. I love the bones of you, but … I can't anymore. I'm sorry.'

'Can't we just talk about it at least?'

'We do need to talk, but only to sort out our lives. Our affairs, or whatever.'

'You know, I didn't sign her off. I never signed her off!'

'You're talking sign off now? Seriously?'

'Yes. I am. The rules. Our rules. You let me down. You broke them!'

'The rules? What about your man, Asif? Think I wouldn't find out? You've been lying to me all along.'

'I have not.'

'Shagging you in the toilets in exchange for a good report? That's what he told Lily. Fuck me, love. Were you that desperate?'

'It wasn't like that. And it was after I'd had to see you *fuck* Lily. Remember?' He rubbed his eyes and then looked behind me, like he was searching for an escape route. I went on, 'I think it's right to say we've both made mistakes, but I *know* we can sort things out; we can get through this, we've been through far worse.'

He peered into my face with eyes so clear. 'But, Katherine, you don't understand. Things *aren't* bad. I mean it's sad, really sad about us after all this time, and I do love you. But now? The thing is, it's not *bad*, I'm doing great.' I shook my head. 'I'm sorry, that's just how things have turned out.'

'So, is that it then? You're just going to give up on us. On me?'

'I don't think we've got anything left to give each other. We're co-dependent.'

'Co-dependent? Well, I can see who's got to you.'

'Stop that. It doesn't suit you. Listen, are you going to be around this weekend? Because I do need to talk to you about stuff. About everything. The flats. About our money.'

Unbelievable. 'The flats? *Our* money? Well, my flat is mine and so's all *our* money. You haven't brought in a paycheck for years.'

'The flat's in both our names since the film, remember? And anyway, circumstances … Things have changed.'

'Changed how? I don't care you forced your way onto the deeds with your stupid, fucking dire piece of shit film that fucked my life forever, it is *my* fucking flat and I want *you* fucking out. Is she there now?' He dropped his head. 'In my flat? Nice. Thanks for that. Do you know what you are? You're a fucking disgrace of a cliché. I can't believe I've poured my time and all my fucking money into keeping you. Trust me, mate, if you've got her in my house right now, you will not have a leg to stand on.'

'Oh, I wouldn't be so sure about that.' Passers-by slowed up to listen to us. 'I think it's best if we just stop this now. This is getting seriously fucking ugly, and we don't want that.'

'Well *we* should have thought about that before *we* moved in that little fucking Snowflake. I'd love to know what, exactly, she's told you about me and her. You know she's only with you because of me? Do you know she was looking me right in the eye when she was fucking you? There! What do you make of *that?*'

'For God's sake, what are you talking about, woman? Your paranoid fucking conspiracies!'

'Mark my words, what's going on with her, it's a farce. It's all about me and you'll find that out soon enough, of that I am sure.'

'Have you heard yourself? Look, just get on with your day, get some rest. I'll be in touch, but please, don't come to the flat and don't blame her. And leave it with the batshit fucking theories will you? You'll get yourself ill again. I've got to go.' He broke into a run again before turning back. 'And please, *please* steer clear of the flat for a while. I'm not there. I'm at Holloway for a wee spell. I'll be in touch.' He turned around again and I watched his unrecognisably hardened form as it disappeared at speed across the park.

Not only had you taken my partner and my job off me, you'd somehow confiscated my flat and evicted both me and Iain. I almost had to admire all you'd achieved if your mission, as I was still sure, was to destroy my life. I burned inside. How I wanted to walk round to my home, let myself in, and hurt you. But that would leave me in serious shit and you sitting pretty in my home. I hated the world.

I dropped the meat and bread in the nearest bin and headed right back to The Rose and Crown.

I started drinking.

I drank all day and managed to score some cheap and nasty coke. I tried to talk to anyone who'd listen. No one wanted to be near me. In the end, I think I ended up talking to myself.

When the sun fell, I went for a walk. I found myself outside my own home. And there you were, dancing in front of a rectangle of yellow light from my living room.

You, dancing in my home. And in my clothes. You'd found one of my shirts and my old leather skater skirt. Your hips slid against the air, your long arms weaved towards my ceiling before you dropped them and ran your fingers down your face. You took periodic sips of water from your fuck-stupid filter bottle and held your stomach as if your dancing has left you dizzy and sick. You little fucking Snowflake. Were you all it took to take my life from me? Were you all it took to steal my home, my job, my fucking partner? Is that all you've got? I walked the backstreets until I found myself on the south end of Seven Sisters Road. I just kept walking.

CHAPTER 19

Katherine

I'd already been up for a while by the time you called on Saturday. What could you possibly want at this time in the morning, I wondered. I couldn't face you yet. You'd hear the darkness in my throat. I'd taken three sleeping pills on the way back to the car the night before, but by the time I finally roused myself, I was still unrested and exhausted.

You rang again. And again. The selfie you took of us, where we both looked so vital, so close to each other, kept appearing on my screen, mocking me, my stupidity, my desperation to believe that somewhere in you, you wanted me to be your friend. How that hateful selfie ridiculed it all as it danced about my passenger seat while I ignored another call from you. I knew I'd have to speak to you eventually, but I let myself enjoy the modicum of control not picking up gave me. In that picture, you were in the thick of your plan to take total control of my life. As long as I refused your call, at least I had some power.

I listened to your voice messages.

'Hi, can you please call me back?'

'Katherine, it's important you call me back urgently. Please.'

'It's me again. I know why you don't want to hear from

me, I know why I'd be the last person you want to hear from, but you need to know something, something really urgent. Can you *please* call me back?'

I wondered, would you ever give me the satisfaction of telling me why you'd done all this to my life? The nirvana moment where you admit your motivations then tell me you'd do anything to put things right?

My phone rang again. I was trembling. It took a few swipes for me to finally stop the phone from ringing and let me hear your voice.

'Lily.'

'Where are you? I've been trying to get hold of you.'

'Out and about. It's early. Where are you?'

'Are you sitting down?'

I looked about at my car as if you could see me. 'Yes, I'm in a café. It's quiet. Is there something you need to say to me?'

'Katherine. Iain's dead.'

Lily

14th April – Some Space to Think

I tell Iain I'll be fine, everything will be fine. But things have gone to a whole new level, so I need some time and space to get my head round it.

The truth is, I need some room to reset who I am. I could be so close to getting everything I've ever wanted. I played my hand so wrong in the past I can't afford to do it now. I called it badly with Ruth and it ended up costing me everything. I can't risk doing that again. I have to get my head straight and I can't have an audience for that. Things have got so real, I have to learn to stop pretending.

So, Iain leaves me in the flat. He's confused too, but he seems to get it. I've told him if he lets me work this out he can have me forever.

I will work this out. *I can totally work this out.* If I do, I think I've got a chance of making things end even better than they could have ever been.

I'm positive I saw KR outside again tonight. I'd been trying to pass the time with some stretches, a bit of yoga. I'd put some music on, danced on my own. When I looked out of the window, I'm sure I saw her stomping down towards Seven Sisters Road. I'd know her dark shape anywhere.

16th April – The Day Everything Changes

I needed a bit of headspace, that's all. That wasn't so harsh, was it? I didn't ask him for forever. I didn't want forever on my own. I just needed to get used to things.

I felt a new kind of happiness creep into me. When I realised what was happening, the kind of future I'd organised for myself, I wanted to lock it down. I wanted to stop faking it and start living it.

I got on the bus to Holloway before six, watching the sun rise over Finsbury Park. It had never looked so beautiful. It had never actually looked beautiful. It was time to tell Iain everything. Let him know who Katherine really is. Then, my new dawn, my own exciting new chapter. I'd already tuned-out Gem and Mum. I could keep that going until they came round and started fighting over me again. I thought about how they'd really like Iain, once they got to know him. I thought about how much *I* really like Iain, or at least what he could represent. I thought about how it's funny where life takes you, or in my case, where I take it.

The steps down to his basement flat are greasy and uneven. We'd have to spruce this place up and get it back on the rental market as soon as we could. He should just come back to the flat now. That's what I'm thinking as I let myself in. I start mulling over how we should be beefing-up security on the place as part of the refresh, then smiling to myself over how adult my thoughts have become in the last few days. I'm still smiling as I step quietly through the dingy little hallway.

That's when the smell hits me. Vomit. I'm scared to push open the door to the living room, but I know I have to. I will have to forgive him for falling off the wagon. That's what you do, when you're in a proper adult relationship because that's what I think I'm starting to get to with Iain. But it's impossible for me not to gag as I walk up to where he lies, out of it on a nasty two-seater pushed up against the back wall of the narrow little sitting room.

'Iain. Iain? It's me, Lily.' I'm about to touch him, and that's when time slows right down. My hand, reaching out for a still shoulder, noticing suddenly just how white he is. Sick, cold on his chin and down to his neck and the close-fitting T-shirt he'd just bought himself and seemed so proud of.

I want to cry, *No!* just like in the movies, but if I stay there another second I'm going to throw up too. So, I run out of the room and into the street above. I call the police. I can't bear to look at his body.

The police arrive and begin to lead me away. As they do, I notice the spent bottles and a couple of those little drugs bags. Empty. Traces of lines of cocaine visible on the table.

Oh, Iain, why?

I just needed some time. Not forever.

Now it's too late for you.

But it's not too late for me. I can still have a version of the future I've made come my way. Let's not forget either, where I'm headed now, it's a victory over KR I couldn't have even imagined. I've outdone myself this time. I'll never top this again. I won't have to and I don't want to.

The morning looks changed as the police drive me back to Manor House. Different, but still beautiful.

CHAPTER 20

Katherine

You told me you'd be with the police for a while, so I decided it was time to get back to my flat. I drove in a sleeping pill fug. It was hard for me to focus on the keyhole of the front door once I'd climbed the steps. How many times had he and I gone up these steps together over all our years? Coming in from nights out. Going out for a walk, then the pub. All but doing it, freezing our arses off on that doorstep the Christmas we first got together. I eventually got the key in, but it wouldn't turn. I tried to force it to move, but it refused.

You'd made him change the locks.

And now he was gone. I was on the outside, you were on the inside, and Iain was in the mortuary. How could that possibly be?

I viewed my key, bent and jammed in the keyhole.

I stepped back and screamed with rage and grief, before running back to my car, leaving the bust key in the door for someone else to deal with.

It was hours before I heard from you again and in the meantime, I drafted a hundred bile-filled texts:

Happy now I have nothing? You fucking two-faced lying bitch?

Congratulations, you have successfully fucked me and killed every dream I ever had.

I don't know how you can sink any lower, but I'm sure you'll find a way, you cunt.

But I didn't send them, I didn't want to give you the satisfaction of your total victory.

I swam in my complete isolation. I needed Iain. I craved his scent, the feel of his arms around me. I heard his voice around me all the time. Saw his face, saw men who looked like him everywhere. I desperately wanted to talk to him. I even picked up my phone a couple of times. In the coming days, I found places to vomit in peace in the evenings, so I could experience that familiar rawness in my throat, something to take me back to my past recently gone, Iain's meals, Iain's care. The madness of my grief.

When you eventually called, you told me how he died in horrific detail, and still I asked for more. *Did he give you any indication he was going to fall off the wagon?* No. *What had you fallen out over?* You didn't want to discuss that. *Do you think he'd got off his face with any intention of hurting himself?* You couldn't honestly say. *Why did the police keep you there for so long?* They must have asked you a lot of questions. It seemed like they were trying to see if there was anything suspicious. *And what did they say?* At this stage, they were satisfied there was no foul play, but there would be an inquest to establish cause of death. Only after that would they release the body so you could arrange the funeral.

'You?'

'Yes, Katherine. Me.'

'*I'm* his partner.'

'No, you are not.'

'I think you'll find twenty years together counts for something.'

'Some things, you'll find, count for much more. I will be making arrangements.'

I do truly hate the vocabulary surrounding death and funerals. That black time around my mother. Old ladies I barely knew offering to help with the 'arrangements'. Being asked to choose the colour of the cloth that would line her coffin, like it fucking mattered. Iain and I had always joked about him going before me. 'It's always the blokes who pop their clogs first, and I don't know if you've noticed, babe, but I'm not exactly a health freak. Don't bother with flowers or anything fancy. Just shove me out with the bins on Monday and go and have a slap-up meal on me.' He would go first, and I was going to be there for him, but not like this. Iain, what had you let her do to us?

'Fine, Lily, enjoy. Oh, and one more thing. I want you out of my flat. You know what you're doing is illegal.'

'So why don't you go on and tell the police?'

Silence for a beat, then before I could say anything, you hung up.

Days went by and I was going spare. I had almost no money and nowhere to go and no one to turn to. You joined your aunt in the conspiracy of silence against me. And all the while, I couldn't believe he'd gone. Eventually, I decided there was nothing else for me to do but wait outside my flat and face you, find out what the hell was going on.

Just after 8.30 a.m., the front door opened and it was my neighbour from the flat below. He stepped out backwards, carrying your bike down the steps for you. You moved on quick, didn't you? I saw you flash him the earnest and grateful version of your smile when he placed your bike gently on the pavement. I got out of my car and started walking towards you.

Getting closer, I could see you looked like hell. You'd lost weight. You were as thin as me. Your hair was flat, your skin grey, turning to white when you saw me. Right then, I could see older you, the shadow of middle-aged you falling on your smooth face. And I wished Iain could have seen you, looking that rough, all your novelty and vitality shod, because somehow I do believe his 'love' for you would have faltered. But that didn't matter now and you knew it.

'Katherine.'

'Looks cosy. Enjoying my place? And so much room with Iain gone.'

'Stop. Please.'

'What the fuck's going on, Lily? I want you out of my house, I want our things and I want to know when my partner's funeral is.'

'It not as simple as that.'

'It's perfectly fucking simple. You're squatting in my flat!'

'Gem was going to contact you. The funeral's next Wednesday.'

'Wednesday? OK. Where?'

'Dissenters Chapel, City of London Crematorium.' *That's where I'd have chosen.* Did you actually get close to him? I wouldn't let myself believe it. 'And what did the coroner say? About the cause of—'

'Death by misadventure. Drugs and alcohol.'

'Of course.'

'What do you mean, *of course*? He was doing really well.'

'So, what was he doing in Holloway?'

'I'm not prepared to discuss that with you.'

'You need to get out of my house. I want my home back. My things.'

'It wasn't just *your* home, Katherine. It was his too.' You said climbing on to your bike and pushing off the kerb. You were not afraid of me.

I shouted down my road after you, 'I want my fucking home back, you thief.'

That's when you braked. You stopped and pedalled back to me, fast. You got closer and closer until I had to jump back so you didn't mow me over. Your bike whined as you came to a halt at the last second, your front wheel between my legs, your face close to mine.

'If I catch you outside here at night one more time, I'm calling the police.'

'*You?!* You've stolen my home from me. They'll have something to say about that. It's illegal.'

'So is stalking. Stay away from here and stay away from me.'

You pedalled back, freeing me from your front wheel.

'I want to know why you've destroyed my life.' My words getting louder as you cycled self-righteously down my street and away from me.

The next time I saw you it was at my partner's funeral where it was you, not me, who played the part of grieving widow. Even after Iain had gone, you were invading what was ours, what was real. You'd put yourself where I should be again. You were brazen, beyond shame. You would have pressed that black pant suit you were wearing in my home, using my iron, looking in my mirror before you left. How was it you who prepared yourself for this scene in that way, not me? You looked more haggard than ever, but that might have all been part of the act. I knew I looked far worse, unwashed, untethered, so perhaps I was playing the part of the truly bereft better than you after all. Some small victory, though it didn't feel like one, and there was no one there to see it anyway.

I had no idea who would show up and, as it turned out, there are only four of us: you and me, and you'd brought your mother and Gemma along too.

I sat alone on the empty bank of pews on the left side. Iain's life and now his death, so small. A life without impact. A death without mourners. Family: estranged or dead. Friends: gone. Colleagues: forgotten. The smallest of lives with only a partner, a lover and her screwed-up family left at the end.

Who would come to my funeral? Who would be there for me at the hour of my death? My life in brackets.

You left the front pew to deliver the first eulogy.

'I didn't know Iain for very long, but he had an enormous impact on me, on my life. He was a kind, funny, generous and spirited man, who had recently made some great changes in his life, which makes his passing all the more devastating. I will miss him terribly and I will never forget him.' You looked around as if for a round of applause or something. Why are young people so fucking thick? 'Katherine, I wondered if you would like to say a few words?'

A few words? A few words to summarise his near-fifty years, nearly twenty of those with me? Gemma and your mother dared not look at me. I didn't let myself imagine what version of events you'd told them about your coupling for fear of exploding at you there and then.

I got up. I was woozy. No sleep at all the night before. I'd got to a stage beyond desperation, beyond loneliness. My gym membership had run out. I hadn't managed, or even wanted, to wash for days. I went to my GP for more sleeping pills and he'd sent me away with a new prescription for Citalopram, my old antidepressants. I picked them up, but I wasn't going to take them because I felt I was somewhere beyond depression too. I'd not eaten that day, or the day before. I was putting petrol in my car in five-pound drips. I was down to the last £43 on a credit card on which I had no hope of making the minimum repayment. Iain's funeral? It was just another out-of-body experience I made myself go through.

Limping up to the lectern, then looking out to you, all I could manage was this: 'I met Iain McIvor nearly twenty years ago. I loved him very, very much. He was my world … He was my partner … I don't understand what's happened. I don't know why he's gone. I can't imagine what drove him to the state he was when he left me, left this world. We'll never know why he felt so desperate, why he had to obliterate his feelings that night. I hope he'll be able to forgive whoever it is who put him there … My heart is broken. I love you forever, Iain. My Iain, I will miss you.'

You'd chosen the music well. I suppose he must have foisted his Teenage Fan Club, Sonic Youth, Jesus and Mary Chain tunes on you. When he did, did he dance like a dad, eyes closed, one finger pointing in the air, waggling a single leg, rooted to the floor? Or was it possible you'd actually got to know him? Maybe Iain was just a person whose life story you could tell in small paragraphs, not volumes. You knew he was a man trapped in time, an earlier time in his life. A young wild man in Glasgow, then London. A romantic. A chancer. A loser. In a coffin, the curtains closing as you watched beatifically.

Outside, you raced into a waiting black car and slammed the door behind you, ensuring I had no chance of speaking to you. Meanwhile, your mother approached me.

'I want to apologise for my daughter's behaviour. I'm so sorry for your loss and I hope you'll find it in your heart to forgive our family one day.'

Her accent. Not at all posh. Traces of Nottingham. She was small and plain. She looked like she'd had a hard life. She took my hand. Hers were rough. They reminded me of my mother's hands. She hummed with disapproval, like my mother. In fact I could see your mother disapproved of you in a way Gemma never would. I could tell she didn't know what to do with you. Never had, but in a completely different way to Gemma.

'Elaine, enough. Let's go,' said Gemma, almost pushing her towards the family's car from behind. She stumbled towards it and got in the front seat next to the driver.

'Gemma. While I have you, is there any update on the investigation?' I asked her.

'You want to do this here? Now?'

'It's just I haven't heard anything for a while. I'm ... I'll be honest, Gemma, I'm running out of cash. What's happening?'

'It's over, Katherine. You'll get a letter next week.'

'Saying what?'

'Saying you've been dismissed for gross misconduct.'

'What about the troll? Where did the investigation into that go?'

'It was Asif. Disgruntled for reasons unproven.' She looked me up and down. 'Anyway, we sacked him. All dealt with.'

'Asif?' I flustered. 'But, but what about my statement for your investigation?'

'No longer required.'

'Why the hell not?'

'Come on, Katherine. The massages at the Rosewood not enough? You thought you'd make us pick up the bill for two bottles of champagne too, then treat yourself to a designer leather jacket? Your dress for the awards and a five-star stay in Sussex? Close to ten grand on your corporate credit card. I warned you and you let me down. You made me look like a fool for defending you. I'm a whisker away from a vote of no confidence because of you.'

I hadn't made a fool of her, you had. Just like you'd made a fool of me. Your thefts had been staring me in the face, hadn't they? But I'd let myself be dazzled by the possibility of our friendship. No one was a bigger fool than me, especially because I still thought I had an outside chance of getting one over on you when you were, as always, moves ahead of me.

'Lily stole my Leadership card. She thieved it and fucked me over, just like she did at the Rosewood and the awards. Look at the evidence: she's stolen my reputation, my job and my Iain.'

Gemma nodded. 'Katherine, you may as well know we found your card locked in your filing cabinet. Do you know, I've always had an idea you were lazy, but I didn't believe you were a fantasist until now. Or a racist.'

'*Racist?*'

You'd been holding your ace up your sleeve; keeping it back to prolong my agony, toy with my half-dead body until there was no further sport to be had from me. I should have known, but I didn't, because I'd let myself think better of you. What an old fool I'd been.

'I could have got rid of you on week one. Lily told me you used racist language in the workplace. Sackable offence. But she gave you a chance.'

'Lily, giving *me* a chance?' I tried to address this to you as you sat stony-faced behind enormous sunglasses in your car. 'Now that *is* ridiculous.'

'Katherine, can I gently suggest we stop this conversation now? It's over.'

It was time for Gemma to hear my defensive lines. She couldn't, surely, shake these off?

'Your actions with Lily, the copy camp thing? That's ageism. You failed to take adequate account of my mental health problems. You … you failed to tackle online abuse against me – the troll threatened to rape and kill me and you stood by and did nothing to protect me! You failed to create a safe place for me to work. You *have* to take some responsibility here; at least give me a chance to put the record straight.'

'*Failed to create a safe space*? That doesn't sound at all like you, Katherine. That sounds rather like something *you'd* probably describe as a Snowflake's defence.' She paused to stare at a stain on my once sleek, now filthy, black pencil skirt. 'Unlike you, I have some respect for people Lily's age. We need them. They are smart, they are dedicated, they are a credit to us. They are everything you're not, which is what makes you so afraid of them.'

'I can demand redundancy.'

'No. You cannot.'

'But you must be replacing me?'

'No. Your role's been subsumed into a new one. We have a new Head of Content.'

'Don't tell me.'

'Lily. Lily is our lead on content creation.' She stifled a smile.

'*Content creation*? We used to call it *writing* before the whole world got so *fucking stupid*!' I said through teeth I realised were bared and gritted. I must have looked like a rabid animal. Did that make you even more self-satisfied, in the back of your funeral car?

'This is just totally inappropriate. I'm sorry to see things appear hard for you now, but you know—'

'Leave it now, Gemma. Let's go,' your mother called through the passenger window.

'You've never really helped yourself, have you, Katherine?'

You were watching me from within the car. My hate burned through me. The vehicle began to pull away. I ran forward, slapped my hands on the bonnet. The driver slammed on the brakes. Someone shrieked in the background. Yes, I looked like a woman possessed, a woman on the very edge and I didn't care. You needed to share in what you'd made me.

I walked round to your window and knocked hard near your face with my knuckles.

'You. You! This is all down to you. I know what you really are. I am on to you.'

I wasn't. It was an empty threat at this point. But it wouldn't be, soon enough.

I drove back to my preferred spot in Church Street, burning through eighteen quid's worth of petrol sat in traffic and getting lost along the way. I spent £21 on a bottle of Tanqueray and walked to the park where I sat on my jacket and started to drink it. My phone rang.

'Katherine Ross?'

'It sure is,' I said, pissed.

'My name is Mr Okoh, I'm the executor of Iain McIvor's will, his solicitor.'

'Will? Iain had never had a will. Always talked about it, never got around to it. Typical Iain, really. Anyway, we were still young, weren't we?'

'This is doubtless a difficult time, but I have a need to speak with you concerning the matter of the property you jointly owned with Mr McIvor. Are you able to come into my office?'

'No. No. Just go ahead and tell me now. He left it to fucking her didn't he?'

'Mr McIvor bequeathed his fifty per cent share of the jointly-owned property to his partner at the time of his death and she would like to initiate the process of purchasing your fifty per cent, Ms Ross.'

'Buying me out? Of my own home?'

'It could be the cleanest solution.'

'I don't have any equity! I have debts. I have *nowhere to live.*'

'So, I take it buying out my client isn't an option?'

'I don't have any options. Don't any of you understand? I haven't had "choices" for years! Did he leave me fucking anything? He's given her Holloway too?'

'You still have what is rightfully yours. We can make arrangements—'

'Ha! No. No I don't. I don't have *anything*!'

I hung up, swallowed the rest of the bottle down in ugly glugs that put most of it all over my face, even into my eyes. I staggered to my feet and smashed the wet, empty bottle on the tree trunk. As I tried to get back to my car, it could have been the alcohol, or it could have been the pointless rage taking over my whole body from my flushed face to my clenched wrists down to my unsure feet, but I could barely see where I was going.

Because it looked very much like you had finally won.

Lily

19th April – The Day I Start Again

I never thought it would turn out like this. I regret, like *really* regret, that he's not here, I do, but somehow this has taken my plan to a level I could have never contemplated. I've ended up with everything he had, everything he built with her.

I thought he'd just been speaking with a solicitor to sort things with the flat. A will? That had never even been in my head. I had no idea. I don't know about this stuff. Not really. But I guess I did say a few things here and there about my past home life, how the one thing that would make me truly happy would be never having to worry about the roof over my head. Financial security that would mean I'd never have to feel afraid of being at the mercy of Gem or my mother or the concierge or anyone else ever again. Maybe I've got to the stage where people like Iain will do what I want, even when I'm not trying? What does this make me? All I know is that Iain must have wanted to secure my future, should anything happen and then, something did.

Naturally, the police wanted to know more about me when they discovered he'd only just changed things; wanted to know where I'd been on that Friday night, etc, but my new (lovely) downstairs neighbour soon put them straight.

Obviously, we had to talk about what happened in Leeds, but we dealt with that quickly too.

Now, here I am in her flat. I've accepted Gemma's offer to help me buy KR out and make it all my own. I may be just another millennial borrowing from their family to get on the property ladder, but with my new, paid job, plus the income once I've spruced up Iain's Holloway flat, I have a genuine chance of paying her back. I can get my balance back to zero with Gem, then, who knows, maybe I can walk away forever. I won't need her anymore. I can be free once and for all.

I know how it all looks, but honestly, I never wanted it this way. I'm on my own again, but I've found I'd rather not be. I've grown. I've changed.

29th April – Iain's Funeral

I've never been to a funeral, let alone organised one. But today I'm sitting in the chapel, looking at Iain's coffin, with her on the opposite side across the aisle. I still can't believe it's happening. So surreal. I say a few moving words, then, well, I have to give her the chance to say something. They *were* together, at one time. Not a monster, we can all see that now.

She gets up. She looks like some kind of tramp. Her hair is plastered to her face. Her clothes look rotten. She speaks and she's clearly trying to blame me for Iain's death, but I think again about when I found him. What I saw, out of the corner of my eye, before the paramedic put a shiny blanket round my shoulders and turned me away from the scene. But it's her who gets to say to me: 'I'm on to you.'

She's finally putting the pieces together.

But so am I.

Asif called and now I'm getting the clearest idea ever of who Katherine Ross really is. Now I've found Iain's copy of *Creep Feeder* in his stuff at Holloway, I expect some answers on why *she* got to be such a force of destruction.

30th April – The Day I Get Out of Here for Good

I've finished reading, I know why Iain wanted her out of his life and why he didn't want me to finish the manuscript.

The idea of being anywhere near her makes me sick. I don't like being in her flat anymore. I know I won't be able to sleep here again. I feel her black life surrounding me in the night. I wish the morning would come.

Now I know I don't need to feel any guilt about her being homeless, jobless, broke and alone. People like KR want people like me to be more 'resilient', well, guess what? Now it's time for her to toughen up. Because this time, I won't stop her falling, she can throw herself right into the traffic and she can stay there.

I wrote a post for my blog earlier, just for her for when I've let her put it all together. But I'm not going to post it, not now. Not ever. She can let her doubts and her questions eat her up forever, until there's nothing left of her. It won't take long.

I've packed all my things into my trunk. It's 5.30 in the morning. I can see the sun shining from behind the clouds. I think I'll be able to sleep now.

CHAPTER 21

Katherine

I was a knockout when I was your age, but I didn't realise it, not until the sun had set and the height of my day was over. I thought it would shine on me forever, and I didn't care if it was right or fair to me or anyone else. I never questioned the source of that power nor cared how it minimised me or every other woman until I met you. I let the attention I received in my twenties have me believe I was special. I wonder now how many other women mistake what they experience when they are twenty-one as real power. Surely about ninety-five per cent of the internet revolves around the twenty-something woman: trying to look like her, trying to fuck her, trying to harness her power. Because power through youth and beauty is as fleeting as it is potent. Instead of beating men at their own game, dragging each other down, imagine a world where women protected each other when our lights are deemed to shine the brightest? What if we shielded each other when the male gaze perceives that light to die, at some ineffable point after your twenty-ninth birthday?

But we don't live in that world.

I have less than £3's worth of petrol left and I've decided to drive until my car just stops.

But then, there you are. I spot you near the junction at Green Lanes. You'd pulled up at the side of the road to take a smug sip of your fucking filtered cucumber water. You're getting back onto your bike now, preparing to pedal towards the junction. I move too, sensing the air change as you pick up velocity and your blood speeds in your veins.

Zooming away from me. Way ahead of me. Your life exactly how you'd want it. My London life wound back to the start, but with you playing me. Me but better. Me but prettier. Me but with bigger tits. Me but more charming. Me but with money.

Me, but equipped to win in the world as it is now, as it changes.

And now I have nothing.

Because of you.

I wanted to hate you from the start and now, finally, I really do. I never should have let you stop me with your smile, your fake interest in me, the friendship you manufactured when you saw how much I needed someone like you. You saw every fault in me, every void in my life and you deliberately found a way to fill it. Then you fucked me and made it so my Iain is dead.

I hate you and now I know what I have to do.

I will follow you. I will track you along the route you made our taxi take, only a couple of months ago now, and I will make it so you don't win in the end.

I need you to die, Lily.

I don't care what happens to me after today.

I'd like to have heard your version of the truth, so I could put you straight about what you think I may have done, but I have nothing now, and I care so little for tomorrow, I just want your shining life halted forever.

I think of all those moments; the first time you said my name, the first time I let you off the hook, the first time you made me do something I didn't want to, you cosying up to my Iain at The Brownswood, then straddling him at Greenings. As we edge up to De Beauvoir, along Kingsland Road, I think of Iain when I first shared my thoughts about you with him, how he'd let me down from the start. But then I remember how I'll never feel his hands, his familiar weight on me again and my anger is replaced by pure, deadening grief.

But I don't cry. I never cry. I channel my sadness into rage. Strange, I think this is what you do too. I grip the wheel hard and worry about running out of road before I get to do what I need to do.

Things are as black as it's possible for them to be for me, but it's such a bright morning, the light bouncing off buildings, all this glass in the City.

Five cyclists have died on this junction. Five young lives, just like yours, lost right here where six major roads join in the middle of the City.

Your back wheel fills my sight. I can almost smell your blood, running hot in you in the final moments before it gushes, cooling the moment it flows out onto the tarmac, before dripping into the waiting drains and down to an impassive Thames below.

I know only when this happens can I really begin again. Just like when my mum died.

The lights change to green. I slam my foot down hard on the accelerator.

You turn. You've felt me there, behind you. You see me.

You draw your breath in. Your eyes widen.

324

'Katherine!'

You say my name and it takes your whole face, from your cheeks, glowing with exertion in a vivid morning sun, to your shining black eyes. You believe I am going to kill you, just as I once lived in fear of you harming me.

My dominance over you is total in this moment. You tried to unpick my life, but I could take yours off you entirely.

I am above you.

I am the most powerful person who has ever been in your world right now.

I could wipe you out.

Or, I could spare you.

Because we've been through so much together.

I can see it in your eyes, you see that too.

No one else can understand us but each other.

In a split second, it's decided: I will use my power to allow you to live. Another chance for you. And me. We're one and the same, aren't we, Lily? That's the problem. That's the great thing about us. I'm in your head and you're under my skin. The enjoyment of my victory would not outweigh the pleasure of allowing your life to continue. You won't leave this earth yet. You won't leave my life. It's your lucky day.

I channel my whole body weight onto the brakes and my car comes to a violent halt that makes my own neck snap over the wheel and back again. I manage to catch my breath enough to wind down the window to speak to you in the now-stationary traffic.

'You,' you say, still afraid.

'Yes, but you don't need to—'

And I notice the tipper truck in the background. It seems

larger than it should, filling the frame of the road scene behind you as it blunders through an amber light before the junction.

It happens in slow motion.

It's as if you're being rolled backwards into some mangle. You're being robbed from the road by the legs first. Then the rest of you disappears from my sight.

I can't look.

I can't breathe.

I can't move.

A chorus of indignant horns. People who don't know why they can't push on through the rush hour and carry on the tracks of their normal lives; people who don't realise the tear in the universe opening up in the road ahead of them. Then screams. People flow towards where you are, but I have to get away from you. I mustn't be blamed for something I didn't do.

I get back to my spot in the deliveries entrance off Stoke Newington Church Street. Shaking. My car won't start again. I know that. I have no petrol and no money. All I can do now is hope my phone will somehow ring with news of you before it too runs out of power.

Someone does call, Iain's solicitor, now your guy. It's clear he doesn't know what's happened to you yet.

'It's Mr Okoh, Ms Fretwell's solicitor.'

'Who?'

'Ms Lily Fretwell's solicitor, in regard to the property at number thirty-two—'

'I think I know my own address after more than twenty years.'

'Would you—'

I hang up and ignore his calls. My home isn't my priority now. Because now I know your real name.

It's the skeleton key to your digital life and how quickly its locks yield now I have it. I use the dying power of my phone to discover what had happened to your life before you came to my bus stop that morning.

Fretwell. Unusual, but not posh like I'd imagined.

Yours is a very modern downfall tale. Funny, I think I actually read about your case in the *Daily Mail* or somewhere like it. An unambiguously bright life royally screwed by a youthful folly that would have been consigned to microfiche in an out-of-town library had it happened 'in my day'. But the day is now yours and people like you leave a dirty digital trail behind you wherever you go.

You were writing an article for some college rag. Once I'd read the trial coverage, I found the original piece: '*Getting away with it: women and the art of negging.*'

> *The strategy of deploying a backhanded compliment or kicking off an interaction with a low-rent insult, then following up with a higher grade compliment has been long deployed by male pick-up artists (PUAs). Remarks are pitched to undermine confidence and to gain the victim's approval with the ultimate goal being to have sex with the negging victim. Could reporter Lily Fretwell bag a male beauty using the method? There was only one way to find out ...*

Then a sorry escapade. You'd singled out a rugger bugger type, rolled out some questions designed to bewitch and undermine in equal measure. Sounds familiar. Must have felt like the perfect assignment for you. I recognised your modus operandi: build me up, knock me down, throw me a crumb of your attention. How easily I'd fallen. But it was clear you had a skill here.

I wonder whether you'd pitched the negging article idea, or if your arm shot up at the features conference when your editor asked for a volunteer. Whichever way it was, I could see this was your perfect assignment; getting inside someone's insecurities, homing in on who they wanted to be, who they needed you to be, then weaponizing all this against them. The coverage suggests you really fucked with the guy before you'd even laid hands on him. Your solicitor argued the physical assault happened because your (male) editor told you the splash was yours if you managed to get in his pants, literally, as people your age say all the time when they don't literally mean it.

It got to the end of your 'date', and he doesn't know whether he's coming or going. You've 'got inside his head'. You go to kiss him goodnight and you grab his cock. The trial coverage says he claims he told you 'No'. He told you to stop repeatedly. He was upset, confused. Whatever secrets you've got him to divulge mixed him up pretty bad and you'd hoped that had made him pliable. You'd just left him bewildered. But you don't give up. You wanted to win your story, so you touched him again, attempting some kind of dry hand job, probably because you weren't capable of believing anyone when they told you 'No'. It was likely incomprehensible to you that someone would stand up to your demands, however warped they were.

The boy eventually got away from you. He tells his housemates what you did to him. They convince him to speak to the university, who throw you out immediately once they've spoken to you and you apparently reveal 'a telling attitude to consent and the nature of manipulation'. He goes to the police and it reaches court, his housemates testifying to the distress and psychological damage you wreaked on their friend. I bet you didn't see that coming, did you? Someone calling you out, so publicly not doing your bidding, not falling into line, not being made complicit in their own undoing by you?

You didn't graduate. You holed up with your 'successful businesswoman' aunt as you awaited sentencing. You were guilty of sexual assault, but you escaped custody. You presented remorse, though I do wonder how much of that involved batting your eyelids at the judge. There was a lack of previous convictions and, apparently, they accepted your 'unsettled' childhood as a mitigating factor. But they still made you do ninety hours of community service and the whole sordid episode took your life off its tracks and exposed who you really were.

There's a comment under one of the news stories.

Just wanna say, this does not surprise me whatsoeva. I was at school with LF and she used 2 pull this sh*t all the time. She did some proper mental gaslighting on my mate. Made her want to kill herself. I heard she moved on 2 making some boy lose himself over some dick pics. School got rid in the end, but she's been getting away with this sh*t for 2 long. She's been let off lightly IMHO. She shud get banged-up for things she dun.

Gemma, the first morning, when I saw you in her office, her fingers gripping your shoulders, trying to force you to look into her eyes. She was telling you to behave yourself; be your best self. *Leadership*: your fresh start but also your final chance.

It takes only a cursory search to find this: *It is an offence for those convicted of a sexual offence to change their name or address without permission.*

Gemma and your mother flank you in the pictures of you leaving court, but you look so broken. Though in the picture your hair seems darker than today, you're being so obviously alone means you've never looked more like me when I was younger. Seeing your image is like looking through a window, not into the recent past, but one long gone and buried deep.

I want to dig up the truth of who you are and why you did what you did to me.

But first, I want money.

It's the morning after the accident and I wonder if Gemma will show for work today. Then, a truly maddening thought. Are you already dead? Are they now 'making arrangements' for you? Will the universe cheat me out of you giving me what I want, what I deserve? You shouldn't be allowed to take your secrets to your grave without me alone knowing them.

But you can't be dead because I see Gemma plodding up Borough High Street. I hide in the alley next to St George's, only emerging at the last second when she has no chance of dodging me.

'Gemma.'

She staggers back, her palm spread under her neck in shock. 'What do *you* want?'

'I heard the news about Lily.'

'Then you'll know what a testing time this is.'

She tries to step past me. I block her, my upper body sliding into the air in front of her. 'Is she alright?'

'She's very badly injured. We don't even know if she's out of the woods yet. Look, this is inappropriate.'

'Well, at least she's not dead. I was fretting.'

'Now, if you'll just get out of my way.' The heel of Gemma's hand finally reaches a pane on the revolving door of the building.

'I was fretting. Well into the night.'

She stops without turning back to me, 'What did you say?'

'*Fret ... Well.*'

She lets her hand drop to her side and takes one step back to face me. 'I don't know what you think you know.'

'Everything. I know everything. Every lie you and she told me. No. Don't talk. You need to listen. I was wondering, what price would you put on maintaining the illusion of the perfect family business?'

Gemma grabs the underside of my arm and pulls me back into the alley, before checking behind her.

'Blackmail?' she says through gritted teeth. 'This is pathetic. You *can't* be serious.'

'Why not?'

'You're going to try your luck now? While she's lying in pieces in a hospital bed. What kind of monster are you?'

'What kind of monster are *you*? Between the pair of you, you've left me with no money, no home, no partner. I haven't showered for a week. Your niece's little move with Iain means I've been sleeping in my *fucking car* for a month.'

'You can't blame any of that on me. At best you've been treading water at work, and there must have been problems at home already. You can't blame Lily for your partner's choices. Or his death.'

'Can't I? You don't need reminding. She is a *criminal*. I know the dark things she's done in her past. What else is she capable of? And who else knew what I did with my weekends? Asif? No. Her? Yes. She's been trying to sabotage me from day one.'

'Your failures as a writer and a human being aren't down to her, they are *your* responsibility. The sooner you accept that, the sooner you can move on.'

'Who the fuck do you think you are?'

'Go on. Go fix yourself, Katherine. You are not my family's problem.' She walks around me and is near clean out of the alley.

'Your niece committed a serious assault, then changed her name and *you* let her, you helped her hide her past so you could create your little publishing dynasty, enjoying another adventure in chequebook parenting by playing magazines together. I wonder what your board would think of that. Let alone the media. I know a good few old hacks from back in the day who'd love to run with this, the downfall of the Saviour of *Leadership*. And what, I wonder, might the police make of it?'

'What ... What do you want?' She watches the pavement below her.

'Twenty years I've given as editor. I want twenty-five grand for every one of them.'

'Come off it, I can't just give you half a million. The magazine's on the edge as it is. *You* took it there, remember?'

'You expect me to care now?'

'What about Lily? Isn't she suffering enough? What happens if we don't pay? You really want to punish her, for trying to get her life back on track and me for helping her?'

'As you said, Gemma, your family is not my problem.'

A pause. A forced softening. 'Look, Katherine. I think we should probably just go for a coffee. Right now. Come on, let's go. Let's discuss how we can help you.'

'Going to bring your little box of Kleenex and representatives from "Talent" and Legal? No. I don't think so.'

Another pause, the biting of the upper lip with the lower set. 'I'd like you to understand a few things. You know Lily hasn't had the easiest life. Yes, she's made mistakes, she's gone too far in the past. She needed another chance and I needed an opportunity to make things up to her for the mistakes her mother made, and maybe I made too. Do I need to remind you it's down to her you still had a magazine to work for, and down to her we kept you on, even though you'd taken *Leadership* to the floor? She deserves another chance. Just like you did. Never slipped up in your life?'

'Plenty of times, but that's not the point.'

'Katherine, the business cannot and will not pay you what you want. I would never get it through under any guise, so you're just going to have to find some other way of earning money. Another job, perhaps? But with your wild theories about Lily setting out to destroy you, if I was your doctor, I'd be profoundly concerned. Would you say you were quite well, Katherine?'

'I don't know.' I take a step nearer. 'Do you really want to find out?'

I'm close to her now. Her face is inches from mine. '*Your* money then. I won't report Lily Fretwell or you if you personally get £500,000 into my account pronto. This is the only way this ends well for you. Find it. Get it done.'

'You know you'll be committing a criminal offence.'

'Well, then we'll be equal, so you've got yourself a solid deal.'

'You wouldn't dare.'

'Gemma, as Lily would say, I like, have literally nothing to lose.'

The funds clear at midnight.

As soon as I can, I get myself over to the Town Hall. I get my boots polished, sleep deeply and enjoy a hearty breakfast before calling work. I get through to a new intern. I pretend to be a concerned reader who'd heard you had been involved in an accident.

They tell me where you are.

You can't hide from me anymore.

CHAPTER 22

Katherine

'I'm Katherine Fretwell, Lily's aunt. I believe she's in the high dependency unit?'

And I'm in. It's time to play my upper hand.

There you are, waiting for me.

All alone and a complete mess: neck brace, swollen head, tubes. Clicking. Dried blood around a bloated eye. A nightmare. I wonder how attractive Iain would find you now. Would he have chosen you in your iodine-stained surgical gown, or me, restored again? It would be no contest, surely.

I pull the curtain around your bed, because what happens next is about us and no one else.

'Time to wake up, Lily.'

Your right eye is stuck fast. Your left eye reveals itself slowly. You see me and your lid springs open with a grunt. You try to move, but you're only able to manage the slightest shifts from left to right.

'What ... what are you doing here?' you croak.

'You owe me an explanation.'

'From what I hear from Gem, you owe *us*. A small fortune ... so if you're here for your victory lap ...'

Your eyes close again. You're acting as if you could simply dismiss me. After all you've done. After I spared your life.

'I'm here for some answers on what you've done to me.'

You regard me with your single black eye again and somewhere under the water-logged puffs of flesh, that familiar malice ripples below the surface.

'How about what I *didn't* do to you.'

'Oh, Lily, let's cut the bullshit. Haven't you had enough yet?'

A pause as you ready yourself to study my reaction.

'The troll.'

'What *about* the troll? You'd have to ask Asif what he was playing at.'

'I did.' You're watching me, unblinking. 'When he called me after they'd sacked him. He wasn't your troll.'

'Well, of course he'd say that.'

'You know he wasn't lying ... I worked it out. I know who it was. So do you.'

A shot of adrenaline in my veins I try to talk over.

'Oh yeah, and did you also discover who'd racked up ten grand in my name, on *my* corporate credit card? Who fucked me over on my awards speech in front of hundreds of people?'

'"Slaughtered".'

'What?'

'"Hundreds of kids are literally slaughtered for her drugs". It was in Acceptableinthenoughties's message, after the party. It's *kind* of like what that boy said when you'd bust out your cocaine, but it's so obviously written by somebody old trying to sound young.'

'Asif—'

336

'Asif *nothing*. You logged on as him and you trolled your-self.'

'Of all the madness you've inflicted on me.'

'He didn't want you, but he did want me. You didn't like it one bit, but you did enjoy having an insurance policy against Gemma, something you could fall back on to show she wasn't in control as publisher. When you saw Gem suspected it was me, all the better.'

I breathe.

Skinless.

Exposed.

'Tell the truth for once, Katherine, then maybe I'll think about telling you a few things you'll want to know.'

I turn away from you and walk to the foot of your bed. I can't look at you. The injustice of you. You're lying smashed and broken in your hospital bed, so how is it me whose heart feels like it's about to give out?

'You don't know what it's like to feel truly desperate, Lily.'

'Think I've had it easy? You think people like me are to blame for how bad you feel about yourself ... You throw guilt out to anyone who isn't you for everything you think's wrong with your life ... not caring who you hurt along the way.' You're very angry now, spitting words at me through pained grimaces.

'I was the hurt one! After everything I did for Asif, he'd thrown me aside after five minutes with you. It *all* hurt like hell. My work, my home, my life, my *body*. I was supposed to be so much more than this, *have* so much more than this.'

'But you had so much. Can't you see that now?'

'Is that what this is about? You've come to teach me a

337

lesson about being *grateful*? Go on, then. I'm listening. I deserve to know why you've taken my life down to hell.'

You breathe, manage to move your head towards a bent straw in a surgical cup on the nearby wheeled tray. You close your eyes and your face contorts as we both listen to the water passing uneasily down your throat. I stare at you, gripping my fingers in each hand in anticipation of what you're about to say. You open your eye again and look me up and down; your vision rests on my clenched fists.

'Listen, Katherine ... I'm tired and I'm sure Gem's due any second. You should go ... this will have to wait for another day.'

'No. It won't. I can't.'

'I'm sorry. The pain meds, they make me very sleepy. Come back when I've had more rest.'

I shake my head. 'Do you really think I'm that stupid? If I walk out of here now, you'll make sure I never get in again. You've no intention of telling me *anything*.'

Your gaze shifts to the floor.

'Do you know what you are, Lily, when all's said and done?' You say nothing, but I can hear your ragged breath getting faster. You don't like it when I'm in control; can't bear it when someone else but you is winning. 'You are ten-a-penny. Even if they manage to fix you, those tits of yours will sag, your teeth will yellow and a hundred thousand people younger, brighter and more interesting to the world than you will come along. Iain would have got bored with you soon enough, trust me.'

'You're wrong.'

'Well, he's never going to get the chance to prove me right

338

and that's worked out rather well for you, hasn't it? You've walked away with all my property with no risk of him throwing you to the dogs when you dared to age, like he did me, like he would have you.'

'I'm nothing like you! Don't think that I am … I had no idea Iain was changing his will, but I know why he did it.'

'Oh yes, I'm sure you have a very good idea. I bet you dripped poison in his ear about me, post-coital suggestions he—'

'I'm pregnant.'

A thunderbolt in my chest. I grip the end of your hospital bed.

'Only six weeks, but I am having Iain's baby.' A familiar faux-sympathetic smile detectable on your face.

Words choke my throat. It's all I can do to whisper, 'Are you sure it's his?'

'Yes, and it seems fine after the accident. So you see, Iain would never have walked away from *me*.'

I feel as if I'm about to fall. 'I didn't deserve any of this,' I say quietly to myself.

Seeing me shrink, you find a new strength from somewhere. You shuffle your body an inch or two up the bed, resting your weight on your elbows; it's enough to make me feel like you're suddenly towering above me.

'You've got exactly what you deserve. You're on your own, Katherine Ross. You're completely alone and you're probably going to have to live that way for the rest of your life, just like I'm going to have to get used to bringing up a baby on my own because …'

For a moment, I feel as if you are crushing me to nothing.

'... Because it wasn't enough for you to help him die slowly with drink, was it?'

I remember when I last felt this weak.

It was right before I first realised my own strength. Back at my mother's farm.

It was when I held firm as my mother asked why she kept finding broken pieces of dry-stone wall on her quad bike's track to the far paddock. There was no storm, no rogue animals that might have knocked the rocks into her path. Did I know anything about what or who could be making her daily journey so treacherous? I looked right into my mother's face and I made my shoulders shrug while keeping my voice level.

'What are you saying?' I ask you now, my breath steady.

'When I found Iain, on the coffee table, there were traces of cocaine.'

'The inquest said he'd had loads. I knew Iain, much better than you: the coke made him drink more. This time so much that he couldn't wake up when he needed to.'

'The traces were neat and horizontal.' Your eye rests on me. 'Like Iain said at the party, like lines on the page of a reporter's notepad ... You were there, weren't you, Katherine? You were involved in his death and now I'm going have to rely on my mum and Gem, and history gets to repeat itself and that's not fair! I know it's your fault! I know how far you'd go to take revenge ... I read *Creep Feeder*, Katherine, and I know *exactly* what you are.'

I walk back towards you.

'OK, Lily. What happens now?'

I take another step closer.

'Now ... Well ... Please. Leave.' Now it's fear that undulates

340

under the surface of your skin. I can hear it now, seeping into your voice, see it reaching your wide open eye.

A step nearer.

'Gem's on her way … I think I can hear her.'

We both listen to the sound of nurses laughing at their station at the far end of the ward. Shift changeover. They wouldn't necessarily hear a patient in need.

Suddenly, your eye searches our curtained confine. I could do whatever I wanted with you now. This must be how you felt when you thought you'd won it all: my home, my Iain; when you'd seen me arrive like a tramp, homeless, penniless, a fucking guest at my own partner's funeral. Now it is you who is without power. You try to sit up fully, but whimper quietly. You're too weak, in too much pain.

'Katherine … Please, don't come any closer.'

You're afraid of me. I never wanted it this way, but here we are.

Closer still.

'You know who I am to you, don't you? You don't want to hurt me … I'm begging you … Katherine, stop, I wrote a blog post yesterday, just for you.' I can feel your breath on my face now, coming fast. 'Can I tell you what it said?'

As close as I could possibly be to you now.

'I didn't get round to posting it yet … but in it, I'm asking you if we could start again. Because we have a connection. You understand me. I understand you … You feel it too … You're what I've been looking for … I want you in my life. Would you like that, Katherine?'

You search every bit of my expression and in return, I examine your pale forehead, the smashed swell of your cheeks, those lips.

'So maybe you don't have to buy me out of the flat anymore?' I say to you.

'Of course not,' you tell me.

'Maybe I could help you with this baby?'

'Absolutely. Let's make plans soon.'

'Maybe I should move back into the flat? With you?'

'That … Makes total sense.'

I rest my forehead on yours and wait a moment while our pulses come together once more.

'And maybe I'm not as fucking clueless and desperate as you think I am.'

You try to recoil from me, but there's nowhere to go. 'Katherine, no!'

I grasp your shoulders.

'Do you really think I'm that needy?' I shake you. 'Do you honestly believe I'm going to buy your lies? Now? After what you've accused me of?'

'Stop … Nurse!'

I push you back onto the pillows and clamp my hand over your mouth. You need to hear this. 'Listen to me, I'm *not* going to hurt you. I've never wanted to hurt anyone, I've only ever wanted to be loved. By my mother. Iain. You.' You grunt and squirm, your left eye darting madly about. 'But you *all* hurt me. And you? You came into my life and you killed everything in it.'

Your hands are flapping around like wounded birds before eventually finding my forearms and gripping my flesh, begging me to let you speak, but I'm not done yet. 'Yes, we do have something.' You moan and you whine beneath my fingers; a machine begins to beep uncontrollably, the hospital itself conspiring to not let me be heard. 'There's something between us and all I've ever wanted is to understand it, explore it together.' Your eyes are closed now. 'Listen to me!'

Your neck slumps, all tension, all fight gone from you.

'Lily!'

You don't open your eyes.

'Come on, Lily. It's your turn now. I want my answers.'

Your stillness finally registers.

You've made me silence you forever.

I'm so angry with you for doing this. Because you've cheated me out of what was mine. Again.

Creep Feeder

There are times when a lamb is a lost cause. You do all the usual tricks, blade of grass up the nose, jab of dextrose, shove them in the warming box, but they're done for. Some are just too weak. 'Born goners.' Worse than them are the ones that take the perfunctory and economically-minded attention you give them as love. They don't want to go back to their mothers and their mothers don't want them because they stink of you. Best to keep them at arm's length. This helps even the weak survive.

Perhaps this is what Mother thought.

Perhaps her cruelty was actually love. Giving the girl the gift of resilience. To be able to survive on workhouse rations of food, complementing the diet of insults gnawing away at the girl's soul. Being told for as long as she'd remember how she was the millstone that kept Mother in this hell, how she'd come to nothing, how she was nothing, how she deserved to have nothing and be nothing. No, this could not really be love, the girl concluded.

The born goners, the ones that can't come back from hypothermia, you can see it in their eyes.

Her mother always knows. Shouts at the girl to walk away.

When the daughter was younger, it wasn't easy. Not just watching them die, but after every death or stillbirth, her mother telling her that's what she had wanted to do to the girl at her birth. The girl's heart aches. There have been many days when she so wished Mother had let her die.

A lamb dying is easier for the girl since she's watched dozens of innocents go, but even now she's seen the light of life die in many a newborn animal's eyes, the girl would never say standing by and letting death happen was an effortless thing.

The girl's father's death had not been effortless and neither had watching it been. She knew she was more him than her mother.

One day, when she is eighteen years old, she finds her father's old biker jacket in the attic, slipping it onto her bony shoulders had felt like being held by a ghost. Love. Being loved, the greatest protection anyone can have from the rest of the world. She never wanted to take it off.

When she comes down to feed the sheep the next day in the jacket, the mother says nothing, but when the girl gets to the breakfast table there is no food, just a quarter glass of milk. The girl knows she is being punished. The same happens for five days.

The girl will not give up her father's coat of armour and her mother will not begin feeding her breakfast again until she does.

Her mother returns from the field the first day the girl decides to show her mother who she really is, that she won't back down every time, that she can't be controlled by food. The mother doesn't dare look her daughter's show of strength in the face. Instead, the mother asks the girl to look at the dry wall on the west side of the far paddock, tells her it needs fixing because some stones have found their way into the middle of the quad track. She could have been killed.

On the second day, the girl doesn't see her mother return from the paddock, but when she comes to the breakfast table she finds four lumps of rock where her food should have been. Mother knows, of course she knows what the girl is doing is deliberate, but to start any kind of dialogue on it would be to admit the girl is fighting back. The girl is a fighter and fighters can win. Mother's doctrine is that the girl is born to lose. To recognise the fight would be an act of heresy against herself.

On the third day, the mother doesn't return.

When late afternoon comes, the daughter walks slowly to the far paddock, admires her handiwork, a hidden landscape of stone under muck she'd compacted down to disguise the obstacles that would send her mother's quad flying eventually.

The girl is third time lucky, because now her mother is a different shape; her neck at odds with the rest of her, under her quad, wheels facing skywards. The girl has brought a loaf of bread and a can of lager with her. She sits in front of her mother and begins to tear at the loaf with her teeth.

The mother is no 'born goner.' When the girl returns from replacing the rocks and reordering the disrupted earth with her hands and feet, the light in her mother's eyes burns hot and angry still. Though she cannot speak, her eyes tell the girl all the things she knows already. Her mother's disappointment. Resentment. Rage. This time, the girl may deserve them.

Dusk arrives and the light in Mother's eyes finally goes out. It is done. And now it is time to live.

CHAPTER 23

Katherine

That night I saw you dancing in my clothes, in my flat, I went straight to Iain to make him see the lunacy of you having kicked us both out.

That same night I learnt Iain had given up everything – booze, drugs, meat, dairy, fucking gluten – but he knew as well as I did that there were just some occasions when you have to think *Fuck it*. That's one of the many, many issues with people your age. You just don't know when to say *Fuck it*; have that drink, say exactly what you feel, when you feel it, get off your heads when you need to. To do something in the moment, regardless of the consequences, not decide how you feel about something once you've asked Twitter, or once you've recorded and shared it. To embark on a course of action after you've processed your feelings. To do and say what you want to do exactly when you want to do it is the terrific gift of youth. And there's a well of forgiveness around your bad choices along the way; the gilded idiocy of youth. Your lot infuriate me because you're happy to squander the gift of the impetuous at every turn. Iain, in his heart, he still knew the intrinsic goodness of *Fuck it*.

He was, in fact, a Fuck it King and I loved him for it. There were times when he was ill with drink that I'd think about reining him in, gently disenabling him, but to do that was to change Iain, and I loved him just the way he was. Not like you.

He didn't want to let me in to his Holloway flat that night. Not at first. He was 'going through something' with you. He was giving you some space and he still needed his distance from me. He looked like he had the weight of the world on him.

'I know, you're serious about her, I get it, it's just that I can't believe she's chucked you out of your own place too!?' He tried to defend you, but I spoke over him. 'Anyway, I just thought these might be in order,' I held my bags of wine and meat up, 'while we chat about how we're going to *consciously uncouple*,' I smiled.

He viewed his feet for a second. 'No, Katherine. I've been doing really well. I don't need it anymore.'

'So then, you're well. Come on, one more meal. For old times' sake? You look like you could do with it.'

'No. I'm sorry. This isn't happening.'

'Please. Don't make me beg. Can we just have one final meal, like the old days. Please, let me say goodbye to our life together. You owe me that. You only asked me to move out for a few weeks. Now. Well, now … Please, cook for me? Have a little glass with me? Do this, and I'll make it easy from here on in. I promise.' He didn't look up from his shoes. 'If not for me, then do it for her. You don't want to inflict ugly court stuff on her when she probably just wants her honeymoon period with you. Remember our early days? Magical. Incredible. Are you going to deny her that?' The tears came, right on cue.

'Don't cry, please. It's not you.'

'You're right, you're right,' I said, swallowing. 'So are you going to let me in, or what? One final supper and let's see if we can't make this quick and painless.'

He looked into my face. 'Are you sure you're ready to do this? Things got pretty ugly in the park that day, and, well, you look like you've probably been on one already.'

'Yes, I have been drinking. And thinking. I'm getting there. I just need to sort things out like me and you; not like some old married couple who hate each other. Break bread, have a tiny wee drink. Because we don't hate each other do we?'

Here, I'm being Cool Katherine, I'm-alright-really-Katherine, though I was boiling angry with him *and* you. The walk had sobered me up which made me realise that mad-as-hell me wouldn't be the most effective, the most likely to win him back, and bring him round to seeing what you really were. I needed to be cool, Shit Happens me. Was this your process too? It feels powerful, doesn't it? A sleight of hand, a trick of character. Dialling up this element, dialling down that. Moulding and presenting yourself as the ideal lover, the perfect friend. Short-circuiting your connection with another person. Cheating your way to it. Which Lily were you with him?

'Of course we don't. Come on then, come inside. I'll cook, let's talk, but I can't drink with you, OK?'

'OK, Iain, your rules.'

I was in.

The first drink, he refused. The second too. 'No, no. I can't. Not for me, really.'

'I think you deserve it, don't you? Whatever she's putting you through, I can tell it's hurting you. Give yourself a bit of a break. You know you can get back on the wagon tomorrow, right? Listen, I'll just pour you a glass, then it'll be your decision.'

We talked for a while before he took the meat off me to marinate. He'd left the drink untouched to that point, but took the glass away to the kitchen with him, ostensibly to use the wine to tenderise the lamb.

He returned with an empty glass.

Without looking at me, he filled it to the brim again, a grimness in his eyes. He downed it like a parched man, eyes closed as he gulped. I could see every muscle in him give in to the familiar warmth of booze, of being with me, just like we had been for years. His eyes stayed closed for a while before he opened them again to look straight at me, that familiar twinkle in his grey eyes. My Iain. I *could* get him back. This was working out.

'Fuck it, eh? One last time. We deserve a normal meal together, don't we, love?'

'I believe we do.'

I refilled his glass.

We'd sunk nearly two bottles, the lamb shoulder I'd bought from the Halal butchers on the way pulled off its greasy bone and finished. So, I took out the coke. 'Don't be mad,' I said as I began racking up rows of clean and tidy lines.

'What are you playing at!?'

'I had loads left over from, you know. Thought we may as well go out with a bang.'

He laughed, but I saw that grimness again as he leaned forward and took the rolled-up £20 note off me, shaking his head. But just imagine how deep-down happy he would have been about all of this; to see a familiar face and the resources he needed to feel better: a river of Rioja to rinse off his sadness, a cheap piece of meat for him to cook into succulent submission, and a good amount of coke, so he wouldn't have to worry about running out. *Fuck it. C'mon!*

We talked about the first time we shagged. And the last. I wanted to fuck him again. This was his chance to come back to me. I wanted to show him what I knew he would have been missing. We could reunite and get you out of my flat together. He'd come round to my way of thinking; he'd have to, surely, given you'd managed to evict him from his own home, my home.

'I know part of us was always being with other people, but it was always you. You were the best. No one else feels like you. Nothing else feels like us, does it?' I reached for the zip on his jeans.

'No. I'm sorry. I can't. Kathy, we're too … fucked.'

'But we're not. We're not screwed, not really.'

'No. No, we are … We're gone. And I love her. I need to love her.'

'But she's thrown you out. And can you really say that's it for you and me?'

'Yes. I'm sorry, but there it is. It's really over now. We're just too … fucked.'

'Stop fucking saying that!' I shouted. I shouldn't have raised my voice. It showed I'd lost control and meant he felt able to challenge me back. My plan for the night wasn't working out after all.

'No, I will. I will because d'y'know the biggest fucking

issue here? The big fucking problem at the heart of *all* this is *you're* fucked … I can see that very fucking clearly now. *You're* fucked,' he slurred the 'ck'. 'You've even fucked me up tonight. I can't believe I let you. Again. I can't … I just can't be part of this anymore.'

'That's not fair. Now you're sounding like a cunt! My illness? Are you trying to punish me for that?'

'No. And you know I never would.'

'Iain. I deserve to know why you're punishing me. How has it been so easy to just give up on me after all we've been through?'

'I don't want to. Please, can you not?'

'*Iain.*'

He took a slug of his booze. 'You sure you wanna hear this, because this is going to be hard to hear, it's fucking hard enough to say.'

'*What* is?'

'Your manuscript. The first one. I read it.' He peered at me for a reaction while taking another gulp. I didn't give him any. 'I found it and I read it. You never let me see it. Because that's no work of fiction is it?'

'Is that what you found on my laptop that morning? Why did you bother reading *that*? I wrote that more than twenty years ago. It's early stuff … Fantasy. What were you going to do with it?'

'This is the sad thing. I was feeling fired up about writing again, thinking I could get into it again and I thought, maybe, if you reminded yourself of what you were capable of, it might get you going again too.'

'What I'm capable of?'

'Oh, don't you worry, love. Your secret's safe with me.'

'No secret. *Fantasy*. I had a very hard childhood. You know that.'

'Hey, I promise, I won't say a word, but I don't want any part of it. I have to get well. I've got to protect our future.'

'Our future?' *Still me and Iain? Together?* My heart beat a little harder, an injection of joy, or relief at least.

'Yeah, our future together, mine and Lily's.' My heart fell again. 'I can't get into it, but we've definitely got a future. I've got to look after it.'

'Your future.' I looked at my hands. They were dry and rough, blue cords of veins shooting up above my wrist bones in ways I'd only just noticed. Just like my mother's.

'You're going to regret this, Iain.'

'No I'm not.'

'Well, let's just say if you think I'm going to make this easy for you, let you walk away with half my flat, you're dreaming.'

'And let *me* tell you *this*: if you so much as think about trying to fuck this up for me and her, you'll find Derbyshire Constabulary opening up a very fucking cold case.'

Neither he nor I spoke for a moment.

'Iain, have you and her not fucked my life enough yet? Not taken enough away from me that now you're cooking up this complete crap about my manuscript? Where's your copy anyway?'

'Somewhere safe.'

'OK. Well, I can see you must be very serious about you and her, if it's come to this.'

'I am. I have to be.'

'You're wrong, you know. You've completely misread my intentions when I wrote *Creep Feeder*. But it's OK. Honestly,

I get it. It'll be fine. I won't make things more difficult than they need to be. Your future. My future. Two separate things. I see it. So, let's say goodbye now. Say farewell to the past. Drink to that?' And I filled his glass, put a drop in mine, then watched him down what I'd given him.

'Here, you relax, while I clean up.'

He watched me as I took the rest of the pots to the dishwasher.

He didn't notice when I returned from the kitchen without a glass for myself.

He kept drinking as we talked about the first time we met: at a Japanese bar in Soho, long-closed now. We'd both peeled away from our respective work Christmas parties. Talking with him had been so easy, so funny. We both hated *Titanic*. Everyone else loved it. We didn't. Were we always bonded by our hatred of the stupid things other people loved – vanilla sex lives and marriage, not being able to say, *Fuck it.*

He was getting more and more incoherent, dropping off into micro-sleeps from time to time. In those moments of lost consciousness, I'd take a tea towel and wipe each empty bottle clean of my fingerprints in turn.

In a moment of wakefulness, he said, 'Do you know, Katherine Ross … you're a fucking amazin' woman. I'll always think that, no matter what you've done, no matter what happens to us, and, you know, I never meant to hurt you.'

And yet I always end up hurt. I always end up being made to do things I don't want to do; things that hurt me even more.

'I know you didn't, Iain. But it happened.'

'I never meant to hurt you, babe. I didn't. You're such, such … an incredible woman.'

'Well. I think you should probably drink to that. Why don't you top yourself up?' He clumsily pawed each empty bottle in turn.

Even as I watched him lose control, I could remember how easy it was to fall in love with Iain and how hard it was going to be to do what I needed to do next.

He filled his glass one last time.

'Tomorrow … I'm dry forever.'

All the wine was gone. The drugs were finished.

Iain's night was done.

I had to protect myself from any more hurt. Just like I did with my mother, I had to make sure I was free and stayed free. Sometimes being in control is where that starts. I think you understood that. Not everyone does, but you did.

His thinned-down form had slid down the arm of the beat up two-seater. I was standing over him, observing him, there on his back, knees poking into the air, his mouth agape. Grandad after Christmas dinner here again. And l loved him. I will always love him.

His breathing was regular and shallow.

'Iain. *Iain?*' I shook him, but he was too far gone.

I put my jacket on, went to the kitchen, to the dishwasher. I let my leather slip off my shoulders and put one set of cutlery, crockery and the glass I'd used back into the cupboards and drawers. I also removed the bowl he'd used to prepare the meat that night. Iain and his marinades. Alchemy that could turn tough flesh into supple delight, transforming the undervalued into the much-appreciated, using time against itself on older cuts of meat; with patience, the flesh could become more desirable than that of a spring animal. I thought he'd stick with me. I thought his patience would last forever. I thought there was value in that. A depth between us built up over time. Not always easy, but better than anything you could offer. That's what I thought, and I was wrong. You had a hold on him stronger than mine.

Pinching the bowl between my leathered grasp, I took it back to the living room and placed it on the carpet. On my knees, I hovered above it, forced two fingers to the back of my throat and filled it. I turned to see if he'd been disturbed by my retching. No.

I went to him, used my finger and thumb to widen his already gaping mouth and started to gently pour the contents of the bowl into it.

He spluttered and he gagged, but his head didn't turn. I poured some more, slowly, steadily. More spluttering. I went back to the kitchen to wash the bowl and when I returned, he was still and quiet.

Iain.

My Iain.

Realistically, there was only ever one end for Iain once he'd left me. Some people can't survive without the stronger half of their couple. You were too young to realise this. If someone ushered the exact moment of his end forward, I hardly see that as a major crime.

The police suspected no foul play. A coroner's inquest concluded he'd choked on his own vomit. No forensic investigation. I suppose it's because he was so clearly a sitter for an early death. Not a born goner, but marked for the grave once he'd chosen you over me.

CHAPTER 24

Katherine

Your death too was the outcome of a tragic accident. It's official. I was a blameless bystander, but still, I wasn't invited to your funeral today, despite our connection. But not going today, that's OK with me, really, because there's a part of me that doesn't want to say goodbye to you. The world lacks a certain colour without you in it. It doesn't keep me so alert, so awake as it did with you, so I'd like to imagine you're still here.

It's a good job I'm so busy now, otherwise I'd likely get ill again. I'm starting a new website: www.freshdirection.com. I might actually make some money from it. Imagine. I need to hand over some of the leg work. I'm advertising for my own interns next week.

I'm also contesting the will and things are looking very good there too. Iain's detoxing, combined with your lies and your history of manipulation, made it relatively straightforward to suggest 'the testator was coerced into it without a sound mind'. Both flats will be officially 100 per cent mine, but it's only on the day I know you and the baby are in the ground that I feel able to return to my own flat, a locksmith in tow.

You've made me have to break into my own home. Some achievement. Again, I feel that grudging respect you must have had for me too, surely? When I finally get inside, I also appreciate how you've cleared so much of the stuff Iain and I had collected over the years, chucking out all I'd smashed up. Not even The Film poster is here. My home is blank again. It looks ready for a new start.

But when I think about going into my bedroom cold fear takes me over. I'm afraid to go in there, to be made to imagine what you did in there with Iain, to see for the thousandth time the image of you on him in that horrid garden behind my eyes. I never want to see that image again, but I will. I see it every day, one hundred times a day.

I'm relieved when I find the room is bare, save for your red trunk which is packed and ready to leave. Where did you think you were going?

I look around, as if checking whether you're watching me still, before running my fingers along the beat-up leather straps over the top of the case. I let my fingertips rest on the scuffed gilt of your true initials. I feel a thrill of freedom and power as I unbuckle the straps and flipping the trunk's lid backwards. Such a contrast to when I stole a glance at your laptop case. I'm in total control now. At the very top of the trunk's contents, there it is: your yellow laptop case. My mind wanders back for the thousandth time to that March morning. I bring the case to me, hold it to my face, and the floral scent of your youth raids my sense of control. I throw it to the floor.

When I look again at your trunk my eyes fall on something that didn't belong to you.

My manuscript.

I reach for it, but a knock at my door stops me. I toss the document back on the bed and then, a terrifying thought: perhaps you are not in your grave after all. As I approach my door and take the handle, my heart thumps at the idea of the ghost of you behind it.

Gemma.

'How did you get in?'

'I've come for her things,' she says, pushing past me.

'You have no right to—'

'You have no right to stop me. This was her flat too and her possessions were always hers. Where have you hidden them?'

'I appreciate today must have been very difficult for you, but—'

'You appreciate nothing!' she spits, stepping around me and into my kitchen and living room, pacing around frantically as if she might find you again here, but keeping her arms firmly folded across her black jacket, like she doesn't want to touch any surface.

'We should really arrange another time to do this. I'd like you to go.' I want her to leave so I can be alone with the residue of you in my home.

'Well, we'd all like a lot of things. My niece not to be *dead*, for starters. Where are her things? What have you done to them?'

'Calm down, Gemma. They're in here.' I let her get past me and walk into my bedroom. I follow her and, while her back is turned, I shove it under a pillow before sitting down on it.

When Gemma sees your trunk, new tears take over her mottled face; she turns and flares her nostrils at me, before squatting down to wrap her arms around it. She starts to wrestle the thing backwards across my bedroom floor then and out into my hall. I can hear she's almost outside into the shared landing. I get up to slam the door behind her, but when I do she's standing again, behind your trunk, which now blocks my door.

'The curtains were drawn around her hospital bed. They're not supposed to be on HDU wards unless by medical staff. She died exactly at the point when they couldn't see her. Or you.'

'Lily wanted some privacy.'

'Why on earth would she want *privacy* with you?'

'Gemma, Lily admitted what she'd done to me. She sabotaged my career, deliberately targeted Iain, lied to you about it all. I suppose the accident made her think about her life. All her mistakes and misdeeds. She apologised for everything she'd done to me, and then she said was sorry to tell me she was having my partner's baby. She became extremely emotional, it obviously got too much for her ... Like the hospital said, I suppose she wasn't as strong as she thought she was.'

At this, she slams her hands on the top your trunk. '*You.* You caused her *death*. She didn't want you there, why would she? And why would she say sorry to you after your conduct at the funeral of the father of her baby? After you robbed me? I can't *believe* she tried to help you. But you wouldn't let her. I should have sacked you when I had the chance. You were dead weight from day one. How can *she* be gone and you're here, sitting pretty, in the flat that's half hers, with *my* money. You *will* pay for this.'

'Please, Gemma, by all means start a new conversation with the police and I'll be sure to highlight the lengths to which you went to help your niece when she was alive. Get out.' I feel the hate coming off her. 'Now.'

I push your trunk out of my flat, Gemma stumbling behind it, and kick the door shut.

I hear your case being dragged away, thumping down the stairs like a dead carcass,

Now I have nothing of you.

I return to my bedroom and reach under the pillow to retrieve my manuscript, but there's something else waiting for me there too. A yellow hardback book with a brassy pen attached to it by an orange ribbon. Your diary. It feels as if you have left me a gift.

I read.

I read every word of the writing in your own hand and barely notice when the sun goes down and the light in my bedroom goes from grey to a dirty blue.

It's hard for me to breathe. A new dread descends, a new filter I have to view the world through. No longer beige. Now, everywhere I look, I can see only black.

Your words, from your heart to the page; from the page to my heart.

What you wrote for me at the Rosewood:

I don't know what's wrong with me. Why they don't want me. They're sending me away again. It always feels like someone wants to send me away, just for being me. My soul is thinking, here we go again. Being sent away is the only thing it really knows …

And so many words from your diary, but it's these that wound me deepest:

> When I know for sure she's realised she has nothing left in the world, that's when I'll sock it to her. I'll tell her about the universe of pain she's caused, and why it had to be this way.

Because it didn't have to be this way.

You.

It *was* you.

Her.

Who else would want to ruin me as you did? You needed me. You always needed me, but I wasn't there for you. I have my answer now.

I had always meant to write an epilogue to my first manuscript, but I had buried that part of the story. So I'm writing it now, and maybe somehow you will hear it.

Creep Feeder
Epilogue

There were no neighbours for miles. I'd sent the reporter on his way nine months ago. I was alone. So completely alone. A brutal pain ripped through me, my whole torso tightening, constricting, like an invisible snake had come from within to kill me again and again. Labour didn't seem to hurt the sheep. That's why I thought this would be easier than the alternative. I was wrong. I had so much to learn about life.

The pain burnt, searing through every bit of me. The baby, you, hung between two worlds, refusing to leave my body. I thought my frame would break, my body would split in two. A terrific push from my guts, using every last bit of strength in me to get you out of me. I caught you in my hands. You were slippery, just like a lamb. I nearly dropped you. But I didn't.

You started screaming, your angry gums vibrating. I wrapped you in a towel and put the bottle I'd made up in your mouth while the blood kept pouring out of me. You were so tiny and hungry and innocent. I thought about my own birth. How rough and cold my mother would have been. The tears fell from me as fast as the blood that followed your body out of me.

I knew I'd never be able to do this again. How could I trust myself to know how to put a child's needs first? I'd never seen it done.

I couldn't wait for the social worker to arrive. I needed to get you away from me. For your sake and for mine because every second I looked at you I risked committing the sleepy slate of your eyes and the sweet fullness of your cheeks to my memory. I inhaled the sweet, soft, scent of your head and felt the pulse of milk in my breasts. I was desperate to feed you, Lily.

But to survive, I needed to forget that moment, forget you ever lived. You would only hold me back, inhibit the freedom I'd made so many sacrifices for and I would only be bad for you. Thinking about you, knowing you, would only damage me more.

Precious you, now I know why our blood leapt together, how our pulses found each other: our hearts were the same, and you had come to punish me for giving up on that. I understand this. I punished my mother too. But it could have been different, Lily. We didn't have to destroy each other.

Imagine Iain and me, taking a walk across the park on a wintry afternoon in March. The day before I met you. The day you followed us, when you trailed me down Church Street, plotting to take away everything I'd worked for. Iain and I chat, sip our coffee, the steam puffing around our heads cheerfully, like nothing's wrong in the world, though we know it is. Of course, we know it is.

I hear a voice behind me. Yours.

'Hello.'

'Yes?'

'My name is Lily Fretwell.'

'Hi.'

'I think we might know each other?'

'Sorry, I can't place you.'

'I don't know how to say this. You know me from a really long time ago. I don't suppose I look at all familiar to you?' Perhaps I would shake my head. 'When you were eighteen … you … you had a baby. It's me. Lily. I know you specified no contact, it's just I know you're a writer. I'm a writer too, or I want to be. I thought maybe we could—'

I go to sit on a bench nearby, taking you with me, holding your hand to steady myself.

'Sorry, I know this must be a shock.'

'It is. It's a surprise. A nice one. You're just like me!' I might have said.

'You're just like me.'

'Wow. You're a woman. Of course you are. What the hell happens now?'

'I don't know.'

'Well, that makes two of us.'

'Three!' Iain would have said, in that ideal world where I could have trusted him to stay with me.

'This is Iain.'

And we'd take it from there.

You didn't have to make me watch you and my Iain make another child together, under an apple tree in a nasty house that didn't belong to anyone we knew.

I howl alone into the blank white space around me.

My Lily, we could have protected each other from our pasts and then from the rest of the world. Instead, you took Iain away and you let your need to punish me end your life too. You and your baby too.

Her.

You didn't get the chance to find out, but I know your baby was a girl. I know because I had the dream again last night. I looked like me now: ginger roots speckled with some grey, the black dye finally growing out. I still look down at my bony teenage feet, but this time, I finally push through the gate. The earth can't contain me in its darkness, not yet, and my bleeding pain can't stop me. In the black-red far paddock, I see an upturned quad bike. Trapped below it, my mother as I finally saw her, but there's you and your little girl too, our baby, and all your bones and flesh are twisted together for eternity.

And when I wake, my wrongness and my loneliness over-whelm me.

*

I spend the rest of the morning doing some research before sending an email to Mr Okoh, the wills solicitor:

Subject: The Intentions of Ms Katherine Ross

Dear Mr Okoh,

I would like to make it known to you that in the event of my death, it is my intention that:

The property at Hercules Street, Holloway, London N7, should be bequeathed to my former colleague and friend Asif Khan.

The rest of my estate, including the proceeds of the sale of the property at Portland Rise, London N4, should be used to establish the Feeder Trust which should award bursaries for young people from disadvantaged backgrounds to support their creative careers in London.

In sound mind,
Katherine Ross

I imagine Asif, plonking down his bits of luggage in the hall-way at Iain's Holloway flat. He wrestles the sofa where Iain died up the steps from the basement, leaving it out on the street together with Iain's ghost. He sets up his weights bench in its place while he waits on the Ikea delivery, all the time trying to focus on the chance he's been given, forcing himself not think about what happened in this flat, or about me.

I fill my bag with Citalopram, my Mini with petrol and tap a familiar postcode into my satnav: Unnamed road, Matlock, Derbyshire.

And I know when my sleep finally comes, I won't have the nightmare about my mother and the farm anymore. Now I'm putting right my wrongs, my sleep will be beyond guilt.

After four hours, I finally reach that familiar gate in real life for the first time since I was eighteen. The rough rotting wooden version gone, replaced by something smart and modern; galvanised metal that won't warp and ruin. The pasture on the far paddock has changed too. The grass is lush and spring green. Someone is finally looking after this land. I swallow a fistful of pills and feel I am closing in on peace.

The pills begin to take hold, the sweet scent of the young roots provides some comfort as I ricochet through seizures towards oblivion.

The day is fading now.

Such a beautiful word, as I say it to myself, before I can't speak anymore.

'Daughter ... daughter ... daughter.'

But then: startling greens. Rich, yolk yellows. Illuminous blue. The squeak of fresh grass around me.

Are these colours, these human sounds enveloping me real? Is there someone out here coming to drag me back into life again? I need this to be the final hallucination of my brain, but I know the world better by now. Life is never on my side, even now I've decided I want to leave it.

Lily

(Draft post, 6.04 p.m., 26th April) – Join the Dots, Katherine Ross

Sometimes all you have to do is sketch out the suggestion of a picture and people go right ahead and fill in the gaps. I've made this happen a hundred times before, but never on the scale I planned with you.

A pretty girl, do anything to be a journalist. Red hair, sassy attitude. Won't take a fight lying down. Great liar. Remind you of anyone yet, Katherine?

This all starts with your sins, but the justice you experienced at my hand begins when I met Ruth.

It was the summer before my final year. Ruth and I got talking at an exhibition at The Tetley. I was wandering around on my own, rinsing the last few days I could stay in halls before being chucked out to spend the summer in the dead centre of another load of Gem/Mum mind games. It seemed to get worse after I'd been away, liked they'd been plotting their next tactic in the fallow time without me. The minute I talked to Ruth, I felt better about everything. It was so natural, so easy. It was obvious we were going to be really important to each other.

Ruth was about to start as a fresher and her parents had bought her a house in Headingley. She was already living in it and planning to rent the rooms to people she met and liked. She was beautiful and clever, she had loads of money and freedom and kind, normal parents, but I didn't hate her. She became my true friend instantly. I'd never felt this way before.

She was different. She listened to every word I said without any kind of agenda. With her as my best friend, I knew I could be happy. I loved looking at her, auburn hair that fell in easy waves down her back, her gap-toothed smile and bright blue eyes that seemed to dance when she was trying to find the right way to describe something. She could only see good where I saw the bad things. She saw the positive in everything. In me. After all the negativity in my life, I was hooked.

We'd talk forever and both crash on the futon in the little living room when the sun came up and the Diet Coke and Doritos couldn't keep us from falling asleep anymore. We started cooking meals together, shopped together and built a little domestic bliss. Obviously, it wasn't long at all before we made it official. I would move in. I chose the room right next to hers. The walls were thin and we could carry our conversations, each in our own beds, until I drifted into the deepest, most restful sleeps I'd ever had, the sound of her duvet sweeping against the plasterboard next to me, the most blissful sound I'd ever heard.

Peace. Home. A connection without conditions.

I found I could tell her everything. For the first time, I actually understood what girls meant when they said *best friend*. The devotion, the infatuation, the closeness and the relief of someone getting you and always being there for you. I told her all about me and my past. My mum. Gem. My mistakes. She still liked me. I guess it was a bit like counselling, only that Ruth talked too, about the good things she could see in the world and in me.

I think she understood me better than I knew myself. Sometimes she'd finish a sentence for me and I didn't find it annoying like I would with any other person, because she was always right. If I was struggling to find a way of telling her what it was really like growing up with Mum and Gem tearing me up into pieces, she'd get there for me. Somehow, she understood my pain.

Ruth's parents were academics and she wanted to teach too. She was a committed vegan and was looking forward to joining politically-aware societies once she'd enrolled. I didn't get people who joined things like that before, but if Ruth could see the positives, then there had to be something in it. I decided I would join the organisations she did. She signed petitions and cared a lot about getting the rubbish in the right recycling bin, so I did the same. She'd give any coins she had to homeless people all the time. I copied her. Perhaps I was a charity case to her, but if I was, I didn't feel like it. This was real.

The end began when I saw you for the very first time, Katherine.

Ruth told me she'd been given away like me, but when she was only a baby. Chucked away like a bit of rubbish. Treated like an inconvenience, just like me. I knew that's why Ruth and I were soulmates. I knew she was the friend I'd been waiting for my whole life. Ruth's birth mother didn't want to know anything about her. I knew how that felt, in my core.

Ruth's biological mother had deliberately asked for no contact. But Ruth was smart and she was curious. She found out who it was that had produced a child and threw her away without a glance over her shoulder.

'She's called Katherine Ross. She's a magazine editor in London, which is incredible when you think about it, given what she'd been through. Here, do you want to see a picture? The social worker took it just before I was handed over. She looks so young. So lonely. I'm glad she managed to turn her life around,' Ruth told me.

I took the photo from her.

There you were.

Thin, scruffy redhead with skin as white as milk. You looked away from the camera. You didn't take any notice of baby Ruth. You never did and you never would. It was as if you didn't want her to exist.

You're the same now. You only want to acknowledge people like me and Ruth when it suits you, when you need something from us. The rest of the time it's trying to pretend we don't exist. At best, you give us open disdain and at worse, out-and-out hate. The exploitation being the only reliable and permanent thing about how you interact with us.

'When do you plan to confront her?' I asked Ruth.

'Confront her? About what? I understand why she made her decision. It can't have been easy, but it was the right thing for her. She was only eighteen. I can't imagine what that must have felt like. It was the right thing for me too. I had a brilliant childhood. I don't need anything else from her, now I know how things turned out for her … Lily, are you alright?'

371

I'd thought Ruth was the sanest person I'd ever met, until she told me this. 'This is *so* typical of people like her. *Typical.* You're angry, right? Somewhere inside you? She spat you out like dirt. You *have* to be mad at her? Why should she get away with it? They shouldn't be allowed to get away with it.'

Ruth's smile disappeared. 'Calm down, Lily.'

'Let's take her down, me and you. Let's put her right about how she's hurt you. Let's make her pay!'

'Lily, you're going to wake the neighbours.'

'Think about it, let me do the hard work. I'm good at this. Let me do this for you.'

'Lily. It's fine. I'm fine. Life is good, I promise.'

'This is … deluded! Don't you see, this is exactly what their lot do? Use and abuse people like us? Their children. You can't possibly feel completely good inside. *She didn't want you.* She doesn't want you. People like her only want people like us if we can do something for them. You're damaged goods! Don't you see, that's why we're like sisters. That's why I'll punish her for you!'

'I think … I'm going to be bed now.'

She looked right at me with the same bright blue eyes you have. She didn't flinch, she didn't falter. She didn't cry. Looking back, that's the first time I really saw you. Your eyes. Your hardness.

In the morning, she left before I did. I crept into her room and found the picture of you with her. I wanted to look into your soul, get some kind of insight into the person able to abandon Ruth so easily. I still don't understand how people like you operate. How you find it so easy to run away from the consequences of your choices, to walk away without another thought, to treat the children you make with such hate.

Ruth and I were always coming in and out of each other's rooms, I didn't think it would be a problem if she'd guessed I'd been looking at her things. It was.

'I'd rather you didn't go in my room when I'm not here. Were you going through my pictures today?'

'I'm sorry, Ruth, it's just what you said about your mother—'

'She's not my mother, Lily. Please, let's drop it.'

'I don't want to, because I care about you. I'm mad as hell at her for you, Ruth.'

'Please, don't be. You're actually kind of freaking me out.'

'You're not scared of *me*, are you?'

'No, I mean, not normally, but this, this is a bit weird, Lily. I think you need to chill out … I'm going out.'

She ran out of the house, just like that. I didn't get to explain myself. It was like she couldn't get away from me quick enough. Because I'd brought you up. I wanted to tell her: Hey, *I'm* not the scary one here!

That day, she got a job at the café at The Tetley and started straight away. She didn't tell me her plans, or how long she'd be gone. She went to the cinema without me in the evening and didn't come home until I'd gone to bed. I had to follow her the next day to find out about the job. She wasn't at all happy to see me when I turned up at her table.

Biting down my sobs as I walked home, I began to see what I needed to do. After all our talks, everything I'd told her, her bringing you up seemed to have stirred something deep and darkly held inside her that she wasn't strong enough to face. She didn't even want to punish you. Digging you out from the corners of her mind had changed her. Now I was going to have to punish her for letting that happen and allowing you to tear us apart. I hated you already.

I thought it fair to give Ruth one last chance, after all, like me, it wasn't her fault she'd been given up on and I knew how all we rejects need to come up with our own coping strategies. She'd chosen self-delusion. I texted her:

I'm sorry you've been so upset about your mother. When you're ready, we can talk all about it. Diet coke and Doritos on me tonight? Xx.

But she didn't come back that night, texting me late:

Going back home for the weekend.

I wasn't about to let myself be rejected for what you'd done to her. So, when she got back from her parents, I'd be ready for her. No one gets to walk away from me.

Ruth's weakness was her virtue. I planned to attack that. I'd done some research. The charity she said she donated to, the CEO was a serial harasser. The school she'd 'built' in Kenya, before coming to Leeds, was falling down. The person who'd organised the last march she'd gone on had posted homophobic tweets. Most of our 'recycling' went to landfill and the flights she took on no fewer than three annual foreign holidays with her parents undid any good she thought she was doing anyway. Of course, I wouldn't tell her directly, I'd let her discover it all on her own. My role would be to make it as easy as possible for her to put the jigsaw of her own failings together.

When, and only when, I'd let her pull down all the walls of social earnestness she'd built around her persona, would I present the solution to put her together again. 'Ruth, I love you. You need to look at why you feel the need to give your life over to these empty gestures. All this virtue-signalling that does more harm than good, do you not think you're trying to hide something in you that's broken? Something that won't get fixed until you recognise the reason why you feel you have to put yourself in the right the whole time. It's because you feel so *wrong*. But I can help you. I know how that feels and I know how to take control of this.'

I waited and waited for the key in the door on Sunday night. Finally, I heard it. She was here. It was time.

'Hello? Lily?'

Not her voice. An older man. Her adoptive father.

He was there to remove me, serve me notice, require I leave before the start of term. I wouldn't get to live with Ruth again, I wouldn't get to put things in their right place with her.

It was made clear there would be consequences if I tried to contact her.

It hurt. It hit me so hard. I had lost control of the situation.

I lived in Gem's Norfolk house for the rest of the summer and found a new place to live in my final year. I had no friends, but you, Katherine Ross, became my hobby.

My earliest investigations confirmed my suspicions. A life without a stain, or so it would seem to those who didn't know what you'd done to Ruth and what you'd caused her to do to me. An entitled, unblemished life: you had a great job, a partner who looked like they adored you and not one, but two London flats. I knew you wouldn't have given Ruth another thought. You didn't deserve any of the things you had.

If I hadn't been let down by her, because of you, I wouldn't have thrown myself into the college newspaper and I know you know how that went.

I spent the time after my sentencing trying to make sense of it all. But it was obvious: the minute you were introduced into my life, things went wrong. I committed to take you down for me, for Ruth, but also for every Asif and 'Snowflake' you've ever wiped your hands on. Ruth had taught me something: that it's possible to do things that make you feel better *and* do some good for the world.

I dyed my hair red and fine-tuned the version of me it would take to unravel you. But I didn't bank on meeting my match in you. I had no idea it would get to where it got to with Iain. His death, the baby, I could never have planned or wanted these things. But you know better than anyone that children, and death, happen when you didn't think you were ready.

So, no, I'm not your daughter, but you'd have liked it if I had been, wouldn't you? That would have been neat. Neat and small. My actions a response to one misdemeanour, not thousands committed against people like me by people like you. We're the ones you should take care of, but instead you spend your energy criticising us. You make us work for nothing, rent your properties, but then you look to us for sex, for the future. You despise us when we challenge the way things are; the sub-optimal way you've made the world. Think of me as your Millennial Avenging Angel. Now I've carried out our revenge, backed you right into the corners of a life you didn't realise was blessed, it's time for you to start living differently. Go find your real daughter. Tell her you're sorry. Get down on your knees for giving up on her, for giving her away. Apologise to all of us you've treated appallingly, when we can only dream of the luck you've had. Pay your interns. Stop sleeping with them. Learn from your crimes and maybe you can find a way to get back on your feet again.

Would you believe me if I said I hope you do?

Because although I took you to rock bottom, I've always felt sorry for you, Katherine. And I like how you fight back, just like me. Now our lives are going to be bound forever by your partner's baby. I have a piece of him and I know you'll want a part of that. I think I need someone like you in my life. Someone who gets me. I think you know you need me too. Now that you know the truth of your existence, perhaps you can see that you and I aren't so different, because I don't love myself enough either and I've always needed a mother more like me.

So. Now what?

Author Note

In my twenties, going for a jog involved a process of mental preparation. Like so many women, I had to ready myself for those men who would call or beep from cars and vans and the male passers-by who would comment on my appearance or performance. Was I feeling strong enough to tell them where to go, or would I settle for simply ignoring them that day? That sense of every bit of me being assessed and graded as I tried to exercise sometimes meant I couldn't face running at all. As a younger woman, I hated the way the male gaze inhibited my freedom to move about the world how I wanted to.

Then, one day, I realised the catcallers had fallen silent. I was approaching forty and it felt like my body no longer registered. Even though I didn't want the attention of my youth, not having it disturbed me somehow. How had my self-worth been coaxed into such a warped shape? I baulked at the idea of being moulded by any sense of 'missing' comments by men in white vans as I aged, but I remained fascinated by the confusion and contradictions I'd experienced. I began to imagine a woman living her middle years with the absolute sense of losses accumulating, including her desirability to wider society. How would she relate to a younger woman, one at the height of her visibility and promise? The story of the novel began to grow.

Generation gaps are not new, but the current chasm between unfairly-maligned millennials, of all genders, and resentful mid-lifers, represents something uniquely unnerving. Fortysomethings like me – who enjoyed free university education, cheap housing and the luxury of establishing our identities in boom times – are widely making our lot even better by exploiting the generation directly underneath us, all the while actively belittling their efforts to shape a world that's fairer, more inclusive, and sober (in all senses of the word).

At the sharp end of the housing crisis, Generation Rent provides extra income for their elders while they themselves remain mired deep in debt. Their working lives are often spent propping up diverse sectors through unpaid internships or exploitative contracts, but this doesn't stop their near-daily pillorying in the mainstream media as thin-skinned, avocado-munching, precious 'Snowflakes'. Yesterday's ravers mock today's young adults for being 'woke', for their 'triggers', 'safe spaces' and sobriety. As for Generation X, we somehow feel as hard-done-by as millennials. We're not rich enough, not successful enough, not sexy enough for our liking. And although we still feel it inside, we are, in fact, no longer young. Little wonder we drink even more now than we did in our twenties.

As well as transitioning from hyper-visibility to invisibility, many middle-aged women find themselves being sidelined at work and often paid significantly less than male counterparts. Such symptoms can make female midlife feel like a condition in need of a cure. In this context, it can prove too easy to assume another woman has it easier than you, particularly if that women is deemed at the height of her appeal. Men block women's paths to career progression and self-worth, but women can stand in each other's way too. We aspire to taking better care of each other, but too often we experience the distance to go: from pulling the ladder up behind us if we reach seniority at work, to 'flaming' posters on parenting forums, to bile-filled weekly columns by female writers about other women. Pretending women always default to gentleness towards other each other won't plug these damaging empathy gaps.

In the world of the novel, two women of adjacent cohorts think and do the very worst to each other, believing the other party deserves it. I'd like their story to contribute to a conversation about women across generations more readily finding our common ground and targets, instead of dividing the world along enemy lines.

Acknowledgements

Thank you to Hellie Ogden at Janklow & Nesbit UK for loving the manuscript from the off and interrupting your family holiday to tell me so. You squeezed the best out of the first draft with forensically brilliant editorial ideas, then got it to my equally talented editors, Emily Kitchin at HQ in the UK and Clio Seraphim at Penguin Random House in the US, who have worked so collaboratively to make the book what it is. Emily, you are completely supportive and completely brutal where it counts. Clio, you have expertly plunged me even deeper into my characters' minds. I am very lucky to be working with you both.

Thanks also to Allison Hunter at Janklow & Nesbit Associates in New York who got this to the perfect US editor in Clio and to all the Janklow & Nesbit teams, particularly Zoe Nelson and Ellis Hazelgrove for securing the translations of *Precious You* by enthusiastic editors in many territories, to whom I am also extremely grateful.

The early readers of *Precious You*, in particular, Rachel Stevenson, Frances Corrin, Elizabeth Corrin, Emma Guise, Victoria Lane and my sister Bernadette Monks-Brown, you are all busy, brilliant women who gave me your time and then your invaluable steers on everything from what Iain should be called to the many places where I should up the stakes, turn the screws or amplify a voice. Thank you all.

Particular thanks to Rachel, who told me so emphatically this manuscript would get published I believed her and kept going. Massive thanks also to my exellent friend and www.northernsoul.me.uk Editor Helen Nugent. Helen, you've supported my writing career since pretty much the night our eyes met over a castrated cat in Kensal Green back in '97 and continue to do so to this day. Thank you.

Very special thanks to my twin sister Ruth Thorpe for lending me all those books once I'd decided I was going to write a thriller and giving me the shock of my life when you told me you thought my attempt was 'excellent'. I am sorry I chose my husband and children for the dedication of my debut novel, but hope naming Katherine's daughter after you goes some way to compensate. Did you ever know that you're my hero?

Thank you to all my brothers and sisters: Joanne Johnson, Michael Gilfillan, Christopher Gilfillan, Caroline Mitchell, as well as Dette and Ruth. I could say why you all matter so much and shape what I do, but I'm crying trying to do that right, so I'm going to stop. Please fill in the gaps. I hope we generally do. We miss you, Michael.

Thanks to my second family, especially my mother and father-in-law Gurpal Takhar and Gurmail Takhar. Mum and Dad, you have been so supportive since the start and helped us out in so many ways.

To my own Mum, thank you for being proud of me. Thank you for everything.

Thank you, Dad. You first gave me the idea it was possible

for anyone to get up one day and start writing. I'm so sorry you're not here to see me published (and take all the credit for it!).

Mohinder and Zora, thank you for putting up with a mum who was half-woman half laptop while I was trying to get published and for more generally making me feel like a balloon about to burst, mostly in the very best way.

To my husband Danny Takhar, thank you for a thousand things, from being the best in-house story editor anyone could have, for all those 4 a.m. starts together, for making me see that Katherine and Iain were not married and for telling me after that first sleepless night I met Katherine Ross in my insomnia, 'That's your next manuscript'. For the other 995 things, I will thank you in person.

Helen Monks Takhar
May 2019

ONE PLACE. MANY STORIES

Bold, innovative and
empowering publishing.